T0131851

# GUIDELESS
## THE
# RIVERS'
# COURSE

# GUIDELESS
## THE
# RIVERS'
# COURSE

STEFANO DUETAGLI

# GUIDELESS THE RIVERS' COURSE

iUniverse books may be ordered through booksellers or by contacting:

iUniverse
1663 Liberty Drive
Bloomington, IN 47403
www.iuniverse.com
1-800-Authors (1-800-288-4677)

ISBN: 978-1-5320-8510-9 (sc)
ISBN: 978-1-5320-8509-3 (e)

Library of Congress Control Number: 2019915880

Print information available on the last page.

iUniverse rev. date: 10/14/2019

I never needed Virgil
Or thought of him, but now
That place seems hell enough—

Now in my dreams the spiral
Spirals without end.
I see myself on every level
Smiled at by a carton,
Never Beatrice, smiled at
By this past that hands me on,
Guideless, always going down.

—From "The Warehouse Chute" by Dabney
Stuart (*The Diving Bell*, 1966, reprinted with
permission of the author and good friend)

# PROLOGUE

Time crawls in prison, the repetition of minutes, hours, and days receding into an unknowable distance you don't dare call a future. My years in Raiford crept as sluggishly as an intestinal worm until one day, without warning, it shat me out. After countless years, churning through the bowels of a penal system, dehydrated and leeched of nutrients, I was ejected into society like buckshot hitting a bedpan. I have only flickering images of that last day. My incarceration seemed so protracted I was certain time had ceased to exist. One minute I was in a dank isolation cell chasing cockroaches and the next the Florida penal system flexed its judicial diaphragm and squeezed me through the chute.

Now, I suddenly find myself a couple of hundred miles from the prison, but I'm not yet a free man. You can't just make a thirty-year con free in an instant like pouring water over distilled crystals. Freedom is a more equivocal process if you've spent thirty years in a maximum security prison for a crime you didn't commit. I know exactly how to become free. I might even die in the process, but who gives a shit. Vengeance is the only thing that can set me free. Perhaps I should take the cultural high road and tell myself I seek redemption, but redemption is merely the well-dressed polite cousin of ragged, venomous vengeance.

I'm still battered and buffeted by the turbulence of the anxiety of freedom. That's what Kierkegaard called it. Fuck Kierkegaard. I will not be deterred by abstract, existential philosophies. I'm not anxious; I'm pissed off, vengeful, and I scraped all the anxiety off on the doorsill of the fucking chute. It is simple mathematics. I am $x$, an as yet unknown value. The man who put me in prison is 1, a known quantity. I will find him, find out why he did this, then there will be either $x$ or $1 - x$; that's the mathematics of revenge. I'll violate every rule I hold dear and become all that I should abhor. I'll finally commit the crime for which I was arrested.

Until two weeks ago, I lived among men subject to whatever guideless forces led them to an inevitable stay in the maximum security prison at Raiford, Florida. I was inmate 123047, thirty years a number, stripped of the noun that once was my name. It's the number of years most people spend with a name and a career. Two weeks ago, I lost my number to freedom, my final months of captivity spent in the darkness of an isolation cell, with the thunderous rush of blood through the ears, sledgehammer heartbeat, scratching of rats, and skittering of cockroaches I came to call hors d'oeuvres.

There was no retirement party, no gold watch, no champagne, merely the cruel joke of the chute. I was incarcerated for second-degree murder. I was innocent. Everyone in prison is innocent. The incessant mantra of innocence rang out so fervently that even a newfound God must have believed it. But it wasn't God you had to convince; it was an equally abstruse abstraction called a parole board.

Upon release, I came home to this small, mean town on Lake Monroe in central Florida. I've come to sit on this pristine lake that is a river, its black tannic waters flowing north toward the sea. I'm not anxious, but I am haunted by freedom. I hope the lake, the river, the town, the sun, the dark line of trees five miles away on the far bank will heal me.

Raiford Prison is forever embedded in me like an inoperable tumor eating away at my sense of right and good as it grows, eroding healthy cells, metastasizing as it eats away my sense of self. In that hell, all light was sepia, shadowy striations on walls and floors; sounds were eerily distorted, echoed through caged tiers over long distances, droning, metallic rhythms from the trenches of a dark subterranean city of industry; the olfactory assault was constant—rancid, sweaty flesh, acrid stench of arc welders, industrial cleaning fluid; and the food consisted of steaming cauldrons of gray meat slathered with a reckless excuse for gravy and vegetables tormented until yielding a flaccidity just short of disintegration. It was a wasteland of insidious, malignant degradation.

Worse were the vestigial sounds at night. Ambiguous moans, pleasure and pain indistinguishable, intermingled, ineluctable. Sleep would not come in the early days. I shrunk to the size of survival. Then an iso chamber where survival ceased to matter.

"Clean up for out-processing," a voice came through the tiny window, vaguely familiar, from centuries ago. But never had it formed that phrase, "out-processing." A bare bulb flickered to life, and I saw the reflection of a thing in the cracked mirror over the sink. It attempted but failed a smile, its lips working to turn up at the corners, the smile of a silhouette at night. Two eyes held my gaze with only a vague hint of recognition.

Hell had eradicated all but a number stamped in memory. The detritus of a thing once named stumbled toward the light. My only possessions? A journal and a wallet. A beautifully rebuilt Rolex watch had "mysteriously gone missing," according to the storeroom guard. I wish I could have laughed in his face and told him of the billions of dollars I had in offshore accounts, enough to replace a million Rolexes. But no one could know. It had been a long trek through hell to pick Lucifer's pocket.

"Let's join the angel in the lake. Shut up." *Don't talk to yourself, fool.* I'd lost the self/other distinction. Isolation does that. "I'm a name again, so fuck you." *Jesus, shut up. The guards are staring.* I'm a man named Stuart Walker Purloin, after a poet. In Raiford, gender is meaningless among the shadows of rape and sodomy.

The recidivists said it would feel like this in the chute. Like the guards were playing a bad joke. Letting you think it was over. Just as you reached the gate, a guard would grab you, laughing as he dragged you kicking back inside. Especially if you'd been in iso. The only clock in iso was Old Sparky. Every Wednesday evening, there was a brownout. Lights dimmed, and a mournful hum ascended to a steady, deadly bass note as they fed Old Sparky great gulps of grid juice, tuning him up for the quivering skullfuck—the only dance Sparky knew. Eventually, Sparky was replaced by lethal injection, so those last months as a turd in dark bowels left me no way to mark time other than greasy metal meal trays shoved through the feeding slot. Poor substitute for the lethal pronouncements of Old Sparky rehearsing to weld an inmate's fillings together.

I picked up my shit and was herded into the chute as the prison spat me out like rotten meat. A lone guard walked me toward the gate, our footfalls scratching on gravel, a familiar sound from childhood, stealing oranges that fell onto the gravel yard under the conveyor belts at the packing house, rushing back to a makeshift stall, and selling them to a snowbird headed north, license plates from Michigan or Ontario receding up Highway 17-92. The town would have forgotten me. But not the one whose lies sent me there. Richard Sheldon Richardson will remember me. And die for it.

"I'll find him." *Damn it, shut your mouth.* The guard was staring hard. I kept my eyes straight ahead. There was the gate. And the bus that would take me back to the town on Lake Monroe.

# CHAPTER 1

I n prison, you learn your own way of counting time. When you first get out, relearning how to mark time is difficult. A watch or cell phone is inadequate. Days gathered into two weeks that felt like decades. It was eerie. Time should fly as one ages, but my first week out moved like an old gator on a sunny riverbank, so still it appears lifeless. Until you disturb it. Soon I would do just that. I would disturb things.

I came back to the house that was once my parents'. It's mine now. They're dead. I was having it renovated by a specialty company. They had no idea who was paying them. My father would rather have burned it down than leave it to me. Too late. The renovations were going well enough to suspend work. I needed time to reorient. The crew left for two weeks, and I slept, waking only to eat, piss, shit, and monitor my offshore bank accounts.

My prison journal was tucked in its drawer. It was my lifeline, my remembrances of things prison. The journal was my Proustian madeleine.

After a week of rest, I donned a seersucker shirt and khakis and, broad-brimmed straw hat perched on my thinning dome, left my air-conditioned haven, truly one letter from heaven, to walk the commercial district of the old town. As I turned onto First Street, the heart of the commercial district, I was struck immediately by the bovine nature of people accustomed to freedom. Like milling cattle, no one seemed to notice the needs of others in their immediate surroundings. At first, it was almost endearing, the way they blocked the sidewalk or clogged doorways as if their needs superseded those of others. It was a profound contrast to what I'd endured for thirty years. In prison, it was critical that you remain aware of everyone around you. If you didn't, you might suddenly find yourself with a shiv protruding from your gut like a newly sprouted limb or another trip to a maintenance closet for a degrading Aryan round-robin.

After begging polite passage with the thousandth "Pardon me," I'd had enough of this mass sense of entitlement. At one point a woman, with no concept of the world outside her perceptual bubble, cut me off and swung a fist into my crotch with a careless swing of her arm.

It was the last straw. Without thinking, I blurted, "If you're going to hit it, maybe you should get down on your knees and kiss it to make it better."

She looked at me in horror, and I apologized profusely as I fled the scene. I saw her later getting into a car and was relieved to see an Ohio license plate. She was accompanied by a big, burly man, but that didn't bother me. After thirty years of teaching big, burly men a lesson by pounding my face into their fists, I didn't give a damn if they saw me. I ducked quickly into an antique shop and hid among a cluster of armoires in the back. I felt wretched and thought I might hyperventilate for only the second time in my life. Perhaps the recidivists were right yet again, and the world was not a place for me anymore. Perhaps Kierkegaard had been right after all. I had been physically imprisoned, but he had been imprisoned by the ideals of an unforgiving religion. Was this the anxiety of freedom he had posited? Was I too far gone to live among these people? Of course, I never could, could I?

I couldn't blame this town, but I was willing to share the blame with everything it once stood for. Another set of ideals I could never live with. I even found it difficult to say the name of this town. It has a name, but a thing once named is stuck forever in the shadow of a noun, reified, mired in its own circular logic of existence. But I will acknowledge it once.

In graduate school, a group of us teaching assistants had an office with six desks we shared. We hung a sign on our office door that read the Antireification League. We despised the concept of naming that trapped nouns in Wittgenstein's hell. I didn't know at the time that "ex con" would be one of mine.

So, I'll name it this once: my hometown is Sanford, Florida. But it could have been Mount Dora, or Casselberry, or Deland, or Leesburg, or Valdosta, or Greenville, or Spartanburg, or Roanoke. In those days, they all shared the construct that reified—segregation. It was a time when black people were discounted by the hideous joke that was *Plessy v. Ferguson*. Zora Neale Hurston was born here and escaped to join the Harlem Renaissance. Every black person who could escape the grasp of this town did so. Those who remained somehow managed dignity during denigration.

That was black people. Brown people, Hispanics, were also bad because Castro was some sort of Hispanic, a Commie, and a Cuban, which was a brand of Hispanic excoriated in a mandatory high school class called "Capitalism vs. Communism." Cuba was right on our doorstep. In high school, we sweated out a horrific day when we all thought the Russians would launch missiles at us. We sat in biology class, silent and frightened, until the second hand swept past eleven, the deadline set by JFK for Russian ships to turn back. As the clock clicked eleven, we rejoiced that we hadn't been incinerated. It's a good thing there was no God watching this town; she may have let one missile fly just to teach the rest of the world a lesson.

The town was built and run by white people. I was born a

3

white person. It would have gone well if I'd stayed inside the social guardrails.

The town was originally nothing more than an army fort established at the navigable headwaters of the St. Johns River, one of a series of fortifications built prior to the Second Seminole Indian War. After the war, the population grew, and steamboats began moving goods between Jacksonville and Mellonville—the town's original name. After the Civil War, a man named Henry Sanford established a citrus experimenting station here, and the citrus industry boomed. The town's name changed but not its character.

Life and death were orderly, slow paced. But in an ironic twist, change blew in on a hurricane of money from California. Somehow, the town miraculously managed to lose out on the building boom. I kept up with thirty years of accretive descent through the local paper.

Theme parks invaded. My mental image of the change was a giant black mouse with a white face and red pants, crawling over the land, gorging on miles of beautiful orange groves, eating all that was natural and good and shitting out this horrid plasticity. We called the great mouse's realm the Tragic Kingdom. My grandparents were old enough to curse the two Henrys, as they were called—not the Tudors of England but Flagler and Plant, the two northern assholes who brought the railroads to Florida, Flagler down the east coast, Plant down the west.

The railroads were the harbinger of all the evils to descend on paradise, invaders from the Land of Nod. Adam and Eve were not driven out of the Garden of Eden but taxed out and overrun by people who retired from cold northern cities and flooded south.

Locals watched the inundation of theme parks, toll roads, hotels with lazy rivers, ambulance-chasing personal-injury lawyers, tasteless food chains, tasteless shopping centers selling tasteless merchandise, gated communities, movie theaters, streaming entertainment to anesthetize, private schools to proselytize, businesses to franchise, and morals to compromise. At least that's what the old settlers thought.

On that first walk, I trudged to First Street, the main drag through the commercial district, to acquaint myself with change. The buildings were as I remembered, nineteenth-century brick with awnings or cantilevered roofs over the sidewalks, but not the businesses occupying them. All the department stores and many of the midsize businesses were now antique shops hawking cultural detritus disguised as nostalgia.

As I crossed Park Avenue, businesses became shabbier, blue collar. That, too, hadn't changed. There was a lube shop, a garage, and a gas station on one side, and smaller businesses on the other: a pizza shop, a sandwich shop, and, finally, the crossroads of life, the juncture of hope and despair, a mystical island free of social snobbery, racism, and inequality. Next door to the sandwich shop stood what was now a real estate office, but I saw only what it had once been. Monk's Pool Hall. The Island of the Archangels— Knights of the Rectangular Table.

If rich whites were the town's Pharaohs, the denizens of Monk's Pool Hall were the Nubians. The only people beyond their control. Monk was a black man demeaned by the nickname Crooked Nigger, dubbed so for a scoliotic spine that pushed his left collarbone out and shortened one leg. No one said it to his face, at least not when his patrons were in earshot. His wife, a mysterious woman of Timucua heritage, died giving birth to Bonnie, Monk's beautiful daughter.

I admired Monk and his clientele, men like Jack Knife, Shorty, Silk, the Fagans, Robert the Bruce, as well as the women, Fancy Nancy, Cruel Kate, Big Mabel the obese prostitute, and Bonnie. Bonnie was Servilia of the Junii, wielding an inordinate amount of authority in a strange, sometimes brutal, environment.

I'd known those women well. As a cross-dresser—transvestite in those days—I had shared their reputation as an aberrant. I eventually completed the transition, becoming a transgender male through a series of operations in Holland, only to be thrown into a male prison the moment I set foot back in town. The Knights of Monk's, like heaven's archangels, saved my life many years ago.

Even the local chief of police left Monk's alone. It once came up at a city council meeting, with great public harangue and religious hubris, that Monk's Pool Hall be forced to close. There was a roar of agreement among the law-abiding, churchgoing citizenry, led by a few preachers and their flocks and supported by the chamber of commerce, the women's auxiliary, and garden club. As a small business owner, I attended that night.

As the crowd reached the peak of its indignant frenzy, Chief Benjamin "Big Ben" Butler walked to the center of the room and held up his hands to hush the crowd. Ben was a big man, broad of shoulder, a little round with age, hair still dark and curly, and a face that looked like it had witnessed the Hittite sack of Babylon. An anticipatory hush descended as the crowd was certain that Ben, a no-nonsense chief, would immediately accede to their demands. Instead, the chief, hands on his hips, asked a question.

"Let me ask y'all something," Ben spoke calmly. "Where can we find all the meanest, toughest people in town tonight?"

The angry crowd erupted. "Down at Monk's Pool Hall. That's where they are."

The chief again held up his hand until quiet was restored before asking a second question. "And where will they be tomorrow night if I close Monk down?"

The stenographer wrote something in the minutes about the sound of a pin dropping.

There was a final confrontation when the owner of a local bar, a known competitor of Monk's, shouted, "You sure you're not just afraid to go in there and clear that place out, Ben?"

Ben immediately retorted, "Is that you, Harold Wilcox?"

There was silence, and Ben said, "Well, is it?"

"Yes, damn it, it's me," came a response from the back.

Ben laughed. "Well, Harold, I'll tell you what. I'll call out

6

the National Guard and gather every one of my men, and we'll follow you down to Monk's. All you gotta do is go inside and tell Sharkey you've come to put Monk out of business."

The stenographer typed, "Is there something quieter than a pin dropping?"

Sharkey. The name made me shiver.

That was the first and last discussion about closing Monk's. Little Ben would one day take his dad's place as police chief. Lessons learned.

Monk abruptly disappeared one rainy night, and it all came to an end. Until then, Monk's strange brand of honor was enforced by a few of his regulars, a handful of folks who played on a red pool table at the back of the room, separated from two rows of green-felt tables by a low wall. Few dared step up to the red table unless they had money they didn't need.

The most feared of the archangels was a young man like no other. They called him Sharkey. His nickname wasn't given because he shot a mean stick, though he did. It was said he was slow to anger, but when he was riled, his eyes went dead like a shark's—dead, icy, gray.

After Monk's disappearance, an era ended. The same night he vanished, a conflagration at the Hatfield mansion took them all, including Sharkey, or so I heard. I thought of the Pantheon and an inscription on the tomb of Raffaello: "Living, Great Nature feared he might outvie her works and dying, fears himself may die." Sharkey was a force of nature.

I recrossed Park and turned right before stopping again. Across the street, next to Carver's Barber Shop, now a biker bar, stood the tattered remnants of optimism: the family jewelry shop. The shop my grandfather established and I operated before the transgender operations. Before Lucifer reached up, grabbed my ankles, and pulled me into hell.

I tore myself away from the facade of the old jewelry shop and turned back down Park Avenue, which terminated at the lake. I made a right for a hundred yards and stopped at this very spot. I sat down on this bench by Lake Monroe in this town. I'd dreamed of this moment. Even prayed for it, though I wasn't religious, or more accurately, I eschewed organized religion, shedding that albatross after watching its hypocrisy for too many years.

The lake, which was really a wide spot in a river, flowed under endless cobalt skies that ended at a dark green line of trees five miles away on the far shore. Directly behind the bench, across Lakeshore Drive, was the town. The lake was part of the St. Johns River, dubbed the Nile of America because, like the Nile, its currents flowed north.

English nouns are neuter, genderless. Nouns in other languages have articles denoting gender. In Italian, the lake before me and the bench under me? Masculine. The dark tannin-stained water? Feminine. A masculine lake containing feminine water? Of course, a feminine body might contain a masculine soul. If I'd been born an African frog or moray eel, I could have taken genders for a test drive. Human gender? Byproduct of an unforgiving culture. If one was sent to a male prison, it was assumed one must be male. True by state law, but the fact that I was once a woman named Margarite Ecclesia Purloin meant nothing to the prison administration. It meant everything to my fellow inmates.

For thirty years, I'd lived in an inescapably masculine world, tossed in with thuggish brutes, especially the Aryans. Huge biceps and granite shoulders snatched me up as I scurried along dim corridors, seeking the shadows. I was reduced to a wall-hugging insect, skittering along corridors, avoiding showers with swastika-tattooed Troglodytes. I burrowed into any form of nothingness I could find.

But nothingness was an unstable state. Aryans appeared suddenly, swept me up like a Jewish shopkeeper in Warsaw, rough arms pinning my limbs, panicked breath snuffling over clamped hands. Once I bit that hand and awoke in the clinic, face swollen beyond recognition, blood oozing from my anus. I tried any trick to disgust, urinating and defecating on myself, holding it all day for the inevitable encounter. Lust and cruelty trumped disgust. *Der Geschrei durch den nature*—a face from a humanities class in another lifetime.

I was forced to become Kafka's cockroach while they strutted boldly, *Einsatzgruppen*, protected by sympathetic guards and the impunity of apathy. I was not *Juden* or *Zigeuner*. This was not Nazi Germany. It was American hypocrisy. I was worth less than the unwanted. "The pleasure of amusement greater than the effort to exterminate" was stamped on the passport of my existence just as authorities at Ellis Island had stamped the papers of the unwanted with "cost of supervision greater than value of labor." American complicity in the deaths of millions.

I dropped my eyes to the tanned-leather binder in my lap. I had pulled it from the drawer in my house this morning and placed it in a satchel over my shoulder, and, walking stick clicking on the sidewalk, I had made my way here to the river.

"This is the record of my life," I spoke aloud. This journal is *un diario*, masculine, as is the binder, *un legante*. A masculine leather binder. "Apropos, eh, Ralph? Nazi pig fucker." Ralph. No journal would be complete without Ralph. Every memory of Ralph hurt. Ralph remained a disembodied specter, a human oxymoron that haunted my dreams.

I opened the leather binder and stared at the first note on the inside cover: "Dante said people who choose to be sad in the sunlight are sad in the black filth. I crossed the Acheron into hell, the mire still sucking at my feet, pulling me down. Mozart echoes in Sparky's chamber. Leonardo lives in a shattered mirror. In hell oblivion is exquisite."

Those initial words sent a shiver of horror through me. I had to look up to prove that I was home, sitting by Lake Monroe. The dark waters were there, just below the concrete seawall at my feet. Hyacinths were rising and falling at the juncture of the seawall and the concrete abutment that formed the south end of the marina. Beyond was the yacht basin, with rows of floating berths where yachts of all sizes were moored, masts and upper decks nodding out of sync as if each were agreeing with a different voice rising from the lake.

I looked down at the seawall. It was a concrete levee that ran for seven miles from I-4 to Mellonville Avenue, constructed first in the 1920s and then updated while I was in prison. Nothing along those seven miles was more important than this five-foot section at my feet. Right here I could stand, walk three paces, and step on the very spot where three decades ago, the local police had pulled a broken body from the river. That was before the old seawall was elevated, before the road was moved back, before the sidewalks were replaced by a wide paved swath called a river walk with pretty pergola-shaded benches and marina shops that at night painted neon brushstrokes on the dark waters.

Thirty years ago, the view from here could have been a different town. There had been no bench or pergola, only the old seawall and a strip of grass where locals sat with cane poles, watching corks bobbing in the water. That was before my arrest. Before my life as a transgender fell stillborn from an operating table in Holland. I had just completed my dream of becoming the man trapped inside Margarite. Margarite was a good woman, but I knew a good man lived inside her like one of Leonardo's prisoners. I'd known from childhood I should have been a boy. I had nothing in common with girls and everything in common with boys, from playing army and cowboys to putting firecrackers up a cat's ass.

I was seeing the town through eyes that, thirty years ago, were Margarite's. At my eleven o'clock, where now an elongated U-shaped marina lay, a long pier once jutted into the lake with a great convex band shell at its terminus. Men in cravats and fedoras and women in dresses and white gloves had gathered there on Sunday afternoons. Beethoven, Vivaldi, or Strauss, Sousa on military holidays, played by the American Legion band had echoed through the streets. It was razed in the name of progress, replaced by this boat-infested marina.

At my nine o'clock had been a small zoo the size of six city blocks. A mandrill named Jigs was the main attraction. Giggling teenagers had gathered to stare at his multicolored face and hindquarters. As a male primate, Jigs watched for human females to stop and gawk. He then spontaneously engaged in unrestrained masturbation. Mothers pulled many a daughter away in disgust, but Jigs's colorful body was like the tattooed man at the circus. He enticed the curious with prurient intent.

Later, the rows of cages were dismantled, and the zoo moved to a zoological park upriver. In its place, after tearing down the old Spanish mission style city hall, they built a new city hall, an abomination of concrete and glass. More progress. The new park had biogenic spaces for animals to roam. Jigs immediately began to escape, always recaptured walking along the seven-mile stretch of Lake Drive toward town. One night he reached his destination, and the next morning, a city maintenance worker found his body lying in the ground-floor atrium of the new city hall in a pool of his own semen on the exact spot his cage had once stood. The legend of Jigs the Mandrill died quickly. Other legends lived on.

Jigs's cage was bigger than my cell, and masturbation was an insufficient distraction for the animals in my zoo.

Final months in dim, throbbing light, alone with an illegible record of a ruined life and the hum of Old Sparky, a ratty cot, a filthy toilet, cold meals shoved through a slot … no worries of being chained in Plato's cave with the illusion of freedom, as there are no shadows in darkness. *Now that I'm liberated, I must read the story of my life. Before I can act, I must remember.*

I scanned the horizon once more, mentally preparing myself for what was to come. This would be a difficult journey through the memories of hell. Finally, I took a deep breath, dropped my eyes to the first full entry, and began to read.

# CHAPTER 2

A nd so it began.

I was a female child born and raised in a small town in central Florida. I was smart, they said, the teachers and school counselors. But in school, I moved through halls of jocks, cunts, pricks, in-crowders, outsiders, deadheads, skateboarders, rednecks, preppies, those who could afford to set the styles, those who pretended not to care, those possessing raw material for Pygmalion's chisel, those deemed of more brittle stuff, those entering a teleological cul-de-sac, and those in the cultural fast lane, though that metaphorical highway in this town was a backroad through wetlands. I was unaware that I'd deflected my own trajectory by a recalcitrant insistence on acting independently. But a consistent sense of self eventually settled in and manifested itself in my insistence on cross-dressing. I loved men's clothes, nice men's clothes. I spent many an hour in the magazine section at Faust's Drug Store, pouring over *Gentleman's Quarterly* and other stylish magazines.

William Faulkner once said of white racial attitudes toward blacks: "The northerner loves the race but hates the individual. The southerner hates the race but loves the individual." I only remember whites hating everyone who wasn't. White was an ideal, not a race, in our town, and I refused to conform to whatever "whiteness" represented. If I was white, it would be on my own terms.

Having named the town and having said it was no different than other towns in the segregated South, I am free to describe a wondrous caveat. Perhaps every town had pockets of resistance against white superiority, but our town had something I'd never heard of elsewhere.

Our town had Monk's Pool Hall, an almost mystical island unto itself. An island inhabited by a strange mixed race of the disenfranchised who cared nothing for the machinations of people of any hue or delusions of superiority. It was insulated from the demands of social order and disguised as a pool hall. A sign above Monk's cash register read "BEWARE: We are segregationists. We love only green. Shoot a mean stick or be segregated from yours."

These inhabitants were rarely seen outside the pool hall, though I know some had jobs other than hustling. Yet, they were whispered about, sightings discussed around school cafeteria tables as if a Yeti or Big Foot had been sighted. They were cool because they didn't care about cool. If you were a high schooler, just saying you got a nod from one of them on the street was enough to dominate a lunch hour. If you were older, the envy went deeper.

Now, years later, as my soul rots in this prison, I have recanted all doubts of the existence of Monk's inviolable code and pray it gives me strength to survive this hell. Their credo? We've got nowhere to go and a lifetime to get there. If you've got someplace to go, then go there, but don't bother us on your way. And don't prey on the weak. It pisses us off.

Monk's island was under the spell of his simplistic sense of fairness that guided the inhabitants. A pool hall saying coined by a small boy summed it up: the red table runs true no matter who wields the cue. Monk kept all his tables physically balanced. All the tables were covered by green felt, the standard back then, but one table in the very back was covered in red felt, and it was where hustlers bet heavily, a table both physically and metaphorically balanced. I once heard Monk covered it in red because it didn't show blood splatters as much.

Monk's Pool Hall was a long, low building bracketed by a narrow weed-strewn pass-through between it and the neighboring building on one side, a wide alley in the back for trash pickup and meter readers, and a spur line of the Seaboard Coastline Railroad on the far side. It faced First Street in a blue-collar section of town. It was a long gray stucco building in the Spanish mission style. It always reminded me of a miniature version of the Alamo. It had a plate glass window on each side of its double wooden doors, which stood open during business hours so that two hinged screen doors allowed air to flow in but kept flies out. On the plate glass windows in arced gold letters with black trim, it read Monk's Pool Hall.

Interior lighting was restricted to long red Budweiser lamps hanging over two rows of pool tables. The fluorescent bulbs had to work hard to penetrate a dense fog of cigarette smoke. The floor was gray concrete littered with cigarette butts doused with a quick spin of a shoe. Cue racks hung on each end of the tables, and there were narrow shelves with chalk and powder canisters set high enough not to interfere with a drawn cue on a tight rubber shot. I'd only been inside once and was amazed at how quiet and salubrious the sounds seemed. It was like a library with little talking, and it was kept low and serious since concentration was at a premium. The main sounds consisted of a juke box at low volume and the steady clack of balls sporadically punctuated by the crescendo of a break shot.

I looked up from the journal. I'd just seen the realty office that now occupied Monk's. The contrast between now and then sent a tsunami of regret and loneliness through me. Memories of Monk and his regulars were greatly responsible for my sanity during my early days in prison. Monk's bound me to something that seemed a talisman against the random violence of prison. I needed a few moments to disengage. Staring out over the lake was the only way to calm my emotions. Only the river looked as it did then. Only the northbound current understood.

I was afraid I might weep if I stared at this view too long, this beautiful river that had flowed through the town since long before white men fucked it all up. I was free and sitting on a bench shaded by a lovely honeysuckle-covered pergola. A breeze wafted off the lake and enveloped me in the aroma of lake water and hyacinths mixed with the sweet smell of honeysuckle. It was all beatific and surreal, filling me with cascading memories of childhood. But it was also devastating. I never had the chance to visit this place before I was sent to prison. Never had the opportunity to see the exact place on this seven-mile seawall where an innocent angel was pulled from the river. I couldn't imagine how frail and lifeless she must have appeared. It was only here that I could read my journal and attempt to recapture the person I'd once been. Only here might I stem the regret of what I'd missed. How much water had flowed past this bench while I was in that horrid place?

The tannic waters of the St. John's River, the Nile of America, flowed from the wetlands of the Everglades to its delta at Jacksonville, sometimes flowing in a singular path, at others splintering as it crawled like a tangled horde of glistening snakes through wetlands before emerging in a five-mile-wide expanse called Lake Monroe.

The moccasin- and gator-infested river formed a chain of lakes, but life on the river as practiced for generations was lost. Progress some said. Fucked sideways said others, as towns erupted on its banks and exploded with people. Northern money some said. Carpetbaggers said others.

The invaders came for the weather, especially during the three to four months when their godforsaken towns were mired in the gray nothingness of whatever kept them up there. Old settlers in Florida had only vague notions of bleak jobs in dark factories.

Or maybe Yankees loved dark, cold days and wore ties or fancy dresses to work. Once here, they always looked the same, like … well, tourists. Some Floridians wanted more of them. Old settlers wished they'd stay the fuck up there.

Old settlers remembered rough riverside honky-tonks dotting the river. Those were gone, replaced by fancy restaurants. Fried fish and gator tail became sea bass stuffed with hummingbird dicks or fish Oscar garnished with pheasant titties. Some thought it fine dining. Others asked who the hell was Oscar and why did he fuck up a good piece of fish?

Corporate folks never sat on the river with friends, holding a cane pole and a cold beer, fishing for their own dinner.

I frowned. "There is unrest even in the plashing of the current." I glanced quickly around. No one heard, so I continued lecturing the attentive air. "Nature is the signal; man is the noise."

In college, I studied statistics. Probability was a disciplined mistress. "What'd you do, puke on the paper?" my father had asked. Life was one big cryptogram to my father.

He was a small man in every way. A cocky Banta rooster at five eight, his body had been unhealthily thin from drink, with severely thinning hair. To combat his aging appearance, he had died his hair black and propagated a vine-like comb-over that started above the left ear and swooped in greasy ropes toward the right. It fooled no one. In prison, I imagined that hair graying and disappearing over a gray skull. I'd never get to see it. I'd been dead to him long before prison.

He'll live on in my memory with that black plastered comb-over. At least it drew attention away from his weak chin, long, thin nose, and thick eyebrows that could have contributed to his comb-over if he'd let them keep growing.

Why my mother married him was a mystery. Never did they reveal any hint of what brought them together. The only conclusion I could draw was that she was pregnant with me. The mystery was greater because my mother was, at least from her photographs, an attractive girl though bound, as are we all, by her times. Her auburn hair was heavily permed, but her face was pretty, with light brown eyes, high cheek bones, a cleft nose, and a dimpled chin. By the time I was old enough to notice, all the brightness and light had faded under the unrelenting demands of an egomaniacal husband.

I sighed heavily. My heart was calm again. I'd walk along the river a bit and then start reading again.

Leitner Dredge sat at the wheel of a red BMW 320i convertible headed south from the neon cacophony of Las Vegas. The top was down and the wind playful, as the sun had not yet scorched away the remnants of cool night air. His curly ash-blond hair flittered in the wind at the edges of a red baseball cap, and the stems of gold-rimmed sunglasses disappeared into his locks. Leitner's cheeks and nose had begun to redden in the sun, so he'd slathered sunscreen on his face and neck. His face was slightly asymmetrical, his chin slightly lopsided, one blue-green eye appearing to squint slightly, but he had one of those smiles that transformed his face, giving him a boyish look that evoked undeserved trust.

He slid his sunglasses down his nose and glanced at the woman in the passenger seat, Summer Winters, truly her name, she swore. Even after she flashed a driver's license, he'd thought it was a made-up name perfect for a bleach-blonde hustler with oversized tits.

As he glanced at her, he was struck by her beauty, even with the obviously bleached hair. Leitner was not a man bereft of confidence. Still, he knew it was important to keep women under control. It was never a good idea to let a woman think she had the upper hand, even if you thought she was more beautiful than you were handsome. No woman would ever play him.

Summer wore red-rimmed sunglasses, which covered deep brown eyes, and a red Delilah dress. Her feet were propped on the dash, and the wind whipped at her red scarf. Her profile was perfectly structured, and as he stole glances at her, Leitner felt himself getting aroused. She suddenly became aware of his attention and dropped her feet to the floorboard, smiling demurely. He gave a sarcastic snicker as he pushed his sunglasses back into place and returned his attention to the highway.

"It's not like I haven't seen what's under there a thousand times."

Summer's downturned lip quivered. "Then maybe you don't need to see it again." She crossed her arms and turned to look at the empty landscape.

Leitner blew air through puffed cheeks. "Look, I'm not in the best of moods today."

She kept her gaze on the desert whisking past. "I was— until now."

Leitner clenched his teeth. That damn Vegas wedding had been stupid and impulsive. He knew he'd regret it. But he didn't have to live with it. Still, she'd been a great partner, and he owed her.

"I had this dream last night. It's been a long time. It freaked me out a bit."

She turned and looked briefly at his boyish profile and then back out the window.

The sudden tension made him press the accelerator. He glanced at the speedometer and saw it top a hundred on a straightaway and backed off.

"Would you like to hear it?"

"Only if you want to tell me."

He turned his brooding attention to the road and said nothing.

Finally, she said, "Do you believe dreams mean something?"

He said, "Not really. Besides, it wasn't as clear this time. That's something, I guess. There were always mountains, but this time they were just dark silhouettes. And the people didn't have faces; I mean, they had faces, but I couldn't see them. But in dreams, you know who they are. And somebody was missing. He'd always been there. Anyway. Fuck it."

Leitner stopped short of revealing the cause of the dream. Nobody's business but his. He'd heard news of the man missing from his dream. A man recently released from prison in Florida. In last night's dream, he'd been merely the hint of a passing shadow. But they were on their way to Florida. Then the dream. He didn't believe in omens. Still.

She started to speak, but he gave her a quick smile. "It was a bad time. Let it slide, okay?"

She nodded, her eyes returning to the desert.

He sat silently for several miles as the landscape rolled past. He was always struck by how bland the desert looked up close but how majestic it was from a distance. Like people, if you thought about it. But he didn't think about it much. A sap up close was a sap from a distance.

He wanted the trip to go smoothly. He'd give it the effort he could. Until he couldn't.

"Let's just enjoy this. We have a ton of cash and plenty of time. I just need to get to this little town in Florida in a couple of weeks or so. It's supposed to be a honeymoon, right?"

His uncle had left him a message: "Please visit sometime this month. In two or three weeks if possible. May need some serious help."

Summer turned from the window and met his gaze. He saw the hint of a smile flash. *That wide-eyed naivete*, he thought. *How fucking sweet*. He never understood it. But it was the only thing he could stand in the world right now.

"Yeah," Summer said, "it's a honeymoon."

The two had met in the Mandalay Bay Hotel, where Leitner, using his favorite grift, had socially engineered a suite pretending to be a wealthy Russian oligarch. He'd managed a huge line of credit, and all was going well until he found himself at a blackjack table with a Russian businessman. He was caught off guard when the Russian began speaking in guttural Muscovite. Leitner chastised himself; success breeds complacency.

Leitner capitulated with a you-got-me smile, and soon the Russian was proud of himself for sniffing out such a clever scam. They shared laughs, and Leitner invited his new friend for a night cap at "a great place with no tourists, exotic." Night cap had a different meaning to Leitner when he felt cornered. The first nightcap was the diazepam cocktail he fed the Russian; the final one was lodged in the Russian's cranium after Leitner left the bar to "help his drunk friend to his hotel, the Bellagio." He said it several times to make sure everyone heard.

He and Summer joined forces in a circuitous manner that began in Leitner's bed. He was drawn to her physical attributes, especially what turned out to be oversized but natural breasts. Her face was beautiful in a way he couldn't describe. Wholesome and perky while maintaining a sultry bombshell look.

In a strange twist, Leitner's first encounter with Summer was when he saw her at a blackjack table with a Russian. Russians and Arabs were Leitner's favorite targets. Both could be dangerous, but both shared inherent cultural weaknesses: macho egos and misogyny. That's why he agreed to team up with Summer.

"You're a natural at this, Leitner," she'd said. It grated when she pronounced his name, but he let it slide. You could take the girl out of Jersey ... "I admit I'm a hired companion, but I'm not a hooker, and I don't want a pimp telling me what to do and taking my money. I make a good living on my own. But you're a real pro."

She was asleep in the suite the night Leitner returned from his drink with a briefcase full of euros and rubles. Leitner explained what had happened. The Russian had shadowed Leitner's bets at the blackjack table and won so much that he invited Leitner out for a drink. Then the bastard jumped him for his winnings. He was lucky to be alive. In truth, the unconscious Russian had received several silenced pistol shots to the face, a set of fake credentials, and then a swim in the reservoir. He might be found, but no place was more adamant than Las Vegas about security and hiding embarrassing press when it failed. Mustn't scare the tourists.

Summer begged him to partner with her and show her the ropes. Leitner watched her, and she showed promise. He'd always wanted to try a double-reverse grift he knew, and Summer's assets were perfect for it if she'd pay attention to his every word. He finally agreed on the condition that she undergo a training regimen and suspend all her hustling activities until he said she was ready. She agreed without hesitation.

For the next year, the two stalked the artificially darkened subterranean world of Vegas, fleecing every millionaire within sight of Summer's considerable breasts, ultimately finding themselves in the red BMW after planting its owner several feet beneath a cactus stand at the edge of a desert escarpment.

It had been their only close call as a team, and Leitner had decided it was a good time to set out for an impromptu honeymoon. He was furious with himself for not pegging that mark right.

Ten years prior to a cactus burial outside Las Vegas and twenty years after a murder trial in a small town on Lake Monroe, Florida, Assistant District Attorney Robert Manakin stood in his tailored tuxedo at the altar of the historic St. John's Episcopal Church in Tallahassee. Six of his closest friends, three frat brothers from Rollins College and three friends from FSU Law School, were lined up behind him as he stared into the golden-brown eyes of Marilyn Osgood. At nineteen, she was the most beautiful woman he'd ever laid eyes on. The elaborate wedding was newsworthy enough for the local news affiliates and was as much a coming out event for Robert as it was a marriage ceremony.

To Robert's irritation, Marilyn's Baptist mother sobbed relentlessly in the front row across the aisle from his own parents, who sat in perfect dignified elegance. His father had encouraged the marriage because Marilyn would make the perfect trophy wife to parade in front of donors at fund-raisers.

"Once you're married to her, you can keep the parents at bay. Can you imagine her mother parading into parties in those hideous floral dresses? And her father can barely string two words together in a coherent sentence."

Robert's father was a brilliant land developer, and Robert always listened to him. His father had paved his way, but he knew his dad was proud of him for developing the cutthroat skills it took to become the golden boy of the Florida Republican Party.

"Don't worry, Dad. Thanks to you I've been building relationships for the future." He'd assured his dad he could expand the family fortune beyond all expectations. He had no idea his father would be dead within months from a massive coronary. Robert made a promise at his graveside to fulfill his dreams for the family—no matter what it took.

Just prior to his father's death, Robert Manakin, at age twenty-nine, took over as the youngest warden in the history of Florida State Prison at Raiford. Robert intended to have a profound effect on the inmates of Florida State Prison. And then, with the Party's backing, the governor's office. "Then, who knows?" the chairman of the Republican Committee asked. Robert was certain he knew.

# CHAPTER 3

I leaned forward and scanned the surface of the lake to the horizon. The weather was muggy, so I wore a white seersucker shirt and tan linen pants with brown deck shoes. I'd grabbed a broad-brim straw hat and sunglasses as I left the house. The outfit had become standard for me, as it kept me cool while protecting me from the Florida sun. I'd bought a closet full of such clothing. Anything but the royal blue of a prison uniform.

The wind was calm, and the broad waters, five miles from my bench in Seminole County to the far tree-lined shore in Volusia County, was a black mirror over which sailboats tacked into any available breeze, limp sails flickering against the horizon, hulls reflecting off the water in impressionistic swaths of color. The marina to the left sat silently with only the occasional slap of waves against the hull of a yacht as a passing motorboat sent a tandem of wakes through the harbor's narrow entrance, where a blanket of water hyacinths rose and fell with a sound akin to yacht ropes tugging against moorings.

To the right, where the river walk ended and the seawall began, was a scattering of folks, cane poles arced over the river, fishing for mullet, bream, and speckled perch, as they had for generations before river walks or seawalls. The wall was built to keep an angry lake from the town's streets during tropical storms, much like the Aswan Dam had tamed the Nile. When the lake managed to breach the seawall, as kids we tied ropes to the bumpers of rear-engine cars and surfed the flooded streets. It was more fun than any ride at the Tragic Kingdom.

Seeing the old jewelry store had struck me hard. It was no longer a jewelry store but a sandwich shop. My father had apparently tried to sell the shop without success and eventually declared Chapter 11. On one side had been a barber shop-cum-biker bar. On the other was now a pizza parlor.

The biker bar bothered me not at all. The clientele was rough, but I'd spoken with the owner early one evening at the German restaurant, the Willow Tree. We sat at the bar and over a beer the owner, Wilson Smith, told me a strange but familiar tale.

I'd bought him another liter of beer to prime him.

Wilson sat hunched over his beer as I listened attentively.

"I was thinking about closing the joint down. It weren't doing shit. Then, one night a little before closing, this was three maybe four years ago, this feller come in and slipped to the very back table so's he could sit off by hisself. Only some biker diehards was left. They was the kind I loved to see out the door. Nasty drunks with big muscles and bad attitudes.

"Anyway, I noticed this feller kept his hoodie pulled up over his head like he was hiding his face. Turns out he was doing just that, even keeping his head down when the waitress brought him a beer. She'd just took him his second PBR when these two big bikers, nasty sons of bitches, went after a local college kid what come in from time to time to shoot a few racks. I had two pool tables. The kid was good. I'd talked a bit with him. Turns out he earned money for his college books shooting pool 'cause his mama couldn't afford 'em. The bikers lost one time too many and went after him.

"What happened next reminded me of tales about that old pool hall, Monk's. Ever hear of it?"

I smiled. "Of course. I was living here when Monk's was going strong. I knew some of the regulars."

His eyes widened. "Really? I bet you got some good stories. Some older customers talk like the place was full of men who'd chew your heart out and spit it back in your face if you thought you was tough."

I laughed. "That's exactly what people said in my day. And it was true."

Wilson shook his head. "Maybe that explains what happened that night. Because before I could blink an eye, this hooded man steps out of the shadows, whips out a knife, flips it open like a gunslinger, and—*whoosh*—in a flash of lighting slices a big gash in the arm of one biker, who falls to the floor, grabbing at it. Then he pins the biggest biker to the wall. The stupid bastard reared back and took a mad swing at this feller's head, and I swear to you, it looked like that damn biker was a rag doll when the hooded man lifted him up and flipped him onto the floor next to his friend. Before you could blink, he had his knife under the biker's beard, and that poor fucker was staring up into the face of a bad dream."

I caught my breath. "Bad dream?"

Wilson gave a firm nod. "Yep, and I mean a goddamn nightmare. This fella stood up and pulled the hood off his head, and holy shit. He stared around the room, and I swear you could hear every pair of drawers ripping at the seams with the shit being squoze. Hell, I nearly shat my pants and he never looked my way. His head and face was plumb tore up with burn scars, and I'm telling you, folks was trying to look up their own assholes so as not to stare at that face."

I was stunned, but I couldn't stop the smile teasing the corners of my mouth.

Wilson continued, "I remember his exact words 'cause there weren't no other words coming out of no other mouths. When this fella spoke, it sounded like bagpipes being blowed up, but every word was clear. Here's exactly what he said."

Wilson put his chin down and dropped his voice an octave. "I miss me a Camel cigarette more 'n I miss a blowjob. These fucked-up lips won't draw smoke no more. I come in here of an evening for a dose of secondhand smoke and a couple o' beers. Any a' you fuckers want to lose a beauty contest to me? Just start another goddamn fight while I'm in here."

His voice went back to normal. "Then he pulls the hood over his head and walks out. He used to come in about once a month until about a year ago. I ain't seen him since."

I asked, "Can you tell me how big he was? And maybe what kind of knife he used?"

Wilson frowned. "He was a big man, maybe six three or six four. But the way he slung that big biker ass over head, he must have been made of muscle. As for the knife, it was one of those long old-timey folding knives, thin long blade, probably seven inches."

I grinned, shaking my head. "We used to call that a fruit knife. I used to know a fella who wasn't dressed without two or three peeking from his pockets. You say this fella doesn't come in now?"

"Haven't seen him, but no one else has either. And it was strange." Wilson took a quick sip of beer. "I thought he might hurt business, but folks started coming in droves."

I grinned. "Listen, my friend. You've been touched by the spirit of Monk's Pool Hall. It's a gift."

*The red table still runs true.* The thought came with a wave of sadness.

Wilson said, "Yep, I agree. He sure as hell saved my business. I'd like to hear some stories about Monk's. I heard one a long time ago, right after I moved here, about some boys out of Monk's saving a local jewelry store from being robbed by a couple of professionals."

I hadn't known whether to smile or cry, but I held my tongue. Some legends were best left alone, especially when fact is stranger than rumor and truth can't be conveyed in the language of mortals.

I knew I needed to spend as much time on this bench as possible. When it got too hot to sit outside, I'd seek out a haven to wait it out. I leaned back to examine my scarecrow body. I'd lost weight in iso, so I was bone-sack thin, and my thinning hair had gone white as Silk's. Silk, the paradox, an albino—a black man as white as snow. Like gender, skin color is a continuum. What was it that made Silk a black man when he was whiter than any white man? I reached into my satchel and pulled out the journal. I studied its smooth, tan leather binder and set it carefully on my lap but didn't open it. Instead, I gazed again at the lake and then turned to look up Lake Drive.

A block away and across the street sat the old civic center, dark and foreboding now. It had died along with the civic spirit. Back then, there were dances every Friday night outside on a broad concrete patio surrounded by Australian pines that still stood like a row of giant soldiers. Speakers, pitiful by modern standards, mounted to the eaves of the curved wing bordering the patio had pumped drive-in quality music into the night air. High-school kids had wriggled and twisted and courted, a few sneaking off to make out in the shadows, the girls to get some tongue, the boys seeking rare stink finger. Inside were pool and ping-pong tables where younger kids had thwacked ping-pong balls and older ones shot pool, allowing as how they'd soon be ready to go down to Monk's and show them a thing or two. Few ever went near the place.

It was during these weekly teenage rituals as a young girl that I became ultimately convinced I'd never grow up to be a woman. I'd been born in the wrong body. I tried dancing with boys, but it was the girls who fascinated. Not sexually. Regardless of gender, I'd never been much for sex until college; the sweaty panting and rutting about seemed more disgusting than exciting. It was the girls' constant preening and obsession with hair and clothes and the way they chattered in incessant twittering fricatives. I could never be one of them. There was no use trying. And dancing with the boys was perverted. It was like dancing with your dirty uncle who kept grabbing your ass.

I unwound the leather strap from around the binder. In prison my soul had been leeched out each day in a thousand ingenious ways. I wasn't sure my life was worth the oxygen.

I turned my eyes down to the journal and began to read.

I was born Margarite Ecclesia Purloin but transformed into Stuart Walker Purloin. I chose the name Stuart Walker after a poet I discovered in a fortuitous accident while in route to visit my paternal grandparents in Virginia. This was the year before my parents became embarrassed by what they'd bred, before I ruined their lives, or so they would claim. I could never tell them it was the words of a poet that freed me from their bigotry.

We were passing through a quaint town north of Roanoke and stopped for lunch at a corner restaurant. I finished eating and stepped next door to a bookshop to browse while my mother finished her hamburger and my father continued griping about its cost. I entered, and there on the first table was a stack of thin books signed by a local poet. The pleasant lady at the counter said the poet taught at a nearby university. I read the first few lines and was hooked. I used my allowance to buy a copy, which I read until the pages fell out. His voice was soft rain in an arid soul. I fell in love with words between the covers of that book and then his next books and those by the same publisher and then by other publishers in endless expanding ripples over a sea of beautifully crafted words.

That book saved my soul, but in a strange twist, it also saved my life.

On a hot, sunny day years later, as I was bent over a watch repair in the family jewelry shop, I caught sight of movement out of the corner of my eye. I glanced up, and there stood the strange boy who swept floors at Monk's Pool Hall, planted statue-like, staring at that worn book of poems propped next to the cash register. He wore a striped T-shirt, jeans, and sneakers. Of all the glitter in that jewelry shop, it was a book that snared him.

"Do you like books?" I asked.

He nodded without looking at me. Then he spoke in a voice, low and strange, that sent a chill through me. "They can't hurt you. You have Virgil to guide you."

I was stunned and managed only to stutter, "Sorry ... I don't understand."

His voice softened. "Sure you do. Yes, I love books."

I stood and laid the watch on the counter. "Would you like to read that one?"

He rotated his head without moving his body and smiled. "I already did but thank you. It was excellent."

I was surprised at his grammar, which was far beyond his years, and that he'd read such an obscure work. But I was stunned by his eyes. I'll never forget them. They seemed too large for his face, though that was not uncommon in small children. What was uncommon was the size of his dark brown irises. Only a thin halo of white encircled them.

I forced a laugh. "How would you manage to find a book by a Virginia poet?"

He gave me an impish grin and pointed. "I borrowed that one. I glued it back together for you. You must have read it many times."

It seemed each word he spoke surprised, but now I thought he must be engaging in childish fantasy. I said with a polite smirk, "I'm sure you didn't read that one."

He turned his forefinger upward, and I followed with my eyes. It took a moment, but I saw what he was pointing at. "The air-conditioning vent? You snuck in through there?"

His grin turned to a frown. "Yes, ma'am. I borrow books from all over town."

I stared at him and then shook my head, not sure I was connecting his words with my thoughts. "You climbed through a vent in a jewelry store to take a book?"

The grin returned. "Yes'm. I'd look silly in jewelry. Besides, I don't steal. I always put the books back." A slight frown crossed his face. "I like you. You're different. You must be brave to be a transvestite. I just stopped by to tell you how easy it is to sneak into your store. If I'm able to do it, then ..." He shrugged, shot me a big grin, and scampered out.

The encounter was disturbing. A small boy with an encyclopedic vocabulary had broken into ... no, he had broken nothing. He'd simply dropped into my store with ease, taken my book of poetry, and then returned it. Therefore, he had entered twice.

I hurried to the front and pulled the small book from its place by the register. It had been meticulously glued back together. I took a quick inventory of my stock. Nothing was missing.

The next day, I called a contractor to make security improvements. They swept in with practiced efficiency and left assuring me my shop was now "robbery proof," especially with the state-of-the-art panic button that summoned the police.

I didn't mention the small boy but was baffled by his comment about not being hurt and having Virgil to guide me. His words were familiar, and soon it hit me. I went straight to a poem in the book.

> I never needed Virgil
> Or thought of him, but now
> That place seems hell enough ...

It was true: prison was hell enough. Perhaps the boy was a prophet I failed to heed. There would be spirals into Dante's ever smaller rings. In prison, the poet's words became a mantra of hope.

Virgil would appear in many forms, the first time sooner than I expected and called forth by the small boy with strange eyes.

I looked up from the journal. Why was it so hard to plow ahead? Stupid question. Each page of the journal brought back memories. Virgil. There were three rivers important in my life: The Shenandoah gave me poetry; the Arno gave me peace; and the St. Johns gave me life. Then I had three Virgils, without whom I would not have survived: Sharkey, Alphonse, and Maestro. Then Mr. O, with a little help from an old friend, had made me rich. It was true that money didn't lead to happiness. Maybe it paved the road, maybe not. I had so much now, I couldn't spend it all if I had another lifetime. How many billions does one need not to seek more? With a computer, a project from a mob boss, Mr. O, and a little guidance from an old friend from college, suddenly I had enough to do whatever I wanted. Payments from Mr. O, Bitcoin trading, hacking … Well, it's in the journal somewhere.

If only I'd stayed in Europe after the transition. The day I returned, I became a convenient solution to a murder. A body found floating in Lake Monroe. Someone I knew. Someone I would never have harmed. Now I'd returned to find out why my very existence had become a convenient scapegoat. I knew how, but I wanted to know why. And I wanted to ruin the man who put me there. Sheldon Richardson. Perhaps he would die. A life for a life. I knew he still lived here. He was out of town. I'd sent him a message asking him to meet me. He wouldn't turn me down. He would be too afraid to turn me down. He knew who I worked for in prison.

Leitner Dredge and Summer Winters crossed into Arizona on Highway 93 and onto the brown plains south of Hoover Dam. The day was sunny and the desert air devoid of humidity, so Leitner acquiesced and put the top down. He wore a black ball cap he'd retrieved from among several hats in the trunk next to the dead man's luggage, which had yielded, among other pleasant surprises, a Glock handgun. He was confident that as long as the body wasn't discovered, they could keep the car. He'd check area news feeds occasionally and steal some backup plates should he need a bridge before switching vehicles. Last time he'd kept a poor schmuck's Mercedes until he was done with it and then torched it. He doubted that body was ever found.

Summer wore a sheer white scarf over her head, a white sundress that dipped seductively in front, and red lipstick below large white-rimmed sunglasses. Leitner had masked his surprised response to her striking Marilyn resemblance.

Summer was pouting because he'd refused to stop at the Hoover Dam, which he found beyond irritating. It was as if she'd forgotten that they'd planted the owner of their car in a shallow grave. It was too soon to stop. It was time to twist his hold a bit. He couldn't let Summer dictate a goddamn thing on this trip. He knew she couldn't pout for long.

She turned in her seat. "Leitner, baby?" He winced as *LOYT-nah* spilled off her tongue. "Can we at least stop and see some of the sights along the way? You said we ain't in a hurry, and we're really close to the Grand Canyon and many other wonderful sights."

Leitner kept his eyes on the road. "I did say that. And I'll be happy to stop at some of the sights. On two conditions."

"Sure," she said with a huge red-lipped smile. "Anything."

"First"—his look was a menacing sneer—"pronounce my fucking name right. It isn't *LOYT-nah*," he exaggerated with a whining falsetto. "It's Leitner, like turn on the light, not like loiter. Got it?"

Her face fell, and her lower lip quivered. "I can't help the way I talk"—talk came out *twawk*—"and you never complained before."

"This isn't before. This is now. How about you give it a try. Can you say light bulb?"

She said it slowly and got close.

"Excellent try. Now just put -*ner* on the end. Not -*nah*, -*ner*."

She said his name slowly, frowning as the syllables rolled from her tongue.

"Not bad," he said. "Just keep practicing every time you say my name, and soon you won't sound like a Jersey bimbo when you say it."

"I'm sorry," she said, looking down at her hands wringing in her lap.

"Now for the second thing." He reached over and slipped his right hand under her skirt until his fingers found the crotch of her silk panties. He scratched gently at her clitoris, and she moaned softly. "How about you lean over here and put those luscious red lips around my cock. You keep sucking, and I'll tell you when we reach the Grand Canyon. How does that sound?"

A smile leapt back onto her face. "You got it, Leitner." She said the name properly. "If we can stop to see stuff, I'll suck your dick all the way to"—Leitner knew Summer's light did not burn bright—"that other ocean."

Leitner shook his head and gave a frustrated sigh, but seconds later when he felt Summer's warm, wet mouth, he put his head back and pressed the accelerator. Life didn't get much better than a convertible, a long, straight road, and a gorgeous woman on your cock.

# CHAPTER 4

S omewhere in the margin of one of the pages I'd written, "A lame gazelle among lions must treat each breath as a gift." I remembered my emotional state when penning that phrase.

I glanced up, relieved that there was no one nearby. Many men in prison began talking to themselves, especially in iso. Most ex-cons learned to say nothing.

I looked down and began to read.

After high school, I left for college. My parents became exasperated with my lifestyle, though my only real crime was not dressing like a girl. The implications overwhelmed them. They thought college would "straighten me out." Everyone from the Baptist preacher to a psychiatrist had failed.

The psychiatrist was a conservative asshole right out of some cliché TV show. My sessions with him ended with a shrug and a psychobabble-laden excuse for washing his hands of me. The excuse, in layman's terms, was "sometimes people are just wired wrong."

My father never ceased his relentless efforts to "cure me," incessantly expressing his disappointment. He made it known that

I was holding him back with my aberrant public displays. From what wasn't clear.

Throughout my early life, my father sat at the head of the table after my mother spent her fastidious Baptist energies preparing a tasteless meal, usually something with ground beef and tormented vegetables, bragging about all the things he could do if only stupid bosses could discern his genius; ahead of his time; a little money to give flight to his entrepreneurial spirit; blah, blah, blah.

I took over the family jewelry shop after my grandfather's death. My maternal grandfather was a brilliant man but a dreamer. My father possessed only the latter. My grandfather had worked to establish the small shop in the face of increasing competition from mall-based chains. His edge was a talent for tinkering. Mall stores were volume retailers that wouldn't change the batteries in precision watches much less service them. My grandfather learned the workings of high-end pieces and could even rebuild a Rolex as well as licensed Rolex specialists. I adored my grandfather.

When he passed away, my father was helpless. That was the year I came home from the University of Florida. I'd been there six years graduating magna cum laude in statistics with minors in finance and computer science as an undergraduate and then staying to get my master's degree in statistics. I will always reflect lovingly on my time at UF. I came home more committed than ever to my life choice.

My father's disappointment was evident, but he had no choice but to ask me to run Purloiner Jewelry. Purloin was my maternal grandfather's name. After his death, I insisted the name stay the same, arguing with my father that it was an established brand. My father was incensed, but he'd learned nothing about the business, and he didn't care to. I became his ticket to a life of ease, so Purloiner it was, and Purloiner it stayed.

I had plans of my own, but my parents had financed my college, so I traded six years of college for six years at the shop. In truth, it was my grandfather who'd paid for my education, but had I refused to help, my father's lack of talent would have left my mother destitute.

I was amazed at how much I loved the work.

My father's recalcitrance was not surprising. For narcissists the future remains shrouded in the fog of dreams. My mother stood up to him once and received a black eye for her fortitude. I snuck into his den that night and threatened him with a butcher knife, telling him if he ever did that again he'd lose the hand that struck her. I was twelve.

He came at me, and I gave him a gash on the arm so deep that we had to rush him to the emergency room for stitches. He whined like a goat in labor and openly blamed me to the hospital staff. At my murder trial, the incident was dredged up by the prosecution—evidence of my violent nature.

"Ladies and gentlemen of the jury, her ... excuse me ... his"—a titter of laughter from the gallery—"own father? The one who raised him, fed him, clothed him ... after a manner"—more laughter—"the lack of gratitude exceeded only by the violence of this ... this thing's nature."

"Objection, your honor. The prosecutor is poisoning the jury with an issue completely unrelated."

"Sustained."

"Excuse me, ladies and gentlemen. I meant, of course, this person."

I built the jewelry shop into a successful enterprise, but I was always a comment on everyone's lips as they drove past the store. "That's one of our finest jewelry shops; the owner is a transvestite. You know how artistic they are," as if such knowledge should be on the chamber of commerce tour.

I've always wondered what they'd say if they witnessed my worst days in prison. Those experiences almost made me blame myself for the punishment I received. Then one day, for reasons I can't explain, there arose in me an impenetrable psychological firewall. Our deepest perversions can get tangled like fishing line. Sometimes you must toss the reel away and get a new one.

My fortunes in prison changed trajectory in an unexpected way just as I was about to suffer a horrific mutilation. My Alphonse became a Virgil.

A member of the Aryan Brotherhood whose lust far outstripped his acumen was convinced that since I had once been a woman there must still be a vagina tucked away somewhere between my legs. He recruited a couple of his fellow anatomical geniuses to hold me down while he attempted to reopen the treasure box with a razor blade.

I was seconds from mutilation when a benefactor appeared out of nowhere. I was in a dimly lit maintenance closet, lying in a fetal position, holding my hands over my carefully constructed genitalia. Suddenly the door was kicked open. I heard grunts and screams of pain followed by Aryan feet pounding a getaway.

My savior was Alphonse Ibn Rashid, his shaved head shining like a halo when he rushed into the closet. He adopted the last name in prison after a rapid and necessary conversion to Islam. Alphonse was a giant black man from a tiny hamlet upriver from my town who'd been incarcerated for killing two game and wildlife officers.

Before prison, Alphonse owned a crab shack on the river, steaming and serving blue crab and a variety of local "river food" like fried fish, turtle, braised rabbit—river soul food—and the best swamp cabbage salad anywhere on the St. Johns. Life on the river was tough, but for a black man, it was also dangerous.

The two officers were part of a burgeoning "protection" industry involving the extortion of postintegration "uppity blacks" who opened small businesses. When Alphonse refused to buy "insurance," they burned his smokehouse and told him his dock and boats would be next. Alphonse fed them to the river, and it took dental records to identify one of them. He was arrested, but there was no evidence of murder. They charged him with one count of manslaughter; there were no remains of one of the extortionists.

Though foxholes and prison cells throw men together and many forge relationships out of stress and loneliness, some men never admit their deep affection for another. For me there was no moral dilemma, not because I was transgender or homosexual but because persistent gratitude nurtured by kindness breeds affection, especially if the object of that gratitude is a fine human being like Alphonse, who adhered to a moral code with which I was familiar. I found out my beloved Alphonse was the great-uncle to someone from my hometown, a denizen of Monk's Pool Hall. A black man as white as snow. It explained his integrity. He treated me with greater respect than my father treated my mother. I was loved and protected.

My affection led me to take up a habit many feminine counterparts in prison practiced. I began to wear a tiny bit of makeup. I rarely wore makeup before prison. In fact, I remember only one occasion. In prison it was a means of distinguishing spousal roles. With my relatively delicate features, I was quite a stunner. Alphonse had himself a prize. I stayed with Alphonse for the remainder of his sentence, nearly five years, even harboring silly dreams of home and hearth with Alphonse at my side.

My father was a staunch racist; the only way I could have disappointed him more than a sex change would have been a homosexual relationship with a black man. I should have written him every detail.

Among inmates is a myth called prison karma. I didn't buy it. But the day after I paired with Alphonse, I almost changed my mind.

Soren Kierkegaard said, "Anxiety is the dizziness of freedom." In college I loved existentialism; in prison it is shit. Anyone who thinks anxiety is in anyway related to freedom needs to spend a few days in general population at Raiford. Fuck the "let's not be bourgeois, we're all free to invent our own paths" Sartre bullshit. I'm not riddled with anxiety. I'm riddled with unadulterated fear and horror, which escalated when I witnessed three vendettas on the same day.

I've been witness to dozens of fights, some bloody and brutal. Inmates suddenly square off and fists begin to pound meat. A punch to the face makes eyes glaze, a man staggers helplessly as his face turns to rivulets of red, a kick to the testicles ends with writhing on the ground. But never a vendetta.

By coincidence, a rookie guard and I witnessed all three on his first shift. It was also his last shift. Ethological theories were confirmed. Men have no moral or neurobiological constraints to prevent them from killing each another. The only difference between me and the young guard was that I was trapped in this horrid place.

Each vendetta exceeded the last in creative murder.

The first seems relatively benign. An inmate walked past me at breakfast and jammed a table fork into the chest of another sitting at the adjacent table. The handful of inmates in the voluminous cafeteria continued eating as if nothing had happened. The grating sound of a fork ricocheting off ribs and plunging into viscera haunts me whenever I hear an oily hinge. The fork wounded but didn't kill. The victim began screaming threats of revenge, so the perp turned, pulled the fork from the victim's chest, and shoved it into his mouth, twisting it down his throat until he drowned in his own blood, writhing on the table in panic as blood replaced oxygen.

I looked up, and the young rookie was one of the guards rushing into the cafeteria. He paused to stare down at the prone body, and his face reminded me of one of the demented peasant faces in a seventeenth-century Dutch painting. Mine was in that same painting.

The second vendetta occurred in the laundry room. I was pushing my library cart through the adjacent corridor and heard a commotion, so I peered through the small round window of a swinging door and saw a team of inmates pinning another to the filthy concrete floor. Four inmates each pinned a limb, one held a work towel over the victim's mouth, while the sixth straddled him, holding a familiar item: a bottle of Texas Pete hot sauce, the only substance that provided recognizable flavor to prison food.

A Texas Pete bottle has a familiar bullet shape. The inmate straddling the victim struck the cap on the floor, creating a jagged end; placed the bottle against the man's sternum with his left hand; and jammed his right repeatedly down on the bottle's round bottom. In three or four thrusts, it broke through the sternum and the bottle's contents poured into the unfortunate victim's chest cavity. It is impossible to imagine the excruciating pain of Texas Pete hot sauce spilling into the soft tissues around the heart. It makes me cringe to think of the agony suffered as his body went into violent paroxysms, kicking, writhing, and issuing muted screams in his last moments. He couldn't form words, only regurgitative gargling noises that a dying animal might make.

As I watched in horror, several guards rushed in from one of the many access points of the maze that is the laundry facility, the young guard among them. The perpetrators leapt up and fled into the labyrinth. All the guards pursued save one. The rookie paused to examine the dead inmate with a bottle of Texas Pete protruding from his chest as if some alien body was breaking out after gnawing its way through his viscera. The rookie raised a hand to his face, and I immediately recognized another painting. On an end wall of the Sistine Chapel is one of Michelangelo's most famous figures—a man shading half his horrified face with one hand as he stares down into hell. The young guard could have posed for that scene.

I find I can't gloss over the ultimate horror of that day, the third and most bizarre vendetta. I've always thought the word *surreal* to be misused and overused, but there is no word I can conjure as a substitute.

During afternoon exercise in the yard, I sat alone at the rickety picnic table near the basketball court as some inmates played five

43

on five—five whites against five blacks. Suddenly, all but two men on the teams backed away from a lone inmate, a big man with Aryan tats, a rare bipartisan act, as the attackers were from both races. The victim must have violated every gang rule known to have both sides after him. The biggest black man grabbed the target around the neck as a white inmate began to slap at him with the edge of what appeared to be an ordinary yard stick. It turned out to be what inmates called a trickle tool—a yard stick with a series of razor blades embedded along both edges except for a taped area for a grip.

Inmates smell blood like sharks, and a crowd gathered from nowhere as the victim was immobilized by one inmate as another began to beat a rapid staccato with the edge of the ruler on his torso, neck, groin—any area his twisting, thrashing body revealed in his efforts to escape. The wielder changed from a rhythmic beat to raking the deadly blades over the man's flesh, biting deeper and creating long gashes in the highways of his vascular system. I'd read something about this but forgot where. Later I looked it up. *Lingchi*. Lingering death or death by a thousand cuts, used in ancient China. To witness it in a dusty prison yard was beyond nightmarish.

Finally, the attack ended, and the victim was released to issue an endless stream of shrieks and epithets that echoed from the walls of the nearest cell block as the perpetrators disappeared into the surrounding crowd. The attack lasted perhaps three minutes on the clock but years in psychological time. When it was too late to intervene, a team of guards descended on the yard but did nothing. Perhaps they'd seen this before and knew there was nothing to be done but watch, like everyone else, ghoulishly enthralled by the inexorable ooze of vital fluids.

I scanned the faces of the guards and saw the young rookie. This time his face was unreadable, his stare distant and disengaged.

The wounded inmate stood, feet apart, arms extended, turning robotically and rocking from one foot to the other, blubbering forlorn sounds, the language of lost souls. Guttural noises tumbled from drooling lips as he rotated in short, bobbing sidesteps, scanning his body as dark spots spread over his shredded uniform and his flesh wept in sorrow.

In panic, he turned and stumbled toward the gate leading from the exercise yard. His efforts to run accelerated the bleeding, and halfway to the gate, he paused, wobbling on his legs, his breathing labored. The screams ceased. His blue uniform was almost saturated, the dark blue now like oilcloth glued to his flesh. Rivulets of blood leaked down his face and dripped from the stubble of a scraggly beard. I saw him with morbid clarity, unable to turn away, as he came to a halt no more than six feet from where I sat. Blood oozed from every pore as the vitality drained from a strong man leaving an empty husk in his place. I groped frantically for a stabilizing reality; I must be watching a horror film, and after this horrifying scene, a director would cut the scene, and an actor would leap to his feet unharmed. But this scene was unrelenting.

The inmate dropped to his knees and then toppled to all fours, arms weak and quivering. Only then did he give voice to his final moments of agony. A low growl gathered in his throat and, building, spewed forth in a high-pitched string of guttural words and random phonemes. I can only attempt to recreate the sounds: "No, fuck, nah, me, nah, plea, hep, fucks, gahdam." He closed with a long, regressive howl, "Mama." That plaintive word echoed from the cell block, a plea for comfort or the laying of blame for a life gone awry? Mama, please, help me? Mama, where did you go?

He pitched forward, and his left cheek slammed into the packed dirt, where he lay splayed, the toes of his shoes alternatingly kicking at the ground. There was a single final twitch as his buttocks raised and fell flat. Like many prison memories, this scene never truly ends. No director will step forth; no clapperboard will slam shut to end the horror. I remember a history professor who cited a Latin phrase common to medieval public clocks:

*vulnerant omnes, ultima necat.* They all wound, the last kills. In Raiford, each second wounds more deeply than the previous; sometimes you beg for a final one.

I looked for the young guard, but he was gone. I heard he suffered a debilitating attack of what inmates call prison panic. Prison panic is the overwhelming fear that, once inside, you'll never be allowed out. The young guard fled to the administration building, threw his credentials on the first desk he encountered, and ran to the parking lot, where he drove his pickup truck as fast as possible out through the employee gates. He probably drove until he ran out of gas, trying to get as far from this place as possible.

I write of these events not to describe creative brutality. That's no secret. It's the contrast between the casual curiosity in prisoners' eyes and the horrified stare of the rookie guard. That difference is the measured distance of my descent into hell.

That night I tried to sleep as I clung desperately to Alphonse's steel bicep. He could tell I was in bad shape and rolled me onto my side, my back to his chest. I guided him into me and begged him to make love to me. I was at a nadir, and Alphonse was my sole anchor in this inverted universe. His love was all that prevented me from ending what Shakespeare called my "outcast state."

Five years with Alphonse came to a peaceful end. There was only darkness ahead, or so I thought. Before his release, my Alphonse told me he tried to set something in motion to procure my safety. An extraordinary form of salvation. If it materialized.

Alphonse was paroled after serving half of his fifteen-year sentence for manslaughter, and though he'd killed an officer of the law, the parole board considered his crime to be motivated by passion; again, that Aristotelean, Dante-esque reasoning that crimes of passion are somehow lesser than crimes of reason.

Alphonse acted a final time on my behalf. He'd worked as a contract enforcer for the Cosa Nostra. They hired him on occasion because he was both universally feared and honest. They never worried he'd skim. They didn't like entering gen pop and hired Alphonse to take care of things among the Bloods and Black Muslims, usually involving an inmate who failed to pay for goods or services. The Cosa Nostra weren't eager to deal with the Aryan Brotherhood, too unstable and lacking the sense to know when paying was better than dying. If asked, Alphonse would also handle them. That's how he found me in a maintenance closet seconds from a very bad day.

Before he was paroled, he asked his contract agent to ask the boss to give me a job. And protection. Our last night together, Alphonse told me two things. First, the Cosa Nostra inmates were held in isolated luxury and continued to conduct business on the outside. Second, he promised them I'd be of great use to them.

We were lying together in his cot, his bicep, as big as my thigh, wrapped over my shoulders.

"You can, can't you, Stuart? Do smart things for them?" His voice was so deep I felt its bass notes vibrate against my back.

"What do you think they want from me?"

"I ain't all that sure, but I think they need help keeping track of all they's owed. And they don't like surprises. I'm hoping that's what you can do, the ciphering and keeping track of their money and such."

I snuggled into the crook of his arm. "I believe those are things I can do very well."

"I sure hope so. I don't know what I'd do if … you know …"

"It's okay, Big Man. I feel the same way. Please, get as far away from this hellhole as you can. I'll be fine."

Alphonse was the only good thing that happened to me in prison up to that point. I will always love him. He kept his business with the Cosa Nostra away from me for fear it would cause me trouble. Now, I prayed they'd reach out to me.

There is a piece by Shakespeare I'll never forget, perhaps because it's based on numbers or the erasure of the distance between lovers using a numeric metaphor.

So they loved, as love in twain
Had the essence but in one;
Two distincts, division none:
Number there in love was slain.

I loved Alphonse, and my heart broke when, a month after
he returned home, he was found in his bed at a halfway house in
Deltona shot to death. The halfway house was located on a ring
road around Lake Monroe, and Alphonse's window in Volusia
County looked out over the lake. He would have seen the lights
of my town glittering far across the dark waters at night.

A few days after Alphonse's death, I received an unexpected
letter. Alphonse was barely literate, so I was suspicious, but he
included proof of identity and a warning:

Dear Stuart: It's me, Alphonse. You know it's me cause I'm the
only one knows what we did together the day you saw three people
kilt. That nite was special. So, it's me. I am being hunted. I seen
them. They might be from prison. Waiting for me. They might
wait for you. It is always hot here. But there is a place with ice to
stay cold. Find it. I love you. Your Alphonse.

I found the letter confusing, but I was still grieving. I held
onto the final words of love and put the rest out of my mind. My
sentence still stretched out before me.

Two weeks after Alphonse was buried in a potter's field, two
men, "thugs from out of town," the paper said, were found splayed
atop "the grave of a recently released prison inmate." "Brutally
beaten with a blunt instrument of death," the local *Herald* reported
in typical hyperbolic ardor.

I broke down in tears of relief and almost didn't finish the
article. It was enough that vengeance had been served, and the
men who killed my Alphonse died horrible deaths; fuck 'em both
in their empty eye sockets. I plowed on through the article, and

the last line reported that the police discovered a message carved on the back of the crossbar of Alphonse's wooden cross above the two beaten bodies: "Red table run true."

I found myself alternately laughing and crying, laughing at the beautiful absurdity and crying from grief and a strange elation. Anyone who knew where those words originated would know where to find those avenging angels. I'm convinced the police knew where to look for the killers of "thugs from out of town" and decided it was best to call it square and leave it alone. I felt the same. Justice was done, and it was time to move on as Alphonse wished.

That said, I got tremendous satisfaction from my imaginal replay of a pale ghost wielding the small metal bat he always carried up his sleeve, meting out brutal justice in a potter's field, two men at his side, one holding a fruit knife he would use to carve a message in a cross and the other staring with dead, gray eyes. A message sent to those who would disturb the balance of the red table. Every time I reread the news story of "thugs from out of town," it would inevitably lead to memories of the attempted robbery in the family jewelry shop.

They identified the two men who killed Alphonse. They were cellmates in Florida State Prison, and both were recently paroled. One had been a small-time pro wrestler who went by the stage name Thunder Ned. In prison he had joined the Aryan Brotherhood and had once been beaten badly by Alphonse for not paying prison debts. The second was convicted of armed robbery, primarily targeting small-town jewelry shops from Lake Okeechobee to Gainesville. It was clear the second man had suffered a serious facial wound many years before that resulted in "a badly reconstructed mandible from a blow to the face."

The sight of that mandible being shattered is part of a memory of the robbery attempt. "Two thugs from out of town … a badly reconstructed mandible." It all made sense. It also overwhelms me with sadness when I consider what I could now do to repay

Alphonse for his love and protection. He didn't have to save me in that prison closet. If he hadn't, he might still be alive. He pulled the Aryan off me in that closet to beat him for not paying his debts to the Cosa Nostra and simultaneously initiated our love affair, one I'll cherish until my last breath. Circles within circles.

# CHAPTER 5

A midmorning sun bore down on Lake Monroe, abated only by a strong westerly breeze that rippled the surface. It was a predictable summer pattern, westerly winds gathering moisture to feed the Florida weather engine during its merciless trek eastward until it pounded the eastern counties with powerful late-afternoon thunderstorms.

Before the storms descended, sailboats careened over the lake's surface, ski boats sliced through the breezes, and the Doppler drone of distant motorboats kicked up white contrails, which rolled under blankets of hyacinths before slapping noisily against the seawall. While the lake was a restless collage of activity, the shoreline remained peaceful as fishermen lazily tended lines or watched for bobs disappearing beneath the roiling surface.

I lowered myself slowly onto the slatted seat of my coveted bench. The air was once again redolent of the purple hyacinth flowers rising and falling on waves and the sweet scent of honeysuckle flowers clinging to metal pergolas. I could hear the swish of an occasional car on Lake Drive behind me as pedestrians and cyclists drifted through the haze of my thoughts.

I spoke sotto voce, "I feel so alone today. Guess I just miss them."

A passing bike rider stared as she heard me talking to myself. I reached into my pocket and placed a cell phone on the bench next to me. Maybe it would look like I was talking to someone.

*A badly reconstructed mandible.* I let my mind drift back to the jewelry shop. Even the worst of those times seemed idyllic when compared to prison. Except for the day professional thieves came to steal my stock and murder me. When I was still Margarite.

The small boy with strange brown eyes had warned me that the jewelry shop was vulnerable. He'd scrambled down an AC vent into the shop. Later I heard rumors that the boy was a Hatfield who roamed ferally about town, mascot to the denizens of Monk's. It was eerie how the boy seemed to materialize whenever I was in trouble. I came to think of him as the lightning that brought the thunder, and, my, the thunder was mighty.

Within a month of the boy's warning, a contractor had completed the recommended security improvements: a lockable metal grate over the air-conditioning vent, roll-up metal doors over the front door and plate glass windows, a cage door on the back entrance from the alley, and an electronic safe in the back room.

The contractor's final step was to install an alarm system with a panic button beneath the counter next to the cash register that would automatically phone the police station. He assured me it was foolproof, and I breathed a sigh of relief.

Two weeks later in the middle of the afternoon, two professional armed robbers, one stocky and athletic and the other tall and agile, rendered my new security improvements useless with a fifty-cent pair of wire cutters. The stocky thief cut the relay box, walked calmly down the alley to join his partner at the corner, and the two strolled into the shop. The taller man, lighter in coloring, turned the open sign on the door around, while the shorter man, with a surprising economy of movement, walked to the back, a pistol held at his side in one hand and a large cloth sack in the other. He tossed the sack casually onto the counter in front of me.

"Fill this with all the jewelry and the cash in the register." His accent sounded northeastern, his tone so casual that he might have asked me to bag his groceries in the checkout lane at Piggly Wiggly.

I walked calmly to the cash register and subtly pushed the panic button. Then I stepped back and leaned against the shelves.

"I've just called the police," I pronounced proudly. "They should be here in a couple of minutes." I felt my voice quake, but it came out clear and firm. The security company had assured me that such an announcement would send would-be robbers fleeing.

The two men were dressed smartly in dark suits, white shirts, and paisley ties. Both wore thin cloth gloves to avoid leaving fingerprints. I was struck by how professional they looked, though I wasn't sure what professional jewel thieves should look like. These were sharp looking yet inexplicably rough at the same time. I realized it was something in their eyes, something sinister and predatory. Later in prison I would see that look in everyone's eyes, including the ones in the mirror.

The shorter man, brown eyes amused above his Nixon-like five-o'clock shadow, smiled as he tossed something onto the counter. "I'm afraid not." His voice wasn't threatening. He replaced his pistol in a holster under the back of his suit jacket.

I stared down at what looked like a large, dead plastic insect. I looked up into light brown eyes. "I don't understand."

He chuckled. "That's supposed to call the police."

My lips moved but no words would come. Finally, I managed, "How did you know?"

The taller man said, "We were trolling and caught a fish. We saw a security truck on I-4 and followed it to your door. They're idiots that draw bees to your honey. Tells us who has valuable merchandise to protect. They lie when they say they can protect it." He leaned forward. "May I have your keys, please? We wouldn't want to be disturbed."

I reached robotically into the pocket of my slacks and tossed the key chain onto the counter. He grabbed it and locked the front door. I was dazed and felt like I was hovering high above, watching it all happen to someone else.

The short, athletic man smiled. "By the way, where'd you get that shirt? We heard you were a transvestite. The locals were more than happy to talk about you while we cased the place. But they didn't say what excellent taste you have."

The question confirmed my displacement. I was being held at gunpoint, and this man wanted to know about my shirt. I looked down, though I knew exactly what it looked like—white with silver thread and a splash of primary color in a Mondrian pattern. I forced the words out. "I … um … bought this in Orlando. It's Ike Behar."

The man raised his eyebrows and nodded appreciatively. "I'll remember that. Now, please, would you be so kind as to fill that sack? I assume you're insured."

I nodded vigorously. "Yes, sir. Yes, I am. By the Prudential Insurance Company." I couldn't say why the name of the company seemed important.

"Good. Now, please." He nodded down at the jewelry counter. The taller man up front turned his back to the door, blocking the view inside. The door was aluminum-framed glass with an aluminum bar handle.

I reached out a tentative hand, pulled the cloth sack from the countertop, and stretched open the rope tie. I stared into the empty sack as if I'd lost something in its folds, still unable to get my bearings. In a room full of precision watches, time ceased.

Once-familiar things became foreign and threatening. Four dirge tolls rang in the tower of the Episcopal Church down the street. A long blast of a car horn from a few streets over, an irate person too ensnared in silly impatience to care that I was being robbed at gunpoint. A forlorn train horn rose faintly in the distance as an engine hauled its freight cars out to the main line and then off to faraway places. A flicker of sun on chrome reflected off a passing car as someone went safely about their business.

The shorter man spoke patiently, "Why not start at the back and work your way forward. That way you'll end up here at the front, and we'll be on our way."

I nodded vacantly, walked slowly to the back counter, and stood staring down at the glass and then up at the man by the door.

"My keys. I need my keys to unlock the cases," someone else's voice rose from a deep well.

The taller man frowned but pulled a secondary ring from the fob and tossed it to his partner, who strode quickly toward me, wing tip heels clicking on the terrazzo, and laid it on the counter. I didn't meet his gaze but picked up the small ring and rummaged to find the appropriate key. I fumbled with it but managed to insert it into a serrated bar lock and gently slide the glass door open, exposing my most precious pieces.

I was surprised to see someone's tears pattering on the glass counter and wondered whose they were. I began to remove a row of necklaces and place them tenderly in the sack. I dangled a twenty-four-carat-gold chain with a one-carat emerald over the sack to bid it farewell.

The shorter man said, "There, there, dear. It's only a few shiny objects. The insurance company will have you back up and running in no time."

His voice gave me hope that this was all a joke. "You seem like a nice man. Why are you doing this to me?"

The taller man at the door erupted in a one-note bark. "Jesus, lady, or whatever the fuck you are. Snap out of it. That man will pluck your heart out. Trust me. Just put the jewels in the sack before his patience runs out."

The shorter man turned and stared at the taller man with eyes that were suddenly menacing.

The taller man held up a hand. "Sorry, man. But we got no time for bullshit."

The shorter man turned back to me and said, his voice threatening as if his partner had reminded him of the irrelevance of even a moment's pity, "He's right. Please hurry it up before anyone—"

The words died on his lips as loud rapping erupted on the glass door, startling the taller man. As he leapt away from the door, he stabbed a hand to the holster strapped at his back. He turned and breathed a sigh of relief.

"It's just some punk kid." He stepped aside so his partner could see.

I saw the figure at the door, and panic seized me. I couldn't suppress an audible whine.

"No, no," I muttered. "Not this."

The shorter man broke into a smile as if he were telling a joke but said to me through tight lips, "Just smile like we're friends. Do you know this kid?"

I felt lightheaded and gripped the counter. "I recognize him."

He spoke loudly enough for his partner to hear. "Listen to me. We're going to open the door and let this kid in. You're going—"

I cut him off, "No … please don't let him in. Take the jewels and go out the back … please."

The man's teeth clenched, but he managed to keep the semblance of a smile. "Quit prattling. This happens sometimes. Just do as I say. We let him in. You introduce us as two cousins from out of town. A surprise visit is why you closed early. Tell him we're just leaving and you'll be open again tomorrow. If you fuck it up, I'm afraid this kid will get hurt if he gets a good look at us. Keep talking so he looks at you and not our faces."

My hands were shaking, and I couldn't steady my voice. "Please. This is a bad idea."

I managed a friendly wave toward the door but refused to make eye contact. Maybe he'd just leave. At that moment, something dawned on me.

I stared into the eyes of the thief. "I've seen your faces."

The taller man went to the door to open the lock.

"Yes, you have." The finality in his voice was terrifying. They had intended to kill me from the start.

That sudden realization was strangely liberating, freeing me from conflicting consequences. The "punk kid" at the door transformed into my only chance of survival. If I could calm myself.

I took a deep breath and nodded firmly. "Yes, you're right. We must let him in. We must do exactly as you say."

The stocky man shot me a frown but quickly smiled as the lock snapped open, the door pulled inward, and my future drifted into uncertainty. I watched from a faraway balcony as time accelerated. I knew why time sped up. I'd seen the news clippings. Heard the stories.

He moved inside, a skinny kid with a humorless grin contrasted by dead, gray eyes talked about by anyone upon whom they fell. "Closing early?" his voice was a growling rasp, old and tattered from a long scar on his neck.

I suddenly heard a whisper from another time and place. Then I realized it was coming from the vent above, from behind the security grate, an icy whisper that made me shiver. I missed the first couple words; I thought it said, "It's bliss." That had to be wrong, but the rest was clear. "The tall one, left handed and slow … get to the other. He's dangerous …"

Most folks in town knew this young man with steel gray eyes only by reputation. No one except me and Monk Labeau knew the truth. We were told a horrifying story by a peripatetic social worker named Charley Atwood.

Monk knew nothing until Charley showed up one afternoon a few months after the boy had begun sleeping in a back room of the pool hall. The social worker told Monk a disturbing story from the migrant camps in the celery fields near town. That part of town had once been called Celery City.

Charley Atwood had heard about a young boy whose father trained him to compete in the fighting pits in the migrant camps. The pits were little more than makeshift dugouts hidden in the trees or orange groves. They were lined with railroad ties, the grass and sandspurs were pulled, and mulch was applied to form a crude arena. Men gathered around these pits at night to drink and bet on fights. Those who fought generally had short careers that ended with a maiming wound, sometimes death. Each growing season, the sheriff's men would pull a young man who'd died from wounds suffered in the pits out of a roadside canal.

The social worker's job was to help families in the camps by providing family services and attempting to negotiate improvements in conditions. As Charley later told me, the boy we came to know as Sharkey wasn't the youngest he'd ever encountered, but he was the youngest he'd ever heard of "fighting up." Charley said he first encountered the boy when he and the local sheriff peeked inside a tent and found him shackled to a pole like a fighting dog.

According to Charley, some men put forth their young males to fight. A good fighter could earn far more from purses and gambling than the pittance paid in the fields.

Charley said this young boy had been fighting since he was a child. At first, warm-up fights that pitted him against other children. But the boy was special. So much so that his father had begun forcing him to "fight up" to get better odds. The older and bigger his opponent, the better the odds. The boy was forced to fight men twice his size. But he wasn't superhuman. He became exhausted like anyone and got his throat slit, not in the pits but by his own father during relentless training.

Even after fights, the father demanded that the boy train for the next one and the next one. In one session, he moved a shade too slow and his father's blade slashed deep, just missing his left jugular. Charley told me he got the boy medical treatment and then went to the father's shabby trailer at the edge of the fields to confront him. The father had a lean-to tent attached to the trailer where he kept the boy imprisoned. Charley threatened to turn him in if he didn't stop fighting the boy like a dog.

Charley gritted his teeth when he told me the father's repugnant response. "He is a goddamn dog, motherfucker. I didn't want the bitch knocked up again. Besides, she died of the cancer. I ain't got the money for his care unless he fights." Then the father pulled a knife on Charley. "Time for you to disappear."

Charley said he knew what "disappear" meant and turned to run, but the father was on him like a madman before he could get to the door. He pinned Charley to the floor and was bringing his knife down on his chest when a small arm reached around the father's neck and opened his throat with a fruit knife. The man fell off Charley, and there the boy stood, the ropes on his wrists cut. It was Charley who first noticed the boy's dead eyes. Some of the father's blood spewed into Charley's eye and coagulated. He was nearly blind in that eye for a month.

Charley said he was wiping the blood out of his eyes with one hand and reaching out for the boy with the other, but as soon as the father stopped twitching, the boy turned and walked calmly out of the trailer.

Charley's eye prevented him from pursuing the boy, but he called for help. When the sheriff arrived, Charley said the father had attacked him and he'd killed him in self-defense while the boy had fled into the groves in fright. Charley said they bought the story because it was easier. The father was reviled by the other families. Some thought it was the father, not cancer, who had killed the boy's mother.

Charley laughed when he told me, "They were willing to believe everything except one part of my story. As one of the migrant men said, 'That kid, scared? Bullshit.'"

After his eye healed, Charley went on a quest, searching for the boy. He didn't have a name to go on, so he went from camp to camp, thinking the boy would stay with people he knew, but he found no trace of him until he ran across the Menendez family working the citrus groves. Señor Menendez said he might know the boy. He'd appeared one day at their camp in a grapefruit grove in a remote corner of Lake County. The family had befriended him, or tried to. The boy barely spoke, but one day he showed up at their trailer to say goodbye. He said only that he had found work in a pool hall. He didn't say where. He shook their hands, thanked them for their kindness, and disappeared.

Charley visited every pool hall he ran across in the citrus-growing counties of central Florida, and one day he walked into Monk's. Before talking to Monk, he'd asked around town about him—his character, the pool hall, and so forth. I was one of the people he asked. For some reason, maybe it was because I was obviously different, or maybe because I ran a shop around the corner from Monk's, or maybe it was because I was protective of Monk, he confided in me. Whatever it was, it prompted him to tell me all he knew about this strange boy's past.

Later, Charley occasionally came through town and stopped by the jewelry store to browse or get a battery for his watch. But he mostly came in to ask about the boy who had been given a nickname: Sharkey.

Charley's story was the source of my fear and indecisiveness when I saw Sharkey rapping on the glass door during the robbery. A young man who'd spent his life fighting to survive was walking into a small shop being robbed by two professionals. I had no way of predicting what would happen, but I was certain it wouldn't be peaceful. I could see it in Sharkey's dead eyes.

But once the thief acknowledged my death sentence, indecision was displaced by a vague and desperate trust in the ethos of Monk's. It made sense that they would kill me; that's how robbers were caught, descriptions and identification in lineups.

But an archangel, my first Virgil, ascended from hell and lit on my shoulder. I invited him in and trusted him with my life.

When the child's voice wafted down from the AC vent above, the tall man heard it and glanced upward. Sharkey accelerated effortlessly past him and, without a glance, flicked his right hand out faster than a rattler in a palmetto stand. The taller man went down, gagging, writhing, and kicking at the terrazzo floor as if riding an air bike as he gasped to draw air over a damaged larynx. Sharkey never paused but accelerated again, moving toward the "dangerous one."

I heard a bark from the front door. "Down, Shark, down."

Sharkey dropped to his knees and glided like an ice skater over the terrazzo as a knife whisked overhead. The shorter man turned sideways with lightning speed as the blade spun past his head and clattered into the shelving behind the counter. He dodged the knife easily, but his attention was not on the knife thrower. He must have been as confused as I was as Sharkey came at him. His movements were completely confounding.

Sharkey's thin frame continued to glide toward him as the thief spun in a tight half circle. A gun magically appeared in his hand, and a sardonic grin creased his lips. But Sharkey initiated a series of contorted motions too fast for me to track. He did some kind of kick-thrust off the floor and lay stretched backward, knees bent at ninety degrees, body cantilevered, feet planted but gliding like a dancer's over the terrazzo, his thin body contorting beneath the handgun's lethal arc. The angle of the attack required the gunman to contort his elbow and wrist at an uncomfortable angle. He lost his grip on the gun, which clattered to the floor.

I stood mesmerized as Sharkey and the thief moved in this bizarre choreography. I went numb with fear when I saw the pistol appear like a bouquet of flowers in a magician's hand. It all happened faster than I could track. Two boys were poised at the front door, a thief lay against the display counter to my left, and the door to my small office stood at my back. I began to flee toward the back door but paused and glanced back at the gunman and the boy called Sharkey. In that instant, it became clear how this boy had survived the migrant fighting pits against older and stronger men.

I was awestruck. There was a flash of movement below my line of sight; the counter blocked my full view. But a body, Sharkey's body, levitated from the floor. It was like watching the Chinese acrobats on the *Ed Sullivan Show*. I didn't know how, but he was suddenly suspended in the air at a ninety degree angle to the floor. He kicked hard downward with his left foot, lashed out with his right, fell below the counter, and then, catching his momentum on the floor—it must have been with his left hand—simultaneously delivered a slashing kick to the elbow of the man's gun-wielding arm, which contorted the tendons in the opposite direction than nature intended. I heard a crunch-like noise followed by a shriek of pain.

But Sharkey wasn't finished. I hurried to the side counter and had a full view of what came next. He dropped his shoulders to the terrazzo and twisted his legs to gather momentum that made his body spin. He looked like an inverted golfer, gathering all the torque his body could manage, and unleashed the coiled power of his legs. The knife edge of one foot slashed across the man's testicles, while the other heel kicked violently upward into his chin.

A strange silence followed. I stood frozen in place, disoriented, this time from the sudden reversal of fortune. Sharkey kipped up to his feet like a gymnast as his friends rushed in. I knew them. One was called Jack Knife, a laborer at a meat packing plant who had thrown the distracting blade, and the ghostly albino called Silk. They were Sharkey's ubiquitous companions.

Jack asked, "Calling Chief Butler?"

I realized I was dialing. I pumped the cradle buttons. "I'm not sure it'll work. They—oh, thank heavens. Whatever he did to the security system didn't kill the dial tone."

I put a hand over the receiver as the phone rang at the police station. "Someone hand me that man's pistol."

The dispatcher picked up.

"This is Margarite at Purloiner's. I've had a robbery attempt. Please hurry. I'm holding two men at gunpoint, but I'm frightened. Okay, put me through, but please be quick."

I held my hand over the phone. "You boys get away from this mess. I'll take care of the police."

I thought I could repay them by keeping them out of this. I didn't know how I'd explain overcoming two men, but I'd think of something. Maybe they fought each other over a piece of jewelry.

They made no effort to leave. Instead they circled the now disarmed men. Jack Knife moved over the "dangerous one," who had slumped against the counter at the back, one hand on his damaged testicles and the other rubbing the side of his face. Silk hovered above the taller man sprawled against the counter near the front, who was still rubbing his throat. Sharkey stood between them, an enigmatic smile on his lips.

During my murder trial, the prosecution seized on police reports from that day. Margarite, they asserted, already demonstrated violent aggression when she went after her father with a butcher knife. Then again by her use of a deadly firearm to abort a robbery attempt. The prosecutor cast doubts on rumors of that day, that a teenager overpowered two professional thieves that each outweighed him by fifty pounds. As I listened to the prosecutor, even I thought it sounded farfetched.

"Are we to believe," he demanded, "that a young boy known to everyone as incorrigible, though admittedly a fine athlete, had suddenly turned into a comic-book hero, Captain America maybe, and flew around the room as he overcame these professional criminals? I suppose his two companions, also local roughnecks, turned into the Wolverine and the Not-So-Black Panther to help out." A titter of laughter rippled through the courtroom at the allusion to the albino Negro.

The reaction of his audience gave free rein to his sarcasm. "Perhaps the defense would have us believe the accused is not a jeweler at all but the secret leader of the Avengers and her jewelry store is merely a cover for their true purpose of fighting for truth, justice, and the American Way. Thank the Lord they have taken up residence in our town, for now we can all stop locking our doors at night and Chief Butler can just go fishing every day."

The laughter became louder, and the judge slammed his gavel down. "Silence in the court," he said, though he, too, made little effort to mask a grin.

Order was restored, and the prosecutor pressed his point. "No, say I. It is far more likely that the accused is very handy with a gun and is possessed of a nature so violent that 'she,' for he was a she at the time of the robbery, was able to overcome two seasoned criminals who had the misfortune to attempt to rob a store owned by someone far more violent than they bargained for. What a wicked surprise that must have been. Two professional criminals discovered the real Margarite Ecclesia Purloin. A father discovered it after being sliced up with a butcher knife. Two deadly thieves found out as they lay prostrate and mangled on a jewelry shop floor. And, yes, a sweet, innocent young woman named Sharon Richardson discovered it. All far too late."

The entire courtroom stared at me, horrified by a modern-day Frankenstein.

Jack Knife knelt, reached down and picked up the pistol from the floor where the gunman had dropped it, and handed it over the counter. I took it without knowing what to do with it. The man was rolling his head back and forth and moaning, while his taller accomplice, though conscious, struggled to breathe regularly.

I pled with them, "Please, get out of here, boys."

Silk spoke in a voice like smooth jazz. "She's right about you, Shark. Chief Butler don't like athletes mixing it up. Don't matter why. Jack and me'll get us a couple of brownie points."

As Silk stared down into the face of the taller man at his feet, he let a small metal bat slide from the sleeve of his floral shirt. As an albino, he had to keep his skin covered against the Florida sun. Outdoors, he always wore a wide-brimmed hat, sunglasses, a long-sleeve shirt, and leather gloves with the fingertips cut short. Under his right sleeve was a metal bat he somehow hooked to an armband.

Silk said, "I'm gon' stand right here and hope this asshole kick-starts his nasty again." He pointed the bat at the tall man, who finally seemed to be breathing easily. "If I pound this motherfucker to oatmeal, his friends might think twice before coming here to fuck with folks. Pardon my French, ma'am."

I smiled through an odd disquiet. My shop had been transformed, distorted into an eerie, dangerous place I didn't recognize in the aftermath of sudden violence.

Jack Knife stood over the stocky thief, a pistol in one hand and a switchblade in the other. His black hair was slicked back, and I noticed he wasn't bad looking with his strong chin and bedroom eyes, though he was going through some postpubescent acne. I could see the muscles in his jaw twitching and the clear definition of taut muscles under his black T-shirt. It wasn't adrenaline; it was unabated rage at a world that had discounted him.

Jack spoke through clenched teeth. "Goddamn right. This fucker keeps eyeballing me, he'll be able to scratch his ass and pick his nose at the same time."

The stocky thief's eyes never wavered. "You won't have a nose to pick or ass to scratch when I stroll back into this shit town and feed you to the fish. You stupid yokels have no idea who you're fucking with."

Jack looked up at Sharkey, eyes pleading. "Shark?"

I was surprised at the deference Jack and Silk showed to the younger man. It was a phenomenon typical of prison. Some men had an aura of strength tempered by common sense that others were drawn to.

Sharkey gave a slight nod.

I looked at Sharkey. "Please, go before the police come."

Sharkey turned his face slowly toward me, and I couldn't suppress a spontaneous shiver. Later, in prison, those eyes, that dead stare, remained. If only I could call those eyes down on those who had violated me.

Sharkey said, "In a bit. Professor Jack Knife and Dr. Silk still have to give today's lesson." There was no emotion in his voice.

Sharkey squatted on hydraulic legs next to the stocky, athletic thief, who cast a quick glance over at his partner. Their eyes met.

"I told you, goddamnit. I heard about this fucking town—" his partner began, but Silk flipped the small metal bat like a baton and pushed the butt hard into the side of the man's cheek. There was a wet, slushing sound as Silk twisted the bat. Blood dripped from the man's lips as the soft inner tissue was ground against his molars.

"We got rules. Don't talk in class unless you're called on." Silk's smooth voice suddenly sounded playful, and I sensed that this wasn't the first bloody drama played out at the hands of these young men.

Sharkey spoke to the "dangerous one" with an eerie detachment. "I'm guessing you guys are in gangster school, and this was like a homework assignment. Go to a shitty town, rob a jewelry store, and kill some yokels. That's what you called us, right? Yokels?" He leaned down and stared hard into the man's eyes. "You failed so bad, we got no choice but to kick you out of gangster school."

Sharkey turned his eyes up to the ceiling. "Hey, Kid. What do we do with these assholes? They came to rob and kill your friend, Margarite. He was going to kill her." He stared back at the thief. "Weren't you, cocksucker?"

The thief's nostrils flared. He clenched his teeth but said nothing.

"That's what I thought." Sharkey spoke louder, "Well, Kid?"

My nerves were frayed, and I interjected, "Please, don't involve the boy—"

Silk said, "Ma'am?"

I shifted my gaze, and Silk gestured for me to come closer. I moved along the back of the counter opposite where he stood. He placed the bat on top of the thief's head and said, "Move, and I'll crush it." The taller thief closed his eyes and nodded obediently.

Silk leaned forward. "If the Kid calls down the punishment, nobody dies."

Another rumor confirmed. I whispered, "Oh. Sorry."

A small voice echoed down from the vent, "I've got it. These assholes thought we were the unfortunates. But they were wrong. They ran afoul of the patron saint of the unfortunates—St. Giles."

Jack looked up. "What do I do with that, Kid? This guy's already pretty damn unfortunate."

The small voice echoed down again, "St. Giles was crippled by an arrow. He was also the patron saint of cripples."

Sharkey chuckled, and Jackie shook his head, grinning. "You something else, Kid."

Sharkey looked at the thief, who returned his stare. "Looks like your day's about to get worse."

I watched the thief's willpower cascade. "Look, man—"

Sharkey's hand flicked out and slapped the thief's face hard. I could only pray that those eyes never looked at me like that.

"I'm looking. I see you. I fucking smell you. But I don't want to hear you. Every noise out of that stink hole will cost you." He put his arms over his knees and glanced at Jack Knife. "My friend is a pro down at the packing plant. Best I've ever seen with a knife."

Then Sharkey leaned forward and put his lips near the man's ear. "It's goddamn lucky for you he is; otherwise, he could make a real mess of what he's about to do."

I was again mesmerized by the calm, methodical way this was unfolding. I looked up quickly and saw that Silk and Jack Knife were watching Sharkey with the same intensity as he again cocked his head next to the thief's ear. His raspy voice was easily heard.

Sharkey spoke slowly, "The worst thing you ever did was call these boys yokels. Now you'll see what happens when a worm thinks it's a snake."

Sharkey stood and walked to the front door.

The stocky thief's eyes were filled with panic, but he fought the urge to plead. He released a final burst of bravado. "Don't touch me, goddamnit. I swear I'll come back with enough guns to kill this whole shitty town."

Jack and Silk laughed, but Sharkey held up two fingers. "Add one. Cut this fucker twice. If he keeps talking, cut him 'til he stops."

The thief's eyes widened, and he choked back the threats straining at his lips.

Suddenly, the phone went dead, and I dialed again. The dispatcher said quickly, "Chief Butler's on the way."

I hung up. Shark turned to Jack and nodded. Jack Knife, in turn, nodded to Silk, who struck once with his metal bat, and I heard the taller thief's jaw shatter—"a badly reconstructed mandible from a blow to the face." The man fell on his side, unconscious, arms and legs cocked at odd angles. Jack dropped to his knees out of my line of sight, and I leaned forward, gripping the counter. I heard the stocky man erupt in a long shriek.

Jack Knife stood, and the ferocity in his eyes was more animal than human. "You stroll back into town now, and I'll see you coming, won't I, motherfucker?"

"Please, please, no more," I said. I felt my stomach twist, and a wave of nausea roiled up. I staggered back against the shelf, afraid I might vomit, but I held onto the gun, though it had been rendered unnecessary.

Jack Knife had tucked the thief's foot under his armpit, pinned it to his side, and in a practiced motion slit the bilateral tendons behind the man's ankle, twisted his foot ninety degrees to the right, and slit completely through his Achilles tendon. That was what caused the shriek that had trailed off to a weeping whimper. The nausea came when I looked down and saw that, without the tendons, the calf muscle had snapped upward and hung gelatinously behind the man's knee as his foot wagged helplessly about. His ankle had shrunk to the size of the tibia beneath.

But Sharkey had said to cut him twice, so Jack also slit the medial tendons behind his knee. There was another screeching yelp as the man fell onto his side, unconscious from the pain.

I don't know why, but I moaned, "Oh, God ... please, Mr. Sharkey."

Sharkey's eyes cleared suddenly, and his lips parted in a genuine smile. "You don't have to call me mister. You don't have to call anybody mister. Ever." Then the smile disappeared as quickly as it had come, and I saw a lifetime of sadness in his face. "Laws weren't writ for us. We only got ourselves ..."

He gave me a small nod and then turned to his two friends. "Monk's."

Jack said, "Soon as the cops get here."

Silk asked, "How'd you know to do that, Jack?"

Jack stood over the stocky thief. "Damn, Silk, I been working at a meat packing plant for three years. I had to pick something up."

Sharkey paused at the door and turned to back to me. "The Kid likes you. He's why we come." Then he disappeared, and I slumped against the shelving, breathing deeply.

When my head stopped spinning, I stared up at the vent in the ceiling.

"Hello?" I spoke softly.

Seconds later, two huge eyes peered through the security grate. I was still nauseous but managed a smile. The small face scanned the room in sharp birdlike movements. Then his gaze settled on me, and he flashed a grin before receding upward into the darkness. I heard distant metallic banging as he crawled back through the vent system toward the roof.

Moments later, three squad cars screeched to a stop on the street outside the shop, and Jack and Silk took their leave after a sarcastic encounter with Chief Butler, who'd wondered aloud why Jack didn't quit working at the meat plant and open his own butcher shop; that way maybe he'd stick to cutting up cows and leave people alone.

A few days later, I heard the two thieves were released into the custody of the state police for questioning in other crimes. A few months later, they were out on bail and disappeared, or so I heard. But they would show up again in Raiford.

# CHAPTER 6

Leitner Dredge sat morosely in the driver's seat of the red BMW as it whisked down I-17. He had finally pulled Summer away from the south rim of the Grand Canyon as daylight faded, and he was determined to reach Phoenix before stopping. He insisted they put the top up to gain speed without the wind blast. Summer turned the overhead light on and sat in the passenger seat, pouring over one of the thick brochures she'd picked up at a restaurant overlooking the great striated chasm. It was just before eight, and the sun was setting. If he pushed it, they could make Phoenix by ten thirty.

"Listen to this." Summer stared at the brochure. "The capitol building in Phoenix? The dome has enough copper in it to make ... let's see ... a four with a comma after it, then an eight and one, two ... six, no, five zeros after it. That's what ... ah ..."

Leitner rolled his eyes. "Four million, eight hundred thousand."

"Wow." Summer looked at him, mouth agape. "That's how many pennies you could make with the copper from one dome. I can't wait—"

Leitner spoke brusquely, "You can see it from the car as we leave town in the morning. We can't stay in bumfuck Arizona. We'll pick up I-10 in Phoenix and take it all the way east."

Summer frowned. "Okay, but I like Arizona."

"So does every fucking white Republican that can make a living off the backs of Indians or Mexicans."

"I didn't know you were into politics." Summer stared at him. "You really surprise me, Leitner."

Leitner rubbed a hand over his face and muttered, "*Jesu Cristo Enchilada Misto*. I give exactly zero of a fuck for politics. You don't have to be political to know Arizona would vote for Hitler before they'd vote Democrat. The NRA could kill every baby in the state and no one would give up their membership."

Summer smiled. "Really? You're amazing. How do you know all this stuff? What's the NRA?"

Leitner dropped his head back against the headrest. "Never mind. We'll be in Phoenix soon. We'll get a nice hotel, have dinner, and hit the sack. I'd like to get out of Arizona tomorrow. Las Cruces, New Mexico, is only five or six hours away."

Summer crossed her arms, a pout edging across her face.

Leitner added quickly, "I'll tell you what. We'll shoot for Las Cruces, but if you're a good girl, we'll stop somewhere special, somewhere I know you'll like."

"What's better than Arizona?"

Leitner smirked. "What's your favorite movie?"

"I already told you. *Tombstone*, with all those delicious actors … I mean, you're more delicious, but …"

"Hey, honeybee, no offense. Those are some good-looking men. But if you just be patient and help me get to New Mexico, we'll stop at a real Western ghost town where Billy the Kid, Johnny Ringo, Curly Bill, the Clantons … all of them used to hang out. How would that be?"

Summer looked at him askance. "Are you just saying that so I'll do what you want?"

Leitner smiled. "Look it up. You've got those brochures. Look up Shakespeare Ghost Town and see. If it's not in there, you only have to give me one blow job today."

She laughed. "What a bargain. But you'll have to do better than that. Shakespeare was some writer from like a million years ago."

Leitner shrugged. "Okay, if you say so. But I'd look it up or you'll miss out."

She frowned as she opened the index in the back of the thick brochure and scanned down the names of sights. Suddenly she looked up at him, "You are just amazing. It's right here, just like you said." She leaned over and put an arm around his neck. "Play your cards right and you might just get a special treat when we get to the hotel."

Leitner grinned, and Summer leaned back in her seat, nestling her head against the window. She tucked a sweater under her head and closed her eyes.

Moments later she began to snore lightly, and he looked over at her with a deep frown and then turned his eyes back to the road. He began to click his front teeth together, an unconscious habit. He had to be careful with this one. It never paid to let them get close.

The day broke with early storms, a precursor of a typical summer day when Florida weather roared to life with a vengeance. The humidity began its steady ascent from uncomfortable to oppressive. The snowbirds had flown north, choking Interstates 95 and 75 in their annual migration, and the small town on Lake Monroe settled in for the hot months.

I'd made an alternate plan for the hottest periods when the lake couldn't provide adequate respite from the heat. I moved my daily routine to a local café with patio seating in a brick courtyard accessed through an alleyway off First Street.

I had been searching for a cool spot and discovered this café, with its interior courtyard made comfortable by misting ceiling fans spaced evenly under a lush pergola. The space reminded me of Italy, where outdoor seating was demarcated by rows of terracotta pots. It was an oasis of potted plants, wisteria, and a large fountain against the far brick wall of the building across the alley.

I visited Italy after being released from the hospital in Amsterdam. I'd always wanted to see Rome, but the northern regions of Tuscany and Umbria captivated me. I would return there again, unless something went terribly wrong.

I wanted to spend the day with the journal. I was running out of time. I ordered an espresso, San Pellegrino, and panini and opened the journal on the tabletop.

Raiford is a tiered, linear maximum security prison, an island running on its own sluggish clock, operated by an authoritarianism tantamount to a provincial general in ancient Rome. In this case, the general is called a warden, and his laws are carried out by his praetorian guard. The guards move through the days in regulated shifts, a conveyor belt of stone faces animated only by inmate misbehavior. The system was designed to hammer inmates toward some bureaucratic interpretation of societal expectations, and each stroke pounds the soul a little tighter into the mold, squeezing out the pieces that won't fit—the pieces a man tries to hold on to.

The day Alphonse was released, he said a final goodbye. "I hope I made something good happen for you, Stuart. You know how special you been to me. I did my best."

I hugged his great, hard body, and he lifted me off the ground in a bear hug one last time. Then I waited. He was certain someone from the Cosa Nostra would contact me. I knew Alphonse tried, but nothing happened. I wasn't even sure how they would contact me.

A month passed and nothing. Then, as hope began its inevitable prison decline, I lay on my back in my cot and my eyes popped open as an epiphany struck. The eerie loneliness meant something.

It dawned on me. *Nothing has happened.* No one had contacted me, but no one paid attention to me. It was suddenly as if I were invisible or leprous, an untouchable.

I was sure after Alphonse's protection was removed, I'd be fair game again, but the prison administration didn't even move another prisoner into the cell with me. If I went through the cafeteria line, inmates ignored me. If I sat at a table, anyone else sitting there got up and moved. Even the guards avoided me. Was I was being weighed and measured? I saw nothing out of the ordinary. No one looking away quickly when our eyes met. No one standing in shadows watching. I was invisible among the multitudes.

Two months passed. Then three. I began to adapt and settled into a comfortable routine. I ate. I slept. I worked in the prison library. I read. I wrote. One day I asked Porter, the librarian, if a book I wanted could be ordered. To my astonishment, the answer was yes. It was usually "We don't have the budget, right now." So, I ordered all the textbooks I had used for my graduate program. I wanted to keep my mind sharp.

I waited. My textbooks arrived. When I opened the box, tears slipped down my cheeks. The multiple regression text was an old, used copy. A name was written on the inside cover. The same name as someone from my program in graduate school. I barely knew her, but suddenly she was my best friend, though I silently chastised her for selling that book back to the publisher. What had she become that she no longer needed such a precious artifact?

I read. And waited some more.

I expected the wait to end. Instead, I was forced down a horrible detour that promised to end all hope. From out of nowhere, she showed up. Mrs. Marilyn Manakin, the new warden's cliché of a trophy wife—a drop-dead gorgeous and fucking vacuous bitch.

The prison grapevine had already spread the news of the appointment of a new warden long before he set foot on prison grounds; he was the youngest warden in the modern era, whatever that meant. What event could demarcate eras in this shit hole? A day without shit? We knew his whole history before he put his ass on the throne of his office "up front." He was a well-connected, ambitious political climber who would do whatever it took to make his mark. Inmates knew with certainty that some of those marks would be on their backs.

We'd also heard about his trophy wife—an ex-cheerleader, majorette, homecoming queen type and ice queen from a small town not all that far from Raiford. She went to Florida State University, where she met Robert Manakin, former student body president at Rollins College, a well-heeled private, before entering law school at FSU. The day after Robert graduated from law school, they married. Marilyn didn't finish her degree. She was nineteen. Her Baptist parents were ecstatic; marriage to a well-connected man was far more important than a meaningless teaching degree.

Robert Manakin spent a mere three years as a prosecuting attorney in Tallahassee before being appointed warden of Florida State Prison. He and his supporters had the governor's office in their sights via the Office of the Attorney General, but first Robert needed seasoning and a few years to build his base. The Republican Party felt he could be governor by his thirty-fifth birthday. Marilyn was the perfect first lady, but she, too, needed experience—the proper volunteer work, the right parties and gala events. She was already a diamond but as yet uncut.

One day I was returning my book cart to the library, having completed my rounds of the cell blocks, and standing at the circulation desk next to the prison librarian stood one of the most beautiful women I've ever seen. She reminded me of another beauty I once knew, Monk's daughter, Bonnie. Both had raven black hair and an icy demeanor, but Bonnie's skin was like polished copper while Marilyn's was white as cream.

Her eyes were huge golden brown orbs. I wondered how eyes could be simultaneously seductive and inquisitive; hers were like that until she turned them on me. Her arched brows were perfect, though they rose noticeably when she saw me. Her cheeks tapered to a perfectly dimpled chin, though she sucked them inward when angry, which she did in that moment. Her lips were full, though she pursed them when riled. Her nose, perfect and dimpled, flared the moment I walked up to her. Her perfect ivory teeth clenched. In short, I watched every perfect feature transform.

She stared at me as I parked the cart next to the circulation desk and looked eagerly at Porter. He had a library degree and a first name, but he was just Porter, a strange-looking man with oversized eyes behind thick glasses and a long, thin body save for a pot belly that made him look like the boa constrictor that had swallowed a pig. But he knew his books and did his best to provide the inmates with a decent selection, though law books remained at the top of the prison bestsellers list. Every inmate was always a day away from his appeal.

Porter waved me over eagerly, and Marilyn Manakin seared me with her brown eyes. She was wearing black pants and a sleek white blouse but had on heeled stilettos, so I had to look slightly up to meet her gaze.

Porter said, "Mrs. Manakin, this is Stuart. He's the best library helper I've ever had."

Marilyn Manakin's distaste was instantaneous.

"Stuart, this is Mrs. Manakin, the new warden's wife. She has kindly assented to volunteer here in the library."

I reached out a hand, but Marilyn Manakin merely stared at it. She looked up, and her eyes bored into mine as she spoke. "Mr. Potter, is this the ... what do you call it? Transgender inmate?" Her voice was sultry; the Southern accent rolled off her tongue like sweet milk.

A slight frown crossed Porter's face. "My name's Porter. I suppose so, but we—"

Marilyn Manakin spit vitriol. "I will be volunteering in this library, but I demand that you keep this ... this whatever it is away from me. Is that clear?"

I could see Porter's jaw flex. "Certainly, Mrs. Manakin. I'll make sure Stuart works only the circuit carts out in the blocks. The only time you might even see him is when he parks his cart, that is if you're even here at that time. Will that be all right?" He clearly shared my disappointment. Books and bigotry are incompatible.

She picked up her purse and slung it over her shoulder. "I would prefer the cart be parked over there by the door if I am behind the circulation desk. That will keep it a safe distance from me." I didn't know if "it" meant me or the cart—both, I assumed.

She turned and gave me a wide berth as she walked to the library doors. Before pushing through, she turned and shot me one last hateful glare.

I returned to waiting, this time with the added burden of Marilyn Manakin's hatred. It wasn't her beauty that made it painful; it was my boundless naivete, the hope that someone who wished to be around books might unexpectedly be my friend. Prison again managed to crush optimism.

I was relegated to pushing the library cart through the blocks, which meant I lost my privileges among the shelves I so cherished. I rarely saw Marilyn Manakin, and most days I parked the cart beside the circulation desk before going back to my cell. On the rare occasion she was still behind the counter, I left it just inside the door and turned without looking at her. Sporadically she'd be off with her husband and I could again wander among the shelves. But eventually she'd reappear, and I was cast again into exile.

Alphonse had been gone for six months, but I still read the short newspaper clip and his letter once a day. I had all but given up hope of being approached by Cosa Nostra. Then one day, I was sitting alone at lunch, reading the newspaper clip hidden by the cover of a book, Dante's *Divine Comedy*.

I was deep in thought when the cafeteria went suddenly quiet, a complete cessation of the clatter of trays and chatter of inmates. It didn't invade my concentration until I sensed someone else's presence. When I looked up, a man I'd never before encountered sat quietly across the table. He seemed to have appeared from thin air.

He was surprisingly handsome, with olive skin, black hair, and full lips pulled back over perfect white teeth as he gave me a quizzical half smile. He studied me as he might a strange specimen he'd just stumbled upon. He wore a prison uniform, but it had been professionally laundered with sharp creases. One can tell prison hierarchy just from the spots and spills on a uniform, but the man sitting across from me must have received a new one each day.

He had piercing, almost black reptilian eyes that never blinked. I almost expected a nictitating eyelid to flicker over them. His black hair was just long enough to slick back from a widow's peak on his forehead. He was reminiscent of James Dean, with slightly sharper and darker features. I'd once read that Ulysses S. Grant was so taciturn that he could be silent in several languages. I thought this man might give Grant a run for his money.

After staring at me for an eternity, he got down to business. "Someone wishes to speak with you." The accent was New Jersey or New York. Not unusual in Florida.

"To whom shall I be speaking?" I asked.

He grinned, and I could tell his sarcasm rested just beneath the surface. "To whom …? To whom is the person who will decide when it pleases him to make himself known to you."

I attempted a bland smile, but my heart was accelerating. "Of course. So, do I get to know when this conversation will occur?"

The man's grin never wavered. "I wouldn't presume to deem it a conversation. It'll be more of a he talks, you nod your head in agreement. Capisce?"

Definitely New Jersey; they always dropped the final vowel on Italian words. *Mortadella* became *mortadell*, *prosciutto* became *prosciutt*, and so on.

I smiled. "Capisco, maestro di morte." I loved Italian and had been studying it from a book I found in the library. It wouldn't hurt to practice. I risked the jab about "master of death."

He chuckled. "Old Alphonse said you were smart." The smile disappeared. "Your Italian accent is terrible, and it's easy to go from smart to smart-ass. Catch my drift?"

I felt my bowels shift but thought it best to try to maintain a facade of confidence, for a facade it was. Something told me this man wouldn't hesitate to snatch my life between his slow snakelike blinks.

"Your drift permeates the very air, Maestro." I'm sure my voice quivered.

He managed to smile and frown at the same time as he leaned forward on his elbows and stared at me hard for excruciatingly long moments.

Finally, he grinned and sat back. "You'll do fine if you never show disrespect. Il rispetto e tutto." He pronounced the Italian perfectly.

This man was both dangerous and clever. But that gave me instantaneous hope. I could relate to clever people. My prison depression was always the product of the randomness of brutality. This man was not random in anything he did. If this man and those he represented could provide the opportunity to control random error in my life, I would do all that I could to help them eliminate the random error in theirs.

I nodded firmly. "Non dimentichero. I won't forget. Do you have a name?"

The frowning smile flashed. I didn't think some men would like him looking at them that way, but for some reason I wasn't afraid. He hadn't come to kill me.

"*Maestro di morte* is good. Call me Maestro for short, but don't forget the rest."

I reminded myself that he hadn't come to hurt me. "How will this occur?"

He stood, hands clasped in front of his crotch. "It'll be obvious to a smart guy like you. Arrangements are being made." He turned to sniff the air with a look of disgust. "*Dio*, the food in here smells like shit."

He turned, and the expensive shoes clicked toward the exit. Every inmate's eyes dropped as he passed, and a guard held the door for him.

Another month passed without incident, though I was leery of an inevitable confrontation with Marilyn Manakin.

# CHAPTER 7

I'd done everything I could to avoid the Bitch Warden; she'd already earned that unflattering nickname. She'd been vilified for her snobbery. I loved my job in the library and was livid that I might be banned because of her bigotry. The internet was becoming increasingly common, but inmates had little access to computers outside the library. For me, hope was glass under the shoe of the narrow minded. I remained a species of one, and a species of one always teeters on the edge of extinction.

Maestro had come and gone, and I was again thrust back into chaos, a world in which the wife of an ambitious warden could with a casual shrug destroy my haven from insanity. And that is exactly what the Bitch Warden did.

As I pushed my book cart from block to block, I'd become excellent at matching the reader to a book. I had begun to earn a reputation as a book wizard, blizzard for short, because I so unerringly suggested books that enthralled and provided a gap in time during which an inmate forgot where he was for a while. I'd never had a positive nickname, so I was flattered. But it was short-lived.

"Hey, Blizzard, I loved that last one. Got another like that?"

"Let me see what I can do."

The Bitch Warden continued to stare at me with what I considered to be every flavor of hatred. One afternoon when I pushed my cart through the library doors, I saw a real whack job from the Aryan Brotherhood at the counter. He was huge and muscular but weaving like he'd been drinking the homemade sterno that passed for liquor in prison. I was relieved to see a trustee behind the circulation desk and a second inmate at the counter. The Bitch Warden was nowhere to be seen.

I turned to hustle away, but the Aryan grabbed the trustee by the shirt and pulled his face close, dragging his body halfway over the counter. "Where's the sweet poontang today?"

I paused indecisively.

The trustee stuttered, "She ain't here. She's the warden's wife for Christ's sake."

"I don't give a fuck. The warden ain't here. Said he was going somewhere, but his bitch is here, and I want to see her." He was in that most dangerous of drunken states between loss of inhibitions and fixation. And why would a warden tell an Aryan he was leaving? Of course. The only difference between a warden and an Aryan is the uniform; Praetorians wear many guises.

The second inmate cast a wide-eyed look my way.

I couldn't abandon him without trying, so I made something up. "Hey, Dave, you still waiting for that book?"

He forced a smile. "Yeah, Blizzard. I hear you can find anything."

I looked at the Aryan. "How about you? I know just the book for you."

He looked at me like I was bad meat. "Fuck no. You two faggots get the fuck out of here. I got business with pootay." He was wavering.

I took a huge gamble. "But don't you want to read the words of your great leader? Have you never read *Mein Kampf*? Hitler's mani—um, Hitler's dream for the white race? It's like your Bible, right? I think we have a copy."

I saw indecisiveness cross his face. Of course he'd not read it, but he showed the dissonance that rises from the arrogance of loudly proclaimed ideals.

He released his grip on the trustee. "You got a copy of that book? Right here in this shithole?" He was winging it, but so was I.

"Yes, of course. It's popular among your brotherhood. I mean, it might be checked out already. We can hardly keep it in before it flies back off the shelf. I could reserve it for you. Would you like to leave your information?"

His dissonance grew. "You're full o' shit. I don't get fucked with. I do the fucking ..."

He muffed his line, so I cut in quickly, "No, I promise. I can check now, but I promise to hold it for you."

This was a dangerous moment, rechanneling his anger. My guess was that he'd drunk his booze fast and worked up the courage to come after the warden's wife, but the alcohol was just now flooding his system.

I stepped forward and grabbed a pen and pad of paper off the counter. "Look. I'll take your info, but I'm on the blocks every day. When I find it, I'll put it on the cart and deliver it to you."

I couldn't tell if this might be working or if he just wanted to sleep it off. He nodded wearily, eyes blinking in that rapid slowness of stupor as he made a contrived effort to appear thoughtful through the gathering haze of alcohol.

"Maybe it's time you faggots read it. It's the ... the Bible of ... future."

I looked amazed and shook my head. "You know, I was just telling that to a trustee the other day. We must stay on our guards, right?" The Aryan frowned, and I said, "You know, we have to keep the faith."

He nodded with a sneer. "Goddamn right. You just bring that to me. You got it, faggot?"

"Absolutely. Thank you for coming in here today. This was very enlightening."

He nodded with a head-bobbing smugness and walked unsteadily to the door. He turned to give us a final threatening frown and staggered out into the corridor.

We waited a moment to make sure he was gone, and then the guy I called Dave breathed a heavy sigh. "Good fucking job, Blizzard."

My relief was short-lived. The trustee gave me a strange look and nodded toward the door. I looked, thinking maybe the Aryan was coming back, but no one was there. He nodded more forcefully, and I got it. He was signaling for me to get out quick, but it was too late.

Marilyn Manakin stepped from between the shelves. I noticed she'd gradually altered her clothing so that her dresses had become sack-like and hid her enticing figure. She'd also cut her black hair shorter; it was now shoulder length though somehow still stylish when framing her perfect angelic face. But this was no angel. I realized she'd seen the Aryan come in and had hidden. Perhaps there'd been a prior encounter. If so, why hadn't the stupid bitch had guards nearby? A fleeting hope sparked; perhaps she'd thank me. She spat on that spark the second her lips moved.

The vitriol that spilled forth was unwarranted and devastating. "I knew you were a deviant and a murderer, but now I see you're also the lowest form of Nazi scum imaginable. If it were up to me, you'd be on death row. I'd pull the switch myself. Now get out and don't come back."

The inmate I'd called Dave tried to help. "Ma'am, it's not what you—"

She turned on him. "Shut your mouth unless you want his trouble."

I don't know where I got the nerve to respond. As I tossed my library lanyard onto the counter, I felt I had nothing left to lose, so the words spilled forth. "Goethe said there's nothing more frightening than bigotry in action. Normally I'd suggest books as an antidote for bigotry. But you probably dropped out of college precisely because you're illiterate."

My heart was broken, and I was frightened, but I mustered the dignity to hold my head up as I strode out of the library for the last time. Maestro seemed like a lost dream. He was gone, and I was banned from the library. I was also certain that my tirade would bring retribution, and that cycled into severe depression.

I was devastated, but just as my depression set in, everything spun on its axis yet again.

Even in the well of despair I felt upon entering prison, I don't remember a depression as deep as the one following my angry outburst at Marilyn Manakin. I'd been surviving on a thread of hope, and it seemed that Marilyn Manakin had nonchalantly cut that thread. I was wrong.

Early the following morning, I was certain a horrible fate was at hand when two guards showed up at my cell. I assumed the Bitch Warden had sent them to punish me for calling her an illiterate bigot, but the smaller one, a rational fellow named Kiser, said, "Gather up your shit. Leave what you can't carry. It'll be brought to you."

Where were they taking me? I had no choice, so I grabbed up my few belongings but paused at the cell door and pointed. "Can I take those books?"

The biggest of the guards, the ignorant walleyed brute, Ralph, stepped in close. "Get the shit out of your ears. Didn't you hear what he said? The rest will be—"

"Back off, Wilkinson." Kiser, a man whose rodent-like features made him look undeservedly sly, pushed me gently aside and pointed to the cot. "Sit there for a second, inmate."

I did as he bade, and he whispered to Ralph. Ralph leaned to the side to look at me around Kiser's head with his good eye. He'd lost his left eye in a cell block riot, and it had been replaced by a prosthetic, a realistic replica that moved almost in unison with his good eye. No one dared make fun of it. He'd busted many a head for even the slightest reference to its slight dysfunction. He was an Aryan sympathizer I knew from my earliest days when he turned a blind eye, pun intended, to my abuse at the hands of the Aryan Brotherhood. He blamed the Bloods and Black Muslims for anything that went wrong, including the loss of his eye.

He stared over Kiser's shoulder, and his head bobbed once. After that, he ignored me. Almost. I was surprised that they didn't install the standard restraints on my arms and legs before I followed them down the long cell block to a freight elevator that dropped deep into the substructure of the prison. We exited the elevator into a long tunnel through the old stone foundation. As I stared into its depths, I could see bare light bulbs stretch into an interminable distance. We moved out, and they guided me along the center of the narrow space to avoid steam pipes and electrical conduit.

I didn't realize until that moment that I was claustrophobic. I'd never been enclosed in such a tight, narrow space. As we moved deeper into the interstitial bowels of the prison, it was all I could do not to turn and flee back toward the elevator as panic gradually threatened to overwhelm logic. My breathing became rapid, and I was certain they would stop suddenly at some hidden isolation chamber where I'd spend the rest of my life chained to a wall like a medieval prisoner who'd offended the queen. The panic rose, and I imagined myself in a dark coffin-sized enclosure. The tunnel shrunk, and my body wouldn't squeeze through. Another step and I'd be trapped. They'd keep me alive on rat meat, and I'd slowly suffocate in these black depths. I tried to close my eyes and walk, but the rough concrete floor was too uneven.

I blurted out, my voice quaking, "Could you officers tell me where we're going?"

Ralph turned on me, but Kiser immediately stepped between us and put a hand on Ralph's chest. He said only, "Don't." Then, keeping his eyes on Ralph, he said to me, "Inmate, it's best if you just do as we say and keep your mouth shut. Got it?"

I said, "Yes, sir." Something in Kiser's voice contained a nuance of reassurance.

We moved on, Ralph and then me and then Kiser. The fear of being halted in front of a steel door made me alert to any indentation in the wall, but I could have sworn we stopped and a door into a black cell swallowed me. But the tunnel began to slope slightly upward. After another five miles, which was perhaps forty yards, we came to a dead end at the very kind of rusty steel door I'd been dreading. Panic rose again as Kiser took out a ring of keys and inserted one. A padlock snapped open. Behind me hung an infinite row of low-wattage bulbs, a downward arc into infinity. Through that door, I wasn't sure. Kiser stood back as Ralph shoved hard. Metal scraped over concrete.

I expected it to reveal a tiny cell with chains anchored in round bolts in the wall, but we exited into an open stairwell and, in tandem, clinked disharmoniously up a long zigzag set of metal stairs. The stairwell widened, and we paused at yet another door. When Ralph pushed this one open, a blast of sunshine slapped me in the face. We stepped into a distant prison yard, a wide expanse in a remote area of the prison grounds. In one direction were baseball fields, and in the other, the double-wound concertina-topped fences. Beyond those fences, to my endless wonder, lay cultivated fields and open farmland as far as the eye could see. I was Dante emerging from the depths of the inferno. I paused to revel in the childlike pleasure of sun on my face. It was hot and humid and glorious.

We proceeded along a wide sidewalk across the open expanse toward a two-story building that stood alone at the edge of the grounds. When we reached the building, Kiser had us pause at a sliding metal door. I'd seen this structure from afar and had deemed it to be administrative offices. Later I found out that it had once been just that. But not anymore.

Kiser pushed a buzzer next to the metal door and stepped back into the view of an overhead camera. It was as unassuming as any other concrete-block building inside the prison fences, but that's where the similarity ended. I heard a motorized whirring as the metal door slid open, and we stepped into a small space before a second door that opened only after the exterior door slid closed. I later found out that the second door was to keep others out rather than the inmates inside.

Just as I was about to step through, Ralph grabbed my arm and jammed me against the outer wall, his forearm against my neck and his nose inches from mine.

Kiser stepped beside Ralph and leaned close to his ear. "Don't say a goddamn word, Ralph. You'll only cause trouble for yourself."

Ralph looked at him with a disdain he must have been storing for years. "Shut up. If this fucking ... whatever it is gets to leave gen pop, I'll have my say."

Kiser shook his head. "Jesus, you dumb fuck. You never get it, do you?"

Ralph made his best effort to stare at me. I never knew why he didn't wear a patch over that eye. It would have looked far more menacing than the cockeyed, doll-like visage he was left with.

Ralph's anger had reached saturation. "You don't know it, but all those times when your ass was getting torn up by the Aryans? It was me. I wanted them to fuck you in your queer trannie ass until you drowned in their cum. I don't care what crimes they did to get in here. At least they're real men. I was waiting for that nigger of yours to get out so I could come after you myself. So just know if you're ever put back in gen pop, I'll be waiting. I almost had you when one of these wops showed up. I won't miss again." He grabbed me by the throat and squeezed. "I'll fucking be waiting."

Kiser stepped in. "Let him go, Officer, or I'll have no choice but to have you brought up on charges of abuse."

Ralph pushed me aside, and Kiser caught me before I fell.

"Go ahead, Mama Kiser. Protect this freak. But you won't be around if he's back in gen pop. Then you got no idea what abuse looks like."

I've never been much for quick comebacks, being mostly the type who always thinks of things I should have said long after the opportunity to say them has passed. But the prospect of being free of the Ralphs of the world gave free rein to my mouth.

I said, "Of course I knew it was you setting me up. You're too stupid for subtlety. And you're the real prisoner here, you walleyed fuck. You chose this pathetic life because you're too chickenshit to live among people who can fight back. Prisoners come and go, but you're fucking stuck here forever, and you're so fucking stupid, you've got nowhere else to go. Who's the real prisoner, fuckhead?"

Ralph's rage was uncontainable, but Kiser was prepared. For the second time that morning, he stepped between us, pushing me out of the way and wrapping his arms around Ralph's shoulders in a bear hug. "Ralph, don't do it. You want to get fired over one inmate?"

Ralph's anger overwhelmed his ability to articulate, and all he could do was spit and sputter. "Fucking faggot cocksucker. I get you back to pop and you're a dead fucking fucker."

I grinned at Ralph and made his anger escalate. I couldn't keep my mouth shut, though I should have. I couldn't resist a final jab. "I'm sure to be passing through gen pop occasionally, Ralph. Make sure and keep an eye out for me. Fucking cyclops."

Kiser said, "That's enough, inmate."

I responded contritely, "Sorry, Kiser. Thanks for not letting him at me."

Kiser grunted and led me through the interior metal door. Ralph had no choice but to follow. His body was shaking, though he was clearly aware that he held no sway in this domain. He was like a belligerent serf suddenly called to the manor house.

We entered a single office with a lone guard at a wooden desk behind a high counter. I couldn't see any more than that one room, but if it was any indication, this place was not a typical cell block. It was like an office in a business on the outside.

The guard, rotund yet muscular with a bald spot in salt and pepper hair, stood and, without benefit of transfer papers, nodded to Kiser. Ralph stood stone-still, staring a hole in me.

The guard sensed his anger and looked at Ralph. "Hey."

Ralph was so focused on me that he wasn't paying attention.

The guard repeated more loudly, "Hey, you. Guard."

Ralph finally realized that he was being addressed and turned his vile attention away.

The man pointed at the door. "You can go now. Get out."

Ralph's denigration was complete, but he wouldn't let go. He took a step forward. "What the fuck do you mean, get out? I'm an officer of this prison—"

The guard cut him off sharply, pointing toward the main prison, "Over there you're an officer of the prison. Over here, you're exactly jack shit. Now get out before I put you in a cell with some gen pop inmates. I bet you're real popular on the blocks."

Ralph looked as if he might break free of his sanity and attack the guard, but Kiser grabbed his arm and forcibly led him from the building back through the single access door. I watched as Kiser pushed a resistant Ralph along the sidewalk back toward the blocks.

I was left with this lone guard, who stood and pushed through a low swinging barrier. He opened a manila folder and stared first at it and then up at me. It must have contained my photograph. They seemed to be avoiding any official record of my transfer.

Satisfied that I was who I was supposed to be, he said, "I'm Holt. A syllable you don't need to remember. You won't see much of me. This is your new block. You'll sleep here, eat here, and do your job here. Whatever that is. Follow me."

He was a tall man, and I felt like an errant child as I tossed my laundry bag full of belongings over my shoulder and followed him into the interior of this, my new home.

At first I tried making casual conversation, thinking it wouldn't hurt to ingratiate myself with this one guard, but he stopped in the middle of the corridor and turned to me.

"Look. Stuart, right?"

I nodded.

"Look, Stuart. I don't mean to be rude, but you get no points for making friends with me. I love this job. It's the best job in the prison. I get more from the tips these guys give me than my pitiful salary. But to them, I'm just like the doorman at their fancy hotels in Miami. Frankly, I like it that way. I'll never accidentally cross these guys if I remember my place. You're with them now. I'm glad you want to be polite to me, but it's best if you forget I'm here. I'm just trying to set you off on the right foot, *capisce?*"

He said "capisce" as a country boy from north Florida would say it trying to imitate one of these guys it was his job not to guard but to serve.

"*Capito*, Signor Holt." Those were the last words I said to Holt for a very long time. He was right. He was not there to be my friend. But when I asked for something, I somehow knew it was Holt who saw that I got it.

As we moved into this new habitat, I couldn't help thinking it was like Dorothy's awakening in Oz. I'd spent years in a drab, gray, brutal world, and suddenly everything was Technicolor. The hallways were bright and clean, with brightly colored walls, white acoustical tile ceilings, and white terrazzo floors, all spotless but with honest-to-god colorful paintings spaced along the walls. Every step took me deeper into Oz. Or Wonderland. Or paradise.

Holt led me past a small public space that perhaps served for visitation, a game room with a pool table, and a gym full of modern equipment. But no people. We stopped at an elevator at the end of the corridor. We entered and rode up to the second floor. An elevator to move an inmate up one floor? This must be Wonderland. I also noticed that there was a button in the elevator for a third floor, which was odd because it couldn't be seen from outside.

We exited into a wide hallway and turned left. I followed Holt to the last door on the left, number 29. He reached out a key, which I took reflexively.

"This one's yours."

I looked down at the key on a metal ring and then up at him. "I don't understand."

He chortled. "I couldn't believe it when they told me they were bringing a non-Italian over here. Never happened on my watch. But, my friend, you are in for a surprise. This is like an apartment building on the outside. Except you can't leave. I just gave you a key you'll never use. There's no one here to steal, as if anyone would be stupid enough to steal from these fucking guys."

He shrugged as he backed down the hall. "Why you'd want to leave is beyond me. It's like living in the goddamn Waldorf-Astoria."

I turned to the door and muffed the key several times before inserting it correctly into the lock—that's how long it had been since I'd entered through anything other than an electrically controlled cell door—but I finally unlocked it, stepped inside, and despite my intentions to remain guarded, burst into violent sobbing. It was triggered when I saw my books already placed carefully in a small bookcase against the wall. They'd beaten me here.

The tears were automatic because I was still a cyclical luteinizer, and one of the few vestiges of womanhood in my physiology was occasional tears when dealing with stress, distress, or eustress. I knew the difference. This was pure eustress—the good kind.

The apartment was small, but compared to a cell, it was palatial. It was, in fact, a two-room suite. I entered a spacious combination living room and bedroom with a full-size bed under an actual window. There were bars on the outside, but it let in natural light. The prison world of dim mustard haze and random echoes had worn me down. I was developing an inexplicable form of light sensitivity that was turning me into Stoker's Renfield. I was certain I'd eventually be huddled in the corner of a cell, eating cockroaches.

There was a small sitting area with a loveseat and narrow easy chair around a glass-top coffee table and a small closet, where two clean sets of prison blues hung. My size. To the left was a narrow galley kitchen with a two-burner stovetop, a sink, and an under-cabinet refrigerator. And then heaven was revealed when I opened a double folding door and there before me in all its glory was a small bathroom. Small but with its own shower. I could use it anytime I wished without being bent double while some fucker soaped up his dick. I giggled like the village idiot.

I barely had time to put my things down and use the toilet—my toilet—when there was a knock at the door. I hurried over and opened it.

"Maestro."

"May I enter your humble abode?"

I laughed. "Yeah, I didn't realize I'd be roughing it like this. And I'm really gonna miss my cot lice. They've become like family."

He smiled as he settled onto the loveseat. "It's time to meet the boss. We call him Mr. O. When members of the organization do time in prison, all real names disappear. It's a sign not to turn rat. If you don't have a name, neither does anyone you ever knew. The *o* is a circle; he's at the center."

I nodded. "I thought it would be for *Omerta*—your code of silence. Or maybe *Orcus*—the Roman god who punished oath breakers."

He stared at me for a moment. "Alphonse was right about your book smarts. I admire you for it. You don't even mind sounding like a total dipshit. Takes courage. You might want to remember the only thing guys in here read is a racing form or letter from home."

I couldn't suppress another idiotic giggle. I stood, thinking he wished to leave, but he remained seated.

"There's one more thing," he said. I sat back down, and he continued, "Everyone knows you used to be a cunt."

I bristled, and he immediately held up a hand.

"Sorry. That was rude. I do that on purpose sometimes. Outsiders don't understand. I meant, woman. Personally, I don't give a shit what you were. But Mr. O is old-fashioned. To him you changed how God made you. You shouldn't presume to know more than God."

I frowned, a bit disappointed in this reflexive misogyny. "So, what do I do? I can't change back even if I wanted to."

He nodded, and I saw a flicker of regret. "Look, just don't talk about it. Mr. O owes Alphonse a debt. You're the payment. Do what he asks, but don't bring up your past. Mr. O takes people for what they can do, not who or what they are and especially not who they think they are."

I said, "I think the world's problems would be solved if everyone thought that way."

He stared at me hard, and I could tell he'd been assessing me. Mr. O had decided to bring me in. This man was doing his own evaluation.

He smiled as he stood. "Now you're thinking like one of us. You're smart. The boss respects what smart people can do. But sometimes those skills are just a means to an end."

"Then how do I avoid my past and earn respect if I'm just a means to an end?"

"You become one of us. We do everything together, here; we never fuck around over in gen pop. You'll never need that kitchen except maybe to keep wine cold. We eat meals together, play poker together, watch football. But maybe use your own bathroom. Standing next to the guys will only make them think a woman is watching them piss. These men will rip your heart out, but they won't piss in front of their own wives."

He stood. "Mr. O doesn't have a good side or a bad one. He's a smart businessman. Too smart to be in this shithole. Do what he says until he figures it out. That's how you stay useful."

I was scared shitless as we left my room and walked to the elevator. I wanted this meeting to go well. In the elevator, Maestro punched the three, and as we rose, he turned to face the back. It was only then that I noticed the elevator opened in both directions, which explained why I had never seen a third floor; it was a half floor you couldn't see from the blocks. The rear elevator door opened, and we stepped into a semicircular anteroom with a shining black linoleum floor and three doors, each a different color. Two huge men in inmate uniforms sat next to the middle one.

The two men stood. They were giant, stocky men from central casting. The prison uniforms only served to accentuate their menacing demeanor.

I stood behind Maestro as he approached and said, "This is the new guy. New guy, this is Big Al and Tony."

*These names are straight from the Mafia manual*, I thought.

Once again, I felt like an ant under a magnifying glass in the hot sun until Maestro addressed me while staring at the two large men. "This is just for appearances. These guys got the easiest fucking job in here, sitting on their fat asses, trying to look tough."

The one on the right said in a thick Jersey accent, "You know I can hear you, shithead."

Maestro retorted, "You saying I'm lying? You assholes are so soft, you couldn't save us from a bunch of Girl Scouts."

The big man grinned. "Hell no, you ain't lying. And I hope we do get attacked by some Girl Scouts. I love them chocolate mint cookies."

I would eventually get used to this. But at that moment, I was so relieved, I wanted to burst out in an idiotic fit of laughter and perhaps do a few tricks like turn somersaults around the room like a trained monkey or pretend to hit myself in the head and fall to the floor as if I'd knocked myself out.

Instead I stood quietly as the two nodded and Maestro said, "He's waiting for us."

The one called Tony opened the door. "Sir? They're here."

If Big Al and Tony were perfect stereotypes, the man sitting behind the desk in the tasteful room on the other side of that door was anything but. His age was difficult to ascertain, probably late fifties. He was tall and fit with neatly cut gray hair, and he spoke in a neutral American accent. His face was tan, and he had an aquiline nose and a strong chin. He looked more Caesarian than Mafia. He was the first inmate I'd seen wearing anything other than prison garb; he was clad in a black loose-fitting warmup suit.

Mr. O sat in a high-back leather chair behind a large desk of dark wood on an oval rug. I thought this office must rival the warden's. It may once have been the warden's office.

He stood and waved a hand at two chairs in front of his desk. We sat and waited for him to speak. There were no introductions. He knew who I was.

"Would you like a coffee?" He sounded like a banker, courteous and professional.

"That would be very nice." I'd learned not to turn down an offer of coffee from an Italian. It was a ritual of hospitality, like tea to the Brits.

Moments later, a door opened from an adjacent room, and Big Al entered with a tray containing three cups of espresso and a container of sugar. He offered the tray first to Mr. O and then me and Maestro.

Mr. O watched me intently as I picked up my demitasse by the handle, put a single small spoon of sugar in the cup, and stirred it slowly. The crema was perfect. In fact, it was the most delicious espresso I'd had since leaving Italy.

I sipped, and I could tell Mr. O sensed my genuine pleasure at the aroma and flavor.

I tried to sound appreciative but not maudlin. "Delizioso. Grazie mille."

Mr. O smiled and got straight to business. "Alphonse was a good friend to the family. Faithful and honest. He wasn't educated, but he was smart. He said you're both. A business degree, I believe. Can you keep financial accounts?"

"Yes, sir, I can."

"Everyone living here has duties. We may be in prison, but business continues. One of our accountants has left us. He served out his sentence quietly, so he'll be welcomed back to his old position." A hint of a frown flashed across his face. I took note.

"I'd like you to replace him. It's simple accounting. We like it that way. But you will use a computer with encryption. I assume you can use these newfangled things."

"Yes, sir, I can." The University of Florida again served me well. I'd been fascinated by computers from day one. They were like complex digital watches that did what you told them.

Mr. O nodded at Maestro. "Will you arrange it?"

"Of course." Maestro's deference was obvious. Another stereotype dispelled. There was no aura of menace, no hidden signals, in their interactions. But I could tell that something was eating at Mr. O. I can read people; it's how I survived as a cross-dresser in a hick town. I recognized the signs of dissonance. He was distracted even as he spoke.

Unexpectedly, Mr. O stood. "Thank you for coming. Our previous accountant left some materials for you. Those, too, will be delivered."

I was surprised that the encounter had been so brief. Then I thought, *Why would I expect an elaborate human resources onboarding process?* Maestro and I stood. The only stereotypical activity took place at that moment. Maestro stepped around the desk, and Mr. O reached out his hand, which bore a large ring on the third finger. It was set with a red stone. I couldn't see it well enough to analyze the gem. It looked like the papal ring.

Maestro bent formally, kissed it, and then moved next to me, and in that moment, I inadvertently said something that would change my life.

As we turned to leave, I said politely, "If there's anything else I can do to help, Mr. O, you have but to ask. Anything within my realm of knowledge."

I moved with Maestro toward the door, and Mr. O said, "Unless you're a fortune-teller, keeping the books will have to do."

I stopped in my tracks and turned back to him. There was that disquiet in his tone again.

My intuition was humming. "Sir, I'm not a fortune-teller in the conventional sense, but I'm good at predictive modeling. I know how to extract information from unexpected places and remove error from predictions. If you'd like to tell me what your needs are, I might be able to help."

He stared at me for a long, uncomfortable moment. I prayed I hadn't offended him. I stood as still as the stone on his finger while Maestro hovered ghostlike behind me.

Finally, Mr. O cocked his head and said to Maestro, "Bring this one back tomorrow. For lunch. You come too. We'll eat, then talk."

A red BMW convertible left Cochise County, Arizona, and entered Hidalgo County, New Mexico, on I-10. There was nothing to indicate the border crossing save a road sign and a slight variation in the highway's surface. It was early afternoon.

"Dry heat, my ass," Leitner said. "I could piss out the window and salt would hit the asphalt."

Summer covered her mouth with her hand to hide a smile. She'd been pouting since they left a truck stop on I-10 in Arizona. Leitner noticed she'd leaned against the passenger door to create as much distance between them as possible. He needed to defuse her. He'd fucked up, but tough shit. The last thing he needed was for her to go off the rails out here in bumfuck.

"That's my girl." He leaned forward and grinned at her.

Summer forced a frown. "I can't believe you. You almost killed that man back there. All he did was smile at me."

Leitner slowed, pulled onto the emergency lane, stopped the car, and hit the button to close the canvas roof against the sun. He sat slumped with his hands at ten and two elbows resting on the steering wheel. *Jesus, here we go,* he thought.

He turned to her. "Look, kiddo. If that guy stared any harder, his eyeballs would have popped out of his head and rolled between your tits."

Summer's voice was placating. "You should be glad when men stare at me. It should make you feel good that I'm with you and not with them."

Leitner's anger flared. *Is this silly bitch serious?* There was an innocent logic to her pea-brained thoughts, but Leitner never trusted women. The marriage had been a stupid impulse he'd regretted the moment it was done. His right hand left the wheel. *I should slap the shit out of this stupid cunt.* He paused. He'd let this play out. She couldn't be as naïve and trusting as she seemed. Sooner or later the real succubus would emerge. He wanted to see how long it took before he left her in some roadside motel with her throat slit.

He sighed. "Look. I'm not good with trust. And I'm sure as shit not good at letting some loser gawk at my woman."

Summer stared at him. "My god, what do you think I am? Even in Vegas, I played those marks and never once had to fuck one. Thanks to you."

He stared out at the highway ahead. "Maybe. But I bet you sucked half the cocks in Vegas before me, especially ones with a winning poker hand."

Her face turned into a mask of hatred, and her voice was enraged as she grabbed her small bag from the back seat. "You fucking bastard. I really cared for you, but if that's what you think, then fuck you." She pressed the release on her seat belt and fumbled to open the door.

Leitner was stunned. The dumb bitch's suitcase was in the trunk. He reached over and grabbed her arm, but she ripped it away, leaving a scratch on her forearm.

"Get away from me," she screamed. She managed to open the door and scramble out as Leitner grabbed at the hem of her dress but missed.

She didn't look back as she trod as fast as her white stilettos would allow along the emergency lane. Leitner got out of the car and leaned on the fender.

*Goddamn her*, he thought, but he shouted, "Come on. There's nowhere to go out here."

The doppler drone of an approaching rig sounded behind them, and Summer turned to hold out a thumb as she backpedaled clumsily up the desert highway. Leitner heard the hiss of air brakes, and a nondescript semi pulled over thirty yards ahead. Summer cocked each leg to remove her shoes and began running toward it in her bare feet, her shoulder-length hair swaying and shoulder bag bouncing off her back.

Leitner paused, thinking she'd stop. She didn't. She was really going after that truck. He launched after her.

"Stop, goddamnit, Summer, stop. They'll fucking kill you." Leitner's voice was lost as two other semis roared past, but he kept shouting, "Summer, goddamnit. Stop you crazy bitch."

Leitner calculated that he could catch her just before she reached the truck. The ball cap blew off his head as he leaned into his sprint, his athleticism kicking in. He was closing fast as Summer's bare feet slapped the pavement, her dress fluttering around her knees.

The driver's side door of the semi was suddenly kicked opened, and a stocky man with a greasy red ball cap pulled low and a halo of dark curly hair protruding around the band leapt from the cab as Leitner got within ten yards of Summer. Just as he reached out a hand to grab her arm, a second man appeared from the opposite side of the trailer, aiming a sawed-off shotgun at Leitner's chest.

"Leave the lady alone." The man was huge. He glared at Leitner from under the bill of an identical red ball cap; neither had identifying letters or logos. The shotgun was shouldered against a denim shirt above jeans and cowboy boots.

Leitner froze and held up his hands. He cursed himself silently for leaving his handgun nestled next to the seat in the BMW.

Summer ran to the man on the driver's side but paused to look back at Leitner, who, hands up and palms out, tried to reason with the trucker aiming the shotgun. The big man stalked across the rear of the truck and stood with his back to Summer. His plaid shirt was unbuttoned over a ribbed T-shirt.

"Look, man, my girl and I just had a little spat. It's okay. Just ask her."

The man with the shotgun stood in his line of sight to Summer, his cheap-ass plaid shirt flapping in the desert wind, obscuring Leitner's view. He couldn't see what transpired, but he thought he saw the driver grab Summer's arm and push her up into the cab. He couldn't tell if she went voluntarily.

"Let's go, Farley," Leitner heard the driver shout from the cab.

Farley took a few steps toward Leitner, and for a moment Leitner thought the bastard might shoot him on the side of the road, though he could hear traffic in both directions.

Finally, Farley gave him a brown-toothed grin. "Don't worry, Boudreaux. We take good care of her. But I see you again, I'll blow your nipples through your shoulder blades."

Farley cackled as he continued to hold the shotgun on Leitner and backed around the end of the trailer to the passenger side. Leitner could see his legs as he broke into a run for the cab.

Leitner turned and bolted for the BMW. When he dove into the passenger seat and grabbed his pistol, the truck was already accelerating onto the highway. A semi had to go through a lot of gears, so Leitner had the Beamer on its tail in seconds.

Leitner Dredge was unaccustomed to thinking about the well-being of another human, so the unusual emotions plaguing him at that moment caught him by surprise. He asked himself a simple question: *Am I chasing this fucking truck because two assholes took something that belongs to me? Or am I chasing it because I care about this bitch and deserved her anger?*

He backed off the truck. He couldn't get into a shootout on the highway. He was in a stolen car and might get Summer killed. It might be a long haul; a semi could run farther than a car without stopping for fuel. That's when Leitner Dredge made a tentative decision. He'd follow these fuckers and decide why later. He knew one thing for certain: the two fucking rednecks would pay. Then he'd decide what to do with Summer. Another thought hit him. Maybe these fuckers wanted him to follow; otherwise, they'd have shot him and left his body in the desert. Could they really be planning to receive payment to get her back? He ran the odds. Yes. And that's when they planned to kill them both.

Leitner slammed his hand down on the steering wheel several times, screaming, "Fuck me." He'd just handed two chump-change artists something they didn't have brains to plan.

Leitner Dredge's anger settled into a lethal bitterness. "You think you caught a sucker? I can't wait to show you assholes what you really reeled in."

# CHAPTER 8

I placed the leather bookmark at my spot and closed the cover of the journal. I'd come down to the lake early while the temperature was still tolerable. A soft breeze wafted soothingly from the east. I smiled into its freshness as I stroked the soft leather of the binder.

The binder as well as the bookmark had been made by a fellow inmate, a kid named Tommy. I once possessed a truly beautiful binder purchased in Oltrarno, "across the Arno," in Florence from one of the fine leather shops. The city was known for its elegant leather goods, the exotic scent of which permeated the streets lined with shops.

That binder had been confiscated along with all my other personal items upon incarceration. I knew I'd never see it or my Rolex again. I had described it to Tommy, who was skilled in leatherwork. The hide for the leather was unexpectedly procured by Maestro, hide that the young inmate had secretly cured and tanned in a prison shop.

The binder was imprinted with a misquote beloved by inmates to indicate their newfound, and essential, religious conversion. The quote wrapped around the binder from front to back. It read "Live simple so others may simply live." The correct quote was by

Mahatma Gandhi: "Live simply so others may simply live." The prison version inadvertently meant live ignorant so others may live. In a way it was better advice for inmates. Live as a simpleton. Know nothing. Say nothing.

I lifted my gaze to the lake, my eyes not registering its vast beauty as I saw only memories painted on the far shore. As Dante had reached the trenches of Malebolge, I too was entering a level of foreboding for which I was never prepared. I once thought the brutal encounter with two jewel thieves in my small shop had prepared me for all the horrors that might befall me. This world kept spiraling down. I reached into my pants pocket and retrieved a tissue to wipe a layer of sweat from my forehead. I squeezed my eyes shut for a moment to clear my mind. Clear my mind? Self-delusional. Inane. My mind would never be clear.

"You must read, and you must remember." I said it aloud, not caring if I was heard. The journal was now a permanent part of my dress. It lay open in my lap like rune signs to a faraway world. I pulled my eyes from the lake and forced myself to read on.

I'd arrogantly announced to wall-eyed Ralph that I'd be visiting gen pop, but I wasn't stupid about it. I never entered the blocks without Maestro. I even took up occasional duties in the library. Porter let me know when the Bitch Warden would be away, and Maestro escorted me to and from the library when he had business on the blocks. Ralph wouldn't dare invade the space the warden's wife now ruled, and contrary to his persistent braggadocio, he wouldn't risk having at me when Maestro was around.

I befriended the freckle-faced, redheaded Tommy Johnson. I met him in the library soon after his incarceration. He was barely out of his teens and frightened of the savagery I suffered in my early days. I decided to pay forward the kindness I'd received from Alphonse and took Tommy under my protection, though the real deterrent was my position with Mr. O. It should have been foolproof. Some fools exceed proof.

Like me, Tommy was imprisoned for second-degree murder, but unlike me, he was admittedly guilty of his crime. His story was a classic tragedy. He worked as a meter reader for the City of Cocoa Beach until he saved enough money to open a little surf shop. His girlfriend helped him build his business, but in a story as ancient as Euripides, she had seduced someone far slicker than Tommy and convinced Tommy to hire the guy to help build surfboards. They pushed Tommy out of his own business.

The day the two announced their love and concomitant takeover, Tommy had smiled and left. The following day, as they opened the shop, Tommy showed up with his father's twelve-gauge and a hacksaw. He nearly pulled it off, but he overlooked one of the girl's pinkie fingers, which the police found in the tire well of Tommy's old Ford. The judge accepted a plea of second-degree murder in a crime of passion, though Tommy had taken a full day to ponder his retribution.

Tommy had a guilelessly manifested dark side, an eerie twist on sociopathy. He wasn't amoral or nonempathetic. He was simply so naïve and introverted that he rarely engaged in social interaction, which accretively disconnected him from society. We were sitting alone in the cafeteria at lunch one day when he pulled out a change purse and said, "Look at this."

At first his conversation wandered. "The day she took my store? She said I made her skin crawl. But, Stuart, before? If we had five seconds alone, she'd go for my zipper. I don't get it."

I wondered how he could not know, but I said, "Look, Tommy. Your last name, Johnson, is perfect for you. I don't mean anything perverted, but you're pretty well known by those who've seen you in the showers. I hear you're packing more salami than an Italian deli."

He held up the change purse. "This is the last present I got from her."

"A gift?" I asked.

"No. When I was, you know … before they caught me."

As I looked at the object, it hit me. "Wait. You don't mean ... is this what I think it is?"

"Yeah." He smiled shyly. "She wouldn't need it, and I wanted to remember her. Daddy was a taxidermist. He taught me everything there is to know about it."

Tommy had created a change purse from his ex-girlfriend's labia majora by applying his father's lessons more broadly than intended. He'd managed to maintain a scattered forest of her dark pubic hair along the outer rim. When he pressed the ends and it opened, the pink flesh was disturbingly lifelike and supple.

I couldn't stop staring at it; it was fascinatingly disgusting. I once had labia. Did a Dutch surgeon make a change purse out of my leftovers? Nazis had horrifying things made from the flesh of those in concentration camps. But Tommy wasn't a Nazi.

That change purse would remain another item indexed in my mental book of desolation. I asked myself many times why I wasn't perpetually horrified, not just by Tommy's purse but by everything. Three vendettas in one day. The helplessness and horror of brutal rape. The leeching degradation. I realized there must be a corrosive parasite at work. It had turned my moral integrity into chyme and was still digesting. It bred in this prison. Had it wormed its way into my soul?

I didn't know it at the time, but Ralph was doing to Tommy what he'd done to me, facilitating his abuse. One afternoon I received a note that Tommy was in the hospital ward. I begged Maestro to escort me to visit him. When we got there, Tommy was in horrible shape. He'd been beaten so ferociously that he had to sleep on his stomach, and punches to his abdomen had resulted in a ruptured spleen.

I begged Maestro to let me stay the night, and without his typical safety tirade, he agreed. As the night wore on, Tommy's condition worsened, but all I could do was give him his meds and apply ointments to his damaged tissues.

Around four in the morning, I was dozing next to Tommy's

bed when I suddenly felt my body levitate off the chair. I was still in sleep paralysis, so my body was limp and my mind disoriented until someone punched me so viciously in the right kidney it made my entire body seize up.

It was dark. The only light was a red exit sign and the distant cycles of oscillating spotlights painting eerie nystagmic stripes on the linoleum.

The punch dropped me to my knees, but I was immediately hauled to my feet by men on either side. A hand grabbed my chin in a vise grip and lifted my face. I stared into the rabid eye of Ralph. Only one other bed in the ward was occupied, an ancient lifer waiting to be transferred to hospice. I suddenly wanted to go with him.

No one could help. There was only a night nurse on duty, and she'd be crazy to interfere. Everyone was afraid of Ralph and his Aryan thugs.

Ralph was positively giddy with anticipation, and I felt my bowels shift dangerously.

"I fucking knew it. I knew you were a dumb shit. Who's smart now, you fucking faggot?" he said.

He gave me a quick slap and afterward clapped his hands like a little girl excited about a tea cake. It wasn't a hard slap; it was a slap that said he wanted this to go slowly. He wanted to savor every second of my annihilation.

"I knew you'd come shove cream up this queer's ass. It was me. I told these guys"—he nodded at the two men holding me—"just give this surfer queer a special dose and you'd come running like a cunt. I've got you now, you fucking piece of—"

Suddenly Tommy's voice whimpered, and I heard him say, "It's bliss." That phrase echoed from my past, further disorienting me. I'd heard it from a little boy through a grate in my jewelry shop ceiling during a robbery.

Ralph frowned down at Tommy. "He's as fucking crazy as you are. But now? Holy shit." He preened, strutting back and forth in front of me, working himself into a killing frenzy. "Jesus Christ,

I can't wait to skin you alive, you worthless fucking faggot piece of shit."

I was dead anyway. "I see you still have that redneck mumble that sounds like you've got a cock in your mouth."

He grabbed the nape of my neck in one hand and clamped his other around my jaw so tight I felt my teeth cutting the inside of my cheeks. He stared wildly into my face, the one eye wobbling wildly.

"Keep talking, faggot. I told you what would happen, didn't I?" He slapped me so hard, I understood the concept of seeing stars. "You're so fucking stupid. You walked right into my trap. Tell me how smart are you now, fucker? Say it. Who's smart now? Me or you?"

My legs were shaking, and I felt erratic motility in my bowels. I was suddenly more afraid than I'd ever been. Most attacks were designed to humiliate. This man wanted to kill me while all the lessons from those I should have heeded mocked me. Ralph was right. I was the stupid one.

I started to say, "Me …" as I went limp.

At that moment, someone began clapping slowly from the darkness near the ward entrance. I heard footsteps on linoleum. Ralph spun around, and the two henchmen holding me looked over their shoulders, me bobbing between them.

Still nothing.

The two men dropped my arms, and I fell to my knees. One said, "What the fuck, Ralph?"

Ralph spoke through clenched teeth. "You just grab that fucker." He turned to scan the darkness as the two picked me back up and held my arms.

Three long shadows slid across the linoleum toward us, shoes clicking time on the floor. Into the light stepped Maestro, flanked by Big Al and Tony, arms at their sides, each holding a silenced pistol down one leg.

Maestro's grin did not match his eyes as he approached Ralph. It was nightmarish. There was only one other person who'd ever affected me that way, and he died in a fire. Tony and Al stood back, stone faces staring at the two Aryans holding me.

Maestro stared at Ralph. "He's right. You do mumble like you've got a dick in your mouth." Maestros hand struck like a viper, and Ralph wobbled on his feet. "Let me answer your question for my friend. You're the dumbest motherfucker I've ever even heard about." He pointed at the two holding me. "You maggots know who you're touching?"

The two men dropped my arms like they were made of hot steel and simultaneously shook their heads. I fell onto all fours as one said, "No, sir. We don't know him … We're sorry."

Tony pointed his pistol at him. "You lying sack of shit. You'd fuck your mother in the ass if this walleyed fuck told you to."

Maestro's stare was mesmerizing. "You telling me you don't know who this man is?" He looked from one to the other.

"This asshole officer said he'd put us in iso if we didn't help." The man's voice quavered.

"That's a fucking lie," Ralph yelled. "It was their idea. Fucking Nazis."

Maestro's hand moved in a blur, and a stiletto blade snapped open with a loud click. I could feel fear exuding from the two. The one to my left began farting as his parasympathetic system kicked in. I'd been farting the whole time, and it was hard to tell who stunk worse.

Maestro looked from one to the other and nodded toward the door. "I see either of you again, I'll slice you thin enough to read through."

The two turned and ran for the exit as Ralph screamed, "Get back here, you chickenshits. You'll pay for this."

Maestro waved an angry hand at me, indicating I should get away from Ralph. I stood and stumbled toward Tommy's bed. Then he turned to Al and Tony and nodded toward the door. "You two go on back. Best you're not seen over here. Find out where those two Nazis bunk. I'll fucking slit their throats myself."

Al and Tony nodded, and Big Al looked at me. "They owe the boss money."

Maestro said, "They'll pay. Then I'll slit their throats."

Big Al nodded his head at me as he turned to leave. "See you soon."

Ralph's eyes went wide, and he began to shake. It was as I expected. Alone, without his Aryans, he was a coward. I sat on the edge of Tommy's bed. He lay on his side, eyes bulging with fear. I put a protective arm over his shoulders.

Maestro moved around Ralph in small sliding steps, his voice a low whisper. "I heard you were bragging about killing me." His eyes widened, his nostrils flared, and he spoke the next words through clenched teeth. "He's here with us. Do you feel him? *Ombra della Morte*. He's in this room. He's come for you."

Ralph began to sputter nonsensical threats. "You fuck. Can't come near me. They'll fry your ass. You … you fucking better leave right now …"

Maestro was scaring the hell out of me, so I couldn't imagine what Ralph was going through. I knew that once Maestro positioned himself, it was over.

Guards inside didn't wear pistols. They used tasers and gas, though guards like Ralph always carried a baton to bash heads. In a sudden movement that surprised me with its swiftness, Ralph unclipped his baton and swung it violently at Maestro's head. It was fruitless. Maestro ducked under the wild blow and danced to Ralph's right side. It happened so quick, I didn't realize it was over.

Maestro stood shoulder to shoulder with Ralph. Ralph's eyes were wide, his good eye unfocused, the prosthetic one bobbing wildly in his skull. His legs seemed to weaken, and he tilted against Maestro's shoulder. I heard a viscous sound and looked down at something shiny and wet at Ralph's feet. Then I looked at Ralph's belly. His stomach began to bulge, and it was then that I saw a long slit across his entire abdomen. Ralph put his hands over his torso and stared down at his intestines, slick with blood, oozing through his hands onto the floor. The smell of partially digested food was sickening.

A guttural scream gathered in Ralph's throat, but Maestro pirouetted lithely and with another slashing motion slit Ralph's throat and then backed away like a matador, arms cocked, after the death blow. The scream died in a wet gurgle. Ralph dropped to his knees and fell forward onto the raw meat of his innards.

I stood motionless. I wasn't afraid. I was angry.

I turned on Maestro. "Now I see why I didn't get my safety lecture. You knew Ralph would come after me."

Maestro merely nodded.

I clenched my jaw. "Surely you didn't let this happen to Tommy on purpose ... did you?"

For the first time, Maestro was not the sarcastic, jovial friend that escorted me around. This was Maestro the professional killer. He stared at me coldly. "I told you. We don't fuck around in gen pop. This guy may have been your worst nightmare, but to us, he was a nuisance disrupting business. The boss, our boss, wanted him dealt with. He's dealt with. End of story."

He was right. I was the only one frightened of the Ralphs of the world. I had to learn where I was. What I was. "It's just that I know what it's like to be brutalized like Tommy."

"Well, now you don't have to worry about it. The boy will be okay. You'll see to it."

I had no idea what this would trigger. I could only guess it wouldn't be nice. And it wasn't. If I thought I was in hell's lowest level, I was wrong. Sometimes this hell is at its worst in the absence of violence.

I closed the binder and took a sip of espresso. I'd walked uptown from the lake to the small café on First Street as the heat climbed. Having relived the tale of Ralph's demise, I looked at the binder and tapped a forefinger on it absentmindedly. "Nice tattoo, Ralph."

Before Maestro let the night nurse call for help, he sliced the hide off Ralph's lower stomach, buttock, and thigh, muttering something about a Sicilian tradition for disrespecting enemies. That was the flesh Tommy used to make my journal binder and bookmark. The misquoted Gandhi had been tattooed across Ralph's right buttock.

*Why would Ralph have an Aryan tat on his ass?* I wondered. Then I thought about how protective Ralph was of the Aryans. If there was a deeper connection, I hadn't discovered it. But I never looked for it.

When Tommy presented the binder to me, he was proud of it and happy to have made it from Ralph's flesh. I wondered what Tommy's father would have said had he known the tasks to which his son had applied his skills. I also remembered the change purse and wondered if there was a menagerie of human parts Tommy had hidden away somewhere.

Later, when I visited Tommy, I asked him about what he'd said when Ralph showed up.

"Did I hear you say, 'It's bliss'?"

Tommy looked puzzled, but suddenly a light dawned, and he laughed, though it brought a shock wave of pain. "I have a new friend. When I get well, we'll be together. He's a Black Muslim. The Muslims call Ralph *Iblis*. In the language of their bible, um, the Koran?" Tommy pronounced it like *corn*. "That word means Satan."

My memory had flown back to a robbery in a jewelry shop many years before. Could it be that a small child hidden in the air duct had said Iblis rather than "it's bliss"? Yes, of course it could. He remained the smartest human I'd ever met. Like a young Averroes, he'd probably memorized the Koran … and the Bible and who knew what else.

I wanted to move on, to remember my past life in this small town. But the journal beckoned. I opened it at the bookmark.

My first lessons inside the Cosa Nostra block were enlightening. I immediately learned that Cosa Nostra business runs the same on the inside as the outside: seamlessly. I was learning things about organized crime in South Florida I never thought I'd be privy to, and it was fascinating.

The Columbians dominated the cocaine trade. The Cuban Mafia ran numbers. The Mexican heroin trade was gaining traction, and the Russians had slowly expanded their presence in human trafficking. Some of the Cosa Nostra were attempting to operate like a corporation, though not all Cosa Nostra families were so inclined or had the requisite understanding of the legitimate corporate world.

All of these organizations were the object of the US Department of Justice's investigations into the crime of racketeering, which is a bundle of thirty-five "predicate" offenses laid out in the RICO Act—the Racketeer Influenced and Corrupt Organizations Act—including everything from murder and arson to illegal gambling, bribery, and wiretapping.

I concluded that RICO was an excuse to classify entrepreneurs operating off the grid as criminals so that the IRS could grab their piece of the pie. I was convinced that if you could create a way to convey agreed upon taxes from the Cosa Nostra to the IRS, all racketeering charges would disappear. It was naïve to think racketeering was anything other than unpaid taxes on lucrative albeit unconventional profits, murder and mayhem excluded, of course.

Later I would discover another burgeoning world that would suffer a similar fate. It would become my world, the cryptoworld. I would soon learn the arbitrary nature of governments and nations.

Mr. O was used as an example by the feds to demonstrate the futility of dodging legitimacy. The odd thing was, in his case, he had simply agreed to do the time for someone else. But something about his situation stunk.

Maestro told me Mr. O was doing time to cover for his Philadelphia benefactor by taking someone else's place. For political reasons, he'd allowed himself to be incarcerated by the state and sent to a state prison rather than a federal health spa. Like I said, something rancid this way comes.

The aftermath of Maestro's vengeance turned into yet another heteroclitic episode that vies for a place in my curio cabinet of bizarre incidents.

A crew of inmates were conscripted to attend Ralph's memorial service at the prison chapel. There was no serious investigation into his death. Maestro had no intention of killing the two Nazis after all. He convinced them to turn themselves in as Ralph's killers. An unfortunate incident in the mangler room. The case was quietly closed lest an investigation reveal a crooked guard on the take, a Cosa Nostra vendetta, and an unmanageable can of worms.

The chapel held a few hundred people, and prison services were held in rolling denominational time slots, though Muslims tossed their prayer rugs in designated areas for their five prayers a day.

There were about eighty inmates in attendance, clumped together in the middle of the large hall. Why I was chosen, I'll never know. Maybe someone wanted to give Ralph the last laugh. Or maybe my lottery number came up. I found myself in the second row of the chapel, listening to a litany of platitudes about Ralph's life as a prison guard, a husband, and a father. I was listening to the biography of someone I'd never met. Little was said of his life as a prison guard, but the words about his private life were a testimonial to a community leader and family stalwart: Boy Scout troop leader, little league baseball coach, president of the local Moose Lodge, and elder of the Starke First Baptist Church.

I could have choked it down but for the presence of Ralph's wife and two sons directly in front of me in the first row. Until that day, I hadn't known Ralph had a family. I always imagined him swilling beer in some shitty roadside bar until closing time and stumbling home to a one-room apartment where he cooked canned beans over a hot plate until it was time to get up and torment inmates. I sat watching my hands during the service until first Mrs. Ralph Wilkinson and then her oldest son, Matthew, went to the podium to speak.

Mrs. Wilkinson appeared gentile and kind as she spoke proudly of her husband's attentiveness to their family, his pride in his sons, his role in the church, his efforts as an organizer of car washes to raise money to send his little league team to the state finals in Tallahassee, his award as citizen of the year presented by the Lions Club, and so on. Who was this man?

It wasn't the roll call of good citizenship that thrust a shiv in my heart; it was her genuine pride in her husband. And her explicit conviction that whoever had caused his death had taken an angel from the earth. But whoever it was must be forgiven in Ralph's name because his God would not tolerate a Christian without forgiveness in his heart.

The oldest son, Matthew, followed with equal praise for his father, who taught him everything he knew. He ended by announcing his full baseball scholarship to Georgia Southern University, which would never have materialized without the guidance and coaching of his beloved father. The younger son wept relentlessly throughout the service.

My confliction need not be stated. As a woman, I can imagine hoping for such a man to become my life partner. As a man, I can imagine envying him for his many blessings. As a prisoner once under his thumb, I can only thank Dante for placing hypocrites in the deepest level of hell. It is almost impossible to reconcile Ralph Wilkinson the caring father and husband with Ralph the Nazi sympathizer and tormentor of helpless inmates. I had to put it out of my head.

Maestro became my friend and savior. My male side admired

him not just for his tough, cool demeanor and his bigger-than-life stroll through this horrid world but also his intelligence and uncanny insight into others. The vestiges of my feminine side felt an animal attraction that my maleness worked hard to combat. He would not have responded well, given the value he placed on his manhood. He wore it like a suit of armor. Yet when the armor was laid aside for the evening, I was privy to Maestro's more gentile side. That's when my battles raged hardest.

I chuckled as I slammed the binder closed. I once called these quick closures "spanking Ralph." I did that in my room many times, but somehow it seemed wrong now. Normal people didn't carry a binder of human hide. I'd get rid of it soon.

I once tried to find Ralph's son, Matthew, on the internet. There was a Matthew Wilkinson who was a lawyer in Starke, not far from the prison. He was about the right age. I hoped it was him because upon my release, my parole papers were stamped and signed by a Matthew Wilkinson, Esq. The red table runs true.

Once again, the journal had triggered memories of another episode many years before, when Margarite was hopeful and happy. A day before optimism crashed headlong into the stone wall of reality.

I sat at the café as a gentle rain was just ending and the sun emerged from a passing cloud. It made everything smell earthy and rich. I called such rains Silk's Tears. Silk loved the rain. I waved to a waiter and ordered a bottle of Pelli, a prosciutto-and-mozzarella panini, and another espresso. It was Monday afternoon. Or at least I was pretty sure it was Monday.

First Street was quiet. Through the alley I could see the old clock that used to sit in the intersection of Park and First. It had been moved to the entrance of Magnolia. The man who had originally erected the four-faced clock was the same man who, in his younger days, had worked on the dredge lines that built the seawall. He worked for the city, and as Margarite I'd always liked him. They called him Whistlin' Sid because he incessantly whistled the same little tune, and unlike my father, he was a man with an easy smile who got things done.

I watched a small lizard crawl along the edge of the terracotta pot next to me just as a tiny hummingbird flickered up to a petunia, dipped its long beak into the bell of the flower, and then flew away so quickly, it was lost in memory before it disappeared into the shadows.

Another memory was clawing to get out. It was time. Time to consider the shadow that had entered my life hidden behind the light of a brilliant smile, damnation hidden beneath charm. I was Margarite, a jeweler, a woman dressed as a man, stooped over a watch, eyepiece in place, behind the counter of Purloiner's jewelers. The bell above the door tinkled, and a handsome young man walked in wearing a beautiful pastel sport jacket, linen pants, and a smile that rivaled the sunrise.

Leitner Dredge leaned against the BMW, staring out at the distant hills south of I-10 as he waited for the gas pistol to click off. He'd had no choice but to stop at Las Cruces, but before he exited, he'd crept up close enough to the rear of the semi to take a picture of the license plate and identification number. It was a private contractor with no corporate logos or other identification. It would make it more difficult to track, but he was confident in his resources.

He'd examined a US Department of Transportation map of I-10 on his cell phone. There was a weigh station about five miles past the New Mexico border just this side of El Paso. It was open, so the truck would have to pull through, and he hoped there'd be a long line waiting to drive over the scales.

He decided to run inside to piss and grab some bottled water and snacks. It might be a while before he ate again.

He'd gotten a good look at the truck as it trundled down I-10. He'd dropped back far enough so the driver and Farley wouldn't see him exit. His only fear was that they would leave the interstate at one of the five remaining exits before the Texas border. He doubted it. They wouldn't risk exiting in unknown territory and encountering a weight limited bridge, which might slow them down. The DOT map listed a series of such bridges on the Red and Pecos Rivers. I-10 ran along the Rio Grande south of El Paso, but the truckers would have to make a difficult border crossing to get Summer into Mexico.

Leitner broke into a grin. The hunt was on, and outthinking his prey gave him irresistible pleasure. The challenge would be channeling them to a trajectory he could intercept. These men had two possibilities of throwing him off. Truckers had their own network they used to bypass authorities. First, the chatter on CB radios as well as a paid service that told truckers how to avoid weigh stations, sending them off interstates. He could lose them that way. Second, truckers knew locals like the Cadillac Man in El Paso who could get them across the Mexican border.

Leitner was a good judge of men, and there was no doubt in his mind that Farley and his friend would flee to their comfort zone. And they were having fun with Summer. Another way of putting it was that they were rapists and kidnappers who were about to take their victim across state lines. They couldn't afford to risk small problems that would lead to big ones. No ... Farley and friend would stick to main routes and play it safe while heading for their home base, wherever that was. Farley had called him 'Boudreaux'. It was a long shot, but he could only pray they were based in New Orleans. That was where Leitner would run them to ground.

The gas pistol clicked off while he was in the shop. He tossed his goods in the back seat and replaced it in the holster. He would change clothes as he drove. He considered changing cars but decided it would take too much time.

Suddenly Leitner paused, his hand on the door handle. Why was he being so impulsive? He was breaking his own rule: never make plans when you're angry.

He mumbled to himself, "Calm down. You've got the advantage."

Leitner climbed into the car and pushed the start button. As he eased out onto the entrance ramp onto I-10, he burst out laughing and shouted, "I'll be waiting for your call, motherfuckers."

# CHAPTER 9

I remembered the tinkling of the bell, glancing up from a watch, and seeing Shel Richardson for the first time. Sitting at the café, staring at the remnants of a panini, my eyes glazed over as my mind drifted back. It was remarkably easy to remember myself as Margarite. I liked parts of Margarite better than Stuart. But Stuart never had the chance to grow into himself.

Shel stood at the door, letting his eyes adjust to the dimmer interior light, and I remember thinking, *What is this man doing in this town?*

He said good morning and asked if I was the proprietor. I thought I was being teased. How many women in men's clothing did he see in the store?

"Am I that hard to spot?"

"I'm sorry?" How could a voice sound like warm snow? "Have I offended you in some way?"

He was smooth and elegant, his accent not quite British. He was tall with ash-blond hair and green eyes—no, blue, no, aquamarine. His teeth were perfect, each lit from inside, and his clothes effortless—ecru linen dress pants, mahogany wingtips, a white open-collar shirt, and a salmon rough-weave linen sport jacket. Every color accentuated his beautiful tan.

"No, I'm the sorry one. I sometimes get gawkers who are new to the area." My voice became a sarcastic parody. "Oh, be sure and stop by the jewelry store and have a look at the town freak. She's a hoot."

He laughed, and it was a wonderful Hemingway belly laugh that made me feel like he'd never laughed with anyone else. "Well, I won't lie. I've heard about the oxymoron who runs the jewelry shop on Park Avenue. A beautiful woman who dresses like a well-appointed man …"

Had he said beautiful woman? It had been a long time since I'd been struck dumb. I used a frown as a defense until I gathered myself.

"Let me start over. My name is—get ready for it—Richard Richardson. For obvious reasons, I go by my middle name, Sheldon, which I also hate, so my friends call me Shel." He held out his hand.

I held my right hand up to show the smudged white glove I always wore when repairing a watch. "Will the intention of goodwill be sufficient? *Jeez*, I sound like a script from Masterpiece Theatre. Dickens, maybe."

That wonderful laugh.

"The intention is more than sufficient."

I couldn't help but smile. "What is it I can do for you on this fine British day substituting warm Florida sunshine for the cold, gray, coal-laden London smog?"

Hemingway laughed. "I'll bet you can't say that again three times fast—cold, gray, coal-laden London smog."

I couldn't restrain another smile. "I'd best not try. I might blow a lip."

He put his hand on the counter as he stared through the glass. "I'm looking for a nice piece of lady's jewelry. I'm thinking a necklace or earrings, perhaps."

Why did my hopes wither? Why were there hopes at all?

"Is it a gift?" I blushed. "Sorry. I really wasn't trying to pry."

He interrupted. "No, no. I wasn't being intentionally abstruse. It's for my sister …"

My relief made me even angrier. I was not interested in men. I was one.

I nodded and pulled a tray of earrings from under the counter. They were displayed on a tiered black velvet tray.

"So, you're both new to our little town?" I held up a hand. "Am I asking too many questions?"

"No, of course not." He continued to look at the earrings. "We were unexpectedly placed in a witness protection program, and we just beat a mob hitman out of our last town."

My eyes went wide, and I could only gape.

The Hemingway laugh burst forth again. "I'm kidding, of course."

I let out a long sigh. "Oh, heavens, you scared me to death. The police chief is my father, and he told me there was a couple to be moved here from New York while they waited to testify in a Mafia trial. Surely they wouldn't be running around loose like you, would they?"

Sheldon Richardson sobered immediately. "Oh, my God. What an unfortunate coincidence."

I placed a cover over the earrings. "Yes … if any of it were true."

Shel's lips turned up in a half smile. "You're so bad. I seem to be making a right mess of this. I really do wish to buy earrings. The ones that you clearly like, the emerald ones."

My head rose and my eyes bored into his. "Yes, I do favor emeralds. I wasn't being nosy, but jewelers—good jewelers—like to know what kind of person is taking possession of their work. I set these earrings myself. It elevates the sale from an impersonal transaction to a mutually beneficial adoption of a lovingly created artifact."

I moved to place the tray back in the cabinet when Shel held up a hand. "Please, don't do that. And that's a lovely way to describe it. I'm going to pretend I'm the first ever to hear it."

I set the tray back down on the countertop. "You are, in fact, the first. But it's been on my mind since I took over this shop."

We locked eyes, and I saw sadness in his beautiful aquamarine orbs, along with something else I couldn't name.

"I moved here suddenly because my sister has special needs, and our previous location was not a viable environment. She needs the warmth of Florida. And, I hope, its people."

As he spoke, I realized I was leveraging anger against doubt. But this man, so very handsome, protective of one he loved, and that something else. His offhand joke about a witness protection program? Not far off. I shook off these thoughts. Not my business.

He told me he was a corporate headhunter, and I said, "That sounds fascinating. But there isn't much industry around here, unless you count the Hatfield Corporation."

I was relieved to hear Hemingway again. "My clients are international, so I can work from anywhere."

I began to speak when the bell over the door tinkled, and an elderly customer entered. My disappointment surprised me.

"It's Mr. Brooks. He's picking up a watch …"

Shel said, "Please, go ahead. I'll look over the earrings if you don't mind leaving me alone with them."

I smirked as I pushed the tray forward and removed the silk cover. "I'll only be a second, so you better be quick if you're going to take something."

I turned and picked up a small package. "Hello, Mr. Brooks. I have your watch right here. It's a great example of the railroad watches they used to give at retirement. The entire casing is twenty-four carat gold. Just had to clean the anchor and the escape wheel. No charge."

Mr. Brooks beamed happily. "Margarite, you're the best. But I insist on paying something. This was my grandfather's prized possession."

I smiled. "How about you buy me a vanilla Coke at Faust's drug store and drop it by next time you come by?"

Mr. Brooks pocketed his package and said, "You got it. I'm coming tomorrow for my weekly haircut. One vanilla Coke coming up."

He left and I walked around the counter to Shel. I looked down at the tray, and my lividity was instant.

"What in hell are you playing at?"

Shel held up his hands. "My God, you're quick. Please, let me explain."

I looked up at him. "Bullshit. Why don't you take your stolen earrings and get the hell out of my shop? And take those replacements with you." I picked them up and tossed them at him. He snatched them out of the air with ease.

Shel took a step back and opened his other palm, exposing the pair of diamond earrings he'd pulled from the tray. "Please, I had to know if it was true."

My face was a mask of anger. I held out my hand, and he dropped the earrings in my palm without hesitation. "Please, Margarite. You can even keep this pair for testing you like this. Please, let me explain. I beg you. I thought the difference impossible to detect."

I said, "Then why didn't you just ask me to compare the two?"

"It was your reaction time. Amazing. I was dubious, so I had to know. If you let me explain, I pray you'll understand."

Suddenly my curiosity was battling with anger. I stared into his aquamarine eyes. His every facial muscle was pleading for understanding. It was a sincere display.

"This better be good."

Shel reached inside his jacket pocket to remove a small string-tied pouch, which he fumbled open to extract two smaller silk pods. He set them on the counter and paused with his hands bracketing the two objects.

He spoke in a serious tone. "I checked around. You really are highly regarded among gemologists in the area. I hope you can appreciate what I have here."

He was sincere, not dishing out false flattery.

"I appreciate your comments, though I think you're exaggerating. It's just the contrast between my shop and the mall hawkers taking over the industry."

He smiled. "Maybe. But I need a serious jeweler, not a mall hawker."

I stared down at the two white silk receptacles and then back up at the two aquamarine gems beneath his furrowed brow.

His voice was pleading. "May I borrow a swatch of black cloth?"

I'd become intrigued, so I retrieved a square of black velvet from a drawer. "So, you're not here to purchase earrings?"

"Yes, of course. I'm going to buy the pair you prefer, the large emerald ones. The stones are perfect, and my sister loves green. I do need to ask if you can set them as clip-ons. My sister can't pierce her ears."

I frowned. "Certainly. It takes only a couple of minutes. But what's inside those silk capsules is the real reason you're here?"

He nodded. "I knew I'd find earrings here, but I admit I was looking for something else." He stared hard into my eyes. "And I think I've found it. But first, look at what's in these pods and tell me what you see."

I picked up an eyepiece. "Okay. Show me."

He picked up the first pod, reached gently inside, coaxed a large stone into his palm, and laid it gently on the cloth. I was stunned as it came to rest on the velvet. I looked at him.

"May I?"

"That's the point."

I grabbed a pair of tweezers and picked up the stone. I examined it first with the naked eye, rotating it in every direction to catch the light. Then I put it under the eyepiece.

"Oh, my. Cat's-eye alexandrite. At least a full carat and a

half. Faceted. And not synthetic." I spun right and turned on an incandescent lamp. "Holy … look at the color inversion." I turned back to the counter and replaced the eyepiece. "Pleochroic in natural light. This is an amazing gem. Ural Mountains?"

He nodded, his smile appreciative. "Yes, it is, and yes, it is. Here. Try the next one." He repeated the maneuver and laid a second stone on the velvet cloth.

This time I couldn't suppress a gasp. "No. It can't be. I've only seen two of these at specialty gem shows in big cities. And neither of those were this spectacular."

I replaced the alexandrite and lifted the second stone, my voice a whisper. "Transparent grandidierite. And, what, two carats? How in the world …" I looked up at him. "These are amazing. I … don't know what to say."

"Say you'll set them for me." He had leaned over the counter, and our faces were inches apart as we stared down at the two rare gems.

"Surely no one is going to wear these without a team of bodyguards."

"No." He chuckled. "But they've been sitting in a safe deposit box. I swore when I cleared that box, I'd not put them away again until they were set."

"They're gorgeous, not to mention extremely valuable. You must be a serious collector?"

"Heavens, no. I mean, I'm a collector of sorts. Sometimes I'm able to negotiate payment for services when I run across the right client. I'm a sucker for rare things."

I smiled as Shel continued, "If I have a hobby at all, it's collecting lint from airline seats. But I do collect the odd rarity. When I settled on this little town, I looked you up."

I shot him a sidelong glance. "That's what you did when you got to town? Looked me up?"

He said, "I asked around about jewelers, and your name kept coming up. The last time these were out of a safe deposit box, I took them to a well-known jewelry store in a well-known city. I'll spare them the embarrassment of mentioning names, but a team of jewelers thought the alexandrite was a moonstone and the grandidierite was a hunk of jade."

I put a hand to my forehead. "No, surely not."

"Well." He grinned. "It wasn't quite that bad … but close."

"That's why you tested me?"

"Yes. And I'm very sorry. I would have returned the earrings and called it a practical joke. But your eye is amazing."

I cocked my head, thinking. "These are large stones that must stand alone. No wrapping them round with other distractions. A platinum pendant with the stones in a prong setting, lots of prongs, but it will show off their color better. I'll check the Mohs rating …"

I stood from the café table as my first encounter with Shel Richardson faded. I left cash with a large tip on the table. Money was of no concern. I put a Benjamin down for a fifteen-dollar tab. I had more than I could ever spend, and I enjoyed making a young waiter happy for a few minutes.

The sun was low in the sky; it was time to return to the lake. I walked out to the street and climbed into my car, or rather my father's old car. The huge engine of the blue 1958 Chrysler Imperial roared to life. While my mother had sat home night after night to save money, my worthless father had denied himself nothing. The jewelry shop had paid for this behemoth. I worked while he spent most of his time at that damn country club, playing golf followed by boozing it up in the bar.

Shel built my reputation. It was the string of purchases from him and others that had paid for my father's lifestyle. An increasing number of customers began coming into the shop as Shel spread the word. Even the Hatfields would shop nowhere else.

Shel built it up, and Shel brought it all crashing down. It was my work for Mr. O that eventually uncovered the truth. What would have happened if a few improbable coincidences had not occurred? But they had.

I took my place by the lake and opened the journal.

Events became so intertwined, it's impossible to tell a linear story. But it all knits together.

I begin with *Ulysses*. Known as the greatest novel ever written, it is full of riddles. It was banned in the US for its final orgasmic line. Now it's considered genius. *Ulysses*, one of my favorites, led to a devastating chain of events.

If I had focused only on my new duties, forsaking all else, pretending I lived in Mr. O's kingdom and that Robert Manakin ruled an outer kingdom far away, my new Virgil, Maestro, would have guided me from hell. If only I'd listened. But I didn't. *Ulysses* and my hubris led me to a deep trench in Malebolge. I could help someone if I took one simple step. But if I made that step, it could hurt the very person I wished to help. And Maestro, my third Virgil, tried to warn me off.

I missed the library, and with Ralph gone, I could swing by occasionally and peer through the windows for the Bitch Warden. Finding her absent, I'd duck in for a quick look at the new arrivals. As a result, I stupidly stumbled into a trap of my own making. Hubris kilns the bricks with which the road to hell is paved.

Late one morning after I left the hospital ward, the day Tommy was finally released, I risked returning to my room via the long way that took me past the library. I peeked in—no Marilyn Manakin. I pushed through the door and headed straight for the shelf with the new arrivals. I couldn't believe it when smack in the middle of the second shelf at eye level, and out of order, was a tattered hardback copy of James Joyce's *Ulysses*. That book, of all books, drew me into its vortex. I particularly related to part 2, episode 6, "Hades." Corpses do not rest easy in Hades.

I suddenly realized I was dawdling, so I turned and hurried to the front desk. An elderly inmate was behind the counter, which I realized wasn't as disheveled as I remembered. Then I noticed the entire circulation counter had been rebuilt. Marilyn Manakin was at least able to accomplish what Porter could not.

I handed the book to this new attendant inmate. His lethargy made a noble cheetah of the lowly sloth. Then it hit me. He was stalling. I was the sloth, lobotomized by my lust for a book. Marilyn Manakin emerged from a tiny office behind a row of reserve shelves, another new addition. As she approached, I noted that she no longer attempted to cover herself in drab, bulky clothing. Perhaps she'd grown tired of not being herself. I could understand that. But I also understood her hatred of me. I did the only thing a reasonable person could do: I turned and fled.

"Stop." Her voice was commanding, but if I could just get out into the corridor, I could disappear, so I kept going. Just as I reached the door and began to push through, she shouted, "Do you want this book or not?"

I was shocked. I must not have heard her correctly. My momentum carried me through the doors, but I quickly turned back to her. Could she possibly be serious? Both doors, on strong hydraulic hinges, snapped back and slammed into the back of my head. I dropped like a brick. Two inmates rushed over and guided me unsteadily behind the circulation desk, through the makeshift reserve shelves, and into the small newly constructed office tucked away in the back corner.

Someone handed me a damp paper towel, and I buried my face in it. I didn't think I was bleeding, but I felt woozy and embarrassed. My failed exit would no doubt lead to further humiliation by this hateful woman.

Marilyn leaned back on a small desk. She was wearing black slacks and an attractive silver-gray shirt. Bright red lipstick etched her full lips against her ivory skin. I sat on a metal chair and kept the damp towel pressed to my eyes with the heels of my hands until her sultry voice wafted through the haze. "Are you feeling better?"

I dropped my hands, still clinging to the damp towel. For the first time, I noticed her ample breast and that her large brown eyes were sprinkled with gold flecks. "I think so, at least my head, not my pride."

It was then that she uttered the first nonthreatening words I'd ever heard from her lips. "Pride is not just a deadly sin; it's overrated and doesn't protect us from anything."

I frowned. That sounded like an intelligent insight. I said, "True. Pride is merely the thin veneer that hides the soul. Aluminum plating on cheap tin." I didn't wish to offend. "I mean, of course, in my case."

She frowned. "*Hmm*. I never really thought about it that way."

An uncomfortable silence descended.

I risked a question that had nagged since we first met. She could only get angry for impertinence, which was our status quo anyway. "Why do you hate me so? You don't know me. I mean, apart from the obvious things. You're the new warden's wife and I'm a transgender incarcerated in a male prison for murder."

I closed my eyes and leaned my head back against the wall. "Never mind. I just answered my own question." I stood up unsteadily, prepared to leave. "I would love to borrow that book, if you're serious about lending it to me. I promise I won't come here anymore. I'll get books elsewhere."

She stared at me, and her confusion was obvious. Then something struck me. Maybe it wasn't confusion. Maybe it was distress. I had been tall as a woman, but as we stood face-to-face, we were the same height.

She sneered and crossed her arms. "I'm sure you have other sources for anything you want."

I could feel her closing herself off, and it made me sad. I'd said something inane, and I regretted it immediately. "I'm sorry. That was stupid. I just meant that I'm aware you don't want me around. My whole life has been people either not wanting to see me at all or seeing me only as a freak. It's easier to retreat."

It was strange. She wanted to give me a chance as if she were a flower desperate for the water of understanding. But why me?

She said, "The night nurse in the medical ward … we went to high school together. I didn't know her very well, but she was always nice. And she always wanted to be a nurse. Even if it meant working in a place like this."

She paused as if deciding whether to bother with this conversation. Then I recognized the look on her face. She was desperate to continue.

"She told me how kind you were to that young man who'd been beaten almost to death. She also saw that guard beating you up. She didn't see everything. She hid, terrified. But she's the reason they knew you weren't the one who killed the guard." She uncrossed her arms, and a frightened little girl appeared. "She said you were very tender and caring. You never left his bedside."

I was careful to avoid implying that she felt the same way. "Please tell her I greatly appreciate her kind words. I don't get many."

She fixed me with a stare. "Why are you here? You don't strike me as a murderer or one of these thugs. You're smart …"

I found it difficult to meet her gaze. Her beauty was unusual and made me feel hideous. This horrible place had taken its toll. But inside, damn it, I was a good human being.

I looked at my hands. "I won't bother asserting my innocence because everyone in here does that. The incessant cry of 'wolf.' As for me? Incomprehensible circumstances I hope to understand someday led me to this fate."

"Why not appeal? Everyone else does."

"An appeal only works if there are procedural errors in the adjudication of your case. When an entire town reviles you, the lawyers have little time for procedural errors. The trial took hours, and the jury deliberated for less time than it took to eat their lunch. I suppose euphemistically they ate mine."

She chuckled. "I see."

I worked up courage and stared hard into her eyes. "Go ahead and ask me."

A frown flashed. "What do you mean?"

I cocked my head and stared at her.

For a moment she stared back. Suddenly the words came. "Why did you do it … become a man?"

At that moment all risks seemed worth taking to save a soul. I don't know how I knew she needed saving, but I did.

I said gently, "Shouldn't you ask me where I found the courage to become who I really was?"

Her eyes flickered wide and then closed. When she opened them again, they were full of monumental sadness. Every thread that might connect us was being stretched thin and taut by the conflict roiling inside her.

At that moment, as if he had radar for shitty timing, Robert Manakin burst into the tiny office accompanied by a team of guards. He never moved in gen pop without an entourage of fawning supplicants. Practicing for the governor's office, I suppose.

"Ah, there you are." If ever there were a voice of male self-confidence, his was it. "Did you forget we have to leave for the event?" Without pause, he looked down at me. "What's that doing here? I thought you kicked it out of the library."

I stood and did my best to deflect his ire. "I'm sorry, Warden. This was my fault. I thought I could stop in quickly to get a book I wanted. I didn't see Mrs. Manakin and thought it okay. I had an accident, and Mrs. Manakin didn't want me bleeding all over her library."

She gave me an imperceptible nod. The warden didn't give my answer a thought. "Well, best get to wherever it is you're supposed to be, she said."

I scurried toward the door, but he said, "Stop."

I halted and turned. It was never good to draw a warden's attention. They normally wouldn't bother to wipe their shoes on your face. I stood at what I thought might look like military attention as he put his mouth close to my ear.

"Did she not tell you to stay away from her?"

I kept my eyes fixed straight ahead. "Sir, I apologize profusely. Had it not been for the accident, I assure you I would never have been in proximity to Mrs. Manakin. It won't happen again."

He stared hard to make his point and then nodded at the door. "Make sure of it. Now get out."

It was a strange encounter. If he knew I was living in Mr. O's cell block, he was demonstrating a strange animosity that violated a devil's bargain. Of course, it could merely have been my presence—the inmate who was once a woman always to be treated as an insect. It seemed I was destined to be hated by the Manakins. But something was off. It was true the Manakins were a nagging presence, but the encounter with Marilyn was different. It certainly nagged at me but not in the same way as before.

I hurried out of the library as fast as I could. I thought about taking the steam tunnels. It was shorter. But if someone caught me down there, it would be like the old days of Vikings and villagers, and I was never the Viking.

I left through the usual side door off the laundry room, scurried along the sidewalk beside the fences, waited while Holt opened the gates, and ran for the safety of room 29. As I sat on the edge of my bed, my thoughts swirled. Something wasn't right with the Manakins. I'd seen hatred in the warden's eyes today. Before I moved into this new block, he'd never noticed my existence. As for Marilyn, her gaze had transformed from hatred to confusion. I knew my life was not my own, but neither was hers. She was as much an inmate in this hellhole as I.

I rolled into bed that night but slept poorly. Nightmares came in waves. Before I fell asleep, a final thought overwhelmed me. It should have been obvious all along; it was only when I lived as a man that I came to truly understand the plight of women. I worried for Marilyn Manakin. I was right to do so.

# CHAPTER 10

Folks had become accustomed to seeing me in my father's beast of a Chrysler Imperial, so the families along the seawall gave a mere glance when I docked the blue land yacht next to the curb. There were several families there most evenings, the very folks who, in an earlier generation, had fallen under the invisible protection of Monk's Pool Hall. It was always with a mixture of sadness and embarrassment that I turned off the rumbling engine and struggled to my place on the bench. I was relieved when several of the families began to return my innocuous wave as I stepped to my bench next to the river.

The journal entries had begun to wear on me. For me there was no buffer between a sense of being and a sense of purpose. I was trapped in an old axiological question: Is there existence without purpose? Perhaps money answers the question for some; it is often viewed as an end in itself. A wall of isolation can be built with wealth, making those inside feel safe and superior. But what I sought lay outside that barrier. It was my sole purpose to look beyond the distorted wall of money if only to stare into two aquamarine eyes. I admitted that desire had transformed into obsession. So be it. I'd probably die anyway.

Once back on my bench, I made sure to wave to a few of the

regulars and settled back to stare out at the wonder of the river. This was the beginning of a special, albeit brief, season. The tannin waters along the seawall frothed and roiled in sunlit flashes of silver as schools of mullet pleached in their breeding frenzy. Mullet spawning season drew folks to the lake to harvest buckets of these fish, which would end up in slow smokers and pickling pots, providing meals for months. Smoked mullet dip on saltine crackers had long been one of my favorites.

The seawall was rife with local families, some with cane poles, some with small nets, and even a few talented swamp fishermen with frog gigs so thick did the schools of fish run. There was mullet enough for all, so there was no competition for a fishing spot, and families happily shared picnic baskets and bottles of beer, wine, and sour mash or moonshine.

As I sat on the bench, I noticed two families I'd befriended. I stood and pointed toward the car, a signal that a cooler lay within and was open to share. The two men hurried from their positions at the seawall, and I tossed the keys to a large man called Big Tom. He hurried with his friend to the trunk, smiling broadly, white teeth flashing against black skin, and the huge deck popped open as he released the latch. His friend reached in and extracted a case of German beer from watery ice.

"Thank you, sir. We been hoping you'd show up today," Big Tom said, grinning as he paused to drop the car keys back in my hand.

"My pleasure, Tom. You folks enjoy."

I smiled as they hurried back to families yanking mullet as fast as lines hit the water.

I lowered myself back onto the bench. Amid this salubrious activity I felt danger building like a Florida storm. I knew its source, and as with a storm warning, I could only do my best to prepare. Reading the journal was bringing memories vividly back into focus. Events were regaining clarity, and a transgender named Stuart was emerging from the fog of mad dreams and the insanity of an isolation chamber.

I'd lived many years as Margarite. Stuart's developmental years were preempted by a murder trial. I'd never had the opportunity to get to know myself as Stuart. Stuart lived under a cockroach shell in prison like an inverted Kafka character. Instead of a man becoming a cockroach, I began as a cockroach who aspired to become a man. In the process, I might become the murderer I was accused of being. I waited to hear from Shel. Then what? Vengeance? Redemption? Useless words unless contextualized. It was that context I was seeking.

I watched Big Tom and his family go happily about their business. They occupied the moral high ground here. Maybe they had their bad moments. But their worst crimes were born of innocence. I was the interloper disguised as an advocate for their well-being. Dante had not created a place for me among the innocent.

Weather patterns had changed as prevailing winds came briskly from the Atlantic, bringing morning showers that passed by noon and rumbled off toward Tampa, gathering energy for an electrical finale in the lightning capital of the world. Old Man River, he keeps on rolling along, oblivious to the eradication of innocents, and innocence.

I pulled the journal from my satchel and glanced down the seawall littered with happy faces. Old Man River kept rolling along, giving up his bounty to those with patience. I, too, was patient. And I, too, was fishing for something. It saddened me that my catch would be tainted by the acrid taste of revenge.

I turned from the happy life along the seawall, pulled the journal onto my lap, and opened it. Richard Sheldon Richardson. I muttered aloud, "Soon, you son of a bitch. Soon." I began to read.

After my initial meeting with Mr. O, Maestro walked me back to my room. As I entered, he said, "I'm not sure what you were talking about, but I hope you can deliver on this prediction modeling stuff."

I stood in the door. "I think I can if Mr. O will trust me enough to give me access to the information I need."

Maestro leaned a forearm on the jamb, frowning. He was taller, and my forehead was at his chin. Again, I noticed the James Dean similarities.

"Tell him what you can do and what you need to do it. Don't expect a decision right away; he thinks things over. If it's a go, he'll let you know. If he doesn't? Never mention it again. I heard he once had a guy's tongue slit because he kept making promises he couldn't deliver. Some say it was his own brother-in-law. His sister never said a word, just divorced the fucker and moved on."

I snickered. "Can you imagine me with a split tongue? Two tongues to talk with?"

Maestro smiled. "Good point. I can't shut the one up. Don't worry, D. He'll find a use for you or you wouldn't be here."

I looked at him quizzically. "D? You've called me that twice now."

"I gotta call you something. I told you we don't use names in here."

I asked, "Why D?"

He looked at me with those hooded eyes. "We called the last accountant C. D's next."

I was disappointed, but he shot me a big grin.

"I'm kidding. When I first met you in that shithole cafeteria, you had a book with you. What was it?"

I frowned. "Book?" I suddenly remembered. "Oh, yeah. It was from the library. *The Divine Comedy* by Dante."

Maestro nodded. "Dante—a great Italian, right? Name starts with what?"

I grinned like a pencil neck trying to befriend the quarterback in high school. "I like it."

It was a rough night that should have been heaven. It was quiet, with no bizarre night noises. It was the first time in years I'd slept in a real bed rather than a prison bunk, but I couldn't sleep. I tossed and turned, trying to picture Mr. O's world, what I'd need, what methods I might use, and the random error I'd have to sort. I finally drifted off and awoke surprisingly fresh. It was ten o'clock.

I couldn't believe it. No one woke me. No night stick rattling along bars, no cold water thrown, no warm stench of some asshole pissing on me between the bars. I put my hands behind my head and spoke to the heavens, "Thanks, Alphonse. I promise to make you proud."

At eleven thirty, Maestro rapped on the door. I was ready.

The Italian lunch with Mr. O was fantastic. He could have hung out a sign and gotten a Michelin star. I'd traveled all over Italy and thought how sad it was that I had to go to prison to taste genuine Italian cuisine again. One of the inmates in Mr. O's circle was a restauranteur swept up in an insurance scam. Little C, they called him. I had no idea at the time how the authentic ingredients were procured. I assumed you could get anything you want in prison if you have money and connections.

That day, we started with antipasti, salami, olives, smoked squid, and prosciutto on slices of cantaloupe and then a small pasta course of *pepe e caccio*, followed by a fish course, which that day consisted of roasted oysters from the coast an hour away, and then a meat course of pork tenderloin with a fig-balsamic reduction; the hogs were raised a few miles from the prison at a minimum security facility. We finished with a selection of Sicilian cheeses. The wines were Sicilian and delicious. I hadn't had any alcohol since starting my sentence, so I was careful not to overdo. It took tremendous willpower; after two glasses I borrowed a technique from my college days and began to moderate my sipping behavior.

There was no business talk. We ate quietly and appreciatively. Maestro and Mr. O made occasional small talk in their Sicilian dialect. Even with my passable Italian, I understood nothing. After eating, we moved into the office, and Mr. O and Maestro lit cigars. He offered me one, and out of politeness I lit up, after

I figured out the end needed to be clipped before it would draw. Mr. O found my naivete amusing and gave me a brief lesson on cross clipping a Churchill.

Mr. O said, "I get these from a little place in Ybor City. You can smoke one all the way down without the ash falling. Perfect roll."

He took a draw and blew a perfect smoke ring. Then he looked at me. "Tell me about predictive modeling."

I took a deep breath and ran through a high-level overview, avoiding a depth that might be insulting while delving deeply enough to let him know it was a powerful, sophisticated methodology. I described the basic techniques—regression solutions, including penalized regression; probit; logit; canonical correlation; factor analytic techniques; structural modeling—and even made a jab at neural nets. I used everyday examples. He listened quietly as I finished.

I concluded with, "If I know what you want to predict, that's called the dependent variable, I'll need as many independent variables as possible that might contribute to that event or set of events. If I have clear measurable variables, I can narrow the probability of the event happening to a point that you can act on the data."

He sat quietly as I concluded my treatise. After a full two minutes, he leaned forward with his elbows on his knees, the cigar between two fingers. "Let's say there was going to be a prison riot. That's the, what'd you call it, dependent variable? What independent variables would you need to give me an idea if or when it might happen?"

It was an excellent question for someone who didn't think in scientific terms. But, of course, he was a businessman, so he had come up with a perfectly relevant scenario.

I took a deep breath. "Good sample question because there's an array of data I'd want to include, some easy to find while others would require more digging. I'd most want historical data: when prior prison riots occurred and under what conditions. I'd also look for temporal variables, time of year, season, and time of day and then ambient conditions like weather, phase of the moon, sudden changes in the prison population, what events—"

Mr. O held up his hands. "Okay, I get the point. Those seem like easy things to get at. What were the things you'd have to dig for?"

I was deep in thought by then, and my voice became low and serious. I think that was fortuitous. Mr. O liked thoughtful people.

"I'd try to find out exactly where riots began. What cell block and what tribal units. The characteristics of the prisoners in past riots. All receding in time until the patterns disappeared. Specific conflicts occurring in previous days or weeks, a racial conflict, for example, something that motivated groups of people rather than individuals. There are always triggers for aberrant group behavior ..."

My voice trailed off as I became lost in thought. When I realized I'd drifted into internal dialogue, I looked up. Mr. O was staring at me with eyes narrowed. I noticed what he'd said about my cigar was true. The ash had grown long without falling.

I muttered, "Sorry. I get lost in my thoughts sometimes."

I expected Mr. O to thank me and say he'd think it over. But he continued to press. "What kind of equipment would you need?"

I blew out a long breath. "A powerful computer, some statistical software like SPSS with R add-ins, SAS, and some other specialized software would be helpful." I paused, again realizing that I was getting too technical, so I ended with, "I could make a list."

Again, Mr. O went silent, staring at me. I realized he wasn't trying to stare me down. He, too, was lost in thought. It was a look that may have rattled his enemies. Finally, he took a long slow breath and closed his eyes. Maestro pinned me with a frown, and when I met his eyes, he raised his eyebrows.

Mr. O opened his eyes and glanced at Maestro with a half smile. "What do you call this one?"

Maestro gave a flicker of a smile. "I call him D."

Mr. O nodded and turned to me. "Okay, D. I'm going to tell you what I need, and you tell me if you think you can do it." He pointed the cigar at me. "But if you have doubts, tell me up front. You got it?"

I nodded. "You've already saved me from the hell of gen pop. I'll do my absolute best."

He shot a quizzical look at Maestro and then turned his gaze on me. "I know." Without pause, he launched in. "Our business interests by their nature create conflict, the biggest over turf and the assets that go with it. Lately things have gotten … strange. Organizations have different interests and the confusion of ethnic groups and unusual business models make it impossible to create a grand council like the old days, like the movies portray. Such an effort would be a total cluster fuck. The best we can do is form temporary alliances as necessary."

I ventured a question. "You said things have gotten strange?"

He leaned back as he continued, "The cops are changing. They've always been on the take, but now? This new generation knows no loyalty. They'll switch sides for a dime. Feds, local vice squads, all of them just spin around until someone drops cash in their palm. Violence starts like a flash fire and then spreads. Cops even participate now. I need to predict when conditions are ripe for a turf battle and, most important, what alliances are being formed." He again pointed the stub of his cigar at me. "So … can you model that?"

My insides were broiling. This was too good to be true. "Like I said, sir. The more information I have, the better my predictive model will become. I'll try to reduce the error term to zero."

They stared at me like I'd grown a second nose.

"Sorry. Statisticians are data dorks. Based on what you've just said, I might even be able to eavesdrop on these alliances, including the cops. I'm not sure how deep I can get, but I'll be able to gather intelligence."

The seconds ticked by, and I could feel my heart pumping wildly. The problem was already gnawing at my forebrain like a mathematical tapeworm.

Suddenly Mr. O stood. "D, thank you for dining with me today. It's been enlightening."

My heart sank as he walked Maestro and me to the door. Al opened it from the other side, and just as I stepped through to the oblivion of financial spreadsheets, Mr. O put a hand on my shoulder.

"Why don't you give him"—he pointed at Maestro, and I realized he never referred to him by a name; he was a ghost—"that list, computers and such."

I tried to contain my excitement. "Yes, sir."

On the way back to my room, Maestro was quiet until we got to my door.

"Good job. Hope you can deliver."

I smiled. "If you get me what I need, I know I can. I'll make a complete list. I don't know if you can get my dream machine, but the closer I get, the better I'll be able to help."

It was Maestro's turn to smile. "I'll get you your dream. And information? We've got guys in here who lived through everything with Mr. O. They forget nothing. Piece of cake."

He turned to leave, and I said, "Maestro?"

He paused and looked over his shoulder at me as I said, "I'll make sure you're the one who knows everything. Information is power. I'll feel safer if I'm not the only one who knows all the pieces."

He smiled and gave a small nod of appreciation. I'd bound Maestro to my fate, but more importantly I'd garnered his trust. We were partners in this endeavor.

The red BMW sat idling in the emergency lane of I-10, a hundred yards back from the weigh station outside El Paso, close enough to watch trucks accelerating in the reentry lane but far enough away to remain unnoticed. Leitner Dredge sat hunched over the steering wheel, eyes at half-mast, concentrating. He was willing Summer to get in sync with him.

He held Summer's iPhone in his hand. They'd used IMEI and GPS Tracker to watch each other's location in Vegas hotels. It was an excellent way to track each other while they were running a mark to ground through the underground labyrinth of Vegas.

He'd retrieved the iPhone because these truckers were idiots. Everyone was an idiot when they thought they had the upper hand. They'd tossed the iPhone from the truck cab just to be safe. The dumb shits didn't take the battery out. He turned it on remotely and found it using the apps. As predicted, they'd not attempted to bypass the weigh station, and Summer had been smart enough not to fight them. He'd taught her patience.

As he sat watching the weigh station, he remembered why he owed her this. She'd been an excellent judge of men but had never worked in close tandem with a partner. She needed more training in social engineering to learn how to close a deal in a way that left a mark grateful for being fleeced like a schmuck. He'd taught her his two-man con. Or, as she'd corrected him, a "two-person" con. Wasn't she precious?

It was one of the oldest in the book, but it was almost foolproof if you were a good social engineer. Leitner knew he was one of the best because he'd learned from one of the best—his uncle in Florida.

He spent a full month with Summer, identifying marks and making initial contact. He wouldn't let her take things to the next level until he was certain she could play her part, and that meant practice. Finding a mark tossing $10K chips around like M&M's was the easy part. The tough part was transforming from a seductive vamp to the sad, bored housewife in Vegas for a fling. She had to learn how to close.

Foreigners, especially rich Middle Easterners, were the best marks because their sense of betrayal by a wife was almost inbred. Fuck another man's wife but keep your woman out of circulation. Being cuckolded was a sign of weakness in most cultures, but in the Arab world it was a mortal sin. Saudi men could drive across the causeway to Bahrain, change clothes on the way, fuck a harem of strange women for a couple of days, and then put the thobe back on for the drive home. But woe be to a wife caught fucking another man.

After weeks of training, Leitner turned Summer loose on a Saudi drinking Remy Black Pearl by the bucket and losing his ass at the blackjack table. He was perfect: young enough not to be bored by a life of excess, with a long, privileged life still ahead. Leitner waited until the mark had lost six hands in a row and then sent Summer to sit next to him. Of course, the odds were in his favor. The Saudi lost one more hand, and then Summer, cooing and preening, leaned forward and blew on his down card. Miraculously, he won three straight hands. By then the beautiful blonde American with majestic tits had sunk the hook. They left the blackjack table arm in arm. Leitner positioned himself by the elevator and watched the iPhone app.

He waited until Summer had time to get the mark into bed, feed him a dosed cocktail, and then use her considerable bedroom skills. Leitner had been with more women than he could remember but none more talented than Summer. She'd get the mark worked into a frenzy.

At that point, Leitner began pounding on the door, screaming, "Sarah. Sarah, for God's sake, are you in there? Sarah? I'm not leaving until I see you. You're my wife, Goddamnit."

Summer did her job, cajoling the mark, "I can get him to shut up." The door opened, and Leitner rushed in, pointing his snub nose thirty-eight at Summer.

"You bitch. How could you leave our kids without their mom? I'm a cop for Christ's sake, and you make me look like a schmuck in front of the entire station." Then he turned the gun onto the

Saudi mark. "Is this the bastard? Did you fuck her? Is she in love with you?"

"No. I swear. I did not know she is married ..." the man stammered.

Leitner went into his great dramatic persona, weeping openly one second and then wildly furious the next. "Just because you're rich? You think you can steal my wife because I'm an honest cop who earns shit?"

Summer began her scene. "Harold, I'm sorry, but life just gets so boring sometimes. I was too young to be married. But I loved you. I still love you, I swear."

The Saudi was caught up in the sad domestic tragedy of two poor losers. Summer was no longer the alluring blonde; she'd been reduced to a pitiful, bored housewife with no future.

Leitner was in the Saudi's head now. The man wished only to extricate himself from this pathetic domestic scene. The doctored cocktail had his head reeling and his senses blunted. Then the gun in his face had pumped a cocktail of neurotransmitters into his limbic system.

The Saudi pleaded, "Please. I can help."

As he backed toward a briefcase, Leitner pointed his pistol, shouting through tears, "Are you going for a gun? Maybe you should. We can all just fucking die right here. I've got nothing left to live for." Leitner had practiced that line endlessly. He'd briefly joined an acting studio to learn when acting descended into scenery chewing. That line had to be delivered perfectly.

"No ... I swear. Please let me show you."

"Show me what?"

The Saudi ran to the briefcase and opened it. He brought it forth like a chef delivering a prize dish. He was, in fact, delivering the only dish Leitner craved.

"Here. Harold, right? Take this. Take it and make your lives better."

The briefcase was full of cash—dollars, euros, and riyals.

Summer stepped in. "Take it, Harold. It's okay. Please. Let's take what this nice man is offering and just go home, okay? You don't need to hurt anyone. Please. Not like last time."

Leitner risked one last ploy. "So, you fuck my wife and throw me some cash. I thought I came here for a wife, but you send me off with a whore? Someone who fucks for money?"

"No. I swear. It's a gift. Here." The Saudi scampered to the nightstand and grabbed a $50,000 Rolex. "Take this. That money is like this, a gift from one friend to another. A watch is a useful thing, yes?"

Leitner forced his voice to a calm snivel. "It's a beautiful watch. I always wanted one like that."

The Saudi put it on top of the cash. "It's yours, from a friend. Go with God."

Leitner, still sniffling, took the briefcase in the crook of an arm and looked at Summer. "You'll come home now?"

"Of course, Harold. I love you, I really do." This was where she had to give the Arab a quick practiced glance of relief that Harold wasn't supposed to see. They had, in fact, practiced it relentlessly. Leitner insisted that glance was the coup. It said, *"I think we'll be okay. I'll get him out of here. You'll live through this."*

Then she was to say to the Saudi, "I'm sorry you got pulled into our"—a frustrated shake of the head—"shitty little problems."

"No, don't worry. This has made me miss my family very much. Please."

Sarah and Harold walked slump shouldered and defeated from the room and then hurriedly fled the hotel. Marks rarely went to authorities. What would they say? I'm a schmuck? If they did, he and Summer couldn't be identified. Few men remembered anything about Summer but her tits, and she always left hair from a hotel bathroom at the scene just in case it got to DNA sampling. Leitner wore a moustache here, a goatee there, and differently tinted contacts. But as Leitner always said, mustn't scare the tourists.

And now, after his run as a skilled grifter, living like a king, Leitner found himself watching a fucking weigh station in a desert shithole.

They'd hit a dozen more marks and netted nearly $3 million in various currencies before the last one went bad. He should have known not to chase that one—the owner of the red BMW. He was an American businessman in Vegas for his own grift. The slick fuck didn't go for the forlorn husband routine but feigned being suckered. When he reached for what Leitner thought was money, he pulled a Walther. The fucker made the lone mistake of letting a whimpering, apologetic Leitner within arm's reach. His briefcase contained six different business cards, three passports, and matching driver's licenses. He'd pegged Leitner and Summer and was going to squeeze them. It was a shame Leitner had to shoot him in the head. There weren't many regular guys out there anymore.

If only Summer kept her wits. Leitner thought, *Come on, babe. Tell them I've got a trunk full of money. Tell them we won big in Vegas. The money is theirs for the taking. Tell them I'm a chickenshit lawyer from Shitlick, Idaho, you're playing.*

There it was. The truck pulled out of the weigh station into the merge lane. He knew they had to stop soon. Truckers carrying a load ran the tanks low to make weight. He prayed the phone rang before they stopped. Summer would not remember his phone number. No one remembered phone numbers; you just spoke into the fucking thing or pressed someone's face. But you know your own.

He spoke aloud, "Use your head, kiddo. I found your phone. Tell them to call it. Tell them ransom is waiting. That's what they want."

The truck eased back onto the highway, and Leitner let it get a half-mile lead. They were still in west Texas hill country, and he could see the truck's silhouette for a mile.

Suddenly, Summer's phone rang. It startled him, and he took

some long breaths to calm himself. He wouldn't answer. This was where he got his edge. He already had the app TrueCaller open and typed in the number that had just called. He had to slow down to multitask, but he still saw the truck round a sweeping curve as it crept along the edge of El Paso in heavy traffic. Bingo. The number was registered to a Mrs. Jennifer Polk of Slidell.

He quickly dialed a second number. When a voice answered, he said, "Code name Fountain. I need help with a trucking crew. Please say these words to our friend: Remember Wanat. Repeat that please. No, never mind. Close enough. I need the name of a trucker associated with a Farley Polk. Works out of New Orleans. Repeat the name. Good. Please hurry."

The seconds ticked by as he followed the truck out of El Paso. He was counting on these fuckers being involved in illicit activities. They had that chump-change asshole look.

Five minutes later, his phone rang, and he almost dropped it answering. He was hesitant to pair his phone with the car's Bluetooth. If they found the body of its owner, they'd find him in minutes.

"Hello. Yes. Let me repeat that. Pierre Ardoin, registered in New Orleans. Tell our friend I may need assistance. I'll call his special line. Thanks."

Leitner spoke aloud as he dialed the number from his own phone, not Summer's. "Please let these fuckers lead me to NOLA. Please, said Br'er Rabbit, don't throw me in the briar patch."

The phone was answered immediately, and Leitner took a gamble that Farley was still in the passenger's seat. "Am I speaking to Farley Polk and his friend Pierre Ardoin who took something from me?"

A hand was held over the phone, and Leitner heard a mumbled argument.

When the voice returned, Leitner could tell the anger was masking confusion. "So what if it is, asshole? You want back what we took?"

*Bingo.* A coonass accent if ever he'd heard one. It was more country, Lafayette, maybe, but they'd work out of NOLA; he was sure of it.

Leitner took a deep breath. *Slow and steady*, he thought. "Yes. I'd like that very much."

"Then listen up, Couyon. Your friend told us you had a lucky streak, won a hundred K in Vegas." *Bless you, Summer. You remembered your lessons. Chump change.*

Leitner feigned indignant anger. "Fuck me. Goddamnit. The stupid girl told you how much we won? Jesus Christ." He let heavy breathing subside. "So, I got lucky."

Farley was a fucking cliché, which infuriated Leitner even more as the man continued, "We don't be greedy folk. Let's say you give us ninety-nine for the girl, and we let you keep a thou, for gas."

He heard Pierre chuckling in the background at Farley's genius sense of humor.

Leitner continued his act. "Goddamnit. I already spent five hundred getting this far." Leitner focused. He needed to hear a sign that they believed they had the upper hand.

It came. Too easily. "That's your problem, Boudreaux. So, here's what happens. We call you back. We make the exchange in New Orleans day after tomorrow. We'll call exactly one hour before we meet to tell you where. Make sure you in the city and waitin' for the call. Best you follow directions just like we say. Fuck up one thing? The Cher goes in the river."

Time to inject uneasiness. "Have you touched her? Because if you've been fucking her, she's no good to me. You may as well put a bullet in her head right now. I won't give a shit."

Again, a hand went over the phone. Leitner knew they'd been raping her. They were pigs, and pigs always rutted. Maybe he could keep them off her until he made them pay.

"Hell, no, we don't touch her."

"Good. I'll wait for your call."

Leitner disconnected, immediately went to his contact list, and dialed a second number. It went straight to voice mail. When the beep came, he said, "I need men, fast. Good money for three, but I need them tomorrow. One needs to know the off-register trucking circuit. He gets a bonus if it works out."

Leitner knew where the bulk of the criminal underbelly operated in New Orleans. Across the river in Algiers. Every industry had its territory and methods. That's why NOLA was fascinating. These fuckers thought they had home field advantage, but the opposing quarterback had once been on a team there. He had a "family" friend. They'd fought in Afghanistan together. He and Leitner were bonded in disillusionment. His friend's father had tried to tell them: America was no longer a country but a poorly run multinational corporation.

Leitner had been a fixer for his friend. Whenever he asked Leitner to NOLA on business, he would tell his men, "Il n'y a pas de problem. Le Boucher vient." There's no problem. The Butcher is coming. That had been his nickname during his time in NOLA. Another artifact of his time in Afghanistan.

# CHAPTER 11

I let the journal drop in my lap as I watched a young boy sitting on the seawall pull a sprat from the water. He pulled the hook carefully from its craw and tossed it back into the current, letting it grow up to be caught again later.

It was getting warm, but the summer humidity had not yet dropped its blanket over the lake. I stretched my back and readjusted the straw hat that kept the Florida sun from searing a hole in my skull.

The boy's cork bobbed gently on the current as he played out the line. I wondered if Sharon's body had bobbed on the surface before sinking. A macabre but necessary consideration. I knew she must have been killed somewhere else and then brought here. That thought was more likely to burn a hole in my skull than the sun.

I thought back to the day Shel returned for his set stones. A half hour before he was due, my idiot father sent the doorbell tinkling wildly. He rarely left the country club in daylight, but here he was, moving intently around the U-shape of displays as if hastily cramming Cliff Notes before class.

"What are you doing here, Frank?" I never called the bastard father.

"Did you forget I own this store?"

My anger flared. I snapped, "Of course, I remember. Please, it's all yours. I'll get my things and leave."

"Now, now, Margarite"—the only thing worse than his braggadocio were his efforts to placate—"you know I won't be around long. I have a four o'clock tee time."

Moments later, the bell tinkled again, and Shel entered with a young woman on his arm. I was immediately captivated. Frank was reduced to typical irrelevance. The young woman's face was beyond pale. It was diaphanous. Her body was hidden beneath white lace, and she wore a broad-brimmed hat tied down on the sides.

The reason for Frank's unexpected appearance was obvious. No doubt a casual comment at the country club bar had tipped him off. The second they entered, he began fawning over them like a pedophile at a bassinet, preening and cooing malapropisms.

I was fascinated by Sharon's unusual appearance. She was beautiful and easily classifiable as a "delicate flower," yet in her dress and demeanor, her fragility seemed not only genuine but oddly paradoxical, as if in creating her the gods had mistakenly used inappropriate materials, perfectly formed but too fragile for the intended purpose. She was a crystalline hammer. If it was used for its intended purpose, it would shatter.

Frank skittered behind the counter. "Margarite, do you have our Mr. Richardson's special package?"

I had the newly set stones in a small box in my pocket. Shel approached the counter as I extracted it and held it out. Frank grabbed it off my palm and began pawing at the meticulous wrapping. The package eventually succumbed to his ineffectual rending.

He extended the small box officiously to Shel. "Please. You must be the first to see." As Shel took the box from his hand, Frank said, "Margarite, perhaps you'd like to describe our work to Mr. Richardson."

I was livid. "No, please. You're doing just fine."

Frank launched a pathetic and inept effort to impress by unleashing an inane polysyllabic assault on the very industry that kept him alive. He wove a fantasy in which a prong setting became a bevel setting; a round facet miraculously became a regatta cut, whatever that was; and the names of the stones were battered and tortured. His two-minute tirade blasted the jewelry profession back to the days of alchemy.

Before he could complete his butchery, Shel turned away from Frank. "Please forgive my rudeness. Margarite, I'd like you to meet my sister, Sharon."

I looked into crystalline blue eyes. She was clearly much younger than Shel but seemed to suffer from some chronic illness that left her pale and weak.

"I'm happy to meet you, Sharon," I said, smiling.

Sharon removed her hat, revealing long, luxurious blonde hair. With a childish glee, she turned her head and pointed. "Look."

Sitting on the park bench thirty years later, I remembered that precious child in that moment. I had said, "Those emeralds are stunning on you."

I would never forget that encounter. Neither would I forget the pain of her death.

I put a hand to my brow and squeezed my eyes shut but couldn't dam the tears. I realized I'd never had a chance to mourn her. I wept silently and whispered, "Oh, sweet girl." I'd been impressed by Shel Richardson, but I was immediately drawn to his sister. I also understood the "special needs."

Through tears, I looked again at the boy sitting on the seawall. He was reading a comic book as he waited for a bite. He sat in the exact location where they had retrieved Sharon's broken body. I never got a chance to see the scene of the crime. Now I couldn't stay away.

After Frank's tirade, Shel extracted the pendants from the box, letting one dangle from each hand. The stones were miraculous.

The light shimmered off their faceted surfaces embedded in platinum prong settings. Sharon gasped in awe.

Shel handed me an envelope containing too much cash but refused to capitulate when I protested. As I watched those moments unfold, I could already imagine Frank's description of his successful business association with Shel Richardson, exaggerated with each telling at the country club bar.

At that moment, Sharkey entered with Monk's daughter, Bonnie. I always equated Sharkey's presence to watching a dangerous snake in a serpentarium. But snakes were safely behind protective glass.

That weekend, Sharkey had become an instant legend when sports pages throughout the region published a photograph of him during a football playoff game. It was his first and only varsity game as quarterback. He was thirteen years old and disappeared as fast as he'd arrived. But that photo lived on. It became a locally famous debate; it must have been doctored or a trick of the light. The photographer swore his camera was functioning perfectly.

It captured a lithe figure emerging from a forest of giant black-uniformed Boone High School linemen in various contorted positions, arms outstretched, bodies twisting as they attempted to tackle him—a moment frozen in time like the raising of the flag on Iwo Jima. Every element of the photograph was frozen save the quarterback. Sharkey's feet were a blur. If the camera was in working order, the only conclusion was that he'd been accelerating at impossible speed. It appeared to show his feet simultaneously planted on the turf and floating above it as he juked his way through a small opening in the line.

Shel was fascinated by Sharkey before gathering Sharon and pointing to me. "I have more work for you. I'm not letting your genius go to waste."

At my trial, the prosecution used Shel's testimony to drive the stake into my defense. I sat in stunned disbelief. At the time, I thought Shel was just telling the truth as he knew it. He couldn't perjure himself for my sake. How fucking stupid could I have been?

So, here I sat, at the place I wished to remember during those final months in iso, the culmination of prison's extractive metallurgy. I feared it had turned me into an unrecognizable alloy. But the memories contained in the journal were reshaping me into a semblance of a person I once recognized. I'd almost forgotten who Margarite had been. Now I needed to absorb her into Stuart.

I knew what came next in the journal. I helped Marilyn Manakin face her own demons, and we suffered mightily for it.

I opened the journal and began to read.

Robert Manakin's warning was unequivocal, and I had no intention of testing him. Being on the bad side of a guard was bad enough. Getting on the bad side of a warden would make my early prison life as a sex toy for Aryans seem utopian.

The good news was that the warden probably forgot me the moment I was out of sight. I was a reasonable judge of character, and I was certain his threats were aimed at his wife, not me. He was telling her he owned her. Warden Manakin's ambition suppurated from his pores like a malarial disease.

I took ill will from the Manakins as a given, until I received a message from Marilyn. I could no longer call her Bitch Warden. She sent a message to Holt requesting me to stop by the library to retrieve a book being held at the circulation desk: *Ulysses*.

There were many ways this could go wrong. It was idiotic to risk being caught in the library if she were there, but if I didn't go at all, it might piss her off all over again. I could only dismiss the idea that her hatred had softened. My plan was to get in, get the book, get out as fast as I could, and pray I didn't run into Marilyn Manakin.

It just so happened that was the afternoon Maestro showed up with my new computer equipment. I was like a kid at Christmas, though my enthusiasm was tempered by the message from

Marilyn. Maestro could tell something was eating at me, so I explained my dilemma.

He nodded at the technician, a trustee I'd never seen before. "How long will it take you to set this stuff up?"

The technician was petrified by Maestro. "I'll hurry, I swear."

Maestro said, "Don't hurry, kid. Do it right."

The trustee's eyes widened. "Forty-five minutes to put the desk together, another forty-five to set up the computer." His voice shook.

Maestro looked at me. "Do you need to be here while he works?"

I shook my head. "I'll reconfigure it anyway."

Maestro nodded. "Good. Let's go get that book. You wait outside, and I'll go in and pick it up. Nobody can complain about you standing in the corridor."

I expressed my profound gratitude, and we left the trustee to his work. He was ecstatic at being able to do his job without Maestro looking over his shoulder.

We used the shortcut through the steam tunnels to reach the library. I waited outside while Maestro entered. Seconds later, he came out without the book.

He leaned in close to me. "The warden's wife asks that you sign for the book."

The panic on my face must have been obvious because Maestro gave me a bemused smile. "Hey. It's okay. I think she wants to talk to you. Just go in and get it over with. I got a little business down the block. See you in half an hour."

He patted my shoulder and walked away, his Italian loafers clicking their usual rhythm on the concrete floor.

I took a deep breath and pushed through the door. Marilyn Manakin was standing behind the circulation desk. As I approached, she nodded toward the tiny office. My last encounter in there had not gone well, and she could see the concern on my face.

"It's okay. My husband is in Tallahassee today. Sucking up to politicos."

I grinned at her sacrilege. She couldn't help returning a conspiratorial smile. We went back to the little office.

I sat on the edge of a low shelf, and she sat in the padded chair across from me. I noticed she was wearing an attractive sundress, black with white polka dots, cut above the knee. She crossed her legs, revealing a long leg up to the thigh, and I began chasing flies around the room, casting my eyes everywhere but on that thigh.

She spoke first. "When you were here last, you never had the chance to answer your own question. We were interrupted."

I knew exactly what she meant. "You mean the question about how I found the courage to be true to myself?"

She said, "Yes. And please look at me. I won't be offended. Someone needs to see me for who I am."

I was suddenly back in my apartment at the University of Florida a lifetime ago, talking with another young woman conflicted about her sexual identity. I was sure that was what this was about. All the signs were there. She wanted me to see her openly, unabashedly.

I took a deep breath and looked directly into her eyes. Her beauty was a contrast to the ugliness in this place. She told me to look, so I did, scanning her body thoroughly without avoiding the perfect legs receding up her skirt. They were long and shapely, muscular and creamy white. She'd been athletic, track and cheerleading or something. She was fit and shapely with full breasts. The stuff of dreams for male or female.

I decided to speak frankly. "Your beauty is remarkable. I was considered a handsome woman in my own way, but you're a genuine masterpiece. And you struck out at me because I represented something you've been fighting in yourself for as long as you can remember. It's easy for a handsome woman to dress like a handsome man. It's quite another for a beauty queen in a conservative town to act like anything but male bait. That's what this is about, isn't it?"

The relief on her face was transformative. Tears pooled in her eyes, but all she could do was nod slowly. Tears made her appear vulnerable and only enhanced her beauty. I'd been through many such conversions at the university. I wanted to go to her, kneel, and put my arms around her. I wanted to protect her and tell her I'd make everything okay. Instead, I sat frozen to the shelf, but my face must have betrayed my heartfelt concern.

I forced a smile. "Psychologists call it ego-dystonic. The internal struggle to fight against an identity your cultural upbringing tells you is abhorrent. You tried to hate me because I represented all you've raged against. Am I right?"

Her lip quivered, but her voice was steady. "Yes. I was raised in the Baptist Church, which means indoctrination. Everyone pushed me to marry a man like my husband to prove I was the ideal wife and woman. I caved to the pressure."

I spoke as tenderly as I was able. "And now it's not me you hate. It's every second of your false life."

Her voice was a whisper. "Yes."

"I was lucky." I lowered my voice to match hers. "I had a father who made it easy for me. He represented everything I hated in men. I wanted only to be the kind of man he wasn't."

She stared at me, and the emotions moved over her face like wind over water.

I was prepared to take risks. She required the truth. "Do you find the fact that I used to be a woman both comforting and somehow exciting?"

Her eyes widened, and her full lips parted, showing perfect white teeth, but no sound came. I forced myself to sit and wait. This had to take its course. I would not force a conversation for which she wasn't prepared. I felt she'd come this far, why stop short of the truth?

Her eyes flickered to the door. The blinds were closed, and

the door was locked. She uncrossed her legs, placing her feet flat on the floor, knees touching. Time slowed and then hovered. We were captives in the static net of this important moment in her life. The air seemed to sparkle with tension. I'd felt this before, but never had I felt this level of emotional voltage. John Donne called it "sweet amorous delay." But this was beyond romantic poetry. It was blisteringly erotic.

Her gaze intensified, and I felt my body tense. I reflexively gripped my thighs where my hands rested above my knees, my breathing shallow and rapid. I was afraid to move lest I alter the moment, fascinated as a lifetime of rigidity and uncertainty reshaped itself into something I recognized. Raw hunger. An inchoate sexual appetite was cascading, overwhelming reason, every logical distraction swept away by a need she'd kept dammed behind thick walls of cultural inhibition.

Her knees began to separate, and my mind went numb, reason swept away in a tidal wave of anticipation. She spread her legs as she pulled the dress up to her waist and reached a finger down to pull her black panties aside, revealing a thick bush of black pubic hair spread above pink swollen labia. She had become so aroused, I could see the glow of her wetness as she reached her other hand down and began slowly kneading her clitoris with her middle finger.

I was many years Marilyn's senior at the time, but her moment of self-discovery made age irrelevant. I was so aroused, I feared I might explode, undoing what the Dutch surgeon had so meticulously constructed. But I knew I couldn't expose myself to her. Marilyn's fantasy was my femininity. Showing my male tumescence would slay the moment, and I was overwhelmed by a desire to be midwife to the birth of her new sense of self. Perhaps I'd retained a shred of altruism and could help strike a blow against an absurd restrictive society, bringing another deserving child out of the shadows of hypocrisy. It was a remarkable moment for anyone, much less a reviled prison inmate.

I moved toward her and dropped to my knees. If I'd learned anything about sexual technique in college, it had been how to please a woman. I'd learned every nuance of the female body. I moved my head between her legs, running my tongue up each inner thigh. A soft moan issued from deep in her chest. I began licking tenderly at the butterfly wings of her labia, only teasing around her clitoris. I knew we didn't have much time, but I tried not to rush. I licked and flickered my tongue in every crevice.

Finally, I parted her labia and slowly, gently inserted two fingers into her wetness with a slight twisting motion. Her response was instantaneous. She leaned her head back and pulled her knees to her shoulders, giving me full, unobstructed access to a wetness that spread from her labia onto the tiny curve of her buttocks and around her anus. I licked and teased everywhere and then focused on her clitoris. Her musky scent made my erection ache, but I wanted nothing more than to show this beautiful soul what sex was supposed to feel like.

I gently massaged the moist silk of her flesh as I flickered my tongue lightly. I'd had many experiences in the gay community in college, to the point that I knew that the genitals of dark-haired women were more responsive to a heavier touch than blondes and particularly redheads. I increased the pressure of my tongue, licking vigorously, and began to pump my fingers, sliding a third inside her.

She began to moan a bit too loudly, so I reached my other hand up and cupped it over her mouth, neither of us caring if I smudged her red lipstick. It increased her excitement. She wanted to be taken. Many women are that way, so long as they choose you. If they don't … well, then you are a beastly rapist like Robert Manakin. But Marilyn had chosen me to bring her out into a world she'd wasted so much energy denying. I was not her fantasy but her Renaissance. The one who could unlock the door that imprisoned her. I wanted her to cum like she never had.

I pushed my hand between her teeth and stretched her lips

back like a bit in her mouth, and she licked my fingers, sliding her tongue between them as she began to ride my tongue. I licked until my tongue began to ache and fingered her more aggressively. I felt her orgasm building. A guttural moan began deep in her breast, and I clamped my hand hard over her mouth as she began to cum, her juices flooding onto my tongue and into my mouth.

Her body went into paroxysms, and I twisted my three fingers palm up. There is a myth of a so-called "g spot." It's bullshit. But there is a bundle of nerves under the pubic bone that can intensify orgasm if stroked correctly. And Marilyn Manakin went into one of the most explosive orgasms I've ever witnessed. She grabbed my head like a melon and fucked my face so hard, I knew her pubic hair would leave my lips and chin chafed.

She rode wave after wave of convulsions that were sustained far longer than I thought possible, moaning into my palm and grinding her pubic bone into my face. With what was left of my reasoning brain, I was already planning to tell Maestro she punched me because I insulted her. No one could ever know how I really got swollen lips and a chapped face.

Her orgasm diminished gradually, and I pressed my tongue flat against her clitoris to let her control the pressure as she rode out the aftershocks. As the spasms finally ceased, I retracted my fingers from her wetness and rolled back on my haunches as she placed her feet on the floor. The material on the padded chair was soaked with the combination of my saliva and her viscous fluids, but that was of no concern. I was more concerned about her reaction to what I'd just done to her.

I've seen women shed tears after a particularly intense orgasm, but Marilyn was sobbing, silently but deeply, her hands over her face. I gently replaced her panties and pulled her dress down over her legs before crawling around the chair and putting my arms around her. She grabbed me with ferocious intensity.

She clung to me, and I nuzzled my cheek on the top of her head as I, too, shed quiet tears.

I finally managed, "Thank you for that precious gift."

We engulfed each other in the unmistakable aroma of sex. I put a hand along her cheek and guided her face up. I kissed her as deeply and tenderly as I knew how. She responded by probing my mouth with an unimaginatively soft tongue. At that moment, I could only imagine her macho husband plundering that tender, sweet mouth like a maniac with a Weed eater. After a long, deep kiss, I pulled slowly away and moved back across the room to lean against the bookcase.

Her breathing slowed, and for long moments I stared at her while she stared at the floor. I wasn't sure where to go from there, so I offered her an easy way out. "Would you like me to go?"

She looked up at me, tears still streaming down her cheeks, and spoke without acknowledging my question. "I always imagined what it should be like. But it's never even approached what you just did to me. Ever." She cocked her head and her tears intensified. "What am I going to do?"

I knew I was taking a risk, but I owed her an honest answer. "Marilyn ... the gay community at my university lived more out in the open than I ever thought possible. It's one reason I loved my years there. It gave me the opportunity to live like a normal person without skulking in the shadows. But I've never had a more intense sexual experience than what we just shared in a prison library. It shows what's possible if you open yourself to someone who shares your dream and your life choice."

I leaned forward to stare hard into her huge eyes. "You've set yourself free. I feel honored that I'm the only person ever to experience the real Marilyn. You can't go back, but you'll have to learn to fake it for now. Trust me. It's hard to hide who you are once you've broken free from bondage. My attempts at sex with most men were just as yours are. I found it silly at best and repugnant at worst."

I smiled gently. "You must become the superhero you are. You must find a way to mask your true identity until you can find an exit strategy."

She made a failed effort to force a smile. "He's a brute. My husband."

I heaved a sigh. "I know the type. The truly pathetic part is men like that fancy themselves real studs." An idea struck me. "By any chance, do you suspect him of having affairs outside your marriage?"

She snickered. "Of course. You said it yourself. Men like him think they mustn't deny the females of the planet the pleasure of their cocks." She shuddered. "The thought of having that thing in me ever again is. I just can't."

I stepped closer and took a knee. "If you can catch him in an affair, maybe you can negotiate a marital standoff. First stroke his ego; you loved him more than life itself and now he's destroyed your image of him as your hero. You're shattered, heartbroken. But agree to keep up appearances for his career, but he makes no effort to force you to have sex. Tell him you don't want to risk him bringing some woman's disease into your bed. That should buy you some time to figure things out."

She smiled wanly. "It's a great idea. But I'm as much a prisoner here as you are. I never travel with him unless it's to some fund-raiser. How am I to catch him?"

I grinned. "Now, that's something I might be able to help with."

She looked at me askance. "What are you talking about?"

I said, "Just trust me. It might take me a little time, but if he's as arrogant as I think, he'll leave bread crumbs all the way to his dirty little beds."

"Okay. I know you're living over in block E. You be careful. Those men are professionals. They aren't to be trifled with."

She was truly concerned. I'd forgotten how much sex alters relationships.

"Don't worry." I smiled. "I'll be doing them a huge service even as I'm helping you."

I stood, as did she. I turned to leave, but she took my arm and drew me close.

"That was the most intense thing I've ever experienced. But you didn't get much out of it. I'm sorry."

She looked deeply into my eyes, and I said, "I'm not just saying this. I promise. That was the most fulfilling sex I've had with or without the orgasm. You needed the woman in me even though you can have any man you want. If that was all I had to offer, I was happy to give it."

She kissed me gently on the lips and smiled sheepishly. "Do you think you might be willing to let me have the woman in you again sometime?"

I responded too nonchalantly, "Name the time and place."

Then I caught myself. I closed my eyes. They burned. "Marilyn, you're a dream I must force myself to wake from. Someone I couldn't have conjured in my wildest imagination. If I helped you find yourself today, then I've done something I'll cherish. But please, for your own safety, stay away from the pitiful shadow I've become. I'm an inmate in your husband's prison. Nothing more."

Her tears mirrored mine. She wanted to speak, but I put a finger against the bow of her lips. "I will never get the chance to tell the man who runs this prison that his wife is the most captivating creature on earth, and he doesn't deserve her. I'd happily suffer his wrath to share this again. But his retribution wouldn't be aimed at me. You know that."

Her lower lip quivered, and I couldn't fathom my reversal of fortune. The fear I'd felt when I walked into the library had become a forlorn sense of loss as I left it. It made no sense. But the heart rules the head, and love is irrational on its best day.

She said, "I refuse to close the book you've opened. And I promise not to chase the shadow of the man, but I can't promise I won't seek the woman again."

I smiled broadly. "My name was Margarite. Before. But please don't make the mistake of saying it aloud in front of anyone."

She said, "Okay … Margarite. I'll stay away. But just maybe I can convince my husband that it's good for your rehabilitation for you to continue in the library." Her lip quivered again. "I feel horrible. I can't believe how I treated you."

I should never have let her pursue this line of thought, but like I said, love is irrational. Or better put, if love is irrational, infatuation is pure insanity. "You'd be better off telling him you think someone needs to keep an eye on me. That I'd be a conduit into E block, which by the way, I didn't even know had a block letter. He'll respond much quicker to conspiracy than altruism."

She smiled. "Okay, Margarite." She kissed me sweetly on the lips, letting her tongue flicker over mine. Margarite. Who had she been? Somehow Stuart and Margarite melded that day in the prison library as they brought new life to this beautiful child.

I gathered the shards of a shattered heart and slipped out. When I exited the shelves, Maestro was leaning against the circulation desk with his back to me. The attendant was as far across the library from him as he could get.

He turned with a quick smile. "Ah. There you are."

I tried to keep him from seeing my chin and lips, and I didn't think he could possibly suspect anything.

Before we entered block E, he turned to me. "I kept that library dude away from the desk. It sounded like you needed some privacy. I can't lie, I'm envious as hell, but you're playing with fire, D. We don't get tangled with the prison administration. We make deals with them but don't get involved in their lives."

I gave him my most serious look. "You amaze me. But I'm no fool. I begged her to stay away from me. For her sake, not mine. If she's just my friend, it might be useful to have someone close to the warden. Something stinks about the way things are going. I don't know why I say this, but I'm certain she could help me, and in turn, I could help Mr. O."

He frowned as he considered this. "Mm-hmm. If you say so. But don't be stupid. Sex is lethal because it makes people stupid. They talk. Broads or guys. Don't matter. You fucking talk about each other because you can't help it. Every time I hear you utter that broad's name, I'm gonna pop you in the mouth. Capisce?"

I smiled. "For a cold-hearted killer, you really do understand human nature. Capito, Maestro."

He was right. Her name battered the back of my teeth a hundred times a day, pounding to get out. My tongue tried to shape the word Marilyn with every word I uttered. When I got back to my room, I silently thanked Maestro and Mr. O that a beautiful desktop computer was waiting there. As I launched into my exploration of its power, my last thought was that I hoped Marilyn was being careful not to speak my name. She must forget Margarite and Stuart.

She didn't speak my name. She didn't have to. I managed to fuck it up without her.

# Chapter 12

I paused in my reading and lay the journal on the bench beside me. I needed time to savor the memory of that afternoon with Marilyn, an afternoon that almost made thirty years in hell worthwhile. I hadn't forgotten that afternoon in the library during my last months in iso, but the details had blurred. The journal brought the experience back with erotic clarity. When I put the journal down, I realized I had an erection. It had been years since my custom-built penis had been erect. I hid my midsection with my satchel as I stumbled to my car for the short drive home.

The next morning, I sat at the kitchen table in the house that was once my parents'. I lifted my demitasse and took a sip of espresso, pondering a final conundrum. Through the bay window, I watched a murder of boat-tailed grackles scorch a cobalt sky, competing for purchase on a great sycamore in the backyard. As random as their swirling and diving seemed, there was an underlying order to their movements. An order missing in my thoughts.

As Margarite, I was a talented and stable craftswoman. But as Stuart, the muddled survivor, I managed to accumulate great wealth. Money bought things, like the espresso maker sitting on the granite countertop in this refurbished kitchen. Money reduced stresses in life. They said money couldn't buy happiness, but the road to happiness was paved with it.

For me that road did not lead to a quiet, peaceful village. That road had yet to be carved through deep forests of hatred and bridge canyons of fear and trepidation. I faced a final hill beyond which I could finally rest. On that hill stood a man, Shel Richardson, who held the final answers. Why were we—Margarite, who never harmed him and Stuart, who he never knew—banished to hell? When I finally met Shel, he wouldn't yield easily. I knew him. Before he agreed to meet me, he'd have his own contingency plan.

I turned from the window and gazed at the beautiful Nuovo Simonelli Aurelia II espresso maker on the counter. Its price tag was nothing now. My love of good espresso was a legacy from Italy and Mr. O. I adopted Mr. O's espresso formula—a single spoon of raw cane sugar and a dab of Sambuca known as Café Corretto. The day couldn't begin without it.

As I sat over my espresso, I heard thunder roiling in the east. A low-pressure front was coming. The clear morning sky would soon be overtaken by thunderstorms. A low-pressure invasion reminded me of younger days. In school, kids moved morosely along the corridors with little energy. Even the typical drone of teachers was slower, and it seemed to take all their effort to push the inanities forth. A tropical low-pressure front sucked the air out of the lungs and the cheer from the heart.

It was on such a day my mother had lost her battle with emphysema and died quietly in the master bedroom upstairs. Frank was, as usual, at the country club when death entered her bedroom, leaving only the shell of what had once been a wife and mother. The body wasn't discovered until the fool teetered home full of booze and anger as he entered and didn't smell dinner waiting.

I'd been in prison for over two decades by then. With Mr. O's help, I was approved for an accompanied furlough to attend the funeral. During that time, I hadn't been outside the prison fences. Holt was on a state retirement track, called Drop, and was training his fortunate replacement. He left his hand-picked trainee in charge of block E and drove me the three hours south to my hometown.

Mr. O had served more than seven years by then. He should have been paroled. Something was wrong. Mr. O thought his lawyers were in the final stages of procuring his release. Instead, there was one delay after another. In the end, Mr. O would become deeply indebted to me for unraveling the web of deceit surrounding the delay. The aftermath would be a shit storm for a lot of powerful people.

I could wait no longer. Time was getting short, so I opened the journal on the kitchen table and continued to read.

I was shocked when they let me go home for my mother's funeral. I put in a standard request to attend, expecting an instant denial. Perhaps it was because I was now with Mr. O or someone just forgot to say no. The approval created a mixture of excitement and fear. A mother's funeral should be a time of solemnity and dignity. I tried my best. But there was also fear at seeing people who had hated me. Added to the apprehension was an undeniable schadenfreude. I'd kept up with events and was aware of the town's steady decline.

Of course, when I arrived, my sole focus was the death of Sharon Richardson. I'd never seen the place by the river where they'd found her. It was a very old case by then, and I knew I wouldn't be able to prove anything, but I wanted to see it for myself.

Thanks to my father's boundless narcissism, the visit began horribly. When my mother finally succumbed to his relentless demands and constant hounding, she died alone. The stupid bastard didn't even bother showing up at her funeral. I never expected him to contact me in prison, but he also prevented her from doing so. She died with no chance to say goodbye. As much

173

as he'd poisoned her against me, she would have wished it. She wrote me once on cheap paper and a prestamped envelope to let me know she didn't believe that I was guilty.

I didn't need to be present to see her final years play out. As her life wore on, her fading spirit was eroded by the constant flow of his corrosive influence to the point that putting one foot in front of the other would have taken all her energy. He was a chain-smoker, and the secondhand smoke from living with him had destroyed her lungs. COPD they called it. The steady destruction of her pulmonary system had stolen her breath even as his relentless demands had leeched her spirit.

The funeral was at the First Baptist Church three blocks up Magnolia from our house. A mere handful of people attended. After a lifetime in this town, there were fewer people there to see her out than had been in the church choir in its heyday. The choir, too, had dwindled and muffed its way through Rock of Ages, her favorite hymn. I recognized only one person, a lady who'd once been in a quilting bee with my mother. I was thankful she didn't recognize me.

The town was at its nadir then. After the amusement parks opened, it became a blue-collar bedroom community for Orlando. Most of the grand houses in the historic district had been broken up into small apartments, while the brick streets had been paved over with asphalt, altering for the worse the ambience of the district. Later they would spend more to scrape the asphalt off and reveal the old brick than it originally cost to pave it over. Whislin' Sid, the old public works director from my youth, warned them they'd want to restore the town's beauty, but no one listened. Of course, he was long dead, along with the few reasonable men who'd been the engine that once kept the town going.

I begged Holt to let me have a few minutes to walk around town on my own, and he kindly acceded, giving me two hours before meeting him at the German restaurant on First Street. Much had changed since I left for prison. It wasn't worth casting blame. The simple fact was that a once thriving community had become a bastion of unfulfilled potential and lost hope.

I walked down Magnolia Avenue to the old house where I spent my childhood, knowing my father wasn't there. For some reason the blue Chrysler Imperial was parked in front of the house. Odd. Maybe one of his cronies picked him up or he was holed up with some woman. I overheard a conversation from an elderly couple in front of me. Their Baptist ire was turned on high as they whispered indignations about my father's cavorting. It stoked my anger, though it didn't surprise me. I wished it was him in the cheap coffin.

As I stood staring at the house, I recalled an earlier time when I had stood at the picketed gate at the front porch. My father had an affair with one of my mother's church friends, and she stood on the steps, screaming at me in a rare disregard for what the neighbors might think. She lay a lifetime of misery at my feet. If only I hadn't been an abomination, her husband would have been a successful leader in the community and the two of them would have had a marvelous life together. Because of me, he was running around with other women, friends had turned against them, and I'd made an outcast of a great man.

I turned and walked away, knowing Frank had finally beaten the remains of motherhood out of her and she'd become a simple automaton espousing his shallow tenets. Still, it was devastating.

That night, I awoke in the wee hours and began to weep. I couldn't stop. I found a paper sack in my room and sobbed into it to prevent hyperventilation. Sometime after sunrise, my body, stomach muscles aching from wracking sobs and eyes swollen, gave up. I slept until the following morning. We stay too long with our parents. Good ones don't need so long to teach us all they know, and the bad ones have too much time to destroy us.

I don't know why, but I decided to take some pictures of the old house and the blue Imperial sitting out front. Tolly had loaned me a camera for the trip. He was a big gruff man nicknamed Tooly for all his gadgets. He was a serious photographer and set up a small darkroom in an old maintenance closet in the block.

Those pictures changed my life. And Mr. O's.

The rains ended suddenly, and the sun stabbed spears of light through dissipating clouds. It was as if God hit his "sun switch" and illuminated his creation. I hurriedly showered, dressed, picked up Ralph's ass, and decided to walk the few blocks to the lakefront to what I now called Sharon's bench.

When I got there, a young couple was sitting on the bench, wrapped around each other like a Giambologna serpentine, so I strolled down the marina to a small restaurant overlooking the lake and ordered a snapper sandwich, fries, and a beer. By the time I returned, they'd moved on.

I stroked the smooth binder as I scanned the lake. The casualties of a damaged life awakened and rattled the chains of the past.

Leitner Dredge pulled the BMW to the curb a block from the warehouse where the two truckers were holding Summer. Lagging several blocks behind the BMW and out of sight of the warehouse was a steel-gray van. He stopped briefly, which was a signal for three men to slip quietly from its interior, after which the van pulled around the block, out of view. He was relieved. The Algiers specialist he asked for had been precise. He glanced through the side window between two warehouses and saw the lights of the city glittering across the Mississippi.

NOLA was one of the few habitable cities left in North America. In the next few minutes, he would add to his memories of this place. He savored what he was about to do to these two fucks. Something he learned from a man in a dream, a man he knew in Afghanistan. He'd had the specialists draw every detail of this block. The test of accuracy was to look toward the city at this intersection. He saw exactly what the man said he'd see; across the river was a narrow stretch of the city near the Superdome.

After the three men deployed, Leitner took his foot off the brake, and the car crept forward. The warehouses were dark, and a scattering of functional streetlights shot a few buzzing fingers of orange across the potted roadway. The infrastructure of this great city was an example of planned neglect.

He drove slowly so his men could keep up. They'd be shadowing him in the dark alleys behind the warehouses to the address given to him by the two dumb fucks. They'd cased the area and seen no signs they were being followed. Farley and Pierre were no doubt confident that they'd snagged some tourist asshole who won big money on a Vegas lucky streak.

That last phone call had gone as he'd hoped.

"Hello?"

"Listen, 'cause I say this once. There's a warehouse by a parking lot where truckers stash they rigs 'tween loads. I text you the address one hour before you show up. Bring the money; come alone. There's a door on the side of the warehouse opposite the parking lot. It'll be unlocked. Go in that door. Your phone's got a flashlight. Turn it on and aim it at yourself. If they's a gun in your hand, you and the girlie die. You got that, Boudreaux?"

Farley and Pierre would have friends with them.

"I got it. But look, I don't know that place, so I don't want to come all the way inside, okay?" Leitner forced his voice to quaver. "I'll stop inside just like you say. You bring the girl over near the door, and I'll toss the envelope full of money to you, okay?"

The hand went over the phone, and he heard muted jocularity.

"Sure, Boudreaux. We do it just like that."

Leitner smiled. He needed to get them near the entrance; no need to chase them around some huge warehouse. They planned to toss him and Summer in the river once they got the cash. He wanted them brash and confident until the end.

He pulled the BMW carefully onto the weeds and dirt of the uncurbed street. His worst fear in the operation was getting a nail in a tire. He stepped from the car. It was a sultry night, but he put on a waterproof jacket to avoid blood splatter. He gazed tentatively at the building, craning his neck to continue the scared-rabbit routine in case he was being watched. He edged slowly forward and then paused to lift a shoe as if looking for dog shit. Anyone watching would see a spoiled asshole afraid of his own shadow. He climbed the few steps of a loading dock to the door he was to enter and pulled out his cell phone as he tested the knob. The catch released, and the door creaked open on noisy hinges. A noisy hinge. How clever.

He took a couple of steps inside and shined the flashlight on his body, keeping it below his eyes to prevent night blindness.

He heard a voice. "Where's the money?" It echoed from the interior of the vast space. Leitner could see only within the halo of his phone light. Other than that, there were a few mere slivers from broken windowpanes high overhead.

"I need to reach my hand in my jacket pocket. Is that okay? You won't shoot me, will you?"

"Just do it slow. We don't shoot."

Leitner shifted the phone from one hand to the other as he reached into his jacket pocket to retrieve an envelope with some strips of blank paper inside. As he did so, he cast the flashlight down at the floor and then back up. That was the signal for his men to move in.

Suddenly, five flashlight beams appeared. The dumbasses just gave away their count and location. Farley and Pierre came forward slowly. The other three trailed them, casting their eyes into the shadows on either side of Leitner.

Finally, he saw Summer held firmly between Farley and Pierre. Her white dress was torn and filthy. He couldn't see her face well, but it looked like she had a couple of minor facial contusions and was no worse for the wear. It might even serve as a lesson.

"Okay, toss the envelope this way."

Leitner spoke pleadingly, "Look. Can you at least let the girl take a couple of steps forward so I know you'll really let her go?" He needed her out of the line of fire.

"Sure, Couyon." Pierre let go of Summer's arm, and Farley pushed her violently toward him. She fell forward and screamed as her legs and arms scraped on the rough plank deck.

Leitner heard three dull pops, and three flashlights hit the floor along with three bodies.

One of the remaining men yelled out in surprise. It was Farley, still holding that stupid shotgun, trying to aim into the darkness. Another pop, and Farley screamed as a bullet tore through his kneecap. Leitner had given strict orders. Do not kill these fucks.

Farley dropped to the floor screaming and holding his knee, while Pierre put up his hands and started talking nonstop. "Farley talked me into it. I wanted nothing to do with it. It was her goddamn idea. I swear to God, mister. She begged us to take her away."

Leitner's team emerged from the darkness wearing tactical night gear. They'd been watching these idiots the whole time as they stood in the dark preening like tough guys.

One of the men placed four small tactical lanterns around Farley and Pierre. Leitner stepped into the eerie circle of light. Summer lay on the floor, sobbing, but Leitner made no immediate move to comfort her. The lanterns illuminated a storage warehouse with hundreds of crates scattered about.

He looked at his team one by one. "Thank you, gentlemen." He pulled three envelopes from his jacket and doled them out. "As agreed."

The three stepped forward, and Leitner dispersed payment. One of the men pointed at Pierre. "Chickenshit there was squeezing your girl's tits the whole time they were squatting here in the dark. I'd kill him first."

Pierre began blubbering, "I'm sorry. I'm so sorry. She told us you had money, and it was her and Farley's idea to get it from you. I didn't want to. I got kids and a wife."

Leitner pointed the gun at Pierre's forehead. "Of course she told you about the money. She's a pro, you stupid shit."

Leitner caught the eye of one of the team and nodded toward

Summer. He knelt beside her and helped her up while examining her face and murmuring placatory phrases of comfort.

Finally, she settled into sporadic snuffling and looked up at Leitner. "Leitner." She was careful to pronounce it as he wished. "You should kill these bastards for what they did to me."

Leitner didn't acknowledge her. Instead, he said to the men, "Zip these fucks. Then, if you would, I'd appreciate it if you'd take her to the hotel where you met me. We have rooms there. See she gets settled in and then call a doctor."

One man used zip cord to bind Farley and Pierre. Farley wanted to nurse his shattered knee, but the man yanked his hands behind his back and zipped them as Farley screamed and Pierre continued blubbering his blame at Farley and Summer. Then he blamed a father who had drank himself to death and a mother who left him with a nasty aunt.

One of his team took out ball gags to shut Pierre's whining and Farley's painful screams, but Leitner waved him off. "I need to get at their mouths."

That sent Pierre into a screaming frenzy. "It was their fucking idea, goddamnit—"

One of the men slapped him hard, and he settled into a drooling, childlike whimper.

Two of the men leaned Pierre and Farley against a packing crate as the third took one of Summer's forearms and guided her toward the door.

As they reached the door, Summer said, "Wait. Please." She turned to Leitner. "I'm so sorry, Leitner. I swear, if you give me another chance, I'll do whatever you say from now on."

Leitner turned to stare at her. Seconds later, he gave the flicker of a smile. She turned and left with her escort.

One of the men asked, "What'll you do to them?"

Leitner's smile was sinister. "Something I learned from a master."

The day after Summer's rescue, Leitner's contact called to tell him he was clear of any problems related to the incident. One of the cops on his payroll had been first on the scene. Two men delivering an unclaimed load of pipe valves and O-connectors from the airport had called it in. They were two locals who were still puking when they called 911.

The one who called it in said they'd thought it was an animal that'd gotten in through a broken window, until they looked behind a crate and started tossing their cookies.

"He blamed it on *housan de diable*. A voodoo devil," Leitner's friend said. "When NOPD arrived, they found three shot professionally and one dead of infection. One was still alive. I don't know what you did to him, but the cop on my payroll said, and I quote, 'I don't know what this asshole did to deserve this, but I hope I never do it.' One of the older cops said he'd seen a spate of killings like this many years ago. The cops hope this is a one-off and that the man who created this signature isn't back. They hope he's long gone."

Leitner chortled. "Tell your cop friend not to worry. He has his wish; he's long gone."

Leitner and Summer crossed the Alabama border on I-10. They'd stayed in NOLA for two more days while she regained strength. Summer was grateful that Leitner had made no attempt to touch her. He'd paid for a suite so she could have her own room. As they drove toward Mobile, she sat quietly in the passenger seat, staring blankly through the side window. Occasionally and without warning, her emotions cascaded and she'd begin sobbing relentlessly.

Leitner reached in the narrow back seat and rummaged around in a tote bag. He pulled out a small pistol and dropped it into the purse at her feet.

"Humor me and keep this with you. Call it insurance."

Summer looked down at the butt of the gun rising above the

leather rim of her small purse. *Too late*, she thought. *I needed it in that truck to kill myself.* But she said nothing. She turned again to the window. The aftermath had left her exhausted and depressed.

Leitner had been more thoughtful than she'd expected. No blame games. He'd said only that he wanted to get to Destin, Florida, by evening. A few days on the beach would do them both some good.

Summer felt zombielike, but it was good. It kept her from thinking about what had happened. At some point she'd confront it. But not yet. She'd become increasingly frightened of Leitner. He became almost manic after killing people. He'd acted the same way after killing the man who owned the BMW. She'd cringed at the first thing he said when he got to one of the Audubon cottages in New Orleans after killing those two truckers. "Fucking with me was a big mistake." She wondered if he wasn't addressing her as well. There was something twisted in him, but there was nothing she could do about it. Not yet.

# CHAPTER 13

I lifted the journal gently from the seat of Sharon's bench, turning it over in my hands. The tanned cover had darkened with age.

"Gosh, Ralph. You might end up a nice Hispanic tone before long. How about I dye you a nice ebony? Alphonse would like that." I was talking to myself less these days—a good sign.

Someone was ghosting my conscience. A spectral form brooded at the edges, distracting me. Shel. Always Shel.

He'd done as he promised and increased my business. The Hatfields, known to prefer shopping in New York, began coming into the shop. Mrs. Hatfield started her long health decline and came in less frequently. I liked her very much and missed seeing her. I even liked Jeffrey Sr. Everyone feared him for some reason, but I found him polite and generous of spirit. He even asked after his youngest boy on occasion, which was odd.

He'd say, "Seen my youngest running around lately?"

I'd report a variation on the same theme. "Yes, he stopped in just to say hello. Such a brilliant child."

Mr. Hatfield would nod, always with a sad smile. One day the boy disappeared. Rumors spread that he'd been committed to the mental hospital in Chattahoochee. The news was incomprehensible. A second rumor followed. He was diagnosed as criminally insane. I refused to believe it, but it was true that he was incarcerated in an asylum. The world was aflame with improbable calamities.

I liked Jeff Sr. but could not abide Jeff Jr. I couldn't pin down exactly what made my skin crawl. He was a star athlete and an honor-roll student, but there was an underlying arrogance as he strutted around town with his entourage of sycophantic teammates. To prove his manhood, he pursued a showdown with Sharkey. Be careful what you ask for. It was an after-school fight brought on by Jeff Jr.'s bullying. I read about it in the sport page of the *Herald* because it ended Jeff Jr.'s football career. I could have told him that fighting Sharkey would be like riding out a Cat 5 hurricane in a canoe.

I opened the journal. I was getting close to the end. It was time to reach out to Shel Richardson. I was driven to finish the journal before we met. I opened to my last stopping place and read on.

It took almost a week to set up the computer to my exact specifications, or I should say the specifications I was taught by a brilliant computer geek and close friend at the university. The first and simplest thing I did was install a bookkeeping program. It started out as my soul duty, but now I had to plan for far more sophisticated work. I'd been given everything I needed, from a rocket motherboard to state-of-the-art systems cards. I immediately fell back into my university routine of working late into the night, staying awake on caffeine and adrenaline.

I also hadn't forgotten what I promised Marilyn.

As that thought crossed my mind, I plugged an ethernet cable into the wireless router and the router into the ethernet port on the wall. Then I configured the router and hit the play button on my new world. At the university, I, like my friend, was a complete computer geek. Even at the jewelry store, I kept up with the technology of the day. But I hadn't touched a computer other than a sluggish machine in the prison library for nearly two decades.

Maestro had somehow arranged for me to have the same internet access as the prison staff. Our block had once been an administration building, so Holt simply had my ethernet jack turned on. No one questioned it because no one really kept up with such things. When I slipped that ethernet cable into the slot, I became immediately enthralled. For perhaps a week, I did nothing but explore the far reaches of the World Wide Web. I rarely ate or slept or showered.

Finally, Maestro began to suspect something was wrong and stopped by my room. I guess when I opened the door, he could tell I'd become an internet zombie.

He said only, "I thought this might happen. You're the type. Snap out of it. You got a job to do."

I nodded vacantly. I showered, shaved my scraggly beard, and staggered off to join the others for dinner. Then I got down to the serious work.

I installed two powerful statistical and data warehousing tools. Since my youth, both software packages had undergone radical changes for the better, which stoked my enthusiasm. The hard part was not using these tools; they couldn't be easier, having shifted from card readers to graphical interfaces. The hard part would be getting the proper array of predictor variables. I knew the technique I wanted to use: penalized regression. An ironic name, I thought. Puns aside, it was a powerful predictive tool. I had some catching up to do, so I experimented with Firth, Ridge, Lasso, and Elastic Net, names that made sense only to a nerd.

Then I began to interview Mr. O's men, but I needed his approval. Again, Maestro smoothed the way. I'd already extracted huge amounts of data from geographical sources, weather history, population shifts, crime statistics—in short, as much as I could find from public sources and, nefariously, from a few not-so-public sources. Hacking into the systems run by state agencies was hardly a challenge.

What I needed most was the kind of data only those on the ground would know. Then I had to quantify it. No database could tell me every detail of criminal operations. For example, if a restaurant was torched, was it an order from a crime boss or did a restaurant owner simply decide to cash out the insurance on a failing business?

I began recording focused interviews with the men and then figured out ways to quantify as much as possible. I needed details. If a crime, C, occurred on day X, at time Y, what else could they tell me about it?

It was amazing how much these guys knew. Who perpetrated it and when it began, not the time stamp of record, but before? Prior signs, a piece of a plan they heard about, warning signs, perhaps a smaller skirmish as a precursor to a big event. Slowly and meticulously I built out the database. I was in heaven.

Mr. O's men, as Maestro had foretold, were like quarterbacks who could recount every detail of a game or golfers who could remember every shot in a tournament in vivid detail. I just kept smiling as the data poured in.

If I put the men in small groups, they'd correct each other. "No, that wasn't the Ice Man—that was Tony the Torch, remember?" "Oh, yeah, that's right. The Ice Man did that other job, the one where that Russian ended up in a canal out on the parkway." It was a gold mine of the macabre.

Maestro dropped by occasionally to see how it was going, but there was never any pressure. He knew I'd become absorbed in the computer and worked late into the night hopped up on Red Bull and espresso. I began to lose track of time, and still they were patient.

Next, I began sniffing data space around the prison.

Finally, after two and half months, I was ready to test a model. I used historical data to see if the model would predict a past event. I divided up the data sets by gang activity. One class of activity kept coming up: the so-called Russian Mafia or Bratva. Their main cash flow was from human trafficking, and Mr. O hated everything about it.

My first test held up perfectly. The model was random except for Bratva, so I focused on the Russians. But the Russian model kept collapsing when I entered the "date stamp" into the model. It drove me batshit until I realized I'd made a rookie mistake. I didn't physically examine that variable carefully.

I switched to the raw data file and burst out laughing.

"You stupid asshole."

The date was always the same.

Any statistician knows that predictive modeling depends on variation, and there's always an error term with variance. With a constant, there's no error term, or more accurately there's zero error; zero into anything is zero. No variation, no need for a probability estimate. But that knowledge made my model incredibly accurate once I simply controlled for the date.

I wondered what was so important about that date. I went back to the men. We were sitting in the game room, and I asked, "Who pulls the trigger on Russian Mafia turf wars? Who gives the go?"

Three men said almost simultaneously, "Vory v Zakone—the Thieves in Law."

This group was on the FBI's transnational criminal organization list. It was clear that the date was crucial, so I asked another question. "Who specifically would make the call to instigate an operation against a rival gang?"

Again, the answer was unanimous: "Shusha."

The man's full surname was Sushanashvili. I began homing in on him, looking for the possible significance of the date, May 9. Every noticeable operation by the Bratva in south Florida began on May 9. Why?

One day while I was wracking my brain, Big Al stopped by, and in frustration I told him the problem.

He shrugged. "Shusha is a very religious man. I'd check there."

Within minutes, I leapt up from my desk and shouted, "Take me, Big Al! I want to have your baby."

The answer popped up faster than an inmate's pecker on connubial visitation. May 9 in the Russian Orthodox Church was Victory Day, when war heroes were celebrated. A day when war and religion intersected. It wasn't the last time I'd worship Big Al for his acumen.

My model was complete. I quickly ran it, and then I ran to Maestro. He was in his room asleep. I didn't realize it was three in the morning. I pounded on his door. He opened it, and I was astonished; if he'd been asleep, there was no sign of it. He looked as he always looked, alert and predatory.

"I have to show you something," I blurted. "We shouldn't wait on this."

He gave a customary frustrated shake of the head. He seemed persistently bemused by my antics of late.

He met me in my room, and I guided him to the computer. "Look at this."

He glanced at the screen and said, "Somebody crapped all over your little TV."

I sneered. "Very funny. All you have to do is look at this date right here." I pointed to a number embedded in a complex data run.

"Yeah, I see it. So what?"

I looked up from the screen with enthusiasm. "When the Russians make a move, it's always on May 9. Their boss is superstitious; it's always on a single religious holiday."

Maestro gave me a sidelong glance. "Wake the fuck up. Today's the first not the ninth."

"That's not all. They always create a diversion on May 1. Today."

He frowned. "Get dressed and come up to Mr. O's. I'll meet you outside the elevator."

Minutes later, the printer finally spit out the last page. I grabbed the pile and ran for the elevator. As promised, Maestro was waiting.

I hadn't seen Mr. O in a couple of months, and he seemed genuinely glad to see me. Maybe it was my elation at presumed success, but it made me feel good anyway. He sat regally behind his desk in a burgundy paisley robe. He seemed pale and tired, but then again, I'd awakened him in the middle of the night.

"Hello, D." Mr. O's voice was its usual baritone, but it sounded as if he had a cold.

"Are you feeling well, sir?"

He gave me a little smile. "Just allergies. Maestro says you've got something for me. I trust our patience is paying off?"

I didn't know the wait had been an issue, so I said, "I'm sorry it took so long. I just wanted to get it right."

"And have you?"

"I believe so, but the good news is we can see if I'm right immediately. Today."

I knew not to try to explain all the stats, so I used the printout only as a reference. I laid it on the desk across from him, and he leaned forward between me and Maestro, who sat quietly looking on.

He responded similarly. "Ah, Egyptian hieroglyphics."

I laughed. "Sorry. I'll give you nice charts next time, but this couldn't wait. I just made my first run. The key piece was finding a date that drove me crazy at first."

I circled two dates on the printout. "The model predicts that Bratva will make a diversionary move today in anticipation of a more ambitious action on May 9. It's been their pattern. If we were talking about a shit storm, I'd predict this one will be a hurricane. The hard part was predicting where."

I looked up at him with wide eyes. "They're due to make a major move. It happens cyclically. All signs point to this year. And before every operation, they carry out a diversion on May 1, even if it's something minor. The diversions are similar, and they're always highly touted in the newspapers. I'm sure they're smoke screens, but the cops make a big deal about a crime bust, calling attention to their diligence against evil crime bosses. But the big events? Swept under the rug."

Mr. O asked, "Why bother with a distraction at all?"

"Great question. It took me a while to figure it out. It's a sacrifice to the cops, but I think it's also a message to someone else. Every time the real move is made, the cops are slow to react, but the two big moves …" I paused. My next point was a bit of a risk, but the model didn't lie.

"Go on, D. Let's hear it." I realized Mr. O was anticipating my answer.

"The Italians had to have known. Both head fakes were against Italian money laundering schemes, and the major moves took out competition for both. The Italians made no effort to disrupt the move. They went dead quiet."

He sat staring at my printout, but his mind was somewhere else.

I felt I needed to explain, so I began, "It was as if they hit a pause button on all business—"

He cut me off, and my suspicions were realized. His eyes narrowed, and for the first time I saw a look on his face that rivaled Maestro's in terms of its clear threat to world peace. "That *puttano* motherfucker. Cutting deals with *selvaggi*."

I had never heard Mr. O use words so foul. I sat frozen, afraid to speak.

He leaned back, hands teepeed under his chin, deep in thought. I was in shock, but Maestro sat snakelike, not even breathing from what I could tell. I noticed something else about Maestro in those moments. It was as if he ceased to exist. I know they could hear my breathing out in the anteroom, but Maestro was as obscure as a water moccasin in tall grass.

After long moments, Mr. O heaved a great sigh and leaned

forward. "Tell me what you expect today." His voice had returned to its calm timbre.

I spoke tentatively. "My guess is there will be some move against a money-laundering operation. Probably against the Italians or the Bratva themselves." I knew it sounded improbable, so I added quickly, "I predict the point of it all is aimed at Miami Beach hotels. I'm not sure why—"

Again, he cut me off. "Sex trafficking. They take over that territory, they control sex trafficking, hookers, white-slave auctions. The Cubans aren't into that. But it's the lifeblood of Bratva. They can serve every Arab oil magnate, American corporate pervert, or Russian oligarch … Miami is perfect for it. Naïve young girls, children with too much money and time to spend it."

I looked at Mr. O as he finished what I was going to say. "If they go after some little money laundering operation, it draws the heat off, gives the cops something to brag about, and seals a partnership. We own the hotels; they use them as a front to hide sex trafficking. Everyone makes money. I never wanted to get into that awful business. But I'm in here."

I spoke in a whisper, afraid of the answer. "Sir, if you already knew what I was going to tell you, why did you need me at all?"

He gazed at me with a fatherly smile. "It's one thing to suspect; it's another to have proof. And still another to know when these things will happen. You've earned your keep many times over, my friend."

Maestro asked in a dead, cold tone, "Do we intervene?"

Mr. O said, "No. Now that we can read their map, we'll decide when to blow up the bridges. It's too soon. Let this one play out. Give them confidence in their relationship."

I piped up, "I have some ideas about a disruption strategy."

Mr. O chuckled. "I'm sure you do. And when the time comes, I'll unleash you on these pigs."

I said, "Shouldn't we wait to see if I'm right about the diversion?"

He stood, his body slumped and tired. "You will be, D. You will be. Now, you two get some sleep. We'll read about it in the papers tomorrow."

I paused in my reading, remembering how genuinely sad Mr. O had been when I confirmed his suspicions. I looked over at the marina. Boats bobbed gently on the steady current sweeping along the lake. I was remembering everything with such clarity now, and even before I read the next section, tears began to build. I pressed the heels of my hands to my eyes and rubbed gently. I couldn't stop now. The past was converging on the present. So much was lost in the mist, innocence engulfed by horror.

It was in college that I made the decision to pursue the transgender operations. But responsibilities delayed it, and it was four years before the two-year testosterone therapy began. Afterward, I flew to Holland for the series of operations: so-called "top therapy" to remove my breast tissue and begin to rebuild my chest to a more male profile and the phalloplasty to give me a functioning penis—the one I ultimately declined to use when the opportunity with Marilyn presented itself. It was a decision I'd never regret.

I forced myself to read on. I was running out of time. Shel Richardson was out there, and I felt his long talons reaching out from his past to tear me apart before I could expose him for the monster he was. I read on.

While I was in college, I met a young boy, a member of the gay community. As it was for me, getting accepted to UF was his dream, and once free of domineering parents, he awakened into a dream he'd hidden all his life. He was sixteen; he'd flown through Lee High School in Jacksonville and graduated two years early. He was accepted to UF on scholarship, a fact that made his naval officer father, a bigwig at Mayport, proud. It was the only thing that ever made the bastard proud of his brilliant son. We found each other and became fast friends, hanging out at Witch Hazel's, the best gay bar in G'ville, and exploring our newfound freedom.

I told tell him my dreams of becoming male, and he told me of his to do the reverse. We joked about exchanging genders and shared a very deep relationship, two burgeoning lovers confused by the clash of gender awakening and naivete. It bound us together. Until I was sent to prison.

I think of this now because this boy, perhaps a woman now, was the best hacker ever to wear a white hat. We'd hear about a talented hacker's exploits, and he'd say, "child's play," and show me how to improve the code.

I was never his match at a keyboard, but what he taught me stuck. He loved the challenge of slipping through defenses and browsing around, though he occasionally sought to right a wrong, like the time he noticed a bank was delaying the posting of interest payments to its customers to reap another day or two of interest for the bank. It was only fractions of a penny on each transaction, but if you considered the millions of transactions a day, the theft added up.

He put a bomb in their system. Every time a customer used one of the bank's access terminals—this was before ATMs as we know them today—a message would be printed on the receipt that read, "Ask your friendly banker about your lost interest payments." He then planted a similar bomb in the admin computers of the bank that said "Stop stealing interest payments or the G2 will crash your system."

There was no G2, or more accurately, we were the Gainesville Two, but it sounded cool, like the G8. We laughed our asses off when the bank president put out an official statement saying his computer security team had found an anomaly in their system that was holding up transactions. He proudly announced they'd patched it and that this was just one more way they were serving their customers, whom they valued greatly.

I'd been out of touch with the cyberworld for a very long time, but if I could somehow reconnect with my close friend and ex-lover, he, or she, or they, could bring me up to date and perhaps even help me. My friend had been G1; I was G2. I desperately needed G1's guidance. I had to reach out.

The computer revolution was in full swing, but state organizations like prison systems were always miles behind. They had a wired system and even some wireless capabilities but were woefully behind in security.

When I first plugged into the Raiford system, one thing was clear: there was a firewall between the prison and the outside world but virtually no intranet security. And I was sitting behind the firewall. In other words, I was already sitting inside the vault of the bank I wanted to rob.

I did what any neophyte hacker would do; I downloaded and installed Linux and partitioned a section to run virtually. Next I downloaded and installed Wireshark, a packet grabber; enabled PuTTY; and added some "secret sauce," a term my friend used for small bundles of coding and tools gathered over the years. Then I was ready to go.

When I discovered how primitive the internal security in the prison system was, I stood and did a tribute imitation of my friend. I leapt from my chair and began stomping around my room, shouting, "You stupid shits! Why not just erase your security code and let me grab root? You just handed me the keys to the kingdom, you lamers."

I didn't realize it was two in the morning, and one of the guys from down the hall stormed to my room and banged on the door. "Hey … D … shut the fuck up. I'm trying to sleep over here."

I went to the door. It was Tolly.

I said, "Sorry, Tolly, but these are the dumbest cocksuckers this side of Redmond, Washington. The dumbasses are still using Telnet. Can you believe it?"

Tolly frowned and stomped off, shaking his head. "Christ save us from smart people."

The world was going SSH, but Raiford prison was still Telnet. Telnet was old technology. It meant emails behind the firewall were not encrypted. With Wireshark and PuTTY, I could capture packets from the air and examine them at will. It was unsophisticated, which matched my skills at the time. All I wanted were communication packets from Warden Manakin. Anyone riding back in on his email? Vulnerable.

The other thing I needed was access to the so-called deep and dark web. Both had always existed, but legal bureaucracies can't abide what they can't control, so they immediately confused the two, dubbed both the dark web, and assumed it was full of nasty hackers. If G1 was still active, that's where I'd look.

I downloaded Tor, an onion browser, to get into the deep and dark web without being traced. An onion browser skips IP communications through random and secure servers all over the world to maintain the anonymity of the source computer.

I also needed a shadow bank account, which Maestro helped coordinate. When the time came to help Mr. O, I would need cryptocurrency ready to use in the dark web. That's why I needed help from G1.

I took a leap of faith and used an old 2600 blast com to send a message into the ether. It was a message to G1 from G2. I only hoped G1 was still monitoring the web like the old days and would be intrigued enough to capture it. I sent a call out into deep cyberspace and prayed for an answer. I resurrected an old chat room we'd established in college and placed an encrypted messaged there.

The message read "G-2 to G-1. Alas, poor Bella. So sad he never visited our old haunt."

This was the key to an old Vigenere cipher. It was falsely

attributed to Vigenere. Bellaso, thus "Bella-So" was the real inventor. It was unbreakable because the answer to the riddle had almost as many letters as the message, making it a perfect polyalphabetic cipher. Our "old haunt" was Witch Hazel's, and the hidden message was "Gmail: dsjewlry." One repetitive letter—near perfect. I'd set up a secure email account just for this. I cast the internet packets into cyberspace, bowed to the internet gods, and waited.

The day after Maestro and I woke Mr. O, news affiliates in Miami reported that a small securities firm had been raided and all assets confiscated, including $500,000 in bearer bonds. The state attorney's office in Miami was convinced it was a laundering operation for the Carbonchio family of the Cosa Nostra. The state attorney general praised the local office for their diligent surveillance, which as it turned out, had been going on for two years.

Maestro dropped by my room with a note from Mr. O. He was impressed by the accuracy of my prediction. He'd written, "Minor operation, just as you said. Beautiful work."

Maestro sat down on my small couch, and I asked, "What next? Who's Carbonchio?"

A look of pure evil crossed his face. I swear a nictitating eyelid flickered over his eyes.

"Mr. O said I should fill you in on some things. He wants you to keep doing what you're doing but focus your work. Keep your computer eye on something." He paused and then said, "And he wants to reward you for your good work."

I held up my hands. "Oh, no … having this room and all these toys is reward enough."

Maestro raised his eyebrows and pursed his lips. "Did you forget who you're talking to?"

I smiled sheepishly. "Okay. I won't lie. I've been hoping he'd help me build a little wealth. I might actually get out of here someday."

He nodded. "That's more like it. He's decided to reward you by giving you the amount those assholes found in bearer bonds in that raid."

My eyes went wide. "What? You don't mean … really?"

He chuckled. "Half a mil ain't a bad start. You need to set yourself up a bank account. We got connections to help. The money's gotta stay offshore. You'll be able to get to it, but by then, you'll be on your own to handle it, just like a grownup."

I said, "Please, tell Mr. O how grateful I am."

Maestro said, "You can tell him yourself. He wants a meet once a week or so. He wants you to keep him posted on that model of yours."

Maestro leaned forward and spoke in a conspiratorial tone, a tone that made me listen very closely. "Carbonchio are Mr. O's partners. In English, the word means carbuncle; in the old language, it means a red stone, what we call a bloodstone. The group took an oath to work together to protect the organization. There are four members of Carbonchio including Mr. O. They wear a ring with a bloodstone. You've seen Mr. O's."

"Oh, yeah. I saw you kiss that ring, like the movie."

"Jesus, that fucking movie. It's close, I guess. A sign of respect. They're capos, but the big boss, the *capo di tutti*, is in Phillie. Mr. O's in here as a favor to him. One of the Carbonchio fucked up big time, but he's a first cousin of the boss in Phillie. Like that movie you love so much, he's what you call a made man. This is one of the traditions Mr. O would like to see changed. Too many idiots get made just because they're related to someone. As a first cousin, the man who fucked up is higher up the chain. Mr. O agreed to cover for him and do the time. The boss is grateful. He's why we got this life here. But something's gone wrong. Mr. O doesn't think the boss in Phillie is part of it, but the first cousin? He suspects he's trying to move the other three out. He wants to follow his cousin as *capo* so bad he can taste it. He'll sacrifice anybody to get what he wants. The soldiers hate the bastard."

He took a deep breath. "Mr. O won't say it, but I will. He's an idiot named Marco Cipolla. If a rock is dumb, this asshole's a fucking quarry. He's got bowling balls for nuts and a lentil for a brain. Goes after turf even if it gets his own men killed. It's why they hate him, but they're right to fear him. He's too well connected for anybody to take him out."

I believe it was at that moment that I realized for the first time how deep into this strange quasi-movie world I'd wandered. I would be stalking people who owned senators and had prison blocks converted to country clubs. It made me feel like one of those tiny suckerfish who cleaned shit off sharks while they went about their shark business of eating things.

I asked, "So, what should I do?"

"Not much right now. Unless you can figure out how to make Mr. O look completely innocent of any meddling while we fuck this guy up the ass."

I stood up and threw my arms out. "I can do that. That's what I've been trying to tell you. I can't kill anybody, but damn it, right now Mr. O needs to let my technological world into the fight. I don't know which end of a gun the bullet comes out of, and frankly, I don't want to know. But you need to listen to me."

Maestro stared hard at me as I sat back down. Finally, he said, "Listen. This ain't no fucking around. If that man thinks Mr. O is manipulating things from in here, they'll get him paroled just to kill him. We can't see everything out there."

I said, "Mr. O wants updates from me. That'll be my first thing. We can move slow. If he wants, we can take years to get this done. My sentence is fucking forever. But I will get out someday. I'd like to be wealthy enough to spend my elder years in something approaching luxury. That means I want Mr. O to win both because I respect him and it helps my chances."

Maestro shot me that frightening frown-smile. "You finally get it. Mr. O can't force this. You need to understand the other side. This cell block was the old prison administration office, already in good shape. But it was renovated over two years before we got here. That's how many strings the man in Phillie can pull. Mr. O wasn't dragged here in handcuffs. He checked in like it was a hotel. He wants to check out again without worrying he'll get popped the minute he sets foot back in Miami or Tampa."

He looked down at his hands. "For me, in here or out there? It's all the same. They let me come in easy because I had a good military record. Gave me the lightest tap possible. But I came in to protect my boss. Once we were here, Mr. O had his lawyers apply for early parole to test the waters. It was killed without a review. That was his first hint something was wrong."

He stood to leave. "When you talk to him, go slow." He pointed at my computer. "You play that thing like a piano, and you're good at it. But this ain't no commercial jingle we're playing here; it's fucking Puccini."

He opened the door, and I said, "You were in the military?"

He flashed a small grin. "I done a lot of things. Not all of them bad. I was a hell of a soldier. That's good for you." His grin disappeared. "Shit's blowing our way, D. *Lo sento nel vento*. I smell it in the wind."

The next day, Maestro arranged an account for me in the Caicos. I told him I might want to buy some cryptocurrency. He asked what that was. I explained. He laughed. Cosa Nostra Italians at heart are as conservative as the Catholic Church. Telling Maestro I wanted to purchase a disruptive currency was tantamount to telling him I wanted to attend a satanic church. I argued from every angle, but what turned the tide was my ability to set Mr. O's enemies up in a way they couldn't understand and therefore couldn't avoid; illegal services on the dark web could not be purchased any other way.

After an hour of coaxing, he relinquished. "Okay, for Christ's sake. Buy it. But the minute this is over, you get rid of that shit, you hear?"

I smiled. "Just wait. You might not want to get rid of it."

Ultimately, I was as prepared as I could be without guidance from G1. Grabbing Warden Manakin by the low-hanging fruit was going to be a cakewalk. Exploiting the dark web was far subtler. But it was my endgame, and I was counting on the opposition to have their own cyberwarriors. I'd sensed someone probing my machine. It began to dawn on me that I might not be the only person crawling around the prison's computer network. Where was G1?

The journal slipped down onto my lap. My prediction had, in fact, been an underestimation of the trouble that would plague me and the people I loved. Lake Monroe sparkled in the sun and hyacinths sloshed rhythmically against the seawall at my feet as my eyes scanned the distant shoreline miles away.

I shifted from the mesmerizing memories in the journal to the hypnotic scene on Lake Monroe. Boats seemed to creep slowly over distant waters as the wide, dark river swept slowly on its inexorable path northward to the ocean. The relativity of distances slowed everything. Boats on the water and memories in time. Hatreds dulled; love as well. Both were objectified by distance, observable. And like a gemstone, flaws were smoothed by the distance.

I was nearly ready to meet him. Shel the charmer. Shel the fixer. Shel was back in town. I'd left a message for him. He still lived part-time in the house a few blocks down Oak Avenue from the Hatfield Mansion.

I knew he would respond. *Lo sento nel vento.*

# CHAPTER 14

A swath of white sand merging with an azure sea as calm as cellophane met Summer on her first full day in Destin. The gentle warmth of the brilliant midmorning sun and chattering gulls flittering against a pristine cobalt sky were improving her spirits, dulling the horrors from the cab of the semi. They'd arrived the prior afternoon under a morose gray drizzle, but a front swept through overnight, and the day broke clear and bright as the seasonal storm dragged a blanket of dry air behind it.

After her rescue, she had wept steadily for the two days they remained in New Orleans and had experienced spontaneous bouts of sobbing until that morning. Her captors had been so certain that Leitner would walk blindly into a trap, they'd spoken openly of how they'd kill them both once they got the money. That threat was gone, yet she was still trapped. The light of her own existence was diminishing under Leitner's shadow. He no longer considered her a wife and partner. She was a property to be held at all costs. Her gratitude was genuine but so were her doubts regarding his motive for saving her.

Now, days later and miles away, she allowed herself to reflect on the details of the two days and one night she'd spent with two lowlife truckers. Some of it might have been amusing had she known she'd survive it. The worst moments came when they parked overnight at an east Texas truck stop and the two went at her simultaneously.

They had no knowledge of female anatomy, and that made her fear that in their ignorance they'd inadvertently damage her. They were obsessed with anal sex and wanted little to do with her vagina except to look at it to get an erection. She'd kept them at bay on several occasions by telling them they were just too big for her and she needed a rest. It was an ego-stroking game she'd played most of her life.

She'd felt like some primeval prey as they pawed and groped her in the oil-stench haze of the cab like two animals ripping at her body one minute and attempting to engage in fetid-breath seduction the next. Some of their machinations seemed spawned in some barbarously licentious world she'd never heard of much less experienced. At one point, Farley was trying to maintain his erection by kneading his penis, and Pierre said, "Hey, Farley, while you're at it, give me a tug or two; I'm having trouble too." She couldn't think about it without a cringing grin. It had kept them off her for a good half hour. They were helping each other get an erection even as they talked incessantly about killing queers.

*Get over it and get on with it*, she kept telling herself. *You have things to do.*

She suffered only one setback when she went to the hotel pool alone and some slimeball ogled her relentlessly before hitting on her, wearing nothing but one of those tiny Speedos. The sight of his pitiful erection beneath the skimpy suit froze her blood, and she almost vomited on his leathery paunch. Leitner had appeared from nowhere. He told her to go to the beach and wait for him. He had a few words with Speedo man, and she never saw the guy again. She didn't know what happened to him, but she had little doubt that Leitner had something to do with it. She just hoped they didn't find Speedo man washed up on the beach with a bullet in his head.

She improved steadily at the shore, and on the fifth night she entered Leitner's bedroom and crawled in next to him. She needed to feel the warmth of another human. It was a watershed for her rehabilitation, but she felt Leitner had in some way become a distant memory even as she lay beside him. What she felt was irrelevant; she needed to regain his trust.

It was, in a way, her fault. She'd asked the two idiot truckers for help. Leitner had pistol-whipped a man half to death in a desert parking lot for staring at her breasts. At that moment, she had decided she could make her own way. Leitner was too volatile to control. It was possible the two idiots had followed them after she finally pulled Leitner off the man and got him in the car.

Leitner had no idea she'd spoken to them while he was beating a man senseless. Then, when Leitner began berating her out of some bizarre possessiveness, accusing her of having sex that never happened, she had acted on impulse and run to them when they pulled over as she was backpedaling with her thumb out. It had backfired. While Farley was holding a shotgun on Leitner, the idiot Pierre pulled a knife and forced her into the cab. She'd been afraid Leitner would think she got in the cab voluntarily. Much of her initial fear had been that he'd just let them take her. She'd felt trapped by her simultaneous hatred of Leitner's vicious volatility and her dependence on it for salvation. She'd come to understand what was called battered wife syndrome. She could see how it might seem easier for a woman to give up her sense of self and allow a man to dominate her as if she were an animal. But that was not who she was. She would not give up. These few days at the beach had been perfect. There was a sense of freedom that helped her climb out of a deep well of depression.

She was wistful when, after several days in Destin, Leitner said they must leave. But she was almost herself again and looked forward to moving on. Forward was the only direction that mattered.

The night Summer slipped into bed with Leitner, she knew the worst was over.

"I can't yet. I hope it's okay. I promise I'll get better," she said.

"It's okay, kiddo. Let's just crank the AC down and keep each other warm."

Leitner had granted her an extra two and half days in Destin, and afterward she dutifully climbed into their new car, one Leitner had bought in Biloxi, Mississippi. He'd paid cash for a Honda CRV. She knew he was just playing it safe. Still, a Honda was not his style. Something was gnawing at him too.

He opened the sunroof as the bellman loaded Summer's luggage into the back, and once she'd settled in, Leitner aimed the CRV for eastbound I-10. They could make the drive to his uncle's in about eight or nine hours, but Leitner said he wanted to arrive fresh.

"How'd you like to stop for a night at one last special place?"

Summer asked, "Why are we stopping again? I mean, it's fine with me, but I thought you were in a hurry now."

Leitner sighed. "I don't know. Guess I'm enjoying this life on the road. And I'd kind of like you to see this little fishing village. We have to drive right past it."

"Where is it?"

"A little island on the Gulf Coast called Cedar Key. I stayed there once on a lark. Somebody told me about it, and I was headed north anyway. It's as old Florida as it gets; even cell phones don't have good reception. I can book us in a little place out on Dock Street overlooking the Gulf. This little café called Tony's has the best clam chowder anywhere."

Summer smiled, and Leitner said, "The town motto is 'Cedar Key: A quaint drinking village with a fishing problem.'"

Summer laughed; she realized it might be her first laughter since her rescue. "Sounds like my kind of place."

It struck her that Leitner was not just going out of his way to please her; he was stalling. For some reason, he was nervous about getting to his uncle's. She didn't know which she preferred, overconfident Leitner treating her like a bimbo or a nervous Leitner becoming attached to her. Neither of those versions appealed to her, but she had no other choice than to ride out the storm and hope for the best.

I edged the blue Imperial gingerly to the curb and used the open door for leverage to raise my aging bones to a standing position on the grass behind Sharon's bench. I'd awakened with back and leg stiffness and blamed it on the need to order a new bed. I'd had my eye on a top-of-the-line, king-size Tempur-Pedic Cloud with an adjustable base—an expensive bed that allowed me to hide behind my fortune when a bed wasn't the real problem; not today. I limped the few feet to Sharon's bench and dropped onto the curved seat. I wasn't sleeping well, because I was on the verge of meeting the man who sent me to prison.

I was coming to the realization that even if Shel told me what I wanted to know, there was no place for me in this society. I was still struggling with the inanity of the culture I'd been thrust into. The only people I felt comfortable around were the poor families I saw at the lake each afternoon, people like Big Tom and his buxom wife, Charise, and their children. This lake that was a river was becoming the only place that afforded me a moment's peace. I feared I was becoming more emotionally fragile by the day. Forces were converging.

The afternoon was hot, but a violent thunderstorm had raged for an hour before moving through and cooled the air twenty degrees. That would last an hour or two, until the sun baked the moist earth into a sauna. I'd waited out the storm at home before leaving for the lake. A cool, steady breeze from Lake Monroe should keep the air tolerable for the couple of hours until sunset. I was reaching the final journal entries and dreaded the heartbreak it would renew. Heartbreak I had caused with a pitiful cocktail of hubris and naivete with a hefty dash of bitterness.

I'd heard from Shel Richardson. We had a very brief email exchange in which his responses were terse and devoid of familiarity. He would meet me in two days. I'd suggested the café where I found harbor during the heat or rain. He knew it and agreed. I supposed I expected nothing more than to be treated as the stranger I'd become.

After our communication, I'd contacted Maestro. I hadn't seen him since my release, but he always promised he'd come to my little town when the time was right. I didn't have a strategy. I simply told him where and when I'd be meeting Shel. Maestro was ever the ghost. You don't ask a ghost to keep a precise schedule, and I prayed Maestro wouldn't let me down.

For some reason I had begun to call my journal the *Book of Ralph*, a play on the *Book of Kells* or a *Book of Hours*. At first I couldn't understand why such abstruse references kept leaping to mind. I came to realize it was because I was still living inside my own head as a means to avoid confronting the world outside prison. I was persistently overwhelmed by a profound sense of displacement. I knew the statistics; almost half of released inmates were back in prison within five years. Some of them because they simply couldn't handle a world that had passed them by and committed some petty crime to get back in.

If Shel was honest with me, there'd be much pain to bear. It would only exacerbate how disconnected I'd become from this world after prison. That morning, I had my first real encounter with the extent of this displacement.

I rarely kept up with current affairs, but that morning I'd gone on my newly installed internet and was immediately overwhelmed by a flood of random information. One story piqued my interest. It was a series of stories and interviews about the world of the modern transgender. I immediately clicked on it, hoping to reconnect with others like me. One story, an exchange between a reporter and a recent transgender, was devastating on levels I didn't know existed. This woman who wished to be referred to by the neutral pronoun, Ze, a person with whom I should have immediately empathized, was complaining about being "deadnamed." I had no idea what that meant until I realized it was now inappropriate for "straights" to use her old, discarded male name. For some reason, I broke into a sobbing fit akin to the one I had when my mother blamed me for all my father's travails. What universe had I entered where a transgender could openly complain about being referred to by a previous name? I thought of the response I would have gotten had I held up a hand to those fucking Aryans and said, "Hold on, fellows. You can stick your rancid cocks up my ass and beat the shit out of me if I bite your cock when you shove it down my throat, but you shall not call me by my previous female name." That story, mingled with my upcoming meeting with Shel Richardson, made me wish to climb into my new soaking tub and open my veins. It wasn't that I begrudged transgenders everywhere the right to create these new ground rules. It was an abiding fear that I would never be able to relate to or be accepted by my own people. I felt like a character in a movie I saw in prison where a white woman is captured by "Indians" in the Old West and, after years living among them, was reviled by her own kind.

I fled immediately to Sharon's bench, where I flipped to the journal page I'd marked the day before. My confidence was badly shaken. I had to maintain my focus. Call me Margarite, Stuart, D, or cunt. I had to stay on task. I began to read.

For most of the next year, I tracked the activities of Carbonchio, and each week or so, I met with Mr. O to update him until he began to battle some health issues, at which point I used Maestro as a conduit. We watched as Marco Cipolla, with Mr. O out of the way, gradually boxed out the remaining two men with the bloodstone rings. It was obvious what was happening, and we concluded that the cops didn't know anything or, more probably, were being paid to turn a blind eye. And the feds seemed to look everywhere but the right places. There must be a trail of bread crumbs. It was difficult to know where to start, so I simply followed every trail I could find.

It was clear that Marco "the Onion" had thrown his lot in with Bratva, but as I continued to analyze data, I concluded that the whole operational structure was more complicated than even Mr. O had predicted. Marco may have been as dumb as a rock, but someone he was working with in Bratva wasn't. Some of their machinations were insidiously clever.

Worse still, someone was quietly tracking my movements in cyberspace. I realized how stupid I'd been. I should have taken greater care to cover my tracks. I trapped a couple of hacking probes at the prison firewall and then at my server.

Someone was probing my system, but there were no clear signs of penetration. I'd done a good job of masking it, but a top-notch hacker would surely make more devious efforts. By capturing a few key internet packets, I could tell that the same source was keeping tabs on prison communications and passing it on somewhere I couldn't follow.

Through a sheer fluke, I found out the focus of these communications. Warden Robert Manakin. The reason I wasn't being probed harder was because they had Manakin keeping tabs on Mr. O; he was their focus. I discovered this at the same time I began monitoring Warden Manakin's emails. I first captured his email username and password using Wire Shark and was gathering the damaging intel I needed to help Marilyn. I also discovered, too late, that the hacker dancing around in the prison system was better than I thought possible. I felt I could duel with him but only if I had greatly upgraded tools.

For this, I needed help.

It's a limit of a journal that I'm bound to linear descriptions of events that occur simultaneously. So, I must be arbitrary in the order of things. I must follow this next path and then retrace my steps and head down another. It's a proverbial good news–bad news tale.

First, the good news.

Out of the blue of cyberspace, and to my great surprise and pleasure, I received my first email at dsjewlry.com. It was an encrypted execute file with a three-word message: "Install on VM." It had to be G1.

I hurriedly installed the code. I forgot that G1 never used standard encryption for anything. If you wanted to talk to G1, you used G1's secret sauce. If it was G1, I knew what would come next. Proof of identity. I used the code to encrypt all emails to and from dsjewlry.com. There would be an e-bomb in the code. If anyone intercepted the packets and tried to decrypt, G1's bomb would blow up their motherboard. I was giddy with relief. The cavalry had arrived.

I sent a single word in response: "Done."

Two hours later, an email came in: "The dream?"

I responded: "Become the man my father wasn't. Is your dream complete?"

Ignoring the question, the next transmission said: "Favorite city, region, town, and lodging."

"Oh shit," I said aloud.

It had been years since I'd spoken to G1. We had an exchange via encrypted email when I was healing in Italy after my operations. The city and town were easy. I typed in Rome and Florence. Some consider Florence a city, but it's walkable in its entirety, so I always considered it a large town. I had a little trouble with the region, but then I remembered the context. G-1 and I had dreamed of living abroad. At the time I'd become enamored with a beautiful stretch of the Italian coast. I typed the Comune del Levanto. This area included the five stunning villages known as Cinque Terre, back then undiscovered, as well as the beautiful town of Levanto and a little-known beach community, Bonassola. But I sat wracking my brain for the name of my favorite place to stay. There were simply too many to mention, but I had apparently chosen a favorite.

Suddenly, I grinned. *Stupid shit. How could you forget?* After World War II an Italian family had purchased a dilapidated farmhouse with many dependencies, including large stables. They'd meticulously restored every aspect, managing to maintain every ancient architectural detail while modernizing the infrastructure. It had become a riding academy and thus qualified as an *Agriturismo* location. I literally stumbled on it while walking through a tunnel of Etruscan walls just outside the city gates of Viterbo. The place was magical, and the family had revealed to me for the first time how bizarre my own family life had been. As it came to me, I thought, *I must get in touch with them. I must tell them how much they meant to me.* I still harbored a dream of having a place in Italy. It sent a sudden shiver of joy through me when I thought, *I can do that. I will do that.*

I typed, "Podere dell' Arco. Now, for God's sake, talk to me."

Seconds later the response came back: "I did it. I had the operations and married a wonderful man. But I'm afraid I stole your dream. I always thought I'd settle in France, but we live high above the beautiful village of Monterosso al Mare in Cinque Terre. I cannot thank you enough for telling me about this part of your beloved Italy. He's a lovely Italian. We live a dream you helped me build."

I almost wept for joy. "I am so jealous. I'm going to come there right now and slap your bitch face. What is your pronoun of choice?"

"LOL. But we know you can't. I heard about your welcome back to that cultural wasteland we call America. Sorry I never tried to contact you. I couldn't imagine you'd have a computer. Are you out now? If so, please come join me in the land of *dolce far niente*. Oh, and 'she' must do. I'm working up the courage to tell him everything. It's not as devious as it sounds. He's from an old Catholic family, nobility, which means more to them than it does to me. He loves me enough it wouldn't matter. But he has this *Dona* mother who lives in the past."

I took the plunge: "He'll understand. But, no, I'm afraid I'm not yet free. And I suppose you can guess what I'm going to ask?"

"Just tell me what you need. The Italian bandwidth is limited. Italy is wonderful, but as you know, we must take the bad with the good. Great food, great wine, great lifestyle, but technology? *Domani*. However, I can still provide you with the tools to become invincible. I'm still G1."

G1 sent me an encrypted JPEG of her sitting at a café overlooking the marina in Monterosso. She was gorgeous, ageless in a white dress, broad-brimmed hat, and sunglasses, with a handsome middle-aged man with a dark moustache and light suit next to her. The cliff-hanging town of Monterosso rose in its magnificence behind them, aged buildings in ochre, sienna, and red and small fishing boats bobbing in a calm marina in the foreground. That beautiful photograph overwhelmed my efforts to hold back tears of joy, tears of envy, and tears of loss and reconnection with a beloved friend and confidant. I sobbed as I typed, and for the next three hours, G1 and I talked, laughed, and planned.

We agreed never to use names just in case, so the Gainesville 2 was resurrected like the Phoenix. Without G1's help, some young hackers might have sent me to the cybergraveyard. But not with G1 giving me all the armor I needed. Should an enemy sneak up behind me … well, would you like butter with that toast?

I looked up from the journal and smiled. The temptation to skip ahead and read more about G1 was overwhelming, but time was running out. I had only one more full day before meeting Shel.

I forced myself to read on. Now for the bad news.

I penetrated Warden Manakin's email account and captured his username and password, but I failed to consider the obvious; if I knew state agencies were woefully behind on technology, so would anyone watching over Manakin. How stupid could I be?

I began grabbing all his emails. It took little time for his boundless ego to go on display. Some people are so certain of their invincibility that they can't see the world from any other perspective. My father was such a man. Robert Manakin was another pure-bred egomaniac and classic authoritarian misogynist. In retrospect, I should have paused to consider why these emails were so easy to find. Why would anyone let this egomaniac off his leash?

I uncovered reams of self-promoting, boot-licking emails to his superiors on one hand and unabashed efforts at brute-force seduction on the other. Emails to state senators were full of hyperbolic fawning. But emails to the women he targeted were demeaning and demanding. He was of the primitive school of thought that if you treated a woman with respect, it was a sign of weakness. It was depressing how many women fell for it. He wielded his authority as if he were the only child with a piñata stick, and if he swung it wildly in all directions, not caring who or what he broke, he'd eventually get the candy.

I captured emails with incontrovertible evidence of Manakin's infidelities. Why they were so indiscrete was beyond me, but Manakin was only the tip of a filthy iceberg of misuse throughout state offices. I back-traced emails from Manakin to other high-ranking officials and found no abuse of state-owned internet privileges were too depraved. I found abuses ranging from the use of state funds to register for porn sites to trading in kiddy porn. One legislative staffer was running a small prostitution ring using a secretarial pool in his office. And I was the one in prison. I tried to tell myself there were thousands of honest state workers, but it was a rude awakening. I had no time to try to right those wrongs; I had other work to do.

I selected an email thread between the warden and a female Republican Party hotshot with whom he shared a bed. The emails portrayed two narcissists feeding off each other. It was so blatantly morally flawed, I found myself not caring if their dance of mutual extortion ruined her along with him.

As I was capturing the last of a thirty-email thread, something disrupted the exchange. I chalked it up to a server failure in my VPN routing. I should have been suspicious, but my sudden immersion in cyberspace had taken a toll. I was suffering time compression. It happens to inmates with long sentences, but I was in double jeopardy. I fell victim to a phenomenon called "time shifting" with the packaging, repackaging, and reordering of cybertime. I was in a house of mirrors with a different clock on each wall, spiraling downward, and the arrow of time was spiraling with me.

I had the evidence Marilyn needed, and I had to get it to her. I wrote a brief note: "Finally finished Ulysses. Would like to return it. Really loved the scene on page 125. When may I drop it by?" I tucked a printout of the damning email string into page 125 and asked Maestro if he'd drop the note by the library.

He was not pleased. "What's this about?"

I owned up. "The warden's a sex maniac and a crook. I have proof. Please. She just wants to keep him off her until she can get away."

He gave me that frown from Malebolge. "And this is our business how?"

I trusted Maestro with my life; now I had to trust him with Marilyn's.

I blurted it all out at once. "She's gay, Maestro. She abhors that bastard, and I'm just trying to help her. Read these emails for yourself."

Maestro was genuinely stunned. "Wait. Gay? You mean she likes women?"

I nodded. "You and she like the exact same thing."

He said, "Christ, what a waste."

I glared at him, and he put his hands up. "Don't look at me

that way. She's a knockout, and it's a loss to men everywhere. If that's what you call insensitive, tough shit."

I smiled begrudgingly. "I get it, okay? But will you please drop off my note at the library? I'm begging you."

He blew out a long breath. "Let me have it. But this is it, D. No more. How many times I gotta tell you, if you keep this shit up, it'll bite you both in the ass."

I nodded. "Maestro, you're honest to god the savviest person I know, and I know you're right. But please let me help her this one last time. I'll hand her the book and leave. I swear."

His eyes narrowed as he studied my face. He could tell I was emotionally strung out; he also knew I wasn't lying to him. I had no further plans to interfere with the Manakins. Neither did I intend to make any effort to see Marilyn again.

The following morning, I received a response: "Please drop the book by this afternoon at four o'clock." I was elated. I could hand her salvation while gazing one last time at that precious face. That day the hours refused to pass. Clocks froze on the walls as the axons in my nervous system increased the frequency of their vibrations until the slightest stimulus might cause them to fly apart like a million broken violin strings.

Finally, at three thirty, I tried to stroll nonchalantly out of the block. Holt's replacement, a man named Joe Willard, waved me out. Book tucked under my arm, I headed across the yard. It was threatening rain, and I had no umbrella, so I hurried. Just as bullet-sized drops began to hit the sidewalk and hiss across the fields, I reached the side entrance, surprised that no one was at the security point. This took me through the lower work areas, and the random, familiar noises sent chills up my spine. I made my way down once familiar corridors, now distant and strange.

At four o'clock sharp, I slipped into the library and headed for the circulation desk. I was relieved there was no one around to threaten our privacy. I expected Marilyn to wait in the small office until I rang the bell, but as I approached the desk, I heard someone behind me. I turned just as two huge guards locked the doors.

At the same moment, a voice I recognized came from the shelves. "Right on time, Inmate Purloin." My blood turned to ice.

I watched as Warden Robert Manakin stepped from between the shelves. I could only stare wide-eyed, mouth working like a stunned guppy as a sense of foreboding washed over me.

The warden pointed at the copy of *Ulysses* under my arm. "I believe you have a message for my wife. Page 125, isn't it?"

Manakin's two Praetorians moved behind me, and one of them swung a wrecking ball into my right kidney. Fear was replaced with excruciating pain, which dropped me to my knees. *Ulysses* slid from my arm and its pages splashed onto the floor. The second guard stooped to snatch it up, closed it, and handed it to the warden.

The guards dragged me through the shelves into the cramped office. My head slumped as the pain gripped me. I'd be pissing blood for a week. They dumped me roughly onto the lone chair. I tried to twist sideways and rub my back where the blow had landed, but one of them held me in place by gripping my shoulders with the two vises he used for hands. Robert Manakin rifled through Joyce's masterpiece until he retrieved the loose page of emails inserted at page 125. Then he tossed the book casually aside. The world's greatest novel ricocheted off the low shelf and flapped to the floor like a dying butterfly.

"What's this?" His voice was infuriatingly calm. He scanned the page in silence and then crumpled it and tucked it into his pocket before advancing toward me across the small space. He turned to the two guards. "Could I have a couple of minutes alone with the inmate, gentlemen? Just wait for me out front."

I watched him intently as the two guards left.

"So, I guess I get another beating now?" I was preparing myself for what was certain to follow.

He knelt beside my chair and put an arm over my shoulders.

His voice was calm, approaching a sincerity I could never feign as well. "Now, why would I do that? I don't abuse the unfortunates in my charge. I just thought I'd meet with you and share some terrible news about someone we both care about."

The sense of foreboding intensified, and I clenched my teeth and squeezed my eyes shut against the tears burning my eyelids. What had I done?

"I'm afraid"—his dark eyes bore into the side of my head—"it's my sad duty to inform you that my lovely wife, Marilyn, has had a sudden nervous breakdown. I was forced to have her committed to the mental hospital at Chattahoochee. According to the director there, her prognosis is quite good, but she may be in treatment for quite some time."

He stood and looked down at me. "Now, I know she took you under her wing as a kind of salvation project. It's too bad you'll not be able to benefit further from her kindness. I know how much she means to you. So, here you and I are at a crossroads. Two people bound together by the fate of another."

He reached down and cupped my chin in his powerful hand. I forgot he was a star athlete, and I could feel the strength in him. The phrase "badly crushed mandible" leapt to mind. Of course, the pressure was insufficient to leave marks. I'd grossly underestimated this man. He showed no anger and was in complete control. His cool-headedness trumped my turmoil. He'd beaten me without breaking a sweat. I was a wretched failure.

He continued, "I believe the best course of action for the two of us is to quietly wait for our mutual friend to get better. Her prognosis may be good, but you never know when a delicate flower might take a bad turn. With that in mind, I think it best if you stay over in your block and pray for her. You do the work assigned to you and leave the rest of the prison to me."

He let go of my chin. "Don't you think that's an excellent plan, Inmate Purloin?"

Rage. Frustration. Worry for Marilyn. He had me, and he knew it.

"Yes," I managed. "That sounds like the best plan."

"Now get out." He turned to leave but paused. "Oh, by the way. There's no place in this prison for you to hide. You'd best keep that in mind every second of your stay." He turned and strode out as his Praetorian guard fell in behind him.

Where in hell did that come from? No place to hide?

I sat alone in the chair where Marylin had opened herself to me. There was still the silhouette of a stain on the cloth where our fluids had mixed. I reached down and touched that fading stain, fighting the tears to no avail. In moments I had again become nothing more than inmate 123047. I'd failed the one person I thought I could help. Someone I cared for immensely. I heard the library staff returning. I stood and walked away.

I paused at the side exit as the rain pounded the earth between me and Block E. I could see the sky getting lighter as the rain moved through. As I stood there, I kept cycling back to that last statement by fucking Robert Manakin. In that moment, I realized how good the other hacker was.

No place to hide. That's what he meant. I thought he had only probed my machine when it was clear he had silently penetrated it without my knowledge and knew everything I was up to. There was no other explanation. I had to isolate my machine. But there had been nothing about my meeting with Marilyn on my computer. That meant the note from Marilyn had not been from her at all. He had eyes everywhere. My note asking to return the book had never made it to her; she was gone by then.

I had to stop wallowing in self-pity. I'd gotten her into this, and I had to try to get her out. If only I had a clue how.

I watched the pounding Florida rain pass as quickly as it had come, and it let up enough for me to push through the exit door for the interminable walk back to my room. The gray sky hovered just above the distant trees, and the remnants of the storm left a light but steady drizzle as I started back across the yard, each step sloshing in sidewalk puddles. I was glad I'd not brought an umbrella. I was already a wet, teary mess, so the rain felt like a warm, cleansing balm. I glanced over at the double fence topped with coils of concertina. I could see one of the great Alsatians that patrolled the no-man's-land between the double fences hunkered in his doghouse, peering out at me as I slunk by. A wet dog in a wet doghouse. Perfect reflection of a wet inmate, except the dog had a clear purpose. Mine seemed lost. Marilyn would have been better off ... I couldn't finish that thought without dropping dead from unmitigated grief.

Marilyn had erected a psychosocial wall to prevent herself from confronting an element of self-awareness her culture considered abhorrent. I'd helped her break through it, and her pig-fucker husband had used it to have her committed. I knew that Marilyn's diagnosis would be ironclad. There'd be a psychotherapist for sale who'd see to it, even if it meant evoking psychobabble some therapists considered medieval.

I knew how it would go. I'd had friends committed by misguided parents, friends swallowed up by a system that had no place for us. They'd have a field day with Marilyn. Her aloofness would be classified as social anxiety disorder, her efforts to deflect a charge of mental illness, anosognosia resulting from gender dysphoria and ego-dystonic homosexuality, and blah, blah, I'm the doctor, you're the patient, now take your Thorazine.

I was disgusted by the pustulant inversion I'd enabled. I'm a murderer who never killed anyone. But now I had snuffed out the torch of this ethereal goddess who once spread light in this horrific place. I loathed myself. And, yes, I felt sorry for myself.

My one consolation, if you could call it that, was when I got back to my room and booted my system, there was a message from G1 sitting in our chat room. Bless her for contacting me again so soon. She had set up a hidden chat room in the deep web with

NordVPN, her own onion browser, a sinkhole for even the best hackers. We could speak without fear of detection. I still needed to warn her about the skills of the hacker who'd penetrated my machine.

Her message read: "Are you okay? I saw some of it."

I quickly replied: "What do you mean you saw it?"

"I took over the camera system. Saw you go in the library. Watched a thug punch you, but I lost you. Cameras don't go everywhere."

I was frantic with hope. "You're a fucking genius. Always have been. I've been hacked. I thought it was a lamer, but it must be someone with mad skills. Watching everything I did."

"Not anymore."

"Explain."

"He's good, but they're never as good as they think. It's actually a team working out of the Ukraine."

"Can you blind them so I can work?"

"G2, listen carefully. I don't have the power I need to help from here. As I said, Italy is glorious, but part of the charm is precisely because they're old-fashioned. I sent the Ukrainian team off chasing a red herring, but eventually they'll catch on. I'm going to give you all the tools you need to fight back, and I'll send instructions for whatever you need, but you'll have to take the lead."

"I fucked up. Someone nice is in trouble because of me."

"Then recover. You've never been a quitter."

"My friend has been sent to the Florida State Mental Hospital."

"Sit tight. I'm sending some vicious code. I've stayed up to date, just can't play live. I can give advice, but it's up to you. Once you have the tools, damn it, get on with it."

My mood was improving. Suddenly I remembered I wasn't just a pathetic loser with no skills. "Thanks, G1. Can't tell you how much I need you right now."

"I've always been here. What do you need right now?"

"Desperate for help with cryptocurrency."

"Will send instructions on Bitcoin. It's brand new. Dicey but the cryptoworld is screaming for a disruptive currency. It will ride up."

"Bless you. I wish I'd waited for you before trying to engage."

"I'm sorry I can't fly wing. But you can't right a wrong by sitting on your hands. I'll get you the tools; you build the empire."

I wanted to wreck Robert Manakin so bad, I could taste acid in my throat. But it had to be done carefully, and it couldn't be traced back to Mr. O. I had a plan. A good one now that I knew G1 would provide the tools.

I needed Mr. O to turn me loose. If I was going to help Marilyn, I had to focus my attention on Carbonchia. Help Mr. O, and I could also find a path to Manakin. I had an email I'd planned to show Mr. O when we met next. I was certain his anger would give me the freedom I needed to attack his enemies. It was damning.

# CHAPTER 15

*Why had I come here?* I pulled forward on the steering wheel and looked up at the entirety of the massive structure. Fear and safety rarely comingled, yet something about this gigantic plank building rising out of the dust and detritus of a lost civilization exuded a specter of fear mixed with nostalgia for a bygone era.

I scanned the exterior of the abandoned edifice for signs of life. My grandfather said even the saddest houses have light shining beneath the door. In prison, that wasn't true. Alone in an iso cell, I stared unblinking at light under doors, waiting for the shadows of moving feet, the sound of a key in a lock. Something about this place made me think of that. Even in the sunshine, there was something frightening but eerily familiar here. It wrapped around my spine like a scorpion poised to sting, something moving in the depths of a vast hollow interior. I came here because Alphonse had bade me to come. Alphonse would never knowingly lead me to harm.

Tomorrow I would meet Sheldon Richardson at the café. My life was poised for a story only he could tell, a painful story of betrayal and retribution attached to Sharon's death. The circumstances surrounding her murder were shrouded in a mist of possibilities, a conundrum more obfuscated than revealed by logic.

Today I'd finally shored up the courage to visit the abandoned icehouse. That was what Alphonse had tried to tell me. "There is a place with ice to stay cold." Alphonse did not have a subtle mind. A place with ice was an icehouse. In the run-down black neighborhood of Goldsboro was this abandoned icehouse. In the era before refrigeration, it had provided great blocks of ice for train cars and other commercial uses as well as residential iceboxes. When I was young, we still called a refrigerator an icebox.

Monk had owned this building of rough cypress planks in an out-of-the-way cul-de-sac. Once electric refrigerators became widespread, he converted it to a storage warehouse and relied on the pool hall for income. After Monk's disappearance, it had fallen into disrepair, a useless relic lost in the shadows of the past.

*Why did Alphonse want me to come here? What am I to find?* I blew out a long breath and gathered the courage to step out of the car and climb the rickety steps onto a loading dock. It took only a few more steps to reach a front door that once opened into an office. The door looked functional, but there was no sign of life inside.

I walked carefully along the loading dock, avoiding loose planks, peering through gaps in the boarded windows, listening intently. There was only the steady summer drone of cicadas from high in ancient kudzu-draped trees and the metallic popping and creaking of the tin roof high overhead as it expanded in the afternoon sun. I could hear a faint tittering of pigeons rattling their wings, their mournful cooing echoed deep in interior rafters. Another sign of abandonment.

At the end of the loading dock, I turned and crept back to the front door, carefully avoiding the odd rusty nailhead and warped plank. The sun beat down on my shoulders like a hot blanket, making my body heavier with each step. I felt a sudden drowsiness as if the heat were pressing on my eyelids.

I paused and leaned close to the plywood nailed over what had once been a half-paned door, listening intently as I reached out a tentative hand to the knob. It was hot to the touch as I twisted it in both directions. Locked. I pushed gently inward, and a spontaneous shiver rolled over me. The door wouldn't budge. Even the soles of my shoes felt hot. I wanted to sleep.

My forehead drooped against the plywood, and I closed my eyes. My head lolled groggily. Another sudden tremor rattled my spine, and my eyes popped open alertly. I was certain there was someone standing just on the other side of the plywood, inches from my face.

The sensation was overwhelming. I didn't believe in a sixth sense, but maybe I should. I squeezed my eyes shut and felt as if I'd been transported back in time. Men in suspenders and fedoras bustled in and out of the office, and the sounds of industry roared from this huge building in an era when the town's heartbeat throbbed with commerce. Much of it had come through here.

The entire building seemed to be breathing in rhythm with my respiration, and just beyond this half inch of plywood was other ragged breathing and a pair of unblinking eyes. I thought of Maestro's reptilian eyes, but these were milky-white dead eyes. Someone was standing in zombielike stillness staring at me through solid wood. Still holding the knob, I placed my other palm on the rough surface and pressed an ear to the warm wood. The sensation wouldn't abate. Something was watching the opposite surface of plywood, blank eyes now shifting upward to others watching from above.

I told myself again, I didn't believe in spirits or premonitions; neither was I superstitious. But the sensation was menacingly vivid. Fear cascaded, and I felt the erector pili on the nape of my neck raising every hair. Something dead was still breathing.

I pushed away from the plywood, turned, and walked as calmly as I could toward the steps that would get me off that loading dock. I unwittingly stepped on a loose plank and almost tripped as I felt powerful hands reach ghostlike through the door to pull me inside. I felt my flesh crawl as I limped hurriedly to the car, bumping my head on the doorjamb as I scrambled to get in before those talons could dig into my shoulders.

I returned to Sharon's bench and reflected on those few moments on Monk's loading dock. I glanced up and down the river walk. No one was within earshot.

I spoke aloud. "Alphonse, you know I don't believe in ghosts. But if that was you in the icehouse, I could sure use your help tomorrow. It's okay if you're at rest in the fields of your Lord. I'll be okay. But I miss you so." Tears leaked down my cheeks.

I swiped at them with a thumb and picked up the journal.

Mr. O looked up from the email, and his visage was chilling. Maestro sat in typical quietude, a reptile on a warm rock. As Mr. O read, Maestro stared into nothingness under half-mast lids, waiting. When I'd shown him the email, he'd merely grunted, "Mm-huh."

The email confirmed that Warden Manakin was taking money to undermine Mr. O's parole efforts. His lawyers had been baffled. A parole board considers evidence that was inadmissible at the initial trial, yet clarifying evidence brought forward by his lawyers had yielded no consideration.

He'd been sentenced to five to fifteen years for racketeering. That meant he had to stay a minimum of five years unless shown leniency for good behavior. Florida's Parole Commission rules the fate of an inmate, but a warden is the conduit for everything that goes on in his prison. It was a simple matter to undermine the chances of parole even if the parole board was being paid off for a favorable decision. It was a standoff of corrupt parties with Mr. O caught in the middle.

The email I'd handed him was from Warden Manakin to a member of the parole commission; it was laced with damning words and phrases like "recalcitrant," "compulsive," "quick to anger and difficult to control," "obsessive-compulsive disorder," blah, blah. A shrink wrote those words. Probably the one holding Marilyn.

Mr. O stared into space, and I could feel him battling for self-control. It didn't take him long. He hadn't risen to his position by letting emotions override logic.

He turned his gaze on me. "So, tell me your plan."

Maestro leaned forward, his voice as lethal as I'd ever heard it. "I'd very much like to take care of the warden."

I quickly interjected, "I know you're upset, Maestro, but they'd just replace him with another lackey. Our goal should be to expose the core corruption and get Mr. O paroled. We may be strange bedfellows, but we've got an important ally out there if we do this right. The *Miami Herald*."

Mr. O frowned, and I quickly added, "Hear me out. They're a long-time critic of the prison system, they go hard at corruption in the police force, and they love exposing Mob activities. It's a triple threat. Plus, the fact that you're in here becomes an advantage. You'll be above reproach while we turn Cipolla and the Bratva against each other and at the same time give the *Herald* a tale of police corruption that'll stay on the front page for months. If they don't kill each other first, we'll have the syndicate bosses duking it out for the best plea bargain."

Maestro sat back with a half grin. "Then answer Mr. O's question. What's your plan?"

I laid out every detail, and as I finished, Mr. O smiled. "You pull this off, I'll make you a rich man. And I'll be forever grateful."

My first move was to follow G1's instructions to procure cryptocurrency. I knew the so-called dark web was a secure marketplace beyond the reach of nation states where one could, at least by reputation, purchase any kind of service, including assassination. I wasn't really going to purchase such services. I was going to make it look as if someone else did. Bitcoin was the inchoate currency of the dark web, so that would be my transaction medium.

The first thing I needed was a crypto-wallet to hold Bitcoin. I chose one of the options and set it up on my now invulnerable virtual machine behind three layers of security. G1's security code made me invincible. Any probes to my server were dunked in a cybersink.

Next, I found an exchange where I could trade dollars for Bitcoin. It had more steps than a conventional bank account, but thanks to Maestro, I had several fake identifications, including passports and social security numbers. Since I had to have a photo on file with the identification, we decided to have Big Al pose after we made some alterations to his looks for an American passport photo. That part was fun.

Al grumbled, "I look like a douchebag salesman from Turd Bucket, Iowa."

Maestro said, "You'd make a lousy douchebag salesman, Big Al. You don't know what a douchebag is for."

"Sure, I do," Al shot back. "I helped your mother use one to flush you out before you could grow. She was very disappointed it didn't work."

It amazed me how levity trumped fear among these men. I stayed scared shitless.

G1 was right about lack of anonymity in dealing with cryptocurrency unless you had talented people to provide foolproof alternative identification. Another element I didn't have to worry about was excess security on the account I was setting up. It was supposed to get hacked when the time was right. I left a tiny back door for the authorities, *Miami Herald* and, we hoped, the Bratva hackers to sneak through. I would open it at just the right time.

This was the earliest days of Bitcoin, and G1 accurately predicted its ascension. Cryptocurrencies were making state-run treasuries nervous. The blockchain and online ledger system was in its infancy, but it was undergoing security updates and gaining traction even in the conventional industry that eschewed it. At the time, it was merely a means to an end. My attitude would change, but for the time being my focus was the exploitation of the little-understood world of the dark web and its exaggeratedly nefarious reputation. It was nothing the media and law enforcement agencies made it out to be, and that made it perfect for us.

I finally managed to procure $200,000 in Bitcoin for about eight cents each. The opening cost of Bitcoin was fractions of a penny. How it would change.

It was time to set my plan in motion. I went back under the shroud of the cyberworld and again lost track of time while chugging caffeine by the bucket. When I realized I'd suck coffee spills out of the carpet if I ran out, I had one of the guys get me some dextroamphetamine sulfate tablets, the M&M's of hackers, and became strung out on fear and anxiety; they're physiologically different neural pathways, and their neurotransmitters are a nasty cocktail.

Part of my plan was a misdirection of sorts, and if I did my job correctly, it would place me among the ranks of real criminals. I wouldn't be a murderer myself, but I would aid and abet. I could no longer pronounce my innocence, and I was stunned at how important that had been.

With my computer system complete, my predictive model validated, a path into the dark web secured, and an e-wallet full of Bitcoin, I was ready. Yet, after all the preparation and the skills I had brought to bear, I still felt inadequate. Then, through a haze of drugs and sleep deprivation, I managed to throw a logical fuck-it switch. Maybe my Cosa Nostra family was comprised of criminals. But we're all criminals in this shithole. Even the prison administration. As trite as it sounds, survival is the ultimate equalizer.

There was one final essential requirement to make the plan work. It was the one act that would toss me onto Charon's boat and carry me across the River Styx into the underworld. The fulcrum of the plan hinged on Mr. O's people on the outside committing two assassinations at precisely the right time. In Dante's inferno, I now wore the glittering cloak of technology lined with lead that weighed my soul so it could no longer move. I closed my heart and mind. Why worry about morality when revenge was so near?

It was time to advertise assassination services on the dark web. There was controversy regarding the pervasiveness of on-demand assassination on the dark web, but law enforcement had fed the notion, and there was enough evidence to legitimate the possibility. The sordid reputation of this technological underworld fed the nightmares of the public, giving further impetus to law enforcement to play it up in a way that enhanced their image as they trod on civil rights. A newsman's dream.

Finally, it was imperative that we connect Warden Manakin to Marco Cipolla. That was a high-risk maneuver, and those risks soon became apparent. I was almost murdered.

# CHAPTER 16

I'd been living in antipodean worlds, cyberspace and block E.
I was somehow in the prison but not of the prison. I was in a
city of dissent with its many brands of evil, yet I could escape and
tread the world on the magic carpet of a powerful motherboard.

So much of my life had been focused on gender identification
when, without warning, I had technologically transcended gender.
I was in a male body built by science, Frankenstein's monster
to the religiously fervent. Yet in the realm of cyberspace, I was
disembodied, my gender, race, and identity meaningless. I was a
quantum ghost no less lethal than Maestro.

Events were moving rapidly. I had to focus on the trap I was
setting for Marco "the Onion," the Bratva's Shusha, and Warden
Manakin, whose ambition was now free range. He would run an
orderly, model prison if it killed every inmate under his control.
To expand his punitive options, he converted some old rooms
off the steam tunnels into extra isolation cells. They stayed full.
Even a minor infraction resulted in iso time. I remembered my
trip through those tunnels and could only imagine the horror of a
black hole from which even light couldn't escape. Thank goodness
for Mr. O. I was able to dodge arbitrary punishment but remained
wary, though inadequately so.

During these intense weeks as we prepared our tactical onslaught, completely out of the blue, I received an update on Marilyn. One afternoon I was at my computer, watching live feeds from a video camera in Marco Cipolla's fancy club in Miami, when I suddenly saw a blinking icon in the corner. I hovered over it and a message said: "The icon is valid. Look now. Window closes soon." I thought it was G1. It wasn't.

My finger shook as I clicked on the icon, producing a feed from an unknown security camera. The feed was erratic and dropped frames, and there was no sound, but the picture was clear. I leaned forward, staring hard at the image as I attempted to orient. Suddenly it came into focus, and my heart raced. Holy shit. It was a live feed from a group therapy session at the Florida State Mental Hospital.

Seated in the center of a semicircle of patients was Marilyn Manakin. She sat so still I thought perhaps the frame had frozen, but others were moving and shifting in their chairs. The therapist was going around the group, soliciting responses.

When it was Marilyn's turn, she gave a terse response. The therapist, who was at the edge of the picture had done no follow-up questions with the other patients, but I could see him pull his chair closer and dwell on Marilyn. Far too long. Her hair had been cut short, but even in the green haze of a security camera, her beauty was obvious. The therapist in his stereotypical lab coat tried assiduously to draw her out.

She appeared drowsy, as if holding her head up took effort. A psychotropic. I reached out and touched the screen as if I could stroke her sweet face.

I spoke aloud, "You touch her, you fucking charlatan, I'll find you …" I knew my threats were empty.

Marilyn's arms crossed protectively in front of her. When the therapist finally moved on, the feed halted. Seeing her was an indescribable relief.

I immediately entered our deep web chat room: "Bless you, G1. How'd you do that?"

Minutes later a response came back: "Sorry, I don't know what you mean."

I typed, "The security camera at the mental hospital."

A second response came back: "Amazing, but not I, dear man. Seems you have an angel in an unexpected place."

I typed so fast my fingers kept hitting the wrong keys, and it took me twice as long to get a response out: "I pray whoever it is let's me see her again."

"I hope so too. I'd like to know this one. He must be a genius. I just tried to crack that system but only got in the records and emails; no success with the cameras."

I sat back, and my head was reeling. Finally, I typed, "I think I know. It can't be … but it must be; it could be no one else."

"Explain."

I hesitated. I didn't want to be wrong. "I want to be sure. If I'm right? Holy shit."

Summer floored the accelerator of the golf cart and leaned into a sweeping turn as she steered it around the curve at Cedar Key High School, paused to turn right, sped down a long, gentle hill, and turned into the Cedar Key Cemetery. Her blonde hair fluttered in the wind, and a happy grin beneath sunglasses displayed white teeth against an emerging Florida tan. She wore a loose skirt over a colorful low-cut swimsuit and white canvas deck shoes.

Leitner held the hand grip built into the plastic roof and leaned against the centrifugal force of the cart as he sat quietly on the seat beside her. He wore a white golf shirt, a navy swimsuit, and slaps. His muscular body easily absorbed Summer's gleeful abandon as she whipped the cart through the cemetery gates.

As she stopped the cart on the asphalt path, Summer said, "I found this cemetery while you were napping. You were right. This place is a dream lost in time. I love it here. And the way the tide comes in and fills everything, then disappears? It's so strange and wonderful."

They'd been in Cedar Key for two days, and Summer had blossomed. She felt as if a weight was lifted from her heart. She set out on the rented golf cart, most often alone, to explore the island. They'd rented a kayak the previous evening and, with a picnic basket tucked at Leitner's feet, had paddled out to some of the remote island beaches dotting the bay.

Summer parked the golf cart along one of the paved cemetery roads and dismounted. There was a couple standing solemnly at a small group of tombstones. They wandered close.

The man, aging but still handsome, tall with thinning white hair, turned to Summer as she approached. He saw her curiously examining the grave markers. "My family," he said. "My great-grandfather was US marshal here over a hundred years ago."

Leitner turned to stroll through the gravesites, but Summer said, "Wow. And such a beautiful place."

The man's wife, a pretty blonde woman, significantly younger, said, "I married into the family. It's wonderful how much they care about each other and the family history. It's like being wrapped in a warm blanket. My family couldn't care less about each other."

A sad frown crossed Summer's brow. "Mine too." She turned toward the golf cart. "Thank you. I mean it. Those words really help."

The man turned to Summer. "Families are always an odd bunch, but we're all we've got. Family is the history not yet lived."

Summer looked at him and smiled wistfully. "What a wonderful way to put it. And you're right. Family is all we have." She turned, and Leitner met her at the cart.

"What's wrong?"

She spoke with quiet conviction. "Nothing. It's that man and his wife. They just reminded me of something ..."

Leitner put an arm over her shoulder. "Didn't I tell you why I need to get to this town we've been shooting for?"

She shook her head. "You haven't said much of anything other than where the town is and something about an uncle."

Leitner smiled. "Yes, but not just an uncle. He practically raised me."

Summer looked at him blankly. "You have family you're close to?"

Leitner said, "Maybe our family isn't as tight as those folks, but my uncle and I have always been very close."

Summer sat back in the cart and steered it through the cemetery's winding paths. "I'm glad I get to meet him. And someday I hope I get to come back here."

Leitner said, "We're supposed to meet him at a café. His little town is cute. I think you'll like it."

That evening, Leitner made a call to his friend in New Orleans. "Can you send backup? It's that little town near Orlando I mentioned."

A voice spoke, and he responded, "Great. I don't think there's anything to be worried about, but I'll call again if things look ... uncertain. You have the address. Tell them to be there by noon. First Street Café it's called."

I considered my plan to disrupt Carbonchio to be solid, though I worried about the number of moving parts. It was critical that the timing outside prison match what I was setting up inside. Before I got started, I used G1's code to set up my own homemade Linux distro, an operating system containing only the programs necessary for what I planned to do.

I needed an external solid-state drive, and that made Maestro bitch about the short notice for finding more parts. I completely rebuilt everything to control every program and every port. The sorceress had even given me an auto-partition routine in the install. Insane skills. When I was done, I was surprised at how lean but unbelievably fast my machine had become.

Next, I created a dark web site called "Ultimate Solutions" accessible only by TOR and protected by VPN. My link was called Last_Resort.com. A banner under the title read "Don't waste time untying the knot. Let us cut it." I created an encrypted internet form with a series of drop-down selections. The first drop-down included quasi-serious choices like "Ex-Spouse" and "Evil Boss." But the serious choice, the one I would be monitoring for my purpose was "Chapter 96"; it was meant to weed out casual traffic. Only those knowledgeable about the world of racketeering would know that Chapter 96 was the part of Title 18 of the federal code covering RICO—Racketeer Influenced and Corrupt Organizations.

If someone selected "Chapter 96," an IP locator would trace it to source and determine what was behind the proxy. If the proxy was undetectable by normal routines, I would penetrate. That's how I would search for probing by the Bratva hackers or law enforcement.

My role in murder began eating at me. If I hadn't known the despicable nature of Bratva and Cipolla's Carbonchio, I fear I would have folded. Each time guilt gnawed its way past my defenses, I thought about why I mustn't care. Still, I could merely deflect my unease by telling myself I wouldn't be the one pulling the trigger. I agreed with Dante: in hell, hypocrisy was the worst offense. The mathematics of my evil choice was simple. If I denied I was abetting murder, I was a hypocrite. I chose honesty. It hurt.

When the time came, Big Al and I picked two obvious targets for murder, one close to Marco Cipolla and one close to Shusha. Big Al had an encyclopedic knowledge of all things Cipolla and Bratva. He said names, and I looked them up.

My story again diverges. Other threads must be pulled in this evil tapestry. First, I was almost murdered. Second, Big Al saw a photograph that turned my world upside down. Things were like quantum chaos in the apparatus of my being. The essence of chaos theory is a simple phrase: sensitive dependence on initial states, also known as the butterfly effect. I realized that the smallest variations in decisions I was making were having wildly variant results. The perfect example was my simple decision to take a walk.

I needed a break from hours at my computer; I wished only to get some fresh air. I could pretty much come and go as I pleased so long as I didn't venture into the main blocks. After my spectacular failure with Marilyn, I refused to reenter the library, which meant I avoided the blocks entirely. Still I needed a break from my work and began to take walks to clear my head. The Florida sun was an elixir, the only medicine that kept a shroud of depression at bay.

That afternoon, I headed for a haven I'd found nearby, a scraggly wooded area. It was not lush, but it had a scattering of trees and underbrush, and once inside, I couldn't see the walls of the blocks or the wire fences. But I forgot one of prison's primary axioms: forget your mama's name before you forget your enemies. I still knew my mama's name, but I'd forgotten what Alphonse did to the Aryans who were about to mutilate me the day he took me under his wing.

Block E was located at the back of the prison grounds near a couple of poorly maintained baseball fields. It was near the fences behind the outfield that this little biome stood, a cluster of scrub pines intermingled with a few unkempt live oaks amid some palmettos and weeds. I missed the oak-lined streets of my hometown, and here I could sit in the shade for a few minutes and feel like a free man pausing for a rest in the park before heading to a restaurant for lunch or perhaps a movie.

As I strolled parallel to the fence behind the fields, a couple of inmates were policing trash opposite the backstop behind home plate. A guard was not far away, so I thought nothing of it. I should have been surprised by inmates policing such a remote area. Guards were lax with inmates on outdoor duty, but alarm bells should have rung loudly.

I wandered toward the trees, lost in thought. I'd spent too much time with my guard down, and I didn't recognize the inmates from a distance. I was oblivious. They weren't.

As I entered the line of trees, one of the Aryans, a big man with muscles on their initial slide toward fat stepped from behind a bush. "Well, I'll be goddamned. Say it ain't so. The fucking queen of block E. The warden said you might turn up out here."

The warden said? What did that mean? A thunderbolt struck, and I realized I was the focus of a prison vendetta, and it had been sanctioned by the warden.

I held up my hands and began to backpedal. "Please, I don't want trouble …"

I backed into a tree trunk that turned out to be the second inmate, a huge man that must have pumped iron incessantly. Alphonse had saved me from the fat one once, but Alphonse was dead. The tree trunk grabbed me with ferocious strength. I was a rag doll in his hands as he threw me violently to the ground between them. I barely caught myself before eating a pound of dirt.

The fatter one stepped forward. "Oh, you got trouble, Hershey packer. Take a good look at my chin." He pointed to a long scar along his jawline. "That's what your goddamn nigger did to me. But that's okay. I'll look handsome compared to what your face is gonna look like."

I was finally dead. It had come unexpectedly as death does. Something came over me. I snapped, thinking I had nothing to lose, so I started ranting as if insults were bullets. "Go ahead, you stupid troglodytes. I don't care. I'm surprised you haven't drowned in the showers by now. You're all so stupid, you forget to pull your heads out of the water to breathe."

The anger in his eyes told me I'd succeeded. I was tired and depressed; at least maybe death would come quickly.

The tree trunk yanked me to my feet, and the heavy one, an asshole named Hall, stepped forward and threw a punch at my jaw. I raised my shoulder and turned my head away from the blow. It would have broken every bone in my face had it landed clean, but it glanced off my shoulder and hit the side of my head as I flinched. Even blunted, the punch slammed into my temple, making me see double. My parasympathetic system reacted, and I felt a stream of warmth on my thigh. Fear. How many times had I pissed or shit myself in this place? Kill me.

I was suddenly overwhelmed by conflicting memories. All the fear I'd felt during my early years in prison flooded my thoughts. Hopelessness. An accretive dissolution of selfhood; I was a transgender clawing for purchase in an impossible hell. This was followed by anger. Anger at myself for stumbling into this, at life for putting me here, for letting me see a path to freedom only to have it snatched away by these lowlifes and their ineradicable existence. Then I acquiesced. I wanted nothing more than to leave this place, even if it was the hard way.

I watched as that meaty fist reloaded, and this time I closed my eyes for what I knew would be the final time. No shrug of the shoulder. No verbal outburst. Just sweet oblivion.

I heard a voice from somewhere in the distance, but it couldn't be real. Maybe the punch was so hard it killed me instantly without pain and I was hearing the voice of an angel.

Yet, I heard the words clearly: "Freeze, shitbag. Touch him and I'll kill you."

It sounded like Maestro. My head was still spinning. That fist was supposed to end it all. What happened? My eyes flickered open. I was alive. Maestro must be behind me where I couldn't see him, but I could see Hall's face. That was enough.

The two Aryans would have battered me into a grease spot and then used it to slick their hair back. First there was Sharkey and then Alphonse and now Maestro. The three faces of Virgil rose like hot suns. Others may think it bad that I viewed the most brutal of men as heroes. But let them get captured by Nazi fucks whose sole purpose is to grind you into nothing and then talk to me about a moral high ground. Oh, and goodbye, motherfucker.

The muscular man dropped me onto the ground and turned on Maestro.

"You ain't in that wop cage now, greaseball. Get the fuck out or join your faggot friend." His words were tough, but his voice had a nervous edge.

The Aryan Brotherhood knew Maestro mostly by reputation. Prison reps are like any other. Persistent and persistently exaggerated. These Aryan apes had no idea what Maestro could do to back up his demand. I did.

Fat Belly said, "Get that fucking guinea out of here before I kill him. I'll watch this queer."

The muscular Aryan towered over Maestro, but the fight, if you choose to call it that, didn't last long. I call it a teachable moment.

The big man bent down and pulled a shiv from a makeshift holster under the pant leg of his prison uniform and advanced on Maestro. Maestro reached into his pocket and pulled out a strange tool; it looked like a corkscrew, one of those wooden-handled ones. He began darting and weaving around the bigger man to keep him off balance. At first, I couldn't figure out what he was doing. Then it happened. He was looking for a specific opening, and within a few seconds, Maestro's genius revealed itself.

He dodged to the Aryan's right as the younger man made a wide arcing slash with the shiv, but Maestro ducked under his arm and used the momentum to leap straight up so that his chest was at the Aryan's eye level. At the apex of his jump, he punched the point of his tool into the man's neck, which lay completely exposed.

A single hot stream of blood shot from the Aryan's right external jugular vein. I found out later that Maestro had a vascular surgeon's knowledge of the human vascular system. It was he who told me that the right external jugular vein is just beneath the skin, while the left is buried deeper in the musculature of the head and neck. He had built this little tool, which indeed was made of a corkscrew handle, but he'd replaced the corkscrew metal with a sharpened length of coat hanger by soldering it through a small washer to prevent the tool from biting too deeply.

Maestro had punched a hole in the Aryan's right jugular vein, which had, of course, caused a thin stream of blood to spurt out at high pressure.

The older Aryan began backing away, preparing to flee and spouting, "Holy shit, you crazy fuck."

Maestro pointed at him. "Stop. You leave, your friend dies." He turned to the wounded man. "Take a knee and press your middle finger over the wound to stop the flow."

The muscular Aryan had seen the thin fountain leaping from his neck and was completely debilitated with fear. He knelt like Maestro said. Maestro stood behind him and pressed his own finger over the tiny geyser.

"Now, put your finger right on top of mine. I'll release mine, and you take over. There was a blood thinner on my weapon, so it won't clot until you get help."

The Aryan did as he was told, while his oversized friend stood wide-eyed.

Maestro glared at the bulky man. "You need to help him, or he'll bleed to death."

The bleeding Aryan moved to stand, but Maestro said, "Don't move yet."

The younger man nodded once, and Maestro continued, "When you get up and start back to the block, you'll see the guard who's supposed to have you two on a leash. You'd best convince him to do as I say. Your blood pressure will rise, and it'll be harder to stop the blood flow. Your finger will get tired. That's where fat shit comes in. He'll press his finger over it so you can rest a minute. But walk slow. The more you raise your blood pressure, the harder it will be to stem the bleeding. I'd have the guard run ahead and tell the doc you're coming."

He looked from one to the other. Both Aryans were suddenly all business. There were no threats, just silent nods. Maestro waved to the big man, and he moved tentatively toward his friend.

Maestro stepped back. "D, over here with me."

I did as I was told.

The big Aryan helped his friend to his feet, and they stood together looking at Maestro.

Maestro said, "I should kill both you idiots. Let's call this a team-building exercise. But I see either of you again, I'll assume you came to fight, and I'll fucking kill you. Now go. Slowly."

The two nodded and dropped their gaze from Maestro's as they stepped in unison from the copse of trees. The big man had his arm over his friend's shoulder.

Maestro glared at me. He was justifiably furious.

I spoke first. "I'm sorry. I know I fucked up."

He said, "If I hadn't seen you leave, you'd be dead. And right now, I'd be fine with that, but the boss needs you alive, you goofy fuck."

"I really am sorry. I promise it won't happen again." Then I added, "But goddamnit, they knew I came out here. The warden sent them."

He turned on me, and I'd never seen him so angry. "What in holy fuck did you think would happen? How many times did I tell you to stay away from that bitch and her fucked-up husband? He's a civilian who thinks he's got our nuts in a vise. He won't deal directly with us because he thinks he owns us. It's part of the game, dumbass."

I was mortified. He was right. My brain felt like a can full of gravel someone tossed down a staircase. At that moment, I realized the distinction between book smarts and street smarts. When it came to the kind of smarts Maestro possessed, I was Jigs in a full-fanged grin mindlessly flogging my pecker at passing girls.

I stared at the ground and shook my head. "How do you think he knew? Was I being watched?"

He oozed sarcasm. "Gee, I'm not sure, but let's talk it through. He catches you with his wife. 'Oh, but it's okay, we're just having a chat.' She waltzes home smelling like a five-day old tuna sandwich 'cause you got her juiced up about her fucking true self. Then he finds you trying to sneak his emails to her, evidence that can ruin his marriage and his career, but he does nothing about it because you two shake hands and you think you have a deal? He has his numbnut Nazis keep an eye on you, and, holy shit, don't you make it easy. You prance like a Leprechaun into the forest to visit the unicorns with one thumb in your mouth and the other up your ass."

"I said I'm sorry. It was stupid and naive." I couldn't bear his anger. I wanted to change the subject, but I just walked beside him, hoping he'd calm down.

He paused, turned to me, and blasted the world out from under me. Circles within circles. When it came to playing death games, no one was better than Maestro.

"I sold you out to the warden, D. I showed him the note."

His initial words stunned me beyond belief. I could only stand and stare.

"What ... No, you wouldn't ..." I began.

"You're right. I'm bullshitting you." He put his face inches from mine. "This time. But it's what I should have done. It's what I will do if you don't learn your fucking lesson. I like you. But here's a dead-on, cliché line from that fucking movie of yours. I've had to kill people I like before. I hated it then, and I'd hate it now. Don't put this family at risk again. Now *that*, they got right."

His look was deadly, and he didn't blink as he spoke. "If it'd been anybody else, even one of our own family, I'd have sold you out with a smile on my face. It would have been a perfect solution. I get you refocused on the job, and he puts his wife somewhere out of the way where you can't get to her. After you finish your job, if he's still alive, I give you to him to take his revenge. I got no choice now but to look at you as meat. It's the endgame that counts."

Maestro was right about everything. We were all a means to an end, and our end was the same. Lesson learned. I had to become as mentally tough as these people.

As we reached the edge of the ball fields, I risked changing the subject. "How is it you even think up shit like that? I mean a jugular hole punch? What next, a portable testicle extractor? A poison pen pecker pickler?"

He tried not to smile. "If I had those, I'd use them on you right now."

"No, really," I said. "How'd you come up with it?"

He became suddenly pensive. "Guess I don't need to kill every time. Fear is more useful."

"He bled like a hemophiliac."

He chuckled. "You heard me. I put a blood thinner on the tip. I'm still perfecting this, you know."

"Holy shit. How'd you get a blood thinner?"

Maestro stopped as we were passing the fence behind home plate.

"I don't know if he wants you to know, but Mr. O is on blood thinners. I borrowed one of his pills and made a paste. He's not feeling well. Something's wrong."

I frowned. "I don't know what to say. He's a … wonderful gentleman."

"He's not himself these days."

We walked in silence back to the block. Was Mr. O sick? This was bad for all of us. He was the glue that held it all together. The one who balanced the table.

Sensitive dependence on initial states. All things descend to chaos. On a whim I took some photographs. In order to select targets for the two assassinations, Big Al arranged to meet me and Maestro in my room. Maestro sat on my loveseat, and Al stood behind me at the computer to look through profiles of potential victims. Turn away, for I feed the river of blood.

That evening, the butterfly flapped its wings in my hometown, and a hurricane hit me hundreds of miles away. On a day years after entering prison, I had attended my mother's funeral and, with no prior planning, took some photographs with a borrowed camera and digitized them.

I was scanning the photographs on my computer when Big Al came up behind me. "That's your town, D? Very nice. Very, what's the word? Quaint. Yeah."

"I took these photos when I was home for my mother's funeral. Would you like to see a few more?"

"Sure. It kinda reminds me of a town I know in Calabria."

I started scanning quickly through the photos and was just about to close the program when Al shouted, "Stop. Wait. Go back. No, no. One more. No. One more."

Suddenly, a picture of the blue Imperial slipped onto the screen.

Al pointed over my shoulder. "There. That one. What are the fucking odds? I know that car."

I laughed. "No way, Al. That car's never been out of that hick town. You might have seen one like it."

"I tell you, I know that car." Al was adamant. "I'm sure of it. I used to oversee a couple of grease shops down in Miami. I know fucking cars better'n I know my wife's tits. We passed hundreds of cars through those shops, but I never forgot one. I'm telling you, I seen that car come through."

It's hard to describe the seism that wracked my body. I was suddenly overwhelmed with foreboding.

I'm sure they heard the quiver in my voice. "How, Al? How could you know it? It must have been a car just like this one. This one was just always there ... only there."

He pointed at the screen. "Nope. Chrysler made only about five hundred of these for two or three years running. We got this car in; the front bumper was a mess, and the front axle was bent. We managed to find an axle from another Imperial to replace the damaged one. We also found a headlight assembly with no trouble. Bumper was easy. But like I said, they only made five hundred of them. My man did a hell of a job, but there was a problem with one replacement part. Take a real close look at the trim."

My hands were shaking, so it took several tries to blow up the image. I looked at one front fender and then the other. I saw no difference, but Al said, "There, see it?"

"No, Al. I don't see anything different." My voice was shaking uncontrollably, and I was close to tears.

Maestro moved behind us as I went back and forth from one fender to the next until Maestro said, "Yeah. Jeez, Al. You got eagle eyes."

Al said, "In that business, you learn to see details. When you resell stolen cars, you had to be perfect."

I still didn't want to see it. I wanted Al to recant like Galileo under threat of torture, but in my twisted gut, a puzzle I didn't know existed was revealing an unbidden picture. A girl awakens to the pain of a mother's tears, a father's drunken shouts, and the scent of night-blooming jasmine; an angel's dead body drifts from imagination to the horror of reality.

I struggled to form words. "I still can't ..."

He said, "Put the driver's side up. Okay, see the chrome casing around the dual headlight? It's perfect. That's because we took one off a fifty-seven Chrysler. The two pieces were interchangeable. Fifty-eight was a bad year for Chrysler; there was a recession, and people couldn't afford an Imperial, not the way it was made in fifty-seven."

I cringed. My father didn't give a shit. He bought his fucking dream car even as my grandfather's business suffered. I remembered the arguments that left my mother in tears about spending that kind of money.

Al continued, "Look at that chrome eyebrow. This side wasn't damaged; this is what it's supposed to look like. The fifty-eight had an eyebrow that was longer and went more past the wheel well than the fifty-seven. Take a good look. Then switch to the passenger side."

It took me a minute, but once I saw it, it could never be unseen.

"It looks the tiniest bit different." I could barely breathe.

Al said, "Yeah, the fucking guy was in a hurry. Moaned like a bitch. My man made this one by soldering an extension on a fifty-seven eyebrow and shaping the longer end out of chrome. Hell of a job for an ungrateful asshole."

My heartbeat was at hummingbird pace, and I couldn't squeeze back the tears leaking down my cheeks. Al really did have eagle eyes.

"Hey, what's wrong, D? Sumpin' I said?"

My father did not have the wherewithal to get his damaged car to a chop shop in Miami, but I knew who did. I couldn't fathom why unless it had something to do with Sharon's death.

I stood up, and the two men, high-level thugs in the Cosa Nostra, men of no sentiment, stood back and let me slink like a whipped dog to my little kitchen to wash my face.

Maestro said, "You need some time?"

I put a towel to my face and shook my head. "No. We have work to do. Besides, I'm probably wrong." I knew I wasn't. "Thanks, Al. Your memory is the eighth wonder of the world."

Al gave me an appreciative nod as I settled back at my computer. More bones for the burial ground of my past. A gate creaks on old hinges as touch-me-nots shrink underfoot. The echo of steps unheard in the night. The ragged texture of my past refocuses.

But I knew now. I knew. I would live if only to leave this hell and confront the past. And Sheldon fucking Richardson.

# CHAPTER 17

I rose early. It was the day I was to meet Shel. I would reach the end of the journal before we met at the café for lunch. I was compelled to finish it on Sharon's bench with Lake Monroe gliding past. I might never be back. Though I couldn't imagine Shel trying to harm me, I knew he was capable of it if he felt cornered. But I intended to corner him. That morning before climbing into the Imperial, I paused to examine the chrome trim on both sides. Big Al had been dead right.

Leitner and Summer ate breakfast in silence at Auntie Anne's Café in Cedar Key. Summer had found an unexpected freedom on the island. Even the difficulty with cell phone reception was a sign that life here was devoid of the frantic fame-seeking of an American public constantly plugged into everyone else's cries for attention. She was resigned to leaving, but it was with a heavy heart. A rift was forming between this newly discovered life and her life "out there." The one she'd been forced to live.

After breakfast and goodbyes to the staff of the Harbor Master Suites, she watched as the hotel staff put their suitcases in the back of the CRV. She climbed in, and Leitner drove slowly out of town. Mrs. Putney had warned them that the local police were adamant about the speed limit in this small village. Summer was happy he drove slowly. It provided her with a final look at the bayous and expansive marshes as they crept out Highway 24.

Eight miles later, they passed the town of Rosewood, where a race massacre had occurred. A movie was made about it. There was nothing much left, but Summer knew the story. Steve, the man at the cemetery, had told her the whole story, the real story, when she ran in to him again. It made her feel a part of the history of this small fishing village.

Steve had waved to her as she drove the golf cart along Dock Street, and she stopped to let him climb aboard. They rode out to the cemetery, and Steve told her a story about his great-grandfather, the US marshal of Cedar Key. He said his great-aunt Madeleine told him the facts the movie missed. She knew the people who triggered the events. And the family always felt if his great-grandfather, Dolph, had still been a US Marshal on the night of the Rosewood race massacre, it never would have happened. Not because Dolph believed in equality for blacks but because he was an equal opportunity hater; he hated everyone equally, white or black, and he would not tolerate lawbreakers in any color. Summer laughed, and they wandered around the island together for a couple of hours.

Everything about Steve's easygoing nature was in stark contrast to Leitner's wounded personality.

She joked with him, "I hope it's okay if you're seen with someone other than your wife."

He laughed. "Don't worry. No one who knows me would believe I was with a pretty girl like you. They'd swear it was someone else."

She giggled. "Surely they give you more credit than that."

He said, "Shoot, no. They wouldn't believe I'd ever even met a woman with a face so damn pretty it puts the moon to shame much less was riding around the island with her. And now,

Summer, why don't you tell me what's eating at your sweet soul. It's clear something's wrong."

Summer only then realized that there were tears on her cheeks. "Your wife is very lucky. You handle me with such care. There aren't many of you left. It's why I stopped to pick you up. Why I rode around the island with you. I would never stop for a man in the places I come from."

As they approached Dock Street, where he asked to be dropped off, she said, "This may sound a bit crass, but I'll say it anyway. Thank you for seeing me as a woman and not a pair of tits."

Steve said, "I'm old now, but I'm a child of the sex-drugs-rock-and-roll generation. I was told I wasn't bad looking back then, and I don't feel like I missed out on anything. I learned back then that women should rule the world. Men sure have screwed it sideways. Not because women are kinder or gentler. But because they have an adaptable strength of character that men lack. You can throw a switch when things are darkest and shine a light in the proper direction. Men just pull out the guns and start blasting at anything that moves. Please remember that; trust yourself. You're among the toughest I've seen to be so damn beautiful. I'll be seeing you in my dreams, pretty girl."

Driving past Rosewood with Leitner, Summer's smile was sad as she stared through her sunglasses at the remains of the village. She slumped down and put her feet up on the dash. She wore a loose-fitting red shirt that hid her bust and a pair of white cargo pants. She'd bought these clothes at the little shop on the ground floor beneath their suite.

"I've never seen you without a dress," Leitner said. "You look like a pretty little country girl."

Summer smiled. "I think I'm learning things about myself. And I'm learning the difference between men and boys."

Leitner nodded. "Nice sentiment. I think you're growing up."

Summer gave him a wan smile. "I'm getting there."

Leitner's voice had a sudden edge. "When we arrive, I have to meet a man before we see my uncle."

Summer stared. "Are you thinking there'll be trouble? I thought we were just going to visit your uncle."

Leitner kept his eyes on the road. "He said he's meeting someone from a long time ago. Someone who just got out of prison. It's just a precaution."

"Why doesn't he just not meet this person?"

"He feels an obligation. Like I said, it's just a precaution. He wants to meet the guy and get it over with. It'll be okay."

Summer shrugged. "Okay. Maybe I should stay in the car until the coast is clear."

Leitner nodded. "Not a bad idea. I'll leave the AC running. It shouldn't take long."

"Have you ever been to this town before?" Summer turned again to the side window. She knew it wouldn't be simple. Nothing with Leitner was simple. If it was simple, he'd figure out a way to turn it into a fiasco.

"Only once a long time ago. I was just passing through, delivering something to Miami for my uncle."

Leitner watched the road, and Summer felt the acid rise in her stomach. Cedar Key suddenly seemed long ago and far away.

I sat on Sharon's bench with the journal open in my lap. I didn't have time to focus on the blue Imperial. My plan had become the nexus of activities for block E. In my efforts to protect Mr. O and the men surrounding him, I found myself at the center of the very activities for which they were reviled by society. Fuck 'em. Not only was this survival, but I'd found out there were no good guys and bad guys. Everyone involved, from cops and feds to mob bosses, were engaged in the same corrupt shit show. Besides, the best people I'd ever met, the ones with a consistent moral center, even if that center was not aligned with a hypocritical American culture, were social outcasts.

My strategic plan was simple. The complexity lay in the tactical aspects. It was facilitated with the help of a reporter from the *Miami Herald* obsessive enough to follow the bread crumbs I left him. The reporter's byline was Ray Cleaver—a *nom de plume*, as writing an exposé on the Mob could shorten your career. And your life.

I watched the morning sun sparkle on the broad river as it made its glissade northward. It was time to read the last few pages.

I knew at some point the Bratva hackers would glean what was happening and attempt a preemptive maneuver. The trick was anticipating these moves and deflecting them. I was worried I might be outmaneuvered. As it turned out, I would have failed if not for some unexpected help. The Bratva hackers were a team led by an insidiously skilled megageek known in hacker circles as the Ukrainian.

With my help, Maestro and Big Al contacted two family "liquidators" and set up two hits by faux hitmen. Big Al gave me two names. One was a Bratva thug called the Priest. His real surname was Popov, derived from the Slavic *pop*, or priest. He was the Maestro of the Bratva chief, Shusha, which made him one of the most feared Bratva assassins. The second name was Skinny Mike, who played a similar role for Marco Cipolla. I was able to procure good photographs of the two men, and Big Al selected family enforcers who looked enough like the Priest and Skinny Mike that in the heat of assassination, wearing balaclavas and bulky clothes, they would be immediately misidentified as the two enforcers for the opposing mob bosses. Again, Big Al showed amazing acuity. In retrospect, I think Big Al was one of the cleverest men I knew. Book smarts always had its limitations. I was book smart, but Al was one of those guys who could think in three-dimensional space. I had a high school friend like that. Couldn't pass a math test, but show him a two-dimensional set of blueprints and he could immediately see it in three dimensions. That was Big Al.

The plan was to put out a hit on two men close to the bosses but make it look like Cipolla and Shusha were themselves the targets. We would use a dark web ad accessed by TOR to make it appear that the two were being hired, each by the other side, to take out the opposing leaders for someone who wanted it all. That someone would be left to the imagination of each side. Lethal. The dark web was the medium for hiring them and a means of timing the hits. The faux Priest was going after Cipolla, and faux Skinny Mike was going after Shusha. Circles within circles. Which move was sleight of hand and which was the real plan? Neither. It was all about sowing mistrust.

The business relationship between Bratva and Bloodstone was based on Bratva bringing its B-girls from Latvia and Estonia to work the Miami Beach hotels run by Bloodstone or, more accurately, Marco Cipolla. They also used the hotels to kidnap young girls.

We needed to disguise the collusion of the two assassins until either the *Miami Herald* or the Bratva hackers, or both, drew that very conclusion. It had to come from indisputable sources, or at least appear to. The feds could not sit on their hands, and heads would roll in all directions. That's where I came in. Any effort to track the dark web activities and put two and two together had to be disrupted until the back door was opened. Then there would be other bread crumbs leading right back to Shusha and his Bratva hackers and Marco "the Onion." Timing was critical.

The final piece was to find out how Robert Manakin was being paid off to keep Mr. O in prison. This is where the tale bifurcates yet again.

I turned the journal on its side; the remaining pages were thinning.

The first part of my plan went flawlessly. I had set up a route for the Bitcoin to hit an offshore account under the real names of the Priest, Mikhail Popov, and Skinny Mike, Michele Albani. There was a nice symmetry to the first names, two Michaels, one "spare in the flank," as Shakespeare said, the other a false priest, and both lethal assassins like their archangel namesakes.

Mr. O's liquidators would have two targets—a liquidation sale, so to speak. Bad joke. Nothing would spook the two bosses like a very close call in which their bodyguards went down unexpectedly, protecting them from assassination. I begged Big Al to keep the targets' names from me. He knew who Shusha's and Cipolla's bodyguards were, but it was not essential to the plan that I know. I felt it somehow distanced me from the deaths of these two fellow human beings. Hypocrisy.

In late morning two weeks after Big Al identified the blue Imperial, he and Maestro came to my room.

"It's done," Big Al said. "Both were hit last night. Your turn."

I nodded, and the two looked over my shoulder as I deposited $100,000 in Bitcoin into two separate accounts in two different offshore banks. It had already begun its exponential rise, so it took far fewer Bitcoins to make the payments. Later I would withdraw the Bitcoin and quietly close the accounts.

"Did it go smoothly?" I asked.

Maestro said, "Smoother than a walk with the unicorns."

I shot him a sarcastic smile. "You won't ever let that go, will you?"

"No." He continued, "One of our men caught Cipolla at his club. He has a stocky build like the Priest and wore a balaclava. Cipolla's number two was there. Our man hesitated long enough for it to look like Cipolla was the target. The number two was wearing only a bathing suit, but he had a Glock in his pool bag. Our man let him draw it before popping him. He swore Cipolla pissed himself. Said he hit number two but Cipolla did number one."

Big Al laughed. "Chickenshit. Our other man hit Shusha at a restaurant. Same deal. Our man was thin like Skinny Mike. His bodyguard was there, and at first he thought it was the damn

Priest. That would have screwed things up big time. But he got a closer look, and it was a guy named—"

I cut in, "No, Big Al, please."

He said, "Okay, Christ. As I was saying, our man made it look like he tripped over a chair. It let Shusha's man get in front of him. *Bam*. Dude fell into Shusha's bowl of caviar. Fish eggs. What asshole eats fucking black fish eggs? May as well eat rat turds."

I spun in my chair. "I just paid the Priest and Skinny Mike for their work."

"When's the next move?" Maestro asked.

"I don't want to wait. Let's do it now," I said.

The next step was to drop an encrypted message into the email account of Ray Cleaver at the *Miami Herald* through a backdoor I'd opened. The *Miami Herald* had a dark net drop box, an anonymous site people could use to provide information of interest, but anyone with know-how could find it. I wanted to make it look like the Ukrainian's team sent the tip to the *Miami Herald*, but I hesitated. What if we needed them to help trap Warden Manakin? I waited. That could have been a lethal mistake, but the unexpected help I received saved the plan.

The message I left for Cleaver read, "This is a gold mine. You should easily guess the password. Happy Pulitzer."

I'd done my research. Cleaver was a federal courts reporter for the *Herald* and had a hefty social media footprint. I was a bit surprised that it took him so long to guess the password, until I realized exactly how many pies this guy was fingering. The password was "muckraker."

My email contained details of both hits, faux Skinny Mike's and faux Priest's, including the account numbers of the offshore accounts. Only a well-connected reporter would be able to get the names behind the accounts, but Cleaver was an ace. I moved the Bitcoin to another account one step behind Cleaver, giving him just enough time to procure proof of the deposit at a bank in the Caymans. Then the money mysteriously disappeared, but only after Cleaver had electronic and physical evidence of it passing through the accounts.

I knew there was mistrust searing its way through the Miami Police Department and the local FBI office because there was a flurry of encrypted emails between police agencies and several law firms known to represent Bratva and Bloodstone. In their haste to avoid their official email servers, they stupidly relied on phone texts. They may as well have posted them on the Wittenberg Church doors. I'd received a modified hack from G1. She got it from an old friend who was ex-Israeli 8200. I captured every transmission. I don't pretend to understand the details of the code except it somehow could capture, decrypt, or divert email or phone messages from any portion of the transmission, even subverting code in any part of the Pretty Good Privacy chain. Beyond wicked.

One of these exchanges was the smoking gun. An email between a police captain named John Dustin Crawford and Warden Robert Manakin. One email from the police captain to Manakin contained only three words: "Lethal dose immediately."

Leitner followed the GPS directions and exited I-75 at Belleview. Then he drove the short distance to Highway 441 South. Summer sat quietly staring through the side window. She receded into a moroseness that made him wish he'd never mentioned potential trouble.

He'd never been in love. It was emotionally debilitating. For saps. This wasn't love, but it was a bizarre obligation growing from Summer's wide-eyed naivete. He was certain one day he'd wake up and realize the feeling was gone; then he'd dump her. He had abandoned thoughts of harming her. He'd never be able to do it. Besides, the world needed Summers.

After turning onto 441S, they encountered construction delays, and every hick town had a ridiculously slow speed limit, forcing him to crawl through strings of traffic lights. After fighting through bumper-to-bumper traffic in a shithole called Leesburg, he decided to stop and call ahead. He didn't want Summer to hear, so he lied about needing a bathroom. They pulled into a Sheetz gas station, and Leitner went inside. Summer did the same.

Leitner gave her time to enter the women's room and then darted back outside. He dialed a number he'd been given.

A voice answered, and Leitner said, "Do you prefer jambalaya without okra?"

The voice said, "Yeah, okra gives me the shits. Go ahead."

"I'm running behind. Will arrive at twelve thirty. Put one man at the far end of the alley. Another at the entrance. Put one at the front door of the First Street Café and tell him not to let anyone enter after five 'til one; say it's a gas leak or something. I'll get there as soon as I can, but I will be there by one. My friend wants to have a chance to talk to the mark. We don't go until one forty-five. Got it?"

"Got it."

He hung up and hurried into the bathroom.

Maestro and I sat on either side of Mr. O, staring across the desk at Little C, Mr. O's rotund chef, whose weeping made his large stomach bounce. His salt-and-pepper hair was plastered with sweat, and moisture beads clung to his scraggly beard. His white apron over prison blues stretched across a girth that hung over the sides of the chair. He was anything but little, but he was named after his father, Big C, former owner of one of Miami's best Italian restaurants.

Mr. O spoke quietly, but his anger was boiling beneath a veneer of civility. "Tell me everything."

"I don't understand, Signor O. What are you saying?" Little C's snuffling made his voice uneven, and he constantly dabbed at his forehead with a dish towel.

Mr. O leaned forward, eyes hooded, jaw muscles fluttering under clenched teeth. "You can tell me, or you can tell him." He nodded at Maestro.

Little C's head drooped, and his great chest heaved as weeping gave way to sobbing. Little C's next words confirmed what I suspected.

"I'm so sorry, Signor O. They say they kill all my family—all in Miami, all in Sicilia—if I don't do what they say. Please, kill me. I understand. But please, don't hurt my family. You no horrible man like that fucking Cipolla."

I always thought Little C was almost a caricature of a chef—fat, jolly, supplicating, shallow. But I'd misjudged him. There was a deeper loyalty and strength to the man. I was glad. Misjudgment normally led to disappointment.

Mr. O leaned back. "Why poison me so slowly? All that would do is make them send me home to die. Why not just kill me?"

Little C spoke excitedly. "I lie to them. They say they want you dead. I tell them if I poison you with that shit they give me, everyone will know. If I do it slow, no one will find out. They believe me. And when you get sick, they believe me more. But today—" Little C's voice broke. "I am to kill you all the way."

Mr. O nodded and glanced at Maestro. "I think he may be right. If they kill me outright, it causes problems. But now they have nothing to lose. They're the targets, and it's kill or be killed. It's stupid, but that's just how that fucking Cipolla thinks."

He looked back at Little C. "How do you get the poison?"

Little C's face looked like he was chewing a lemon. "That fucking warden. The poison is in the grocery order."

Maestro said, "That's why they never gave us trouble about special orders. Anything we want. How nice."

Mr. O nodded, eyes never leaving Little C. "Who gave you the order to give me a lethal dose?" His anger was abating.

"Messages come from the warden's secretary; she puts notes in when I pick up supplies. One time, I walk in his office, she under the desk sucking his *cazzo*. I can't see her, but I hear her sucking like a *porcellina*. He grinning at me like he own the world. *Stronzo*. Says I should remember who runs this place. I do what I'm told just like the bitch sucking his *cazzo* or I'm dead, my family dead."

Mr. O was calm now. In a way, it was more frightening than his anger. "You ignored them? You didn't try to give me a lethal dose?"

"I couldn't do it. They were very nervous. My cousin call me, tell me about some newspaper story in Miami. I think maybe they will become too … too …"

"Distracted?" I asked.

"Si, Signor D. Distracted. They don't keep their eyes on me."

Mr. O looked again at Maestro. "So, what do we do with this chef?"

Little C looked down at his hands and closed his eyes.

Maestro heaved a sigh. "I don't know. It's a tough one. Do you believe him?"

Mr. O said, "I'm afraid so. My impulse is to cut all our losses, kill anyone whose part of this conspiracy."

Little C's eyes squeezed out more tears.

I thought about defending Little C, but Mr. O said, "C's right about one thing. Cipolla's first reflex is murder. If we do the same, we'll never distance ourselves from trash like him."

Maestro nodded. "Then you have your answer."

Mr. O stared hard at Little C, who'd settled into a low whimper. "Get out, C. You're still my chef." The man stood to leave, but Mr. O said, "Hang on. Look at me, Cesare." Mr. O's voice was uncompromising.

Little C looked with squinting red eyes. "Si, Signor O?"

Mr. O frowned. "They might be dumber than I think. If they contact you wanting to know why I'm not dead, tell them you put all the poison in my food, but it didn't work. I must've developed an immunity. Ask them to get you a different one. If they do that, you will do exactly what that man tells you to do." He pointed at me. "We'll beat them at their own game."

Little C bowed. "God bless you, *padrino*. God bless you. I do all Signor D says. My life been hell. You're my friend, and they want me to kill you? Fuck them."

Mr. O said, "I'd better get the best meal you've ever cooked tonight, you understand?"

Little C waddled to the door. "Veal. Your favorite. Wait until you taste the scaloppini I prepare tonight. *Scuisito.*"

The door closed, and Mr. O looked at me. "What do you think?"

I was already considering plans. I decided on the spot.

"I'll need Maestro's help, but I have the perfect idea."

I looked up from the journal to watch a speedboat make its way out of the marina and split the buoys before slowly receding into a distant haze, its white wake converging at a distant point as it turned north. I wasn't to meet Shel for another hour and a half. I peeled a protein bar, bit off an end, and chewed vigorously.

As I swallowed the last bite, I heard my phone buzz in the satchel next to me. I frowned and slid the cell phone out. I swiped it open and saw a series of text messages. I began to read them, but at first it didn't make sense. Finally, it hit me. I was reading a transcript of a recent phone conversation. A very recent conversation between a location in New Orleans and somewhere out on I-4, near the exit to my town. Nothing could make me alter my plans, but I would be doubly vigilant when I met Shel. I didn't expect him to meet me without someone watching his back. A ripple of fear went through me.

Where had this come from? I discarded my first thought. Ghosts didn't exist.

A man in his late thirties sat hunched over a computer in a windowless room in a massive plank building in a cul-de-sac in Goldsboro, a historically black neighborhood in a small town on Lake Monroe. The only light came from his bank of monitors. He preferred the dark; his eyes were sensitive to light. They were huge brown eyes, the irises so large that there was only a thin aureole of white surrounding them.

He sat back in his office chair, smiling, after he sent a VOIP capture to a cell phone only a couple of miles away, the cell phone of a person he had known as a child. His computer was of his own making. He had built it part by part using a conscripted computer from a talented director of technical support, a young man named Kenneth, at the Florida State Hospital's ward for the criminally insane. He'd spent much of his life there as a patient known as Patient One. As part of his renovations of an old icehouse, he'd installed a satellite dish in a discreet area of the building's high tin rooftop and "borrowed" time on satellites including those run by NASA at Cape Kennedy forty-four miles to the east. A sign above the computer in simple scrawled letters read Mad Hacker—a handle he'd earned while he was a patient in the mental hospital.

He'd observed his old friend's movements from afar and knew carefully laid plans were coming to fruition. As he had as a child, he made a silent commitment to help Margarite, now a transgender prison inmate named Stuart. Four days prior to the VOIP capture, he'd made a roundtrip to the hospital in Chattahoochee accompanied by an old friend, retired Florida state trooper Cleveland Washington. Their mission was brief. As Patient One, he'd been the most feared inmate in the ward. Not because he was violent. It was his uncanny ability to see into the soul of anyone his brown eyes fell on. His friend Cleve often asked him, "How is it you know such things?" The answer was consistent: "It's a curse."

When they arrived, he and Cleve entered the main receiving center of the clinical ward. When the woman behind the desk looked up brusquely to demand their purpose, he could see the blood drain from her face, and she gripped the edge of the counter as she suffered a sudden dizzy spell. He knew she wouldn't call for help. She was a first-class bitch known for intolerance and patient brutality. After handling him for three days, she was forced to take unpaid leave to recover from the encounter, and upon her return she was transferred to the main reception area for intake. She refused to return to the ward for the criminally insane.

As they approached, he said, "Hello, Anita. I need you to do something for me. And do not tarry, my dear."

Anita stuttered, her eyes wide, "I'll do anything; just please don't say things."

Cleve said, "Everything will be fine, ma'am. We just need your help to check a patient out of this facility."

Anita paged three staff members, who reacted similarly to his presence. Between them, they procured the proper paperwork in minutes without notifying the medical staff.

As Cleve Washington pulled a black Mercedes to the front door, Patient One handed Anita a thumb drive and said, "Please instruct Kenneth to substitute this for the patient's current e-file. You'll do that for me, won't you, dear?"

At that moment, an attendant pushed a wheelchair containing a heavily sedated woman hastily dressed in street clothes with a hoodie pulled over her face to the counter. The security attendant refused to meet his gaze. Instead, without speaking, he parked the wheelchair and scurried back through the electronic doors.

He took the handles but fixed Anita with his gaze. "Anita, we may never have to meet again. But you can make that a certainty if you tell Kenneth he must also wipe this visit from the security cameras and erase all records of this patient's electronic file save for what's on that thumb drive. Should that not happen? I'll see you all again. Very soon." He glared at her with his oversized brown eyes and said, "We are clear, aren't we, Anita dear?"

Anita shook her head vigorously. "But Kenneth? Will he do these things?"

He smiled. "I'm certain of it. Now run along."

As the Mad Hacker, he knew G1. He had let her inside his system, and they'd had a brief conversation. He'd even let her poke around at some code. They made a commitment, and G1's last message on his screen was "I have been to a holy shrine. Please don't be a stranger. G-1 had no idea the Mad Hacker was also known as Patient One."

He stood and left his insulated quarters. After walking across a room forty feet above the main floor, he entered a small elevator cage and descended. He entered a second huge room, where two men were playing pool at a red pool table set among others but behind a low wall.

As he approached, he said, "Our old friend's in trouble."

A raspy whisper came from one, a voice that sounded scorched. "The one who dropped by the other day?"

"Yes."

The second's voice was also raspy but much deeper. He was leaning over a shot and, after stroking the cue ball, stood up straight. "Is it just me, or do you boys think assholes just keep gettin' dumber every day?"

I was almost finished reading the journal. I heard sounds of life on Lake Monroe, but there was no time to pause.

The Monday after the contrived hits on Cipolla and Shusha, the *Miami Herald* released a story detailing a murder-for-hire scheme advertised on the dark web. The reporter, Ray Cleaver, wrote in detail about a plot to kill Marco Cipolla orchestrated by Alexandr Sushanashvili, a leader of the Russian Bratva organization. I had opened a port from a remote server, which the Ukrainian had penetrated to discover an identical plan to assassinate Shushanashvili. The Ukrainian had almost found me, tracing my route through various servers, and I saw one of my ports being penetrated by an insidious worm. Then something happened; the port was closed and all efforts at penetration were disrupted. I had no idea what happened. Or did I? In any case, the Ukrainian must have immediately alerted Shusha of Cipolla's treachery, and the war was on. Within hours, those closest to Marco Cipolla and the leaders of Bloodstone were among the first casualties of a burgeoning Mob war.

And so the river of blood flowed. I wanted to disappear from the world of Mobs and gang wars, but of course, there was nowhere to hide. Eight days later, the *Miami Herald* ran a lengthy follow-up story citing "anonymous sources" in which they provided evidence of criminal collusion against several "high-ranking members of the Miami Police Department and an associate director of the Miami branch of the Federal Bureau of Investigation," who had been taking bribes from both the Cosa Nostra and the so-called Bratva.

The final line of Cleaver's article should have made me happy even though it was incorrect: "In an apparent effort to avoid prosecution and the fall from grace of a political golden boy, Robert Manakin, warden at Florida State Prison in Raiford, committed suicide in his office at the prison."

I closed the journal. I'd written it sporadically over the years, earlier entries fewer and more scattered as I spent most of my time skulking in corners. Though I had the journal with me in iso, there had been no way to make entries in the dark. My last entries until recently came after the Mob wars but before my months in iso. I tried to scribble a few lines of gibberish in iso, but it had become a blur. Within weeks of the fall of Warden Robert Manakin, almost everyone in block E was paroled. I was supposed to be paroled at the same time. Something went wrong. I said goodbye to my friends in block E, hugging Big Al and Tony, who left on the same day. Mr. O and Maestro had disappeared as if by magic the day after Manakin died. There was an immediate emergency replacement for Manakin; a new warden was assigned to the prison in the short gap between the Cosa Nostra paroles and my agreed-upon separation date.

The new warden was as arrogant as Robert Manakin but not as smart. I was the last inmate in block E, and he wanted it immediately closed. While I awaited parole, this warden, whose name I never cared to know, moved me out of block E "for my own safety." Kiser and a second guard came to retrieve me once again, and once again we made the long walk across the yard and entered the steam tunnels. But this time, Kiser paused halfway through the long tunnel at one of steel doors in the deepest bowels of the prison. My worst nightmare had come to pass. He opened the door.

Kiser had to physically lead me into the dank cell. He couldn't look me in the eye. "I'm really sorry, Stuart. You don't deserve this. Hang in there. Surely your parole will come soon."

It was nearly five months before my parole was finalized. Five months in darkness is interminable. You begin to hear your heartbeat as the seconds tick by. The roar of blood rushing through the cathedral of your skull is deafening, its every apse an unholy shrine where you find yourself praying to a god you don't believe in to stop your heart. I didn't have the courage to bash my own brains out against the stone walls. Instead, I prayed incessantly that endless night would draw a curtain over me and give me peace.

When I saw Kiser again, he came to accompany me to my parole hearing. I was huddled in the corner. I know I'd eaten at least one cockroach.

Kiser said only, "Holy Jesus, Stuart. That's it for me. My retirement papers go in tomorrow."

I had no memory of my transparadoxical state where I bit the hand that fed me. But I remembered barking like a dog when my food tray was slid into the slot. And I had no memory of my ultraparadoxical state as I kissed the hand that beat me. I remembered only begging to help someone, anyone, to kill me. I had no idea who I was to help or how. But most of my past life had been blurred; even my gender change had become merely some cultural artifact of a lost life.

After my parole was granted, I had gripped the journal tightly, as if it were my only connection to sanity, as I walked the chute. During the interminable dark, I had held but one thought. It became a mantra, a firewall against encroaching insanity.

*What happened to Sharon?*

I would find out today. One more death, even my own, was nothing without that answer.

It was almost time. In a half hour, I would drive the few blocks to the café. As I sat quietly staring out over the lake, a taxi pulled up at the curb. I smiled. The cab door opened and closed, and moments later, Maestro appeared beside me as I sat on Sharon's bench.

"Nice spot," Maestro said.

I smiled. "I love this view. So peaceful. I can see farther than six feet. Thanks for coming."

He sat beside me, and I glanced at him. "Jesus, don't you ever age?"

He smiled. "What? And look like you?"

I laughed, perhaps a bit too loudly. "Good point."

"You ready to go?"

I nodded. "Yes. But we have a couple of minutes. I hoped to catch up on a few things, but for now I'd like to know what happened to Manakin. I mention only his suicide in my journal."

Maestro leaned back on the bench. "How much do you remember?"

"I helped you set him up, but I never knew the end of the story."

Maestro nodded. "Not much to tell. The boss wanted him dead, you planned it, and I killed him. It was the first time I can honestly say I enjoyed killing someone. I was dressed as a guard, thanks to Big Al. I got through the blocks with no trouble thanks to you. Warden Shithead was in his office. When I got to the administration offices, all hell broke loose. There was an all-systems alarm, fake prison riot, just like you promised. The admin offices went batshit, so I slipped into his office. I told his secretary she should get out while she could. She thanked me and told me I should make the evil bastard suffer. Then, *poof*, gone without giving him a farewell blowjob."

Maestro paused and sat quietly.

"And?"

"I did as planned, D. Like Mr. O wanted. He started begging. All the tough guys end up on their knees. I poured every drop of that poison he ordered for Mr. O down his throat."

I stared out over Lake Monroe. I needed just one last look. Just in case.

I stood. "I think I'm ready."

# CHAPTER 18

Leitner took the off-ramp from Highway 441 at high speed, cursing under his breath as he cut in front of a semitruck hauling orange crates and whipped the CRV onto State Road 46. He was twenty-two miles from his uncle's town. Summer sat quietly watching the road.

Leitner autodialed his main contact. "Set?"

The response came. "He's got a pro in tow."

Leitner's mind raced. "How do you know?"

"I know one when I see one. This one's the real deal."

"Only one?"

"From what I can see."

"Are we good, then?" Leitner's reflexive caution piqued.

"Unless he's got reinforcements hidden in a potted plant."

"Okay. I'll be there in thirty."

Leitner was driving frantically down a two-lane highway. It, too, was under construction. A row of orange barrels came out of nowhere at the one Podunk town of Sorrento between him and his destination.

Summer glanced at Leitner's intense expression and then stared again at the road ahead as they whisked through a tunnel of oak trees.

Leitner glanced at her. "Look, I'm sorry. I know it's not what you thought, but it will be. Once I know everything's okay, we'll sit down together and you can get to know my uncle. He's an amazing man."

Summer kept her eyes on the road. "You're expecting trouble. I can tell."

Leitner sighed. "It may be nothing at all. But my uncle doesn't get rattled by things, and he sounded concerned when I talked to him. It's not like him. This town …"

Summer asked, "This town, what?"

Leitner accelerated the CRV around a slow-moving pickup truck. "I'm not sure; it's something he said once. He said this place was different, like living in some old movie where creatures crawled out of the swamps. He's just playing it safe. I hope he's just getting nervous in his old age."

Summer said, "Well, I hope once you two get things sorted out I can meet him."

Leitner smiled and nodded. "I promise."

I sat at an outdoor table in the alley patio attached to the café. The second story of the neighboring building soared like a Bridge of Sighs, covering the entryway to the alley exit.

Mist fans wafted a fine refrigerated spray over the area under the pergola. I'd dressed as usual for the heat, white seersucker shirt, khakis, and tasseled loafers. To ensure we wouldn't be disturbed, I'd rented the patio area for the afternoon. It was an unusual request for a small local café, but the manager had acquiesced when I offered a thousand dollars for a couple of hours.

I stared at the narrow entrance from the sidewalk, nervously twirling a coaster end over end. Precisely on time, a backlit figure stepped into the arched entrance off First Street. My heart accelerated. At last. It was no surprise that, when the man emerged from the sunlight, he was older, but the remnants of his magnificence were intact. During my final months in darkness, the face of a younger Shel had lived in my consciousness.

I stood. "Shel? Thanks for meeting me."

"Hello … it's Stuart, right? I'm sorry. I find it hard not to call you Margarite. You still look like her. I only saw you at a distance during the trial. So many years ago."

I forced a smile. "I'm lucky I look like anyone. You've barely aged at all. I assume you have a painting of yourself in an attic somewhere that ages for you?"

Shel returned the smile. "Well, thank you. I wish I felt so young. And less alone."

An awkward silence descended as the waiter approached the table. I ordered a panini, espresso, and sparkling water. Shel ordered a coffee.

As the waiter turned away, we both began to speak, but Shel deferred. "Please. You asked for this meeting. I yield the floor."

For thirty years, a single question had gnawed at my soul. Any thoughts of clever repartee disintegrated as I blurted, "Why, Shel? Why let me take the blame for Sharon's death? Why let me languish in hell?"

Shel closed his eyes momentarily, and when he opened them, I saw a mixture of resolve and regret. "It was all so complicated. But more importantly," Shel paused and brushed a hand across his brow, "it was an accident. I would never have harmed her; you must know that."

I was stunned. There was no denial or diversion. A strange shiver ran through me, and I became disoriented. My expectations were shattered.

Shel sighed and glanced down at his watch.

I knew he wasn't alone. "You don't have someplace to be, do you?"

He merely shook his head.

I pressed quickly, "So, please, tell me. Who was driving?"

Shel's eyes narrowed. "What makes you think a car was involved?"

I said, "Please, Shel. No games. Neither of us have the time."

Shel took a quick look over his shoulder. "That sounds like a threat."

I leaned back. "I just want to know everything about Sharon's death. I know more than you think, but let's pretend we're still old friends catching up on the past and mean each other no harm. You owe me an explanation. No. Forget that. You owe me a simple humanitarian act. Tell me why I spent my adult life in prison for someone else. My father's car was the murder weapon, so I presume he was there as well."

Shel frowned, and I feared I'd lose this momentum, so I leaned forward and said, "You can't give me back my life, but you can give me peace. I've already served the time. But you must tell me. I know everything but the details."

Shel snickered. "And if I refuse?"

I said, "Maybe I've been waiting to say these words. Talk to me or talk to him."

I nodded over Shel's shoulder, and he spun in his chair. At the entrance to the alley under the high overhang, backlit by the sun, Maestro strolled into the courtyard. As we sat by the lake, Maestro had been relaxed. I watched his graceful movements; he was still relaxed.

Shel watched as Maestro's features emerged from the backlight, and he muttered, "Holy shit." He caught himself and added, "Friend from prison?"

I said, "I couldn't trust you. Please, just tell me?"

Shel glared menacingly. "Well, well. Little Margarite finally grows up in prison. What are you, some pathetic gang moll?"

I smiled. "No. But I may as well have been. Which is why I have absolutely no sympathy for you."

I was pushing way too hard. "Look. I'm sorry. When I sat here waiting for you, I didn't intend to descend into threats. You keep looking at your watch. Don't take me for a fool. You didn't come here alone either."

I'd warned Maestro about Shel's backup, and he'd said, "Mm-hmm."

Suddenly, something changed everything. As Maestro approached the bistro table nearest the entrance, I saw movement over Shel's shoulder. A man with a hoodie pulled close around his head walked to the entrance of the courtyard and, in a quick gesture, flipped the hoodie back to reveal a split-second's glimpse of a horribly scarred face. He replaced the hoodie, turned, walked back out to First Street, and disappeared.

I recognized the face behind those scars. The face of harsh justice, of pool-hall denizens and tough men drifting deftly around a pool table the color of blood.

A specter from the past changed everything. In my youth I never questioned it, and it saved my life. I decided in that moment to trust it once more.

I said, "I'm interested only that you tell me what happened. You've always been a man who honors bargains. I have a bargain like the one you and I made the first time you came into the jewelry store to ask me to set two stones. Do you remember? We never signed a single piece of paper. We never even agreed on price. Do you remember those two people?"

Sadness flashed across Shel's face. "Of course I do. It was a better time."

I nodded. "Then let's make another bargain. I asked that man only for protection from you. I was afraid of you. But I'm not afraid anymore. I'll tell him I don't need him now if you'll talk to me face-to-face. I don't even care who you have lurking about. Would you agree to that?"

Shel said, "He won't really leave. I know people like him. Apparently you do as well. I heard you did quite well in prison."

I smiled. "Then you know he considers this a favor. If I ask him to step aside, he'll honor my request."

Shel's return smile was bland. "Honor aside, you're right. I prefer not to have an enforcer at the next table."

I stood. "All I want is what you can tell me. Is it a deal?"

I knew Shel felt he had the upper hand. I might be alone, or so he thought, but he wasn't. He was confident in his control of the situation.

"Sure. If we're alone, I'll tell you everything."

I moved to Maestro's table. He was looking at a menu and never glanced up at me as I spoke in a low voice. "Maestro, I know this will sound strange, but I need you to leave us alone. Maybe go inside and have lunch. That man will talk to me if you're not a threat."

Maestro kept his eyes on the menu. "That doesn't sound strange. It sounds stupid. I've seen wannabes like him all my life. He has no honor."

"He'll talk if he thinks he's not threatened."

"You know he's got guys around here somewhere, right?"

"Have you seen them?"

He looked up at me. "Come on, D. You know if you see them, they're shit. His aren't shit."

"Mine aren't either."

Maestro gave that smiling frown that had frightened me on our initial meeting in the mess hall. "What in God's name are you talking about? I saw one bum walk in here, realize he was lost, and leave. Nobody else. So, who you got?"

I smiled. "I've admired you from the moment we first met. But now I'm asking you to trust me. There are ghosts in this town. They're stirring. Please. Let me talk to him alone?"

Maestro stared. "So, you're saying if I go inside and get out of the way, I'll see ghosts do what you wanted me to do?"

I snickered. "If you go inside and watch, even the great Maestro might be surprised by what he sees." I added, "If I'm wrong, then I'll pay the consequences. I can't worry about it. But if I'm right? I'll get the information I need. And maybe you'll witness my redemption."

Maestro chuckled. "You've surprised me before. I hope you can do it again."

He rose and disappeared into the café.

# CHAPTER 19

I returned to my seat across from Shel. I could think only about the story I'd waited thirty years to hear. I was worried he'd renege, but as I sat down, he looked more relaxed. I hoped he'd been as eager to tell this story as I was to hear it. He didn't hesitate.

"You must know I was devastated by Sharon's death. I was supposed to protect her. She was everything to me. Afterward, I wasn't thinking clearly, but I never considered pinning it on you."

A sudden frown crossed his face. "May I ask how you figured out about the Chrysler? It was sent to a first-rate repair shop. The repairs were perfect."

I smiled. "No, not perfect. By a strange coincidence, someone I knew in prison recognized the car and knew of a single miniscule flaw. I never would have noticed. I refused to believe it at first. You were the only one who could arrange something like that. My father was inept."

Shel shook his head, a strange smile on his lips. "What are the odds?"

Leitner pulled the CRV to the curb behind a windowless van. First Street was quiet, but one of the men had left an orange cone in a space for him just in case. The delay had been agonizing as the arrival time on the nav system kept backing up. But he was still in the buffer zone.

He turned to Summer. "I'll be back."

She nodded as Leitner stepped from the car, leaving the engine running.

As he left the CRV a wave of apprehension made his antennae hum loudly. Something felt wrong. He didn't believe in a sixth sense, but he believed in intuition. Like that time in a ravine in Afghanistan. Or the sudden flight of a flock of birds in a Maghreb skid mark.

The moment he was out of Summer's sight, he pulled out his cell phone and dialed.

Moments later, a voice answered. "Dauphine."

"This is Mr. Fountain. May I speak to Mr. Armstrong? I'd like to hear his favorite song, 'Black and Blue.'"

A silent pause dragged on interminably.

Finally, a voice, clearly irritated. "What is it?"

"Mr. Fountain would like additional assets for the current project."

"Very late notice. How many?"

"Three."

"When?"

"Apologies, but immediately if possible."

"The exact position?"

"The address in the town twenty miles …"

"Exact coordinates. This ain't the fucking Boy Scouts."

Leitner clenched his teeth, pulled a piece of paper from his pocket, and studied it. "My mistake. Lat 28°48'1.98″ N, long -81°16'23.23″ W corner of the intersection at that location."

A pause. "Double the assets plus rapid deployment equals triple the price."

Leitner spat, "Instructions. Listen closely because mistakes will cost you. Two men meet an asset in place in an alleyway behind the building at those coordinates. Combat armed under civilian dress. The third, wait across the street from the location at the front of the address. Unobtrusive, small arms only."

"Combat ready, add thirty percent. I hope you understand this is a very special favor."

"I'll show my gratitude in the usual manner. Do you see the deployment requirements?"

"Of course. I'm watching as we speak. Assets are in route from east Orlando. Make the deposit now."

"ETA?"'

"Scrambling; twenty minutes from … right now."

Leitner shook his head as he opened the secure browser on his cell phone and entered the proper transaction codes. How could Mr. Armstrong have assets just waiting for deployment nine hundred miles from his home base? He watched the green bar creep along as the transaction worked its way through the system. He was told money was no object. The mark had plenty, and that was why he was here: to get it.

After the green bar indicated the transaction was complete, Leitner said, "Run through protocol once more."

The voice repeated the instructions, and Leitner said, "Good."

The voice spoke low. "And if there's trouble from the natives?"

Leitner chuckled into the phone. "Your assets will get some small arms practice."

"If it's so easy, why double down?"

Leitner was irritated by the question. "It's always best to overprepare."

The voice said, "Happy to hear it. Good assets are hard to find these days."

Leitner disconnected the call and walked along First Street to scan the assets already in place. He was dressed as planned, in clothing he'd grabbed from the BMW. A straw fedora with a red hatband was his key to be recognized. As he strolled First Street opposite the café, he encountered Number One standing under the awning of a storefront, gazing at a window display, wearing a collared shirt and jeans. Even in shirt and jeans, he couldn't detect a firearm. The two exchanged a nod.

Next, Leitner glanced at the glass front door of the café. Just inside, as instructed, was Number Two. A black hoodie hid his face. His job was to prevent anyone from entering or leaving the café until Leitner and the first crew member entered the alley. Then he was to get anyone left in the café out of the building or onto the floor. Leitner did not want complications from collateral damage if things went sideways.

He proceeded to the end of the block, took two right turns, and entered the alley behind the building. He saw Number Three leaning against the rear of the building, next to the alleyway entrance. He was wearing a black tear-away track suit.

Leitner approached. "Mr. Etouffee, I presume?"

The man nodded, and Leitner said, "You'll have two additional members in." He checked his cell phone. "About twelve minutes. You're Three, Four, and Five. If I yell, 'On me,' make tactical entry into the courtyard. I'm told you'll recognize the reinforcements."

Number Three said, "Good. I don't like working with men I don't know."

Leitner quickly glanced in both directions. "What are you packing?"

The man patted his track pants. "Tear-away pants with a twelve-gauge pump on my thigh. Double-aught Teflon."

Leitner smiled. "Jesus, don't spray that death machine my way."

The man chuckled. "Been using this lucky lady for years. Never hit the good guys."

Leitner laughed as he moved away. "Let's keep that winning streak going."

He completed his trip down the alley and ended up back on First Street near the black CRV. He looked at his watch. A half hour until go. As he strolled slowly back toward the car, he paused to watch an innocuous white van pass. The man in the passenger seat tipped a black ball cap as they drove past and stopped at the corner.

The backup. He ignored them, trusting they'd take up their positions. When he got back to the car, Summer was dozing against the window.

*Good*, Leitner thought. *Let sleeping women lie.*

A badly scarred man in a black hoodie watched from just inside the door of the café as Leitner and Summer entered town and sped up First Street. The driver parked the black CRV down the block. He'd been just in time. Ten minutes before, he'd entered the alley courtyard of the café, tipped his hoodie back for a split second so only one person in the courtyard could see him, and then entered the café and pinned gimpy against the wall. He'd wrung everything out of him, and he'd said it would happen just like this. He'd also ID'd the man in front and knew there was another one in back. Jesus, it was true. These assholes never learned. He'd watched gimpy take up a position just inside the café. The stupid fucker really had limped back into town looking for revenge. *Shithead can't say I didn't warn him*, he thought.

He'd watched the whole thing. Gimpy took up his position just inside the café door just like the Kid said he would from the phone conversations he'd intercepted. He could tell this asshole was straining at the bit to start shooting. The Kid told him it was best to neutralize him fast and find out what his dumbass friends had planned. The Kid had played every one of their phone transmissions for the last two hours while they shot pool on the red table and knew everything they were up to. This was going to be fun, and he'd start with gimpy, who was just excited to be here.

The man with the limp had taken up his position inside the foyer of the First Street Café. He was hoping no one would enter until the killing started, but five minutes after taking up his position, some retard opened the door and entered the foyer.

He stepped forward from the alcove. "You can't come in. There may be a gas leak."

The boy with Down syndrome, short and round with a trusting smile that turned to a fearful quiver, said, "But my mama's here. She said to come."

"I don't care, kid. Beat it." He gave the boy a little shove in the chest but not enough to draw unwanted attention.

Tears rose in the boy's eyes, and he said, "Please, sir. Mama said come."

He didn't have time for this shit. "For the last time, you fucking retard, beat it."

The boy gave a low moan and hung his head. He turned to the door and began to cry, tears spilling down his cheeks. "Okay. I'll go if you want me to."

He couldn't believe it. Just as he was getting rid of the retard, some tall punk in a black hoodie walked in. No one had been in for a half hour; now these yokels were pouring in.

As the retard turned to leave, hoodie-man put a hand on his shoulder and whispered, "Hey, little buddy, it's okay. You go on in and find your mom."

The man took a limping step forward. The asshole's voice sounded like he chewed gravel. *What is it with these fucking rednecks?*

He kept his voice low and threatening, touching the Glock at his waistband. "Grab that kid and get the fuck out of here before—"

He stopped abruptly and gasped as a sharp pain wracked his rib cage. He looked down and saw that the hooded man's fingers were locked into the holes of a neck knife. It was protruding from between two of his ribs. He felt a debilitating pain as the crazy fuck gave it a slight twist, and he heard a subtle whispering sound from the wound. The pain froze him.

The raspy voice kept its calm tone. "Go on in, sweet boy. Your mama must be worried."

The retard's face changed to a happy grin. "Thank you, sir." The boy slipped past them as his mother waved from a table at the far end of the long, narrow room.

As the boy stumbled clumsily between café chairs, the hooded man pushed the knife, gently guiding him into an alcove. The hooded face emerged into the light, and his face turned pale. The face under the hood was a mask of burn scars.

The damaged voice spoke in low tones. "Your left lung is losing air. Don't breathe too hard. If I push harder, the blade will slice your heart. If you've fucking grown one."

"Fuck, man, please. Don't push that knife." He couldn't believe it. This fucking town.

"You didn't listen, motherfucker. I told you in that jewelry store I'd see your lame ass limping back to town. I should kill you just for being so stupid. That kid you called a retard is Einstein compared to your dumb ass."

The limping man's face was a frozen mask of fear. This simply couldn't be happening. "You can't be you. What the fuck happened?"

The scarred face pressed close, one milky-white eye half closed. "After I sliced you up, the devil came to see me. He kissed me with fiery lips and burned my face like this. He said. 'Welcome, my brother. You do good work, but you can't come to hell yet. Your job is to stay up here and send me the souls of fools.' And look who limps right back into my knife."

This was bad. He felt his knees shaking as the scarred voice became all business.

"The devil's waiting for you, but I assume you want more life. If I slide this knife out and you get to a hospital, you might make it. So, tell me every fucking detail of what's about to go down. Talk fast, because the longer you take, the less chances you got. And if it don't ring true, I'll cut your heart out to make me a sandwich."

The limping man whose life was ruined after he and his partner tried to rob a jewelry store in this town had longed for one thing; revenge. Now, he'd do whatever it took to get away from this fucking town alive and never come back. What in fuck was he thinking coming here? He'd wanted to shoot this town up so bad he could taste it. Not anymore.

"I swear. Let me go, and I'll get as far away from here as fast as I can. Just like you told me last time. I swear I'll listen this time."

For four minutes, he whispered into the black hoodie. He held nothing back. He wouldn't be here when shit went haywire anyway.

Finally, the damaged lips formed terse words. "Get gone. There's a cab stand around the corner by the old Valdez Hotel a block that way." He nodded toward Park Avenue.

The hooded man reached into his pocket and pulled out a piece of cellophane. "When I pull this frog gig, your lung will try to collapse. Hold this piece of cellophane tight over the wound, and it might not. But wait too long? Say hi to the boss for me. He'll be the one with horns and a pointy tail."

*Oh, Jesus, who are these fuckers? God, get me out of here.* Those thoughts rattled through his head, but he said, "You mean you planned this whole fucking thing?"

"You're an idiot. We watch every move you make. Every whore you bang, every poker hand you cheat at, we're watching. We don't usually give no second chances. There goddamn sure won't be no third. Now get the fuck gone or I'll send you down in pieces."

Leitner was removing the cone in the parking spot a block down from the café. As he opened the rear door of the van to toss the cone inside, Summer lay motionless, looking through half-open eyes at the side mirror as a man exited the café. He limped badly and was holding his side. She wondered if the trouble had already started.

She lay still and quiet, eyes closed save for the odd peek at the side mirror. Trouble was coming, and she had no choice but to wait it out. She saw a second person, taller and wearing a black hoodie, exit the café. He disappeared into the shadows of a stairwell across the street. Were they all Leitner's men? She had to stay strong, but she a bad feeling.

# CHAPTER 20

As I prepared for his story, Shel stupidly said, "You know, there's no statute of limitations on murder."

I spat the words. "Of course I know that. I've been in prison for three decades. I know more about felony law than I ever wanted to know. Do you think I give a shit about the statute of limitations?" I calmed myself. "You've always been a fixer. That's the word you use, right? The man who fixes other peoples' problems? But you couldn't fix Sharon's. Tell me about that sweet girl's death."

Shel's face showed a flicker of sadness, but he again glanced at his watch.

I said, "Come on, Shel. You know I adored Sharon. How was she killed and I made to look like a repulsive monster?"

Shel finally sighed and nodded. "What the hell. I'd like you to know that I avenged you as best I could. I hope that's worth something."

I said, "Why not just tell me the whole story? You're the only one who can give this to me."

Shel gave a short nod. "I suppose you're right. I've got nothing to lose." He spoke in a steady voice. "Circumstances left me at the country club without transportation. There was a phone call, and it was important for me to get somewhere immediately. A terrible thing had happened. It was just before dusk, and a hard rain had blown in not long after I finished a round of golf. The brick streets in town were too slick for fast driving."

Shel closed his eyes with a gentle smile as he continued. "Sharon loved the rain. She was afraid of lightning, but during those lingering showers, she loved to walk and feel the rain on her skin. She was so sensitive to sunlight, the rain was her friend. She'd put on a shirt, shorts and a pair of slaps and walk for blocks. That evening was a Sharon rain. Gray skies meant no burning sunshine, everything was colorless. Except my beautiful angel."

Shel opened his eyes, and the sadness was now tinged with hatred. "I tried to warn your idiot father to slow down. Not because of Sharon. I had no idea she'd be there at that moment. We flew around a corner at Fifth and Oak, and he punched the gas. The car skidded on the wet bricks, and the fool panicked; he slammed on the brakes, which made it worse. The brakes locked, and the car jumped the curb. At the last instant, I caught a glimpse of a figure in white trying to dart away. Her foot slipped; a slap flew. I knew who it must be. I heard the nightmarish sound as the car thumped over her. It may as well have been my heart."

Shel paused, his eyes distant.

I asked gently—perhaps it was Margarite speaking from the past—"She wasn't really your sister, was she?"

Shel looked up abruptly. He picked up a cocktail napkin and wiped a tear away.

"Jesus, Stuart … Margarite—a woman's intuition in a man's body. You're a force of nature. Did you know all along?"

"I came to suspect. I didn't know if she was a wife, but she wasn't a sister. Even when you tried to pretend you cared for me … in that way, I could tell you were holding back the deepest part of yourself."

Shel nodded, his lip quivering as he continued, "She was a relative. Far enough removed to love but too complicated to marry. Her parents died in an accident."

He paused, and I asked, "An accident?"

A smile hinted at Shel's lips, and he shook his head. "You truly are amazing. But that's something I can never talk about. We were already in love. It was the perfect opportunity for us to be together."

I said, "My guess is she was being abused and you saved her." Shel's eyes widened, but I cut in, "I'm not here for that. No matter how this ends, that's something that belongs only to you. I promise."

Shel's confliction was obvious as I said as softly as I could, "Please tell me she died instantly. That she didn't suffer while lying on a rainy sidewalk."

Shel reacted with instant vitriol. "What? You think maybe I finished her off so I could frame you?"

I held up a hand. "Of course not. But my father was capable of anything."

Shel's anger dissipated. "That's for sure."

I was confused. "I don't get it. Something else must have happened? You can skip the shame you must have felt for dumping her body unceremoniously in the lake. That's a memory that no doubt haunts you. But why do that? It was an accident. Even if my father was drunk as usual, I doubt you were. You could have stayed there and explained it to the police and walked away."

Shel drew his lips in over his teeth and closed his eyes tightly. He tried to draw a full breath but snuffled unevenly.

"Please. I need to hear this."

He nodded slowly, and I suddenly saw his age pushing through the veneer.

He continued, "My first impulse was to dispose of the body and say Sharon had to go away for her health. Everyone knew she was fragile. But the circumstances required that we act fast and close it off."

Shel poured some water from a carafe as I glanced over his shoulder. Only the occasional pedestrian strolled past the alley entrance.

He leaned forward. "You must already suspect the rest. The

streets were empty because of the rain. We put Sharon's body into the trunk and drove to my house to pick up a few things. Sharon wasn't wearing anything other than her walking clothes, so we grabbed one of the outfits she wore to go to town and ..."

I said, "And the emerald earrings I converted to clip-ons for her."

Shel flinched as if slapped. "Yes." His voice slowed. "We didn't worry about cleaning her up ... She was going into the lake, so why bother. Then we—" He took a deep breath. "We ripped her clothing as if she had been in an altercation."

Shel slowed again, and I said more forcefully, "I don't understand why. I've made guesses, but nothing makes sense. I sat in court as they marched out all the evidence you and my father provided."

"We drove to your parent's house, and your father grabbed the things we needed ... the butcher knife you'd slashed him with. A pair of your socks. You know the things ..."

I said, "Of course. So, you did the entire setup down by the lake?"

He nodded. "Yes." Shel put the heels of his hands over his eyes, elbows on the table. "We ..." He sucked in a breath. "I ... stabbed Sharon's body with the kitchen knife. We stuffed one of your socks in her mouth and put the earrings on her ears ..." He paused for a moment and then forged on. "After ripping a piece of her earlobe as if someone had tried to rip the earring away. It looked exactly as the prosecution made it look."

He dropped his hands but couldn't open his eyes. "Please believe me. The hardest thing I've ever done ... in a life of doing bad things ... was to stab Sharon's limp body and drag it along the seawall to disguise the contusions from the car hitting her. It made me sick. I puked over the seawall. I drove a bit farther down the lake and lay in the front seat, shaking."

"Was my father with you then?"

"No. I made him walk home. I met him there. The one thing

he had to do was get to an empty dealership and help me cover the car with a tarp until I could get it to Miami. I had to drag him out of the house to help me. I should have just had the thing chopped up and threatened your father with death if he ever talked."

I leaned over the table. "Shel, that's what I keep asking. Why didn't you just do that? What are you not telling me?"

He frowned. "I never intended to tell this to anyone. You see, Margarite ... May I please call you that? Despite what you think, you haven't aged all that much, and your face ... it's still Margarite to me."

I nodded. "As long as you don't make the mistake of thinking Margarite is more vulnerable than Stuart."

Shel said quickly, "On the contrary. I'm guessing it was Margarite who got Stuart through the roughest times in prison. The one who saved both of you."

I frowned. How did he always know how to surprise me? "You may be right, but this is what I've become. Maybe prison ... Never mind."

Shel spoke abruptly, leaning across the table and pinning me with a stare. "I need to tell you something. I killed your father."

My jaw dropped, and I stared at him, dumbfounded.

Shel scooted his chair closer to the table and leaned in close. "You came to your mother's funeral. I was there. You didn't see me because I watched from the balcony of the church. I was there, but your father wasn't."

He placed a closed fist on the table. "After Sharon's death, he wanted money. Said he was too emotionally damaged to work. I gave him some. Of course, he kept asking for more, so I kept him on a dole, just enough to maintain his pathetic life. His country-club friends began to thin out as the town faltered, but he was there every day, pretending to be a big shot."

My anger flared. "I thought the pig was holed up with some mistress I heard about."

Shel was clearly disgusted. "You should have seen him.

Parading around town with this poor creature, a waitress at the country club. It was the only work she could get. A sad, gentle thing with a low-wattage bulb in the attic. But that wasn't the issue."

I said, "Let me guess. He started upping his demands in his pitiful need to impress her."

"It gets worse," Shel said. "The moment we stepped from the car and realized what had happened, your father immediately began blaming you. He insisted on it. He laid every broken dream, every lost opportunity, every snub from anyone who ever said no to him at your feet."

Margarite, the daughter still residing inside me, felt embarrassment, anger, and sadness. But my voice was laced with bitterness. "You didn't have to tell me, because I've always known it. A father who loves only himself has no capacity to love his child. I remember a line from Lawrence, *Sons and Lovers*. I memorized it: 'she had borne so long this cruelty of belonging to him and not being claimed by him.'"

Shel leaned back. "I understand. Believe it or not, that's how Sharon and I often felt. I never felt so guilty in my life as I did when the judge's mallet hammered down after he pronounced your sentence." His lower lip quivered. "I've thought about it many times. I've even put a gun to my head, thinking I could pull the trigger."

I said, "The story isn't over. The thing you said you've never told anyone hasn't crossed your lips. Why would a capable man like yourself, a man always in control, lose it and go along with a fool like my father? And please, include the details of the bastard's death."

Shel's smile was wan. "I saw you at the funeral. It made me remember how genuinely I once cared for you. True, it wasn't a romantic caring, but I honestly felt you and I were joined by more than just common interests."

He shook his head and continued, "I watched until you placed a rose on your mother's coffin and walked away with your prison attendant. He showed you such deference ..."

"Holt," I said. "His name was Holt. He's retired."

"Holt," Shel said absently. "Just as I neared home, my cell rang. It was your father. He needed to see me immediately. I asked him where he was, and he said he was home. His girlfriend had broken up with him. He needed money to get her back."

I said, "So he was there? I wondered why the car was there. I took pictures."

Shel said, "I know. I saw you."

I frowned. "Oh my God, the curtain. When I reviewed the pictures. In one the curtain was closed, but in another it was pulled back. It was you? I thought maybe it was my father avoiding me."

Shel lowered his voice. "He was lying on the kitchen floor. I used a plastic cover from one of his laundered shirts. He wanted money, lots this time. He was sure this girl would go away with him if only he had money. If I didn't give it to him, he would ask someone else."

I frowned. "Someone else?"

Shel nodded. "It's the point of the story. The motive you so rightly perceived. That day your father was full of himself. Ranting about life dealing him out of his due. He could start all over with this girl. I asked him if he'd looked in a mirror lately; he could have been her grandfather."

Shel's face was a mask of disgust. "He was out of his head. I couldn't stand it another second. His laundered shirts were hanging on the door, so I ripped off a plastic cover and wrapped it over his face. He fought like a wild man."

Shel paused, and I said, "And?"

"The last words that slimy bastard heard were, 'This is for Margarite.'"

I said, "I don't know how to react to that. Margarite would be shocked. But Stuart says good riddance."

Shel snickered. "Welcome to my world."

I looked away for a moment, gathering my thoughts. "So, this 'someone else' is the key?"

Shel nodded and crossed a leg over his knee. How elegant he always looked in his beautiful sport jackets, ubiquitous white open-collared shirts that set off his tan, dress pants, and on this day, a pair of sockless Gucci loafers.

I said, "So, we near the denouement?"

Shel raised his eyebrows. "Yes, we do. I'll keep this short because I shouldn't be saying these things at all.

"That night we were at the country club. Your father was with his usual group of clowns drinking cheap beer and laughing at the same bad jokes they told ad nauseam. If I had to hear the joke about the golfing hooker or the Scottish mulligan one more time, I'd shoot them all."

I asked, trying not to plead, "And who is we?"

Shel gave a wistful smile. "Jeff Hatfield Sr."

I put a hand to my mouth. "What? He was with you that night?"

Shel nodded. "We played golf that afternoon. We were dropped off at the club by Jeff Jr. Mr. Hatfield never drank and drove, and we planned on a few drinks after golf."

I said, "If Jeff Jr. was involved, this story is definitely headed for the shitcan."

Shel said, "I agree. Jeff Sr.'s cell phone rang. He got up and walked out onto the patio to take it. He came back frantic. He begged me to go with him right then. I was his fixer, wasn't I? I improvised. I grabbed your father, who strutted out with us like he was the Prince of Wales."

"So, Jeffrey Hatfield was in the car when it hit Sharon?" I was stunned. In all the scenarios I'd imagined, never had someone else been part of it. Especially Jeff Hatfield Sr.

# CHAPTER 21

Summer lay with her head against the car window with her eyes closed. Leitner had returned to the car long enough to turn the AC fan on high and check if she was still dozing. He glanced at his watch and then stepped to the curb. He pressed his weight against the door until it gently latched and then crossed the street. As he reached the storefront next to the café, a man stepped out of the shadows to join him, and together they stood next to the alley entrance, Leitner checking his watch repeatedly.

Summer lifted her head and watched in the side mirror as another man in jeans and a dark shirt stepped from a doorway behind her. He watched Leitner and his companion slowly step into the narrow entrance to the courtyard and then strolled casually along storefronts, looking in the windows. *So, Leitner brought more men. No surprise.*

As she watched, the man wearing a black hoodie slipped out of the stairwell next to the café and crossed the street. Leitner's man watched him until he disappeared around the corner. He then returned to his pretend browsing. All these movements were confusing, but she could never understand Leitner's methods. She wished only to get into the alley with him.

She waited two minutes before she picked up her purse from

the floorboard and stepped out of the car. The pretend shopper was gone.

"*Jeez* almighty," she muttered to herself. *These men creep around like ghosts.*

She moved tentatively along the street opposite the courtyard entrance in the cantilevered shade of the storefronts. When she was directly across from the café, she stepped into the street.

A car stopped to let her cross, and as she approached the far curb, it stopped behind her. A man's voice came from the passenger side. "Hey, baby, you look like you need some help. I bet I got just what you need."

Summer put up her middle finger behind her back and kept walking. A voice said loudly, "Stupid bitch," as the car peeled off.

She saw the man with a black hoodie over his face appear from nowhere. He stood in the shadows where one of Leitner's men had been. He motioned for her to come back across the street.

Summer hesitated but thought, *if he's with Leitner, it'll be okay.* The man held up one finger and tapped his wrist as if to say, *"one second of your time,"* and stepped back into the shadows. She scurried back across the street and tentatively approached the doorway.

When he spoke, his voice was low and his words slightly slurred. A flicker of light revealed a badly scarred cheek, and she took a step back.

His voice was forced over damaged lips. "Ma'am, don't go where you're headed. There'll be trouble in there. Don't get caught up in it."

She asked tentatively, "What happened to the man who was here a few minutes ago? I think he's with my friend, isn't he?"

He chuckled. "He had a health emergency."

She said, "I know there'll be trouble. I came with my friend in there."

"I know. I was told." He turned his head slightly, and Summer caught another brief glimpse of the scars. "But there's something else comin'. Something you don't want no part of."

Summer said, "I know. It's my friend. He's expecting trouble. If there is, then you're right; something bad will happen. He's dangerous. But I have to go in there."

"Well," the voice strained to push words out, "I'm sure your friend's a very dangerous man. But if you gotta go in there, remember one thing for me, okay? If you go into hell, it's best to stay close to the devil if you ain't the soul he's after."

Summer frowned at the strange words. "I'll remember that."

The rough whisper echoed as he stepped back into stairwell. "I'll do my best to help you, if I can."

"Goodbye then." She turned and hurried across the street. At the curb, she looked back, but he was gone. She felt sorry for him. He was just the kind of man who'd be first to die at the hands of a man like Leitner.

Shel said, "This is difficult, so bear with me. Yes, Jeff Sr. was in the car. But he wasn't the only one." His tone changed. "Do you remember that kid they called Sharkey?"

A spontaneous shiver wracked my spine. I could never forget Sharkey. "Holy shit, was Sharkey involved?" A spontaneous memory flashed: *two thugs from out of town.*

"What's wrong?" Shel asked.

I shook it off. "Nothing. I'm sorry. Please, go on."

Shel said, "Sharkey wasn't there. It was fucking Jeff Jr. He was drunk and wanted to prove his manhood, so he went to Monk's Pool Hall looking for Sharkey. The pool hall was empty; Monk must have decided to close early. We never knew what happened other than Junior began arguing with Monk and either shoved or punched him. The little shit. His exact words were 'that crooked nigger just stumbled and killed his damn self.' Bullshit. Monk hit his head on the corner of a pool table and hemorrhaged into his brain. He died in minutes. But we knew Junior caused it. So would Chief Butler."

Shel made a steeple with his hands. "Monk's body was in the trunk and Jeff Jr. in the back seat with his father when we hit Sharon. It was the night of the fire at the Hatfield mansion. Another casualty of Junior's idiocy, I found out. It was a massive clusterfuck."

I was more than shocked. I was devastated. Nothing like this had ever occurred to me. I said, "That was a mystery the town talked about for years."

Shel said, "After putting Sharon in the lake, we took Monk's body upriver, away from the current because nothing would be left after the gators got at it." He shook his head. "As Monk lay dying, Junior called his father. You know the rest. That's why I acceded to your father's idea. I was protecting my client while setting you up for the fall." He looked at me pleadingly. "It was my job to keep Jeff Sr. out of trouble. Sharon's death masked Monk's."

Shel paused and cupped a hand to his forehead. "We were only a few blocks from the Hatfields', so I told Jeff to walk home through the back alleys with his kid and we'd handle it. When they got near the mansion, it was ablaze. As it turns out, a murder trial was a red herring for a series of idiotic mistakes by Jeff Jr. Even the arson that started the fire was glossed over."

He picked up the cocktail napkin and wiped his forehead. "I made a devil's bargain."

I sat staring at the table, unable to think. I'd been seething since Big Al pointed out the flaw in a repair job. I had finally heard the story I'd dreamed of hearing, and now I wished to forget all of it. What was the point? Vengeance wasn't a cure. It was just another manifestation of the disease. I just wanted to sit on Sharon's bench and watch the river.

I could think of only one thing to say: "When I was traveling in southern Italy, I went into a small Catholic church. In the crypt was a young girl floating in a huge glass cylinder of preservatives.

It was how they preserved the bodies of local saints. I stared at her perfectly preserved face; it seemed her eyes would open at any moment as she floated in her timeless chamber. That's how I think of Sharon. A sweet innocent floating in the glass chamber of memory, forever unchanged."

Over Shel's right shoulder, I suddenly saw two men walk into the courtyard. One wore a golf shirt and straw hat. The other was dressed in a plaid shirt and jeans. They looked ordinary, but after thirty years in prison, I recognized predators when I saw them. I wondered when Shel would show his hand. This would not go well.

Maestro finished a sandwich and glass of white wine, put a fifty on the table for a twenty-two-dollar tab, and walked to the front door of the café. It was time to see what Stuart's "town ghosts" were up against. Just as he stepped onto the sidewalk, he caught a glimpse of movement to his left and watched two men disappear into the narrow entrance to the courtyard. He also caught sight of a buxom blonde standing across the street, talking to someone in the shadows.

He got a good look at the men entering the alley. He mumbled to himself, shaking his head and chuckling. "Fuck me, Stuart. How did you get tangled up with a taco bang-bang, Section 8 like that?"

He turned and walked back into the café. This time he found a seat next to a window with a good vantage of the outdoor courtyard. He whispered, "This should be entertaining."

Shel saw my gaze dart behind him, and he glanced over his shoulder. "I'm afraid the cavalry has arrived. I've truly enjoyed this chat, and I hope you're satisfied that I've told you everything. Of course, what I've told you can't be passed along to anyone. I hear you got rich in prison. Don't you think a story like mine is worth something? If you don't, I feel better knowing Stuart may die here today. I don't think I could bear killing Margarite."

My smile was genuine. "Ah, there's the Shel I've been waiting for. And I can't wait to see that stupid grin wiped off your face. By the way, before you think of killing me, you might want to know I've wiped out all your assets. I'd keep me alive."

Just as those words left my mouth, I looked up and saw a lovely blonde walk into the courtyard. Standing right behind her was the scarred face I recognized. He was hovering over her, and I knew the avenging angels had arrived.

The blonde raised a pistol and bobbed it up and down. She was signaling to me. I didn't hesitate. I tumbled out of my chair onto the floor just as she opened fire. I realized she was shooting at Shel. I saw him drop to a knee as I dove. The blonde fired until the gun was empty.

I raised up and saw that Shel had been hit twice but not badly. Both men who'd just entered with pistols turned, one raising his weapon toward the girl. In an instant, the scarred man I once knew as Jack Knife flicked out an arm like a striking cobra, and like magic, a knife protruded from the gunman's throat. Jack had thrown it with such velocity and accuracy that it appeared as if it had popped out of his neck. The gunman slumped to the bricks, grabbing frantically at his throat, and managed to extract the knife, releasing a strong stream of blood. He throttled the bricks with his heels as he bled out.

Jack Knife pulled his hoodie back, revealing his badly scarred head and face as he stepped into the courtyard and stood slightly behind the blonde. Wisps of thin hair floated around his leathery skull like thin sparks of static wavering around a scarred, misshapen Tesla orb.

The man in the straw hat raised his pistol toward the blonde, but with lightning speed, Jack Knife pulled a shotgun from under his long black Mackintosh.

"Toss that pistol, motherfucker." Jack's voice was chain-saw ragged.

I saw movement to my right, and there was Maestro staring

at me through the glass. Our eyes met, and he gave me a small sarcastic wave as if to ask, *"Having fun yet?"*

I gave him an equally sarcastic thumbs-up with a fake smile. I saw him laugh. Discretion should have dictated that I be afraid, but I wasn't. Not even a little.

The man in the straw hat shrieked at the blonde, "What are you doing, you stupid bitch? You fucking hit my uncle."

I thought, *Shel's nephew? It must run in the family.*

The blonde screamed back, "I want your uncle dead! It's the only reason I put up with your evil shit. That bastard killed my sister, Leitner." She pronounced his name in an exaggerated New Jersey accent: *LOYT-nah.*

Leitner screamed at her, "What in fuck are you talking about? You were nothing when I found you. A worthless whore. He doesn't even know you."

She barked, her face full of rage, "You didn't find me, you dumb shit. I found you." She gave a high-pitched imitation of a Jersey accent: "Oh, *LOYT-nah*, you're so smart. I don't know how to hustle these rich men. Please help me." Her voice became low and threatening. "I watched you watching me for months. I found out you were that asshole's nephew. He was in Vegas too, as if you didn't know. I knew if I could get to you, you'd eventually lead me to him."

Leitner rumbled, "I saved you from those fucking truck drivers."

She shrieked, "I asked them for help. I wanted to get away from you the minute you said where we were going. You killed anyone that got in your fucking way. I asked those two idiots for help. They followed us, and I ran for it. I just didn't know they'd be as bad as you and even stupider."

Jack Knife began laughing in a wheezing wail that echoed across the courtyard. Leitner's fury was boundless, and he turned to Jack, who said, "This is better than the goddamn *Secret Storm.*"

I rose from the wooden floor and sat back in my chair but

leaned over the table to keep my profile low just in case. I watched Shel struggle from his kneeling position, holding his left bicep. He slumped back in his chair, pulled off his sport jacket, and wrapped a sleeve around the wound. It looked like the bullet had passed clean through. He'd also received a flesh wound in his lower side, but I was stunned to see him so alert; I'd probably have gone into shock at the slightest gunshot wound. It was another testament to a life of violence. I could never shake such things off and keep functioning.

There was a bizarre pause as if everyone in the courtyard had frozen. It probably lasted mere seconds, because suddenly a series of loud shrieks erupted from the back alley and echoed through the courtyard. As if it was a signal, all hell broke loose.

As the gunman called Leitner screamed, "On me!" I could hear panicked screams from inside the café as people either scrambled toward the door and spilled out into the street or hid in place wherever they could find. Maestro had left his position.

Leitner kept screaming, "On me," and when he paused, I heard Jack Knife laughing. "You just called for the devil hisself."

Then, something from a nightmare occurred. I saw a shadow enter the rear of the courtyard.

A man dressed in black appeared from the alley entrance wearing a black surgical mask, burn scars noticeable above its edge. He was towing something. When he turned toward us, my blood froze. I'd never forgotten those dead eyes. It was Sharkey back from the dead. He slung something across the courtyard, a rope with what I thought must be three cantaloupes tied to it.

Shel hadn't forgotten either. With his right hand, he reached into his waistband and pulled out a pistol. I couldn't let him shoot, so I launched myself over the table, grabbing at his forearm, but I was too late. He whipped around, holding the gun in his palm, and slammed it into the side of my head. The pistol hit me just above the temple, and I fell onto the top of the table. My head spun, and I began fading in and out of consciousness. I slumped down in the chair and dropped my head onto the table, cradled in the crook of my arm.

Shel gripped the pistol to fire, but Maestro appeared like a specter, gun in each hand. He placed one against Shel's temple. "Drop it or die." Shel tossed the pistol on the deck. "Put an ear on the table." I thought I saw through the haze that Maestro guided Shel down on his chair and pinned Shel's head to the tabletop inches away from mine.

My head was spinning, and I could only catch sporadic words as I fought to stay conscious. "Let … play out, dipshit …"

I managed to wave a hand at Maestro. "Don't kill him …"

I heard different voices as things escalated.

"Sarge … what … fuck are … doing here?" The nephew.

"Watching your dumb ass … handed to you … Corporal." Maestro.

I heard screams … no, sirens, tires screeching.

"Drop the weapons and … behind your heads." Big Ben? Dead. Little Ben. *Looks like his father.*

"Can't do that, Ben …" Jack.

"Jack Knife … that you?" Ben.

I turned my head but couldn't seem to lift it. I could only see part of the courtyard through a haze and listen through ringing ears.

"Look over there …" Jack.

"Holy … Shark …? That you …? Thought you was dead." Ben.

"I am … assholes … woke me …" Shark in his throat-slit rasp.

More tires screeched. "Frank, for … sake … those damn newspeople away from here."

I managed to lift my head but was seeing double. I put my head back down.

Screams of anger. "You fucking assholes!" Leitner.

I felt a cold, wet bar towel on my head. Opened an eye. The blonde was wiping my face with a blood-soaked bar towel, a look of concern on her face.

"Holster ... firearms, men." Ben.

"Chief, what in hell are ... doing?"

"Damn it, Lloyd, just do ... see why my father ... never called out at night." Ben. "Let the town do its work."

"Hey, Kid, tell me ... about this one." Shark.

"Please ... let them arrest you ... don't want ... lose you. You're ... a son to me ..." Shel's voice, loud, still pinned to the table, inches from mine. He was pleading with his nephew to give himself up. Even in my stupor I knew that wouldn't be an option. Such predators never give up when their manhood is at stake.

"He's right-handed, slow with ... use his ... you'll kill him in seconds ..." That voice was familiar, older. I opened one eye and saw two huge brown eyes mere feet away from me.

"Run along, son ... got no time ... with children." Sharkey was baiting Shel's nephew.

A sudden primal shriek of anger erupted from the nephew.

I opened my eyes and leaned up on an elbow. I knew I was still reeling because I saw something impossible.

"Jesu e Maria. What in holy hell?" Maestro said.

I must have seen the same thing Maestro saw. Impossible. I put my head down and receded into the beautiful oblivion of unconsciousness.

# CHAPTER 22

I t took nearly a week for me to fully recover from the blow to the head. In another week, I was back on Sharon's bench by the river, reflecting on the horror brought to the First Street Café by armed mercenaries led by Shel Richardson's nephew. Shel's intention all along had been to extort money from me, and he had made the same mistake others had made when challenging the ghosts of Monk's Pool Hall.

The media had dubbed it the "Massacre in the Courtyard." The events had occurred so rapidly that no two witnesses could agree on the details. That was a good thing. It afforded Chief Ben Butler Jr., Little Ben, the option of precluding an investigation under Florida's controversial stand-your-ground law. Trained gunmen tried to shoot up the town and were stopped. End of story.

Little Ben's summation of events in his first television interview was simple and accurate: "A band of professional assassins came to our little town bent on murder. But they came to the wrong town. I hope this is a lesson to other bad people out there. This town is where bad men come to a bad end."

Other aspects of the story died more slowly, but the small-town folks involved closed ranks, refusing to cooperate when

*60 Minutes, 20/20,* and other high-profile newscasts came knocking. Eventually the spotlight moved on after a man known as Patient One and two of his friends, badly scarred men who had wreaked havoc that day, disappeared along with the target of the assassins—an aging transgender ex-con once purportedly connected to the mob.

The story of the massacre in the courtyard died as all tragic stories do in a gun culture like America's. Media attention moved on to the next tragic event, in this case another school shooting.

I, the aging transgender ex-con mentioned in several news stories—also forgotten to my great relief—sat quietly on a bench named after an angel. As I clasped the leather binder to my lap, I mumbled, "Finished at last." I stared wide-eyed at the vast glittering expanse of Lake Monroe on a miraculously brilliant day. It was as if I was seeing it for the first time, the day my grandfather brought me here when I was a girl named Margarite and taught me to toss a baited line hopefully into the current.

I was debating with my wicked soul regarding its fading will to exist. I had been exonerated by the man who admitted to framing me. But it left me hollow and empty. I'd been exonerated, but I remained estranged from a culture that had passed me by and had no place for me.

A spontaneous smile creased my lips as a cloud swept overhead and, in its wake, a white curtain opened. The lake erupted in rapturous light, a five-mile-wide river smiling up at the sun, millions of tiny glimmering mirrors sliding northward to the sea. For the moment I lost the debate with the darkness. Oblivion could wait.

I spoke to myself aloud, not caring who heard. "If I ever had a voice in this great cosmic choir, it was disharmonious and vulgar to human ears." I leaned back and shouted, "That's okay. At least I know who I am now."

A black family fishing down on the seawall turned, and the husband shouted, "Yes, suh! And that damn sure what counts, ain't it?"

I gave him a sweeping wave and shouted, "There'll be beer in the trunk next time, Big Tom."

Tom gave a grateful nod and returned the wave.

I turned my wounded eyes, a fading bruise around one, a healing cut above the other, south along Lake Drive, upriver. The street terminated at Mellonville Avenue, where a small monument commemorating Fort Mellon stood among unkempt azaleas and mulch. Fort Mellon was so named in the 1830s after an army captain, Charles Mellon, the sole white man killed in a so-called "Indian raid" in the Second Seminole War.

How was it that a monument was erected because a single white soldier was killed in the misnomer designated an "Indian raid" but there was no monument to the Seminoles killed by the army that day? These indigenous people were merely protecting homes, a lake that provided fish, and land that yielded game, vegetables, wild palmetto hearts, and palm trees with fronds to roof their huts.

I spoke aloud, "This town never stopped paying for the murder of innocents. But the spirit of innocence survives so long as avenging archangels stalk these streets."

Most importantly, the little boy, now a man, Patient One, had shown how he earned his reputation by revealing Shel's layered efforts to hide the truth.

I saw Sharkey for a fleeting moment as he disappeared in the aftermath of the conflict in the courtyard. I regained consciousness, though I was still woozy, and I was sitting next to the blonde, Summer, and Maestro was still holding a gun on Shel. Sharkey moved opposite the row of verdantly effusive terracotta pots. He'd been wearing a black surgical mask to hide facial scars when the gunman, Shel's nephew, attacked him. The mask was gone, and I saw that his cheeks were smooth as glass. Two faceless ghosts, he and Jack, timeless avengers. Sharkey backed away, those eyes scanning to assure the threat was gone as Little Ben and his men took control.

Sharkey turned those dead eyes on me as he moved silently toward the shadows.

*"Thank you."* I mouthed the words, once again struck by the fluidity of his movements. It was as the Kid always said. Sharkey didn't move; he contorted the space-time continuum. He gave me a barely perceptible nod as the shadows swallowed him. He'd stepped into this plane of existence only long enough to uphold Monk's credo. The red table runs true because Sharkey keeps the balance.

Just as these thoughts emerged, there he was, standing in front of me. The Kid but no longer the child I'd known. He was somewhere in his late thirties now. He had appeared next to Maestro in the thick of things, and just as he had in Monk's and in my shop, he called down the thunder that was Sharkey. He wore a white rough-weave shirt and navy pants. I was always startled by those huge brown eyes that saw into your heart.

"Hello, Stuart. You still look like Margarite. I like both of you."

That beautiful naivete. Why didn't everyone have it?

"Thanks, Kid. Aren't those media people out there after you? I read the news stories. Seems they follow you everywhere."

He smiled. "Nah. Jackie scared them away. A reporter asked him, 'How'd you get those scars?' Jack pulled his hood back and stared at the guy. 'I got 'em kissing the devil's ass. How'd you like to kiss mine?'"

I laughed. "Sounds very clever. Who fed him that line, as if I didn't know?"

He gave a shy grin. "Well, I did tell him about the *osculum infame* once. We were just joking around. He thought it was funny. I was trying to cheer him up." He frowned. "It took a long time for Jack to heal after the fire."

I remembered something. "And Silk died that night, didn't he?"

He turned and his voice was deeply sad. "I have to go now."

"Where?" I asked.

"You know."

Of course, I did. "The icehouse?"

He nodded. "Yeah. We set up Monk's just like when we were young. Why don't you come by?"

I grinned. "I already did. But you know that, right?"

The small grin flashed. "We needed to know what you looked like. It'd been a long time, and you changed genders. The prison cameras weren't very clear. Silk's Uncle Alphonse wrote you so you'd come. So, come by again."

I nodded. "Of course. But I have a lot of questions. Would you be willing to give me answers?"

He said through a wistful smile. "Sure."

I nodded. "Were you watching the whole time Shel and I were talking?"

He gave a slight nod, a deep frown on his brow.

I said, "Then you know what happened to Monk?"

Again, he gave a short nod. "I suspected something like this. The night of the fire at the Hatfield mansion was rife with evil. I just didn't know the details. But Jeff Jr. got what was coming, though that's another story."

"You mean the fight?" He nodded, and I continued, "I'm so sorry you had to find out about Monk this way. I didn't know until Shel told me."

He said quickly, "No, don't apologize. Thanks to you, we can help Bonnie gain closure." He paused, an angry frown furrowing his brow. "That man, Richardson. He hurt you."

I smiled wanly. "You're very smart. I hope we can be friends again."

His eyes widened, and the smile broadened. "Oh, I almost forgot. I have something for you."

He reached into his pants pocket and extended his hand. He held an envelope.

"Here." He grinned. He started to turn away but paused and fixed me with those huge eyes. I swore I could feel them boring into my soul. "God stopped longing for immortality the moment he breathed life into Monk."

He turned and followed Sharkey into the shadows.

I sat back in the chair, staring at the envelope, hope leaping from the depths of sadness like a shiny brim breaking the surface of Lake Monroe.

I felt a presence over my shoulder and turned as Maestro came up beside me. He'd been helping Little Ben sort things out.

"What's this?" He nodded at the envelope.

I tried to smile. "I don't know. I hope it's good news for a change."

He frowned. "Come now, you're fine. And holy shit were you right about this town. I've never seen anything like these ghosts of yours. I could make them rich ghosts down in Miami."

I laughed. "Something tells me you'll never get them out of this town. But why don't you come with me to see them? I know where they live."

He nodded. "I'm game. Now open your letter."

I used a café table knife to slit the envelope and retrieved a beautiful card with an imprint of an illuminated manuscript on the cover. I closed my eyes. I recognized it—a copy of a page from the *Book of Kells*. I opened it to reveal a letter written in an elegant hand. I didn't need to look at the signature to know who wrote it.

Dear Stuart,

I'm not sure where you'll be when this letter finds you, but it doesn't matter. It matters only that it reaches you in happier times. I don't have the words to express my gratitude for all you've done on my behalf. Or to thank your amazing friend. I knew you were a complicated person, but it seems you are far more complicated than I thought possible. I was in mortal danger in that mental institution, and without the help of your friend, I'd no doubt be dead.

I'm told Robert committed suicide. Something tells me that's not the whole story. If I'm right, I hope you don't think less of me when I say I didn't grieve for him.

I also must try to apologize for the unforgivable. Each morning when I awake, I look in the mirror and say, 'I'm sorry for how I treated you when we first met, Stuart.' No matter how many mornings I have left, they will be inadequate to express my regret. But I'll keep trying.

I'm beginning to find happiness now, thanks to you. One of the nurses in the hospital befriended me. She could tell I'd been falsely committed. We live together in High Springs. We're happy, Stuart. She took a job at Shand's Teaching Hospital at the University of Florida—your university. I've started taking classes there. It's like you once told me. The time will pass regardless, so I may as well have a college degree at the end of it. And you were right about something else. I'm smart enough to do this. Your university is all you said it was—a place I can be myself. I love being a fellow Gator.

I wish I knew how to repay you for releasing me from a life as Robert's mannequin, pun intended. How do you repay someone for freeing you from a lifetime of bondage? I wish I could have done that for you. I love my new partner, Laura, but I'll never forget you.

I'm older now. I had my thirty-second birthday recently, yet I feel my life is just beginning, a life you awakened me to. In the hospital they turned me into a drug-induced zombie but no more than the one I'd been before you awakened me with that "chat" in the prison library. I never think about that without smiling. I'm not sure I'll ever have such an explosive conversation again. My dearest Stuart, there is a special room in my heart that is yours alone. No one else will ever be given the key or allowed to enter that special place. It is ours.

All my love, Marilyn.

Maestro sat quietly as tears of relief and loss dripped down my smiling cheeks. If those tears could have become crystalized electricity, I could have strung them along the streets and lit every home in this old town for a lifetime.

# CHAPTER 23

A s I sat staring into the hazy distance of the lake, I witnessed a rare weather display. As the day wore on, the heat abated, but an invective caused an unusual mist to gather over the water. It looked as if the lake was shedding a thin translucent layer of skin like a great dark animal molting. The water was cooling with the current even as the air remained warm, a sign that nature was yielding to Florida's version of midsummer. Yet the air was oddly dry, the sky crystal clear, and the breeze had a soupcon of freshness as if the weather gods had decided to add a dash of something exotic to the thick atmospheric soup.

I'd read and reread the final pages of the journal, in which I had attempted to tell the story of events in the courtyard. Somehow my life sounded empty, as if I, like the lake, were molting a shallow skin with nothing beneath it. Why did it all seem trite in the aftermath? Mine wasn't the worst story in history, was it? I needed to stop feeling sorry for myself.

The lake, which moments before had beckoned me to join it in an unholy baptism, had become once again a sign of hope and my morose thoughts of suicide self-indulgent and cowardly.

I pulled a recent newspaper article from my satchel, written by

Ray Cleaver of the *Miami Herald*, opened the journal, and once more began to reread my final entry.

It's been a more than a week since I met Shel Richardson in the courtyard of the café on First Street. It took time to process his final treachery and heal from his violent attack. I've written of the horrors of rape as if they happened to someone else, but it took three operations to knit my colorectal muscles back together to avoid wearing adult diapers for the rest of my life. And I will likely always suffer bouts of TMJ from having swollen penises shoved down my throat until I thought my face would explode. I thought of all the *Zigeuner*, *Unerwunschten*, and *Juden* who labored in the death camps under Fascism. If he was alive today, Dante would create a new trench in Malebolge for such inhumanity. There are many flavors of horror in prison, and I was force-fed a smorgasbord of its nastiest cuisine.

Yet the shameless betrayal of one man stood out among all other atrocities. The Aryans never pretended friendship before their brutal assaults. I at least enjoyed the delicious vengeance of stealing the thirty pieces of silver paid for my betrayal. The taste was bitter.

I can only recall those last minutes in the courtyard in pristine vignettes of magnificence. Yet there were far broader repercussions. Immediately prior to my stint in iso, a little over a year ago now, a series of arrests were made. In a sweeping dragnet, several high-level members of known crime organizations were incarcerated under the RICO Act, starting with one Enrico Cipolla from Philadelphia.

After Enrico Cipolla's arrest, the US Department of Justice sent a special FBI internal investigation task force to Miami to guide the arrests of those who survived the war while simultaneously overseeing an internal investigation of the FBI's Miami office and the Miami Police Department's Vice Division.

Just over a year later, a second spate of arrests occurred. In the aftermath of the media-dubbed "Massacre in the Courtyard," the internal investigation task force was reassembled to examine evidence from events in a small town on Lake Monroe, prompted by evidence from "an unknown source." One FBI agent dubbed it, "a second installment of documentation" sent to a reporter at the *Miami Herald*. It provided recorded telephone conversations complete with voice recognition data, bank account and transaction data between gang members, and a host of criminal elements, including one of the gunmen in the courtyard, Leitner Dredge, now deceased.

Aside from a crime sweep in Philadelphia, New Orleans, and Miami, a flurry of national media attention focused on a once-famous mental hospital inmate known as Patient One, who had recently been released from the Florida State Mental Hospital in Chattahoochee. The small town on Lake Monroe had once been his home when he made national headlines many years before. This mysterious figure had again disappeared, according to Ray Cleaver of the *Miami Herald*.

The one remaining mystery was the beheading of three men, part of Leitner Dredge's assassination squad, whose headless bodies were found in the rear alleyway of the café. The bodies were all dressed in military-grade tactical gear, while the heads were found tied together in the courtyard, next to a fellow gunman with a lethal knife wound to the throat.

Also arrested was Sheldon Richardson, a small-time fixer and odd-job man for several crime families, who suffered flesh wounds from an unknown assailant during the courtyard massacre. He was released on bond.

There were more arrests, more political backslapping, and more news stories, but the events began to bleed together. I can no longer force myself to care. Five months in deep isolation caused my personality to splinter and nearly disintegrate. The only thread holding it together was the thought of a girl adrift in a glass bubble. I'd discovered what happened to her, and that was what mattered.

I leaned back against the bench, let the journal drop into my lap, closed my eyes, and tilted my face to the sun. I was startled when a large Budweiser truck rumbled behind me and down the street toward the marina, engulfing me in shadow. I chuckled to myself. Nothing should frighten me anymore.

As it passed, another shadow remained, a human one. It stood as still as a post, and I could feel its owner staring at me from behind. My skin crawled, and those erector pili went to work on the nape of my neck. It moved toward me and circled the bench. The slats creaked as the figure sat.

"*Buongiorno*, D."

"Maestro?" Apprehension was replaced by elation. "What are you doing here? How'd you find me?"

"You're joking. I was only here once, but all I had to do was drive along the lake until I saw a giant blue hunk of shit Chrysler, and *eccola*."

I laughed. "Genius."

He leaned close and stared at my head. "Looks like that little pimple on your head is clearing up."

"*Pfft*," I muttered. "I suppose you'll be patting yourself on the back all over again for saving my scrawny butt?"

He laughed but quickly became serious. "I was just about to squeeze one in that Richardson fucker's brainpan. Why'd you stop me?"

I closed my eyes. "I barely remember. Part of me wanted him to know I took everything from him. And part of me didn't want to be the cause of more death."

We fell silent and sat together staring out over the lake. He crossed his neatly creased black pant legs and placed a cream-colored silk sleeve over the bench behind my shoulders. I saw a glint of the sun reflect off his expensive Italian loafers. His dark hair was slicked back, and a pair of wraparound sunglasses shaded his eyes. *Always handsome*, I thought.

We sat quietly, watching boats glide over the sparkling lake, a team of kayaks row past just beyond the marina, and a few motorboats create whitecaps in the distance, their faraway drones wafting across the open water.

Finally, Maestro said, "Tell me what happened in that last moment. I know you were awake then. I'd like to hear it from you. I can't believe what I saw."

I placed the journal carefully on the bench between us. "You mean Sharkey."

He said, "Of course. Did you see the same optical illusion I saw?" He looked down at the journal. "I see you're still carrying Ralph's ass around."

I frowned. "Not for much longer. It's the only thing they let me keep in iso. I hate to admit it, but it was like a talisman. It was too dark to read or write, but just holding it made it seem I was connected to reality."

I leaned forward, pulled my wallet from my back pocket, and extracted a yellowed newspaper article. I opened the ragged clipping carefully and handed it to Maestro.

The old newspaper photograph was faded but legible.

"That's him. I can tell." His voice was oddly somber.

"Yes, it is. It was his one and only football game. He was the quarterback."

"There's something wrong with the …" He turned his body toward me. "This photograph wasn't doctored?"

"The photographer swore it wasn't. No problem with the lens, no overexposure, nothing wrong with the camera." I stared down at the clipping in his hand.

Maestro handed it back to me, careful not to damage it. "It could explain what I saw. He moved into the shadows, and I thought it was a trick of the light. Still. Someone would have to be moving at unnatural speed, like lightning in a bottle, to fool a camera like that."

I gave a slight nod. "Lightning in a bottle."

Maestro stared vacantly over the lake. "The speed completely fooled me."

"Our school was small. Never a powerhouse. In that football game, he single-handedly destroyed one of the most powerful teams in the state. He was barely a teenager. It caused a huge stir. The other school protested. The photo was published repeatedly, but that article is about him being banned from playing because he was too young."

"Too young or too good?"

I nodded. "Way too good."

"Who is he, D? I mean really. And where is he now?"

I rubbed my eyes with the heels of my hands. "A dirt-poor kid raised in the migrant camps. Forced to fight against adults from the time he was old enough to know he had to fight to live, or so a social worker told me."

Maestro pursed his lips and nodded as I added, "What I saw in the alley? I've seen it once before. The first time he saved my life. It's why I don't question his speed."

"And why you asked me to leave you alone? How'd you know he was even alive?"

"Remember when you said you saw only a bum enter the courtyard? That was Jack Knife. He came to give me a signal. If he was there, so was Sharkey."

I turned from the lake and stared at Maestro's handsome profile. "I don't believe in fate. Prison knocks that out of you. But what you witnessed in that courtyard was something I should have, I don't know … respected more?"

I again opened my wallet and pulled out a second news clipping. It, too, was old but not quite as fragile. I opened it and held it so Maestro could see it clearly.

"What's this?" Maestro lifted his sunglasses to look at the news photo. It looked like an abstract artwork, a large room with a stage and a silhouette at a podium with everything behind it in flames.

"My wallet was confiscated when I went to prison. I forgot about these clippings. I found them just this morning when I was looking for the registration for the Chrysler. I'm getting rid of it ... and maybe everything else before—"

Maestro was staring at me hard. "No, you're not. Not after all you've survived. I've saved your ass too many times for you to fucking toss it in a lake. Besides, this lake is nicer from this side."

I smiled, though I couldn't hide the sadness that kept creeping back in, battering at my defenses just when I thought I was free of it. "I won't. I'm just suffering a horrible case of time distortion. Tell me about Leitner Dredge. How was it possible you knew him?"

Maestro chuckled. "Corporal Dredge. Or I should say Corporal Top? The men called him that because he was wound so tight; when he spun out, he caused bad shit to happen. More full of shit than a Sicilian pizza. Wound tight and looking for a fight."

He continued as he turned to stare out over the lake. "A lot of us do stints in the military. Most enlist to avoid doing time; others volunteer to get free training. It's like a contest to see who can get into the toughest outfits. Plus, afterwards the cops don't like coming after fellow vets." He looked at me askance. "And some of us just want to serve this great country."

I looked at him sharply. "What? Really?"

Maestro burst out laughing. "Jeez, D, you're still so ... sweet."

I sneered. "Asshole."

Maestro sat quietly as the levity passed. "I've been in the family since I was old enough to walk a bookie account from one storefront to another. Mr. O took me in when I was a kid. Oldest story in the book, right? Like your movies. He controlled a small piece of turf in Miami for old man Cipolla, Marco's grandfather. He's gotta be spinning in his grave watching Marco get popped faster than a virgin playing squat tag in a dildo factory."

I snickered. I knew he was baiting me. "Better a dildo than a cock. You can throw a dildo in the trash afterward without having to pretend it's amusing at dinner."

I'd never heard Maestro belly laugh. "Point to the transgender."

I smiled. "Thank you. And I'm glad we could keep Mr. O out of this mess. How is he?"

"He sends his regards. He told me you saved him, D. I'm impressed. What happened?"

"It's pretty simple. The feds were trying to freeze his offshore accounts, break his balls so he'd cooperate. I found a way to bring his money in electronically by bouncing it through half the banks on the planet right under their noses. Then I sold his Bitcoin. That gave him short-term capital.

"Oh, that reminds me." I reached into the satchel and brought out another envelope and extended it to Maestro. "Here. I cashed out your Bitcoin. Part of your pension."

Maestro stared at the envelope. "Pension? What the fuck you talking about?'"

"Your Bitcoins. I cashed them out."

He laughed. "Jesus, I'd forgotten all about that shit. Well, at least I can buy lunch with my pension."

I grinned. I'd been waiting for this. "You can buy a lot of lunches."

He took the envelope and ran a finger under the flap. He flipped it open and pulled out a certified check. I'd never seen Maestro stunned, even when he was facing men wanting to kill him. The look on his face in that moment would become one of my happiest memories.

"Christ on a crutch, D. I can't take this. You told me you only paid a few pennies for that shit."

"I did. But don't you remember me telling you we shouldn't get rid of it when we were finished? I held it. I bought a ton of Bitcoin for under eight cents each, remember? I needed two hundred thousand dollars' worth just to pull off the fake payments to assassins. I actually used all the money Mr. O gave me that first time, half a mil, to buy all I could. I kept adding."

I pulled out my cell phone and poked at the browser, shading the screen from the sun. "Here's what Bitcoin is worth today."

Maestro looked at the phone. "You gotta be shittin' me. Nearly eleven grand for one Bitcoin?"

I said, "Thanks to G1's advice, I sold it just as it was peaking. A little over seventeen K per Bitcoin. It was falling, so some of our holdings sold for around fifteen. How many did I give you and Mr. O?"

Maestro shook his head. "Five hundred each."

I shrugged. "Then do the math. And don't worry. I've liquidated three billion worth and still held some back. Now, what were you telling me about the old days?"

Maestro said, "Look. I don't fucking deserve this. It's almost eight mil, for Christ's sake."

I said, "Yes, it is, and yes, you do fucking deserve it. You deserve far more than this. Now tell me what you were saying about the old days."

Maestro spoke quickly. "Bad stories gotta be told quick and dirty. During the *Cocaine Cowboy* days in Miami, things got crazy. Mr. O and the others had to go underground for a while. Before he left, he suggested I get out of circulation. He's the one who suggested the military, so I walked into a recruiting office and joined up. Told the sergeant I wanted special forces. He laughed, said, 'Okay, hotshot,' and sent me straight to Bragg.

"I sailed through. Best scores in the cycle and then off to Afghanistan. Ended up with my own platoon after our second looie ditty-bopped into a Taliban sniper's kill zone first day out." Maestro paused with a sad look on his face. "Those academy kids should spend time on the streets. Good kid. Balls of steel, but no, you know … antenna. You gotta have bullet sense."

Maestro leaned back and put his hands behind his head. "Anyway, Corporal Top was a squad leader in my platoon. I didn't know him that good, and he thought I was a lifer. One day in the mountains, we caught this Taliban soldier. The guys bet he'd say nothing. Those Taliban would sometimes chew their own tongues off before they'd talk. I pulled out a trick I learned from one of Toto Riina's Sicilian death squads to send a message while getting information. *Uccidere i sensi*—slaying the senses, one at a time. It's no fun, but it works.

"I peeled out an eye and put it on a stick to stare back at him. Then I dug out an inner ear, careful not to touch his brain. I put the fleshy part on a stick next to the eye. I told the translator to tell him what his heaven would be like: seventy-two virgins but no way to enjoy it. I took one of his testicles, and he passed out. When he woke up, I ate it in front of him. I told him I was slowly taking his place in heaven. I'd be fucking his virgins with his *cazzo*. He started singing like a canary."

I stammered, "Jesus, you ate his testicle?"

He issued an exasperated sigh and shook his head. "Fuck, no, D. I ate a goat's testicle. In Sicily it's a delicacy if you cook it right. He didn't know it was from a goat. Do you know what your nuts look like out of the sack?"

I said, "Actually, yes, because I saw them before they went in. Remember? I'm transgender. Hello?"

Maestro flashed a grin and leaned forward, his elbows on his knees. He gazed out over the lake and became more intense as he continued, "At one point, while I'm taking this brave Taliban fighter apart, I look up and there's Dredge watching, wide-eyed. He had this crazy look on his face as he watched me peel this guy. The next morning, he was gone. Off to capture his own Taliban one of his squad said. I was fucking furious, but he was a loose cannon anyway, and frankly, I hoped he wouldn't come back. He didn't. He was captured. But a few months later, he escaped and showed up singing his own praises. They quietly gave him a dishonorable discharge. I finished that tour and went home. I didn't see him again until he walked into that courtyard, waving his cock around. Same old fucking Corporal Top, wound tight and looking for a fight."

Maestro finished, "Anyway, after two tours, I went back to work for Mr. O until he was busted. You know the rest."

I nodded. "Yes. I know the rest."

Maestro pointed at the journal. "Did you write what happened two weeks ago?"

I said, "All but those last few moments when Leitner chased Sharkey into the shadows."

I opened the journal to the final empty page. On the verso was something that astonished Maestro.

"Whoa, what in hell? It looks like your computer screen in prison."

I nodded. "It's Leonardo. Mirror writing."

"Holy shit. How would anybody read that? The writing is tiny."

"That's the point. When I first started a journal, my cellmates kept tearing it up because I told the truth. I lost the first several years of entries, so I started learning mirror writing. I was a jeweler, remember? All I needed was a tiny mirror and a magnifying glass. When they found this, they thought I was just a nutjob."

Maestro laughed. "Amazing. It must take forever."

I smiled. "You get used to it."

Maestro and I sat in silence as a few pedestrians strolled by. A young couple waved to me, and I nodded in return. Several yards down the seawall, Tom and his family were packing up their fishing gear for the day after having their usual good luck. Tom could barely carry his fish bucket. He and the two boys waved; his wife was carrying their youngest, so she just shot us a big grin as they climbed into Tom's old pickup.

*I'm going to buy Tom a new truck,* I thought. Big Tom was a story in himself.

# CHAPTER 24

A s Maestro and I sat watching life on the lake, more pedestrians began to show up as the workday drew to a close. I was stunned at how content I felt just sitting next to Maestro on Sharon's bench.

Finally, he said, "So, we just leave the end hanging? We agree Dredge charged into the shadows waving his pig sticker and seconds later staggered out and dropped dead, sliced up like sushi. But the part when he tried to kill Sharkey, we pretend we didn't see?"

I forced a smile. "We saw a man move faster than the eye could follow. That's how a young boy survived the migrant camps. Survival is the ultimate motivator."

"Is that the end of the story?" Maestro stared unfocused into the light mist just beginning to dissipate as it drifted across the lake's surface.

"There are some loose ends. Shel is ruined emotionally and financially. I used my computer to strip his accounts. But he's a sociopath; he'll make a comeback. He put his house on the market. He doesn't know it, but I bought it. He'll have enough from the proceeds to leave town. If I know him, he'll find some rich elderly woman to charm. I don't care."

"What about the blonde? Dredge's wife, Summer?" Maestro asked.

"Sarah. Her name is Sarah." She'd told me her real name, and I thought I'd finally gotten one up on Maestro. Of course not.

"Hmm," he said. "I thought it would be Rebecca. She looks like a Rebecca."

I stared at him. "You knew she was lying about her name?"

He shook his head. "You are truly still so very sweet. She was playing Dredge from day one. She was ten times smarter. We had Dredge pegged in the field. He thought he was so slick he could slide through a keyhole. They're the easiest to play."

I could only grin like Jigs. "Someday, I'll learn. Anyway, when I came to, she was still holding a towel to my head. I gave her Shel's money. Poetic justice. She told me she was going home to … I don't know … one of the landlocked states. She wants to buy her parents a house. They never recovered from her sister's unsolved murder. Then she may come back here. We'll see. I'll sell or rent my parents' house and move into Shel's. It's a beautiful old Victorian on Oak Avenue."

Maestro nodded. "I hope she does come back. I'd like to see her again."

I couldn't help but think that would be a perfect match.

Maestro said, "You mentioned Shel but didn't say what happened to him."

A smile teased the corners of my lips. "Complete capitulation. I took everything from him, and"—I stretched a leg out and reached down to pull a small pouch from my satchel—"he sent me this." I tipped the bag, and a necklace with a large stone fell out.

"Damn. Beautiful. Is it valuable?" Maestro asked.

"It's extremely valuable, a perfect Cat's-eye alexandrite. There was a one-line note that said, 'Stones that change color are rare and beautiful. The same can't be said of people.'"

We sat in silence until I said, "I've decided to send it back to him. I'll tell him he should sell it to help him start over. Without the color changes. I—"

"You want to forgive," Maestro said.

I nodded. "He was brought low, Maestro. He lost Dredge, his only family. I took everything, and I watched him wither. I realized what I'd become if I didn't let go."

Maestro nodded. "You amaze me. In a good way."

We sat silently for several more moments until Maestro shot me a sidelong glance. "And her?"

"Her who?"

"D. Remember who you're talking to."

I grinned. "She's … happy. I paid off the mortgage on the house she and her wife bought in High Springs." I reached again into the satchel and pulled out a book. "She sent me this."

Maestro read the title. "*Ulysses.* Isn't that the book—"

"Yes, it's the book. But this one is very special. It's one of 750 signed first editions published by Shakespeare and Company in 1922."

Maestro nodded, the corners of his mouth turned down and eyebrows raised. "Is it valuable?"

"My guess is she paid no less than seventy-five K for a copy of this quality." I couldn't suppress my excitement.

He said, "Whoa. I gotta admit, no girl would shell out that kind of dough for me. And if she did, it damn sure wouldn't be for a book."

I smiled as I rewrapped the book in the tissue and tucked it gingerly back into the satchel. "A lot of thought went into this purchase. I told her I always wanted to collect rare books, and this is her way of helping me start with something that meant a lot to me."

"Well, she must not be hurting financially to pay that much for a book."

"She's not," I said cagily.

"Okay, own up. What else did you do for her?" Maestro crossed his arms as he leaned back against the bench.

I chuckled. "It was a fair set of trades. Summer ... Sarah wanted nothing to do with the money she had bilked from marks in Vegas with Leitner. So, I traded her Shel's fortune for the remainder of the money in the trunk of their CRV. About two-and-a-half mil. I gave that to Marilyn. Plus, she got a nice life-insurance payout from Robert Manakin's estate that someone we both know and love handed her on a platter."

Maestro rubbed his chin and with a sly grin said, "You're an admirable man. But I still say it's a damn shame, you know. Such a beauty going to waste. Her so-called wife is probably also a beauty. A double loss to mankind."

"Goddamnit, Maestro, how provincial ..." I paused and sneered. "You asshole ..."

Maestro leaned forward and stared as the waters sloshed against the seawall. A boat dropped speed to enter the marina, and a few gulls floated in perfect harmony with the wind, wings spread, drifting on the thermal waves rising from the lake.

Maestro said, "And how about Sharkey and Jack Knife? What of them?"

I nodded. "I think I told you they're living in Monk's icehouse. I'm going over there in a few minutes." I turned to him, eyes pleading. "Would you come with me?"

"Will someone explain these news clips?" he asked.

I said, "Yes. And much more."

"Then I'm in. Looks like I'm going to become part of your little town."

I smiled. "You're welcome to have a room in my new house. It's huge."

Maestro grinned. "I might take you up on that from time to time."

I became suddenly morose. "Maestro? I need to tell you ..."

"Tell me what?" He turned to me.

"There's something I could never write in my journal. I buried it. Deep. But now. I have to tell someone. I have to face it."

He said only, "Get it over with. It's not like I don't know."

I was stunned. "What do you mean you know?"

He said, "You gotta start hiding your buttons. Of course, I don't know exactly what it is, but it's got you tied in knots. You're free, you're rich, yeah, you're still a nerd with a computer, but I already forgave you for that."

The dam burst, and tears erupted, but my voice emerged from the pain with conviction. "When I was a child, my piece of shit father started coming into my room at night. At first he just sat on the edge of my bed and stroked my head, but he called me his 'little guy.' Then he started touching me, saying, 'Gosh, little guy, where's your peepee?' Then one night, he came back from that fucking country club drunk, and this time there was no touching; he just rolled me onto my stomach and shoved his cock in my ass and started saying, 'That's my sweet boy. That's the boy I love ...'"

I collapsed against Maestro, sobbing convulsively. Maestro put an arm across my shoulders and let me cry.

I slowly calmed into a mewling mantra. "Jeez, what am I, Maestro? What am I?"

Maestro gave my shoulder a gentle squeeze. "You're worried you changed your sex to please a sick father? Let me ask you a simple question. Why should you give a purple fuck? Your old man was a worthless pile of yak snot. Every kid I know had some crazy uncle or cousin who tried to diddle him at Thanksgiving or Christmas. I actually put my *pazzo* Uncle Angelo's cock in my mouth once."

I laughed through the tears. "You did that?"

Maestro nodded. "Goddamn right. Then I bit down so hard he emptied his wallet on the floor next to me so I'd let go."

I turned to stare out over the lake but saw nothing. "I wish I could just tune out the demons like that."

He said, "Don't create a problem just to wallow in it. That's what politics are for. Before I met you, I'd have kept killing for the fun of it. We need people around to make us change for the better, to help us think of a better way. The end."

I chuckled. "You make it seem so easy. But I'll try."

Maestro smiled. "Good. Come on. Let's go visit your friends."

We rose from Sharon's bench and turned from Lake Monroe.

# EPILOGUE

My heart soared as I looked out over the Italian landscape. I'd spent thirty years rambling through the levels of hell and now I was nearing Empyrean, the highest level of paradise. I was spending a couple of weeks at Villa Valentina in Levanto while my purchase of a beautiful villa in the hills overlooking the Ligurian Sea was finalized. G1 had agreed to help with renovations. She had the necessary contacts.

A warm early-fall sun painted the Ligurian a fiery orange from my table at a café perched at the edge of an escarpment. I was staying at Villa Valentina but spent a lot of time having my driver take me around this stunningly beautiful area. Today I'd chosen a café high in the mountains with panoramic views of the Ligurian and its coastal mountains. I had decided to rename my new palazzo, Palazzo Vente Nuovo—Palace 29, the number of my room in block E.

Of all the strange events I'd witnessed during events in a café courtyard, the strangest occurred only a few days afterward once I was fit enough to leave the house. I couldn't tell anyone about it. Not even Maestro. I had misled him when I asked him to come to the icehouse as if it was my first time. For now, it was a secret for those of us from the small town on Lake Monroe. Someday I would tell Maestro about it—perhaps when he visited me in Italy as planned.

One morning, I was at home, nursing an espresso and a splitting headache when my cell phone rang from an unknown number. I assumed it was another reporter and let it go to voice mail. Moments later, a text came through: *Please come to the icehouse. Something you must witness.* I immediately got into the Chrysler, drove the mile and half, and parked in the dirt parking lot in front of the massive structure. This time as I approached the door, it opened on its own. No one was there, but I was no longer afraid. I entered and walked deep into the interior. It was a sunny day, but the only lights came through cracks in the planks. I looked left and saw new construction—a twenty-foot wall reaching to the second level.

"Hello?" I called.

A door opened in the new wall, and Neil—a.k.a. the Kid; a.k.a. Patient One; a.k.a. the Mad Hacker—stood silhouetted.

"We've been waiting for you." His voice was low and soft.

I walked across the plank floor and entered a huge room that looked exactly as I remembered Monk's Pool Hall, red Budweiser lights receding into a long narrow room. The cue racks and shelves were the same. Even the rainbow of the Wurlitzer jukebox stood in a side niche. The only difference was the absence of a pall of cigarette smoke.

I followed Neil to the low wall in the back, where a red table sat surrounded by three men. Jack Knife and Sharkey sat on the red felt, facing me, but I could see only the back of the third man who sat on a metal chair set against the waist-high wall facing them. In the low light I could still see Sharkey's burn scars reflecting the light as if he had mirrors for cheeks. They were probably sanded as part of the effort to heal him. Jack Knife pointed to a high-back chair angled so I could see all three. When I walked through the gap in the wall and looked at the third man,

I gasped. There sat Shel Richardson, blindfolded, gagged, and handcuffed.

Neil, Patient One, took a seat in a chair opposite me; we had Shel surrounded. Without wasting time, Patient One, for that's who he was in those minutes, pointed at Shel with a look that was no longer innocent or naïve.

I asked, "How did you get him away from the police?"

Patient One spoke flatly, eyes on Shel, again stripped of the naivete. "The same way I got your friend out of the mental hospital." He looked past Shel and up at me. "He lied to you. He's an excellent liar. He's had a lifetime of practice. They call it sociopathic lying, and this man has elevated to an art. He layers facts as if he's spiraling to the truth, but he circles it like a buzzard over a dying animal. The truth has always been dead to him. He obfuscates. He can fool anyone"—he leaned close and cast an evil glance at Shel—"almost."

I sat staring back and forth between Neil's huge brown accusatory eyes and Shel. Neil signaled to Jack Knife, who pushed easily off the table, removed Shel's blindfold, and peeled the ball gag out of his mouth. Then he walked to the corner of the low wall, pulled a floor lamp over, switched it on, and adjusted it so that it illuminated Shel's face.

Shel started to speak. "You fucking punks—"

In a flash of lightning, Jack had a knife at his throat, his raspy voice dead serious. "You call me punk again, I'll slit your fucking throat and dump you in Lake Monroe like you did to that girl."

Sharkey sat stone still, staring at Shel with those dead eyes. I'd never seen Shel cornered before. I was amazed that he couldn't shut up.

He looked frantically at Neil. "You don't know me. You have no idea about the truth."

Jack Knife shoved the ball gag back in Shel's mouth. "Shut up or I'll shove it down your throat."

Shel stared wide-eyed at him and then gave a small nod. Jack removed the gag.

Neil's nostrils flared, and one side of his mouth turned up into a half smile, "Oh, yes … I do know your lies and your truth, Mr. Richardson." He looked at me. "What did he tell you at the café?"

"I was shocked at the voice that came out of Neil. It was a hissing, evil sound. I recoiled and looked at Sharkey. He said only, "It's Banks. Best not to ask." I looked back at Neil. It was as if he had an alternate personality. Is that why he was sent away to a mental hospital?"

I thought for a moment. I told Shel he could keep some secrets. I caught myself. Hell no. I deserved to know everything, "He told me my father was driving the car that killed the young woman I was accused of murdering."

While I spoke, Neil leaned toward Shel, staring hard at his face. "Could you say that just a bit slower and give me more details?"

Shel snapped, "You're no mind reader."

Neil grinned. "I'm not a mind reader, but I can see the shadows there. Since you think I'm lying, let me see your eyes while Stuart speaks. What have you got to lose? You don't believe me, right?"

Shel sneered. "Bullshit. It's bullshit."

Neil said, "Go ahead, Stuart."

I glared at Shel as I spoke. What treachery had he carried out, now? "I found out that my father's car was sent to a chop shop in Miami to repair damages he and Shel wished to keep secret. I was sure it was how Sharon was killed. He told me the story of that night. He told me my father was giving him and Jeffrey Hatfield Sr. a ride." I hesitated and glanced at Sharkey. "With our friend Monk dead in the trunk. Murdered by Jeffrey Hatfield, Jr., who was trying to find Sharkey."

I could sense Sharkey's tension exuding like electricity, and a low rumble came from Jack's chest, but Neil never took his eyes off Shel's face.

"Keep going." The anger in the hissing voice was evident. It was chilling.

"He said it was raining and the streets were wet. My father lost control of the car, and it jumped the curb and accidentally hit Sharon. She was out walking in the rain. She had a condition that made her sensitive to the sun but loved walking in the rain."

Neil cut in quickly, "Your father wasn't driving ... This poor liar was driving, wasn't he, Mr. Shel Richardson? And I don't believe Sharon was alone. But we'll find out."

Shel began to protest. "Stop this, you fucks—"

But Jack's knife was again at his throat, and this time I saw a red line under the blade.

Neil held up a hand, and Jack backed off. Then Neil turned to me. "I'm going to find the trail of snail mucous this gastropod left behind by having him tell me the truth."

Shel's voice was full of unconvincing anger. "You fuckers will pay if you don't let me go now."

Neil leaned close to Shel's ear. "All the ones who think they're clever are first to give up their secrets; they can't help it. Surely a smart man like you can keep a secret."

Shel stared hard at Neil's huge orbs. His face reddened.

Neil said, "You were driving the car."

Then for reasons I will never understand, he suddenly began to slowly enunciate a series of words as he watched Shel intently. "Monk ... crooked nigger ... black man ... daughter ... car ... Sharon ... rain ... bricks ... sister ... sidewalk ... lover ..."

Shel closed his eyes, but Neil continued relentlessly, "... pool hall ... accident ... desire ... wife ... mother ... father ... wet ... snow ... hope ... white ... loss ... albino ... anemia ... angel ... Chrysler ... chenille ... silk ..."

It went on for several minutes. The handcuffs prevented Shel from covering his ears, but as Neil spoke, Shel's face went suddenly blank, followed by a look of hatred that transformed him. Shel suddenly launched himself toward Neil. The cuffs held his hands around the chair back, but as he careened, he and the chair dropped at Neil's feet, his hands forming claws behind his back.

His shriek was that of a madman. "Shut up, you son of a bitch. Shut up, shut up."

Humans are susceptible to suggestion. That's how lie detectors work. I knew Neil was beyond brilliant, even as a small child. Still, I'd never witnessed anything like what I saw in the dimness of Monk's reconstructed pool hall. He was pulling Shel's mind apart. I'd read the news accounts, stories of Patient One. I thought them highly speculative. He once wreaked havoc at a class reunion. Most of those he targeted left town. Several committed suicide. The stories didn't go far enough. It also explained why he ended up in a mental institution. Better to have him locked away than running amok with the most lethal weapon known to man: the blatant, unexpurgated truth.

Neil moved back, and Shel lay sobbing at his feet, saying one word over and over: "Sharon." Even as his voice weakened, his lips continued to form her name, strings of mucous from his mouth and nose flexing with each syllable.

Neil motioned to Jack, who lifted Shel upright. Shel hung his head, the low moan of her name droning on.

Neil spoke to me in a pitiless voice. "He was driving." He turned back to Shel. "And I believe he killed Sharon intentionally. And she wasn't alone, was she, Mr. Sheldon Richardson?"

Shel's face was a mask of hatred as he screamed, spittle flying from his mouth. Nothing of the slick sophisticate remained. "You don't know what you're talking about."

Neil met Shel's gaze. "You killed her. She had aplastic anemia. My guess is you did something to cause it. You're riddled with guilt." He looked at me. "He didn't deny killing the parents, did he?"

I was speechless and could only shake my head.

"Well," Neil said. "No matter. I found the story of their deaths. Got the parents out of the way and convinced her he could take care of her. Her father was a talented artist. This man made it look like a suicide pact. Poisoned them and locked them in the father's studio. But he locked Sharon in as well. Drugged her, maybe tied her up so it would look like the father tried to get her, too, but didn't give her enough poison. That way she'd be free of any accusations. Lots of paints and solvents in a studio. Sharon wasn't found for two days. Breathed a lot of benzene for those forty-eight hours. Acquired aplastic anemia, it's called. But I don't give a shit about that."

The depths of Shel Richardson's savagery stunned me more than anything I'd heard in thirty long years in a maximum security prison. Even my imagined menagerie of Tommy's taxidermy collection of body parts paled in comparison.

Neil kept mining Shel's memory, and I felt my own mind drift free of its moorings.

"I'm going to tell you what you've done. But here's your one chance. Do you want to say it, Mr. Sheldon Richardson? If I have to say it, there will be no garnish on your shit sandwich."

Shel's anger began to evolve. His facial muscles began to twitch, and his eyes widened. "You don't know. You don't know." His voice became an animalistic grumbling.

Neil said, "Say it. They were together, weren't they, Mr. Richard Sheldon Richardson? You couldn't believe what you were seeing. All you thought sacrosanct was shattered in a single moment. After all those years you've tried to bury it and pave it over. Say it. Tell us how proud you are of yourself, little man." Neil stood up and screamed at Shel. "Say it!"

Shel put his head down on his chest and began shaking his head robotically. "No. I didn't. I couldn't."

Neil sat back down. "Last chance." His voice was suddenly calm.

A whine began in Shel's throat and rose slowly in timbre until it became a loud moan. He slumped forward in his chair and began sobbing loudly.

I had to know. I turned to Patient One. "Please, Neil. Please tell me."

Neil stood and stared down at the wreckage of Shel.

"Everything he told you was true except one critical fact. I'm sure your father was in the car but in the passenger seat. This great manipulator was driving." He shot Shel a look of hatred. "Not very good at it, are you Mr. Richardson? Don't manipulate or hide the truth as well as you thought, do you? I saw men like you by the dozen in Chattahoochee. New ones locked up every day, pathological liars and murders. None of you can hide the truth from someone who knows how to see it."

He continued the story, never taking his eyes off Shel's face. "He was driving that night, and when he came to the corner of Fifth and Oak, he made sure to stop at the stop sign. He would be driving ever so carefully with Monk's body in the trunk. As he sat at the stop sign, the headlights shined across the intersection, headlights and streetlights reflecting off wet brick streets, flickers of raindrops shimmering. Maybe he wasn't seeing things correctly in the strange night rain. Surely the glare on the streets must have confused his vision. But as he stared, his vision cleared, and he saw a girl on the sidewalk across the intersection, a pale young girl he loved passionately, standing in the rain."

He shifted his gaze to me. "She was talking intimately with our friend Silk. Silk and Sharon—an albino and a girl with aplastic anemia. Two snow angels. Sharon liked the feel of warm rain on her sensitive skin, and so did Silk. Many was the time when we were huddled around the red pool table on a cloudy day, and a light rain would begin to fall. Silk—our beautiful white angel of death—would hear it, and we knew what would happen. He'd step in the back room where I slept after Sharkey was old enough to get his own place. Silk would take off his long-sleeve shirt and come out in a T-shirt. Shark or Jack would say, 'It's a Silk rain,' and Silk would give us his big grin and slip out the door just to walk and feel the softness of rain on his genetically altered skin."

Neil closed his eyes and smiled. "I suppose he ran into Sharon on one of her walks and the two made an instant bond. Silk even mentioned meeting a friend who understood him. I never thought anything about it. Two tender souls, prisoners of the sun. But on a rainy night, this thing saw them. He couldn't stand the thought of his lover sharing something so deep and intense with the oxymoron that was Silk. Maybe he even thought they were lovers. Sharon was probably hugging Silk good night."

He knelt beside Shel, who was sitting blankly, eyes closed. "Silk was on his way to meet us at the Hatfield mansion. Before he'd gone looking for Sharkey, Jeff Jr. had kidnapped Bonnie from her job at the country club. His punk friends were holding her. He was going to throw it in Sharkey's face. But Sharkey wasn't there. I knew what the simpleton Jeff was up to. He could hide nothing from me. That was my house. I'm a Hatfield who spent much of my time in the attic, hiding from Jeff Jr. I saw them bring Bonnie in and tie her to a bed. I went to Monk's and got Sharkey and Jack. Silk was on his way to meet us when I suppose he ran into Sharon. We were going to save Bonnie. The night of the fire. I know because we started the fire as a distraction so Sharkey, Jack, and Silk could get in and retrieve Bonnie. I burned down my own father's house to save my friends. That's why I was sent away to a mental hospital."

Shel's snuffling continued as Neil leaned close and whispered, "I think Sharon and Silk were lovers."

I asked meekly, "How could you know all that?"

Neil smiled wistfully. "It's a curse. I see things, the slightest variations in blood flow to the ear, eye movements, other things I can't even describe. I grew up in the dark. Became a perpetual observer of people. I was a prisoner who escaped at night and moved through attics and vent systems to watch people I couldn't be with. My brother, Jeff Jr. did that to me. I learned to read people like books."

As Neil finished, Sharkey spoke for the first time. "I'm going to step on this cockroach now. You boys might want to leave."

Shel said, "Yes, fucker. Kill me." His voice was already of the dead as he sat slumped, almost sliding off the metal seat.

I said quickly, "Please don't. Killing him is a mercy. Let him live with what he's done." I looked from Neil to Sharkey. "Please."

Neil nodded. "I think he's right, Shark." Then to me, he said, "You've been after revenge for a long time. Can you reconcile this?"

Tears burned my eyes. "Vengeance takes many forms."

Neil turned to Jack Knife. "Would you shovel this pile of shit out of our house, Jack?"

I cut in, "I'll get him out of here if Jack will ride with me. I'll take him to the airport and buy him a ticket to wherever he wants to go. I'll square it with Little Ben."

Neil nodded, and Jackie undid the handcuffs. Shel never said another word. Neither could he meet our gazes.

As we got to the door, Sharkey said, "Hang on a sec. I got one more question." He walked up to Shel and gripped his chin in a vise, making him stare into those dead eyes. "Tell me what you done with Silk's body that night."

Shel was already a wreck, and now he was physically shaking.

His voice was frantic. "I left him on the sidewalk. He wasn't … I mean he was a local thug. They'd think he just got run down by somebody he'd pissed off. It would detract them even more from suspecting Mr. Hatfield."

Sharkey squeezed harder, and I thought he might rip Shel's chin off, but Shel merely stared into those dead eyes. Sharkey said, "Did it never occur to you that his body wasn't reported as being found on the street, shit brain? The Kid sees everything with that computer of his'n. Your name ever shows up on it, anywhere, I'll track you down. I sliced up your piece-of-shit nephew just for being stupid. So imagine what I'll do to you. You'll disappear without so much as a marker saying, 'Unknown.'"

I never realized Sharkey was that perceptive. And that wasn't the least of it.

As Jack was putting on his hoodie and fitting out his knives and I was trying to pull the shell of Shel together, Sharkey spoke to the Kid. Jack and I stopped to listen, and it set Shel off bawling like the useless fuck he was.

Shark's voice rumbled up from the depths. He spoke without taking his eyes from Shel's. "That fire. We had the Kid start it. We were ready to walk through hell to save Bonnie. That's where me and Jack got these burns. But I never told you boys this one thing because I thought you'd think I was crazy. I was about to kill that fat shit, Blue, Junior's lineman lackey, when one of his boys come up behind me and was about to cauterize my brains with a shotgun. Silk come out of nowhere and tackled that fucker. Then he picked him up and jumped into the fire, and I swear to God, I heard him say, 'Welcome to hell, motherfucker.' That's how a man like Silk dies. Not gettin' run over like roadkill by a shitbag like this."

Later that sunny afternoon in Villa Valentina, I finally did what I'd intended for some time. I had my driver take me on a day trip to Bocca d'Arno. We drove south through the stunning landscape until we reached the mouth of the Arno River. The driver left me alone while I walked to the water's edge. Three rivers flowed through my life. It was only fitting that I ended things where they met the sea. The St. Johns emptied into the Atlantic, as did the Shenandoah after it met the James, and the Arno emptied into the Mediterranean, which met the Atlantic at Gibraltar. These were the waters of my life.

I knelt as I watched the Ralph-hide binder and journal drift momentarily on the surface of the current. Slowly, as water soaked into the pages, the journal began to tilt on its end, and the contents of my life slid beneath the surface. I thought I might regret letting go, but the relief was overwhelming. Humans weren't built for loneliness, but neither were they built to spend most of their days in hell. Virgil and Dante had merely been passing through. I'd spent most of my life there. Those experiences would sink with the journal.

I scanned the horizon. This seemed the most appropriate ending. My life, like a river, had made its inexorable path from its headwaters to the sea and on to the freedom of horizons without end.

# AFTERWORD

For Sue.
I'm helpless without you.
And our blended family—they've grown
into beautiful, tolerant adults.

The "mean old town," Sanford, Florida, is real, and all
descriptions of its plan are accurate and live on in my memory.
My granddad was Whistlin' Sid, and it's true that he ran the crew
that built the original seawall; established the zoo, Jigs and all;
and dredged up the remains of Fort Mellon. We remember our
pasts emotionally as much as cognitively. There was a Monk's Pool
Hall where all the cool, tough guys hung out. At least I remember
them that way. Monk, however, was based on a wonderful African
American man with scoliosis who ran the pool hall above the
College Inn in Gainesville across the street from my college dorm.

I taught in Florida State Prison at Raiford as a graduate student
at the University of Florida for three years. Most of the horrors
described in this novel are based on either my own experiences
or stories told to me by my inmate students. However, the guards
I knew were professionals like Kiser. Ralph is a composite of the
actions of less-professional guards described by inmates.

To the LBGTQIA and African American communities:

Imagine the day when all humans break free of their cultural imprisonment and we all gaze out at endless horizons. You turned this small-town country boy upside down and changed my way of thinking forever.

And the poet for whom Stuart was named? He's my friend and a poet for the ages.

Printed in the United States
By Bookmasters